What people are saying about …

Too Far to Say Far Enough

"The final book in Nancy Rue's well-received Reluctant Prophet series, *Too Far to Say Far Enough* reminds us all of the struggles throughout the human journey. Rue's characters are flawed, quirky, and believable, while her scenes are contemporary and edgy. Despite a dive into the dark underbelly of prostitution, readers are left with a beautiful reminder to love thy neighbor. If you have always dreamed of zipping up a black leather jacket and hitting the highway on a Hog, or if you just want to immerse yourself in a different world for a while, this is the book for you."

Julie Cantrell, *New York Times* and *USA TODAY* best-selling author of *Into the Free*

"Allison Chamberlain is a gritty, human, thoroughly likable modern prophet. In an era of tamed and timid faith, she models a bold path as she follows the Nudges of God. Author Nancy Rue has crafted a gutsy page-turner, a compelling tale of fear and forgiveness that is packed with both tragedy and humor, which ultimately invites readers to explore for themselves how to answer the call to courageous faithfulness in a hurting world."

Joyce Hollyday, copastor of Circle of Mercy congregation in Asheville, NC, and author of several books, including *Clothed with the Sun*

Praise for ...

Unexpected Dismounts

Praise for …

The Reluctant Prophet

"I love this book! Hop on and ride with this 'reluctant prophet'—but hold on tight, because the call of God not only takes Allison the Tour Guide out of her comfort zone, but the reader as well. An important novel about the awesome, quirky, breathtaking adventure of obeying God's Nudge."

Neta Jackson, author of *The Yada Yada Prayer Group* novels and The Yada Yada House of Hope series

"In Allison Chamberlain, Nancy Rue has created a fresh and unique protagonist to challenge all who follow Christ. How will we change the world? By being willing to leave our comfortable pews and habitual routines to truly *listen* to the voice of the Spirit … and show the world that Jesus called us to love. Not to take care of ourselves, but to take risks in loving others. *The Reluctant Prophet* is a wonderful book with the power to changes hearts and lives."

Angela Hunt, author of *The Debt*

"In her latest novel, *The Reluctant Prophet*, Nancy Rue asks this question: What can God do with broken people? The answer Rue comes up with is humorous, hopeful, and challenging. A story to remind us that God is involved in the everyday, and in love with everyone. You'll cheer this motley band of people who decide love is more important than living a safe, easy life."

Bonnie Grove, award-winning
author of *Talking to the Dead*

"If you believe following Jesus can be an exciting adventure that is baffling at times and even a little messy, with zero tolerance for self-righteous complacency, then *The Reluctant Prophet* is a book for you."

Bill Myers, author of *The God Hater*

"*The Reluctant Prophet* is a bold, wonderful novel. If you have ever felt a Nudge and thought it might be God trying to get your attention, read this book. It might just give you the courage to follow that Nudge and see where it leads. Nancy Rue writes about the tough issues of life and faith with grace, love, and daring. I am so glad God Nudged Nancy to write and so glad that she followed, Harley and all!"

Joyce Magnin, author of *The Prayers of Agnes Sparrow* and *Charlotte Figg Takes Over Paradise*

TOO FAR TO SAY FAR ENOUGH

TOO FAR TO SAY FAR ENOUGH

A NOVEL

NANCY RUE

David C Cook®
transforming lives together

TOO FAR TO SAY FAR ENOUGH
Published by David C Cook
4050 Lee Vance View
Colorado Springs, CO 80918 U.S.A.

David C Cook Distribution Canada
55 Woodslee Avenue, Paris, Ontario, Canada N3L 3E5

David C Cook U.K., Kingsway Communications
Eastbourne, East Sussex BN23 6NT, England

The graphic circle C logo is a registered trademark of David C Cook.

The website addresses recommended throughout this book are offered as a
resource to you. These websites are not intended in any way to be or imply an
endorsement on the part of David C Cook, nor do we vouch for their content.

This story is a work of fiction. Characters and events are the product of the author's
imagination. Any resemblance to any person, living or dead, is coincidental.

Matthew 5:41 quote taken from the New Revised Standard Version Bible, copyright
1989, Division of Christian Education of the National Council of the Churches of
Christ in the United States of America. Used by permission. All rights reserved.

LCCN 2012944301
ISBN 978-1-4347-6490-4
eISBN 978-0-7814-0851-6

© 2012 Nancy Rue
Published in association with the literary agency of Alive Communications,
Inc., 7680 Goddard St., Suite 200, Colorado Springs, CO 80920.

The Team: Don Pape, Jamie Chavez, Amy Konyndyk,
Nick Lee, Renada Arens, Karen Athen
Cover Design: Kirk DouPonce, Dog-Eared Design
Cover Photo: istockphoto

Printed in the United States of America
First Edition 2012

1 2 3 4 5 6 7 8 9 10

073012

*For Lee Hough, who has come too
far to say "far enough."*

"If anyone forces you to go one mile,
go also the second."
—Matthew 5:41

"Every road leads to another road,
Every day leads to tomorrow.
I open doors and let them close.
My heart leads, I will follow."
—Alisa McCance

CHAPTER ONE

Every Monday morning I quit.

Before I even crawled out of bed, sometimes even before I clawed all the way from dreams to the mental pile of stuff I was going to have to try to make a dent in, if it was Monday, I said, out loud so there could be no misunderstanding: "God, you're going to have to find somebody else to be your prophet, because I'm done. You got a recovery group I can get into?"

Sometimes I'd imagine such a group—a place where I could sit in a circle with other people who were in way over their spiritual heads and say, "Hi. I'm Allison, and I'm a recovering prophet."

Seriously. The women of Sacrament House could nobly go to Alcoholics Anonymous and Narcotics Anonymous and Prostitutes Anonymous (okay, I made that one up), and begin to see themselves healing. Ninety meetings in ninety days was a requirement for them.

But there was no Prophets Anonymous. There was no recovery from being one—although at times I would have given up my Harley to escape it—and there was nothing anonymous about it. I knew. I'd tried that.

That particular Monday, however, I skipped quitting. I didn't even give a nod to the stack of not-yet-done stuff teetering just beyond my reach, waiting for one more thing to topple it over. Because that late-August Monday, almost exactly one year since I'd caught twelve-year-old Desmond Sanborn trying to steal my house key, I was standing in front of a judge, about to adopt the boy.

It was enough to make the whole precarious pile disappear.

The Honorable Charles Walton Atwell the Third swept his eyes, decidedly reminiscent of a basset hound's, over the crowd gathered in the gallery behind Desmond and me. Normally a transaction such as this would have taken place in his chambers, but there was nothing normal about our group. We had everything from a social worker, two attorneys, and a real estate broker to a row of recovering ladies of the evening and another of HOG members in sleeveless T-shirts, holding their motorcycle helmets respectfully under their arms. One elongated look at the motley cloud of witnesses overflowing his office, and Judge Atwell had ordered us all into the courtroom. Desmond gave that his signature stamp of approval by high-fiving said judge and saying, "Good choice, Mr. Your Honor, sir."

Judge Atwell now dragged his ancient face down with his hand and went into a pause as lengthy as his chin. I remembered that about him. You could practically go out for a cappuccino during one of those conversational gaps. Beside me, Desmond shifted his negligible weight from one lanky leg to the other. I put a cautionary hand on his shoulder and prayed he wouldn't blurt out, "Mr. Your Honor, sir, you takin' a *nap* up in there?"

Finally His Honor nodded gravely at Chief, who stood looking even taller than his six-foot-plus on the other side of Desmond. I suspected that judicial gaze was as much about Chief's graying ponytail as it was about the solemnity of the occasion. He must have been satisfied with the fact that at least Chief was clad in Brooks Brothers all the way down to his black wing tips, because he said, "Mr. Ellington, you may proceed."

"Who's Mr. Ellington?" Desmond whispered to me. His version of *sotto voce* was like sandpaper on a two-by-four.

"Do you have a question, son?" the judge said.

"I was just askin' who's Mr. Ellington," Desmond said.

"That would be your attorney." Judge Atwell moved his head in slo-mo to regard Chief. "I assume you've introduced yourself to your client."

I could see the spray of tiny lines at the corner of Chief's eyes crinkling, but he nodded with the proper sobriety.

"Oh, you talkin' 'bout Mr. Chief," Desmond said. "No, he introduced hisself to me a *long* time ago. We go *way* back."

"I'm relieved to hear it."

The judge indulged in another snail-caliber pause and then nodded once more at Chief. Behind us, I heard Jasmine's nervous giggle, followed by Mercedes's unmistakable shushing. Like most of the Sacrament House Sisters, they were both virtually allergic to all things judicial. Mercedes wasn't going to take a chance on being escorted to a cell.

"Your Honor," Chief said, using the courtroom voice that made people involuntarily improve their postures, "I introduce Allison Chamberlain to the court."

His Honor and I nodded at each other. I was no stranger to the man or his courtroom.

"Ms. Chamberlain, would you state your name?" Chief said.

"Allison Eugenia Chamberlain," I said, and then squeezed the lifeblood out of Desmond's shoulder. Even though we'd rehearsed this so he wouldn't go into convulsions of hysteria over my middle name, I couldn't trust him not to at least snicker.

He remained snicker-less.

"And do you verify that you have appeared today to adopt this child, Desmond Edwin Sanborn, born August 26, 1999?"

"I do," I said.

"Do you know any cause that would legally prohibit this adoption?"

I knew none whatsoever, although everybody and their sister had tried to make one up. "No, I do not," I said.

"The rights of Desmond Sanborn's biological parents have been terminated?"

I couldn't help cringing at that one. His mother herself had been terminated. As for his father, the monster had never *had* any rights as far as I was concerned.

"Yes," I said.

But I still stopped breathing and sneaked a look at the judge. Chief had assured me this was all a formality, that there was no way anybody was going to protest the adoption at this point. Still, I'd been blindsided on this before.

Judge Atwell nodded as if his head was too heavy for his neck, and I allowed myself a breath. According to Chief, one more question and I would be Desmond's mother.

"Ms. Chamberlain," Chief said. "Would you please tell the court why you want to adopt this child?"

I felt more than saw the sudden slant of Desmond's huge brown eyes, made browner by his cinnamon-shaded, half-African face. During our rehearsals I had threatened to come out with, "Because who else is going to put up with him?" or "I've invested too much in groceries for the kid to kick him out now." I never had told Desmond exactly what I was really going to say, and at that moment I still didn't know myself.

I'd rejected "Because his mother wanted this," and "Because *I* want him to survive to adulthood." Even though both were true, neither was adequate, and if I said, "Because I love this boy more than I have ever loved anyone in my life," I would have, to use Desmond's words, "gotten all emo." I had assured him there would be no emo. As for telling him I had been nudged by God ... Judge Atwell and I had been down that road before.

Evidently endless pauses were the sole privilege of His Honor. He squinted down at me from the bench and said, "Not having second thoughts are you, Ms. Chamberlain?"

"No, sir," I said. "I just can't seem to find the words."

"Now that *is* a surprise."

I looked at Desmond, who despite his new, manly cut-close-to-the-scalp haircut and the tiniest of hairs sprouting on his chin, seemed suddenly as vulnerable as a four-year-old. Then I did what I'd learned to do in situations of the utmost importance: I opened my mouth and let God come through.

"I want to adopt this young man because he's been given to me to love," I said. "And to love him is a privilege."

Yeah. Couldn't have said it better myself.

The little-boy Desmond popped away, and my adolescent Desmond slipped cleanly back into place and presented a fist for me to knock mine against. Somebody, probably one of the HOGs, whistled through his fingers. Judge Atwell banged his gavel, though not much louder than Mercedes's "Y'all got to hush up now. We 'bout to get throwed out."

Another record-breaking pause ensued, during which the judge scowled over the papers in front of him, picked up his pen, put it down, took it in hand again. Desmond was beginning to squirm under the death grip I had on his shoulder, and even Chief reclasped his hands in front of him. It was all I could do not to shout, "What is the *problem?*"

Finally Judge Atwell looked up, this time at Desmond. "I have one question for you, son," he said.

I shot Chief a *This wasn't in the script* look, but he kept his gaze riveted to the judge.

"Ask me anything you want, Mr. Your Honor, sir," Desmond said. "I got nothin' to hide." He grinned. "'Cept the Oreos I ganked from the snack drawer."

I came just short of snapping his collarbone in two with my fingers.

"Petty theft is handled in a different court," Judge Atwell said. "What I want to know is ..."

Desmond gave it eight seconds before he held out his palms, face quizzical.

"I want to know if you realize that most parents have to simply take what they get when they have children."

"Oh, I know that thing," Desmond said. "I seen me some ugly babies, now."

Somebody in the back seemed to be choking on a hairball.

The judge nodded toward me. "That woman standing beside you—"

"Big Al," Desmond said.

"She is not making you her son because she has to; you know that, don't you? She chose you—"

"I got to stop you right there, Mr. Your Honor."

"Desmond," I hissed. "You can't interrupt—"

"Go on," Judge Atwell said. "Let's hear what you have to say."

My eyes met Chief's over the top of Desmond's head. His were sparkling so hard I could almost hear them.

"Big Al *does* have to adopt me. If she don't, she be in some big trouble. We talkin' epic, now."

"Trouble with whom?"

"Trouble with the *big* Daddy. If Big Al doesn't do what God be tellin' her to do …"

Desmond's ellipsis rivaled any the judge could leave. Judge Atwell pulled his chin nearly to his navel as he turned his houndish eyes to me.

"I do recall that about you, Ms. Chamberlain," he said. "You call yourself a prophet, don't you?"

"If I might speak for my client," Chief said.

"There's no need. I think we've tried that case before, right here in this courtroom." For a sliver of a second, something that might have been a smile quivered around the judge's long lips. "And as I recall, God won."

"Amen," someone muttered behind us.

"Now before this turns into a prayer meeting …" Judge Atwell picked up his pen again, trailed his finger down the paper, and wrote with the careful deliberation of a preschooler gripping his first fat pencil.

"Ladies and gentlemen," he said, "this adoption is final." Then he pulled up one corner of his mouth and added, "I think that calls for some applause."

Applause wasn't the word for it. The cheers of thirteen people, pent up for months by the fear of hoping for too much, burst like a tsunami over the courtroom. Arms of all colors were flung around backs, and squeals, whistles, and assorted versions of "amen"— liturgical to downright Pentecostal—rose in joyous cacophony. The only thing powerful enough to bring it all down was Desmond, standing up on the railing that separated us from the gallery and waving his adolescent arms in the air.

"Desmond!" I said between clenched teeth. "What the Sam Hill are you doing?"

"I just got to say something," he said.

Chief wrapped his fingers around the back of Desmond's shirt and transferred him to the floor. I looked frantically at the judge, who was either in the midst of one of his pauses or had simply passed on from shock.

"Can't you control your kid, Classic?" Chief whispered to me.

"Your honor, we apologize," I said, and gave Desmond a death stare.

"Sorry, Mr. Your Honor, sir," Desmond said. "But I got to check something out, now."

Judge Atwell resurrected himself and looked at me. "Are you sure this boy isn't genetically related to you?" Before I could answer, he turned back to Desmond. "What is it, son?"

"I just got to make sure somethin' is right 'fore I leave here."

Desmond glanced at me and added, "Sir." Like that was going to keep me from throttling him later.

His Honor held up two of arguably the world's longest fingers and beckoned to Desmond. He approached the bench with surprising propriety, while I anticipated a lecture from His Honor about Desmond's behavior or his impudence or his grammar. But Judge Atwell merely picked up the paper before him and handed it to Desmond.

He frowned at it, lips moving as his eyes trailed down the page. I had seen the document myself and had had to have Chief *and* Kade—both attorneys—translate. Desmond was only making it through eighth grade English by the skin of his big ol' white teeth, so I didn't see how—

"Yeah, baby. That's what I'm talkin' about." Desmond grinned up at the judge, his marvelous mouth extending lobe to lobe. "You got it right."

"And what is that?"

Desmond swiveled to take in the crowd, which was still in unanimous inhale. "Y'all can call me Desmond *Chamberlain* now, 'cause that is my *name*. Yeah, baby!"

No one waited for His Honor's permission this time. The cheering went on long after Judge Atwell retreated to his chambers. I didn't have a chance to thank him, not with half the crowd bawling on one shoulder and the rest of them pounding on the other. I was sure Judge Atwell was just grateful to have me out of what was left of his hair.

The group was sorting itself into a variety of vehicles out in the parking lot of the St. John's County Courthouse by the time I signed the paperwork under Desmond's scrutiny. Ulysses, Stan, Rex, and the

rest of the Harley Owners Group members had already roared
out on their bikes, led by Hank, who was wearing what she
called her Sunday-go-to-meetin' helmet, an amusing term when
delivered with her Boston accent. Five of the seven Sacrament
Sisters—Jasmine, Mercedes, Ophelia, and our two newest, Gigi
and Rochelle—were loading into the van, having given the
motorcycles a wide berth, although ten months ago they would
have ridden with Evel Knievel if it would have helped them get
high. Besides Chief and Desmond there was only Owen Schatz,
looking far younger than his seventy-something years next to Ms.
Willa, fifteen years his senior. He had evidently refused all help
transferring her from her wheelchair into his Lincoln.

"When did Owen get a new car?" Chief said.

Desmond paused, helmet halfway on. "When he started
seein' Ms. Willa."

"'Seeing' her?" I said. "Like dating, you mean?"

"I don't think they datin'. Just talkin'. There ain't nothin'
goin' on." Desmond wiggled his eyebrows. "Yet."

"Keep us posted, will you?" Chief said drily.

"Oh, please don't," I said. "Who are you riding with,
Desmond?"

It was a pointless question. If given a choice, he was always on
the back of Chief's Road King in a heartbeat, especially since two
weeks before, Chief's orthopedist had cleared him to ride again
after a five-and-a-half month recovery from a leg injury. If *I'd* had
a choice, I would have been there too. As close as I could get.

But Desmond was already swinging a lanky limb over the seat
of my Softail. I fought back the "emo" gathering in my throat.

"You're not dressed to ride with that lady," Chief said.

"What lady?" I said.

"I got my brain bucket," Desmond said, motioning with his helmet, "and you *know* she never let me ride without every part of my body covered up even when she knows Imma get heat stroke."

"You've got the wrong jacket on," Chief said. "Here. Try this one."

He reached into one of the studded saddlebags on his bike and produced what appeared to be ten pounds of leather. I could feel my eyebrows lifting. Granted, Desmond's arms were growing so fast he needed new gear about every three months so his wrists didn't stick out like poles, but I'd just gotten him a denim jacket that should last him until Thanksgiving. Okay, maybe Halloween.

But Chief unfolded a soft, muted-black garment and held it out to Desmond as he climbed off my bike. "Congratulations present," he said.

"That is *sweet*," Desmond said, though he, too, looked a little mystified. It was, after all, ninety-five Florida degrees, each one soaked in equal parts humidity.

Chief motioned with his chin. "What's sweet is on the back."

Desmond turned the jacket around, and I lost control of my emo. Just beneath a full-out screamin' Harley Davidson emblem, the letters *D.C.* were embroidered, thick enough for even Ms. Willa to see from a hundred yards.

It was one of the few times I ever saw my boy without the perfect retort. Chief rescued him by holding out his fist. Desmond didn't tap it. He threw his arms around Chief's substantial chest and buried his face.

That kind of joy was still unfamiliar enough to make me wonder if it really belonged to me.

Classic II, my Red Hot Sunglo Heritage Softail, purred like a lioness beneath Desmond and me as we followed Chief. He might still walk with a slight limp, which I personally found sexy, but he rode like he and the Harley were one streamlined, bad-dude being. I'd been back on my bike six weeks longer, after my own injury, but I never hoped to handle a motorcycle with that kind of hunky confidence.

He led us away from the looks-like-any-other-town-in-America cluster of Walmart, Target, and Safeway, and toward the part of St. Augustine that is like *no* other town anywhere.

Coquina-sided Spanish-style houses cozied themselves between Greek revival–columned mansions and Victorian-era bed and breakfasts trimmed with gingerbread. Live oaks, bowed under Spanish moss, tunneled streets so narrow a Harley was about the only vehicle a person could drive comfortably on, if it weren't for the brick pavement that threatened to jar our teeth loose. From the "sissy seat" behind me, Desmond howled his delight with every bounce, maybe with even more abandon than usual. I did a little howling myself.

As we entered the long sweeping curve of Avenida Menendez that ran along Matanzas Bay, the sunlight glared onto my visor, momentarily blotting Chief from view. Too bad, because the sight of his back pulling denim across his shoulders did it for me like no other. That and his eagle profile. And the raptor eyes that could twinkle with mischief or take my breath right out of my body with their I-know-you-Classic intensity …

Okay. I needed to concentrate. It would be bad form to dump the kid in the bay the first day I had him.

Chief continued to lead us toward our turn-off at Cadiz Street. I could almost smell the sun bleaching the pastel walls of the waterfront homes. Plantation shutters were closed, lace-bordered shades pulled down. My black pants and my own denim jacket made me feel like I was wearing a plastic garbage bag. Other women didn't seem to sweat the way I did. Chief didn't even sweat the way I did. Desmond had to be dying in leather, though he'd never admit it. I'd be lucky to get him to take that jacket off to go to bed.

But despite the rivulets trickling between my shoulder blades, I took a long inhale of a peace that was still as foreign to me as heart-bursting joy. Left to my own devices, I wasn't one for *all manner of thing shall be well*. My MO was more: *When will the other shoe drop? Come on, I know it's going to.* So whenever even my breathing was taken over, I braced myself for the Nudge, the kind that threatened to knock me off the bike if I didn't take heed. And above the purr of the Classic and the uninhibited yowling of my kid, I heard the whisper that was not my own.

Go another mile.

Up ahead, Chief leaned easily into the left turn onto Cadiz, but I stayed on Avenida Menendez. I didn't argue with the Nudges any more. Didn't question them, even though I had no idea what they would eventually mean. This one would initially result in Hank having to warm the lasagna up and Ms. Willa *tsk-tsk*ing about my manners. Chief would just sit on the side porch, feet perched on the railing, waiting. Getting it.

Desmond, on the other hand, yelled, "Oh, yeah!" and clung to me like a long-armed koala bear. I had the irresistible urge to play.

We inched our way amid the trails of wilting tourists jaywalking across the Avenida just about anywhere they pleased to get to their suppers at O. C. White's and the Santa Maria and the A1A Ale Works. A mile would take us to the fort and back, but I didn't check the odometer. I would know when to turn back. The almost violent power that told me to go would thrust us forward until it just as firmly said *stop*. It was a sort of coerced freedom that I never tried to explain. Most people thought I was sufficiently crazed as it was.

So with Desmond calling out, "Oh, yeah!" and leaning with me as if we'd been somehow Velcroed together, I answered the whisper to *go another mile* and chugged behind the tired traffic along Castillo Drive. Finally we broke free at Orange Street and cruised past the crumbling City Gates that kept no one in or out and drove on heedless of the funky shops and pubs that beckoned visitors in search of respite from the heat and the history. I turned left on Cordova, the street tourists seldom made it to when the sun was bearing down this hard.

I teased Desmond with the throttle at the intersection, and he hollered, "That is what I am *talkin' about!*"

Grinning inside my helmet, I gave the Classic just enough gas to make Desmond yell again and let the Methodist church and Scarlett O'Hara's pub go by in one blur. With Flagler College in sight on the right I slowed down, but Desmond was already squeezing my rib cage and croaking, "Copper, Big Al."

I glanced in the side mirror and groaned. Blue lights flashed atop a cruiser. Its *whoop* signaled me to pull into the student parking lot.

I would have blamed God, except that the Nudge had just been to *go another mile*. God hadn't indicated how fast.

I could feel Desmond's skinny body flatten into my backbone. One year with me wasn't enough to shake the aversion to law enforcement that had been ingrained in him the first twelve. I was starting to suspect it was in his DNA.

"Busted," he said.

But as I watched the officer climb out of the cruiser, I shook my head. "Maybe not, Des," I said. "It's Nicholas Kent."

"Well, shoot, we got nothin' to worry about then."

"Let him tell *us* that," I said. "Which means, say a word and you lose helmet privileges indefinitely."

As usual, that guaranteed silence.

I raised my visor and tried to look contrite as young Nick Kent stood beside me, freckled hands on his hips. He was wearing shades, but I could still see his Opie Taylor eyebrows knitted together.

"What were you thinking, Miss Allison?"

"I wasn't, Nick. I'm sorry."

"Do you know how fast you were going?"

Even if I'd had a clue I couldn't have answered with Desmond death-gripping the air out of me. I could practically hear him gritting his teeth. His impression that our favorite cop was going to let us off had clearly faded.

"Forty in a thirty," Nick said.

"Are you serious?" I said.

He nodded solemnly.

This was the point at which I expected the freckles to fold into laugh lines around his eyes, but he kept his boyish mouth stern.

"If you have to write me a ticket, I totally understand," I said.

Nick pulled a pad out of his back pocket, and my heart turned over. He really was going to give me a citation, and any minute now Desmond would crack a molar. I'd have to add dental fees to whatever this was going to cost me.

Officer Kent scribbled briskly on the pad and tore the page off, while I peeled Desmond's arms off so I could breathe.

"Just a warning this time," Nick said.

I took the paper from him and gave it only a glance before I felt the grin melt across my face.

Congrats, Miss Allison, he'd written. *BTW, the coast is still clear.*

"Thank you, officer," I said. "I'll be more careful from now on."

Out of the corner of my eye I saw Desmond's hand come up, fist balled to thump into Nick's.

"You don't gotta worry about that," Desmond said. "Imma keep a eye on her for ya."

"Do it," Nick said. "I'm counting on you."

My next sensation was Desmond's chest puffing against my back. I sneaked a smile at Nick and crept out of the parking lot at a speed just short of falling over. Officer Nicholas Kent was one of the good guys. Staying out of the less-than-good guys' headlights wasn't easy for people who associated with me, and I wasn't going to make it any harder for him. We headed to Palm Row at a respectable twenty-nine miles an hour, while Desmond rattled on about cheatin' death again and I savored the God-joy.

It was the upside of being a prophet.

When we got to our house on Palm Row, the site of just four houses between Cordova and St. George Streets, Chief was, indeed, on the side porch, Italian soda in hand. He didn't ask me any questions, although he did shoot me a puzzled look when Desmond barely spoke and hurled his adolescent self into the kitchen.

"I told him not to tell you something until I had a chance to," I said. "I don't think he trusts himself."

"You ever going to tell me?"

"No."

Chief's eyes grinned. "You're a cruel mother."

"Somebody should have thought of that before they let me adopt him," I said.

Chief reached out a hand, big but always surprisingly soft, and hooked it around my neck to pull me to him.

"He's all yours now, Classic," he said into my hair. "Nobody can take him away."

I pushed my face into the chest I loved and felt his other arm come around me. One would think such a scene would cause anyone who happened upon us to do a sensitive about-face.

Yeah, well, one would have to know the Sacrament Sisters before assuming such a thing.

"Miss Angel? Everything all right? Didn't nothin' happen with Desmond, did it?"

Chief chuckled into my scalp and let me go. I tried not to glare at Sherry and Zelda, who were rushing up the steps onto the porch. Sherry's already almost-translucent face was turning

another shade of pale, while Zelda's very-black one pinched
inward.

"Everything is *fine,*" I said. "We were just celebrating."

"Oh," Zelda said. And then her eyes quickened. "Oh! I'm sorry,
Miss Angel. When I see somebody cryin', I always think somebody
died or got busted or somethin'."

"I'm not crying," I said.

Sherry nodded toward the kitchen door that was even then just
closing behind Chief.

"She was talking about him."

Zelda let out the laugh that was still rusty from underuse. "We
didn't mean to interrupt you and Mr. Chief hookin' up."

Sherry smacked her on the shoulder.

"I didn't mean hookin' up like hookin' *up*! I just meant—"

"I get it, Zelda," I said. "I'll catch him later. I'm glad you two
made it."

Zelda's eyes clouded again. "We almost didn't. Old Man Maharry
was all up in my grill work the whole day."

Sherry glared at her.

"I don't care if he's your daddy," Zelda said. "I don't need him
fussin' at me all the time."

"He gave you a job," Sherry said. "I wouldn't be griping about
it if I were you."

I raised both hands. "We're having a celebration here, ladies.
We'll talk about this later."

Then I waited and watched as Zelda rearranged her expression and
jiggled her shoulders out of defensive mode and sucked in her lips. Four
months ago that display of self-control would have been impossible.

"There's food inside," I said.

Zelda gave up a smile and disappeared into the kitchen. Sherry wandered to the railing, her bony back to me, arms hugging her own feather-thin body. I felt a grab at my gut.

"It is not working out at C.A.R.S.?" I said.

"Daddy's having issues." Sherry shrugged. "It'll be all right."

"So what's the deal?"

She turned to me, eyes pale. "Mr. Chief is right. Nobody is gon' take Desmond from you, Miss Angel."

"You're talking about Sultan." I said.

She didn't answer. She didn't have to.

"Nick Kent just told me things are still cool," I said. "The last news we heard was that Sultan—"

"Just never mind."

Sherry took the steps in one long lurch and marched across the yard, once again hugging her body as if she were trying to hold herself together.

Whatever she was carrying made my own arms ache. That was the down side of being a prophet.

※

By the time I got inside, I knew the crowd had probably already eaten its way through the antipasto and was working on Hank's matchless lasagna. Square, dark-haired, and wise-eyed, she greeted me in the kitchen with a forkful of noodles and sauce already pointed toward my mouth. A string of steaming cheese clotheslined from plate to tines.

"I know you won't stop to eat, Al," she said, "so open up."

As my spiritual guide and Harley-riding teacher, Hank was surprisingly light-handed with the instructions, so when she told me flat
out to do something I did it. Especially if it involved her cooking.

It *would* be an insult not to take a moment to appreciate a
D'Angelo special. She'd even improved Desmond and the Sisters'
palates, though granted, anything beyond what they could cull from
alley trashcans would have been a step up.

"I *will* be back for more," I said.

"I'll hide some for you for after the ceremony. We'll start in ten."

"Where's Chief?" I said.

"He grabbed a paper towel and went out on the front porch."
Hank's lips twitched. "I heard him blowing his nose."

I slid around the bistro table, which was completely taken up
by an enormous basket of the kind of garlic bread that cleared your
sinuses, and pointed myself in the general direction of the dining
room. With any luck I could slip out to the front porch and finish
what we'd started.

"Am I too late for the salad?" said a voice from the side door.

I turned around, straight into a bouquet of lettuce larger than
both my head and the one behind it, which belonged to next-door
neighbor Owen. The man was nothing if not green-thumbed. I
tried not to think about him having something "going on" with
Ms. Willa.

Hank tilted a now-empty basin toward him.

"I'm always a day late and a dollar short," Owen said. "Sometimes
I get so far behind I meet myself coming back. I'll probably be late
for my own funeral."

"You're fine," Hank said. "I'm sure if I make another salad it'll get eaten." She cocked an eyebrow at me. "Don't you ever feed your kid?"

"He's growing like a weed, isn't he?" Owen said. "It's like he has a hollow leg—"

I left Hank to untangle the usual Owen-string of similes and nearly plowed into Mercedes, who was deftly hoisting a tray of licked-clean dishes with one hand and steering Desmond by the back of the neck with the other. It struck me that he was almost as tall as she was now, a fact that did not make her any less capable of cowing the boy better than most of us. Though he was grinning, his eyes were definitely seeking an escape route.

"What did you do now?" I said.

"I didn't do nothin'," he said. "Mercedes Benz just always up in my business."

"It's not your business to be telling Gigi and Rochelle how to get away with slackin' on they responsibilities." Mercedes gave him a shake that wobbled his head, but he beamed her the smile he claimed put every woman in the palm of his thirteen-year-old hand.

"Ain't nobody responsible as you, M.B."

"Then don't make me responsible for smackin' you up the side the head."

Desmond at least had the smarts to look guilty. When Mercedes's black eyes flashed like that and she drew herself up to her full five-eight, I usually felt guilty myself, even if I hadn't done anything.

"Go set Gigi and Rochelle straight, Clarence," I said. "And stay out of the tiramisu until after the ceremony."

Mercedes gave him another jiggle and let him go. He grabbed the hand that wasn't still holding the tray and brought it to his lips.

"Don't you be tryin' that with me," she said. But I could see her pressing back a voluptuous smile.

"Something I should know about?" I said when he'd escaped.

"Just the usual when somebody new come into the House—but nothin' you need to be worryin' about today. This is your day, you and Desmond." She deftly shifted the tray. "Now I need to get rid of these dishes, is what I need to do. Where is Sherry? She s'pose to be helpin' me."

Mercedes disappeared into the kitchen before I could tell her Sherry was outside putting her game face back on.

I tried again to make my way to Chief on the front porch. We now only had about five minutes left before the ceremony and I would have loved to at least finish off that reassuring hug.

This time I got as far as the entrance hall. Who in the world had left Ms. Willa parked there in her wheelchair? Although if Ms. Willa hadn't wanted to be there, we'd be hearing about it. The bluish mane fell over her collar as she leaned back and pursed her entire wizened face at Desmond's framed artwork displayed in the entryway.

"Your boy did these?" Her voice never failed to remind me of a terrier's, though she looked more feline than canine. Since neither animal had an azure tint to its fur, Ms. Willa was actually her own breed. No one ever argued with that. Or her.

"Hard to believe this comes out of him, isn't it?" I said.

From the front porch, I could hear the resonance of Chief's voice in conversation with somebody, and I looked longingly at the door. But I sat on the edge of the old church pew that flanked the wall and pulled a throw pillow into my lap.

Ms. Willa pointed a knotty finger at Desmond's drawing of me, the one I unabashedly thought was the best thing up there. "Is that supposed to be you?" she barked. Yipped, actually.

"It is," I said.

"He made your face too long and your mouth too big."

"It's a caricature, Ms. Willa. See? He's made Owen's teeth huge and his face all pruney. Kind of captures his optimism."

Ms. Willa's nose wrinkled. "Owen goes on about the boy like he's the next Leonardo da Vinci. I don't see it myself."

"I would love to sit here and debate art with you," I said, "but I need to—"

"How's my boutique doing?"

Before I could answer, the front door burst open and a bulging black trash bag entered, followed by Erin O'Hare, Desmond's history teacher. The humidity had frizzed her massive tresses into a mahogany-colored white-girl Afro, which accounted for Desmond calling her Miss All-Hair.

"Sorry I'm late," she said. "I went by my place to pick up these clothes for the boutique. I found some great stuff at the consignment stores in Orlando and got it all for a song."

I came off the old pew like a shot. "Let me help!" I said.

"We've got it handled."

That came from Chief, backed up by Bonner Bailey, who was wearing his Bailey Realty nametag as if everyone in town didn't already know him. Chief took the bag from Erin and Bonner hiked a second one over his shoulder.

"Excuse me, ladies," Bonner said. "Didn't mean to interrupt."

"You're not—" I said.

But they hurried on through, jaw muscles working to hold back laughter. Traitors.

"Ms. Willa," Erin said, "you and I are going to keep the Sisters in merchandise, aren't we?"

"The idea is for them to *sell* the merchandise." Ms. Willa's papery paws were folded in the lap of today's all-puce ensemble, but any minute the claws would come out if I didn't give this my full attention.

"Just tell your two Sherpas to put the bags on the upstairs landing," I said to Erin.

She glanced at Ms. Willa and, with a knowing nod at me, fled the scene even less unobtrusively than Chief and Bonner. I turned with a stifled sigh to Ms. Willa.

"Your building looks great," I said. "The guys have turned that place into a—"

"I've seen it," she said. "I had Owen Schatz take me down there."

"Then you know it's fabulous."

"Harold Renfroe would be pleased with it, I'll give you that."

Her tiny face squeezed in. I was about to get an earful about how Troy Irwin had ruined her first late husband and cheated him out of that piece of prime real estate on St. George Street, as well as the rest of his fortune.

"All right, everyone—it's time," Hank called from the living room.

I thanked God for her as I took hold of Ms. Willa's wheelchair. "We need to get in there," I said.

"I want that shop to be the talk of the town," Ms. Willa said. "I want to make sure the score has been evened."

We were still tapping toward Troy Irwin, and that was a dance I refused to do, not just today but any day. Anytime. Anywhere.

"I'll give you a full report when I come over this week," I said, my fingers already curled around the handles. Then I dropped that onto the Things To Deal With Later pile and steered her to the living room.

The court had made the adoption legal. It was time for us to make it real.

CHAPTER TWO

Everyone was gathered around the trunk-turned-coffee table Hank had covered with Desmond's Harley-Davidson throw. Somebody, probably India Morehead, had seen to it that the contraband Oreo crumbs were shaken from it and had placed a white china basin over the ketchup stain.

India herself wafted in from the kitchen carrying the matching pitcher of water and wordlessly settling the air with her flowing silk and her unflappable class. I'd given up wishing I could be like her when I grew up. Ophelia, who followed her with Desmond's Harley beach towel folded like a king's robe, *could* actually be her own version of India someday. She spent most of her free time away from Sacrament House with her mentor and had distinctly more natural promise than I did. Ophelia's Hispanic beauty often stole my breath from me, even with the echo of sadness in her eyes. I wasn't sure that would ever go away.

"Y'all can sit right here," India said, waving a willowy hand at two red cushions on the floor beside the trunk.

Desmond had left the cocky grin parked somewhere. That was Desmond for "This serious, now." While Hank took her place at the top of the circle, between Zelda and Jasmine, who was, of course, already crying, I risked looking at Kade Capelli for the first time that day.

Kade was the only one who looked unconnected to the group. His handsome Harvard confidence made a better shield than the visor on my motorcycle helmet. If anyone else picked up on the slight stiffening around his eyes or the minute hunch of the athletic shoulders, they didn't let on. I couldn't convince myself that I saw it because I was his mother. I had, after all, only known him for four months.

He was across from Desmond and me, standing next to Chief, arms hanging casily at his sides just the way Chief's were. Though sandy blond to Chief's gray, in posture, he looked more like Chief's son than mine. That was probably because they'd been working together fifty hours a week for the last two months. He'd definitely spent more time with Chief than he had with me.

I looked away before Kade could see my eyes begging.

"The Lord be with you," Hank said, square hands raised.

"And also wichoo," was the reply from the Sacrament Sisters. Everyone else joined in as well, but I always heard the women above the rest, as if they felt the Presence the most.

Hank stretched her arm over Desmond and me, and I watched every head bow before I lowered mine. Desmond and I were surrounded by people who had always brought what prayers they had to courtrooms and hospital rooms and jail cells so that this family could be. They were so achingly beautiful to me, I couldn't close my eyes.

"You've entrusted Desmond into our care," Hank was saying. "Help us to remember that we are *all* Your children—"

Amens were murmured.

"—and to nurture him to the full stature intended for him in your eternal kingdom. For the sake of your dear Son, our Lord Christ."

Hank opened her eyes to meet mine, melting me with her sheer sincerity.

"You are not alone in this, you two," she said. "We can all share in the responsibility. Are we in, my friends?"

Mercedes's signature *mmm-mm* led the response.

"Allison and Desmond," Hank said, "have chosen to wash each other's feet as Jesus did his friends' when he said, 'Love one another as I have loved you.' Any of you who would also like to wash their feet as a sign of your commitment to them are welcome." Hank's lips quivered into the smallest of smiles as she added, "I know this isn't your first footwashing, but let me just remind you that we're not talking about a full leg massage."

I poked Desmond with my elbow.

"Imma hold myself back, Big Al," he said.

I didn't say anything as Desmond sat on the trunk, sans Harley boots, and I knelt and cleansed my son's gangly, adolescent feet of the need to ever run from his life again. I was still under my vow not to go emo. Besides, unless I was speaking the words God gave me, I was very likely to insert both feet and a hand in my mouth anyway.

Desmond took his turn, and in deference to Hank, limited himself to my heels, soles, and toes. I was surprised he didn't take that opportunity to regale us all with the whole story of how he had come to live with me on Palm Row, how he'd become as much a part of my Harley as its handlebars, and how I was going to be impressed at the model kid he was going to be now that he was a Chamberlain.

He just dried his hands and reached inside the leather jacket he still hadn't taken off and pulled out a folder smeared at the corners with chalky fingerprints.

"I made you this," was all he said.

Necks craned as I opened it, to find two drawn figures looking back at me. The hair on one resembled a Brillo pad on steroids, the other long strands of straw stolen from a haystack. But the smiles on both could not have been truer as they extended almost beyond their faces.

"Now that looks like you, Allison," Ms. Willa said. "But that one in the hallway—"

"Anyone else want to make a promise to Allison and Desmond?" Hank's timing was always impeccable.

Every person there washed Desmond's feet and mine, and with each splash of water and press of hand, the pile that had become my life became less daunting. Each of our beloved friends expressed what they could offer Desmond and me, everything from the HOGs guaranteeing enough Harley T-shirts to get Desmond through high school to Sherry promising to teach him how to do an oil change, to which he replied with the charming grin, "I like that in a woman."

We were covered. There was clearly nothing that could take us down.

The only person who said nothing as he washed—just squeezed Desmond's shoulder and kissed me on the cheek—was Bonner. I knew him well enough to drag him out to the side porch after my feet had been washed until they were shriveled, while everyone else made a beeline for the dessert table.

"That was you choking like you had a hairball in the courtroom, wasn't it?" I said. "You know how hard it is to keep a straight face when you do that?"

Bonner sank beside me on the swing, the sun teasing out the reddish tinge of his hair, and studied the crease in his slacks through the inevitable sunglasses attached to him with Croakies.

"You okay?" I said.

"You mean because I didn't say anything when I was washing your feet—"

"You have already given us so much. Any more would practically be overkill. But you wear yourself all over your face, so what's going on?"

Bonner pushed his glasses up his nose. "I just didn't want to say this in front of everybody—"

"Uh-oh. What did I do?"

"Am I going to get to finish a sentence in this conversation?"

"Probably not."

He put a hand over mine. "Look, I know things aren't easy for you financially right now, and I thought maybe you could use—"

"You are not going to give me money."

"I was just going to offer you a loan to tide you over until—"

"I'm fine."

He just blinked at me over the tops of the shades.

"Seriously," I said. "There's a salary for me incorporated into that grant Liz helped us get. That'll last six months if I budget carefully."

"That's a pretty big if."

I flopped back on the swing. "I know, right? Sometimes I don't know where it goes."

"I'll tell you where it goes—"

"I take Mercedes to coffee. I buy lunch for Maharry and the girls. I—"

"You try to save the world instead of paying the electric bill."

I narrowed my eyes at him. "How did you know about that?"

Bonner grinned. "So that really happened."

"You are slime. Tell anyone and I'll cut your heart out."

"Look, Allison—"

"No, Bonner, I'm not going to accept money from you. We're about people becoming empowered to help themselves, and that applies to me, too."

"Y'know, if you'd hush up for about seven seconds …"

He waited. I pulled a finger across my lips.

"I was just going to suggest you have somebody handle your personal finances for you. That way you'd be freed up to do what you're good at."

"Are you volunteering?"

"I'd rather be shot. But Chief would probably—"

I actually snorted.

"What?"

"That would be a total train wreck. It would just be a matter of who came out alive."

Bonner leaned back, arms folded behind his head. "So what's going to happen when you get married?"

I could almost feel the sweat bubbles popping out across my upper lip. "What makes you think—"

"Oh, come on, Allison, I've never seen two people more nuts about each other."

"More so than you and Liz? You two can't keep your hands off of each other." I leaned toward the door. "Where is my favorite social worker, anyway?"

"You're dodging."

"Yes, I am."

I stood up and put my hand down to him. "Thanks, my friend. But I'm fine. I really am."

"The offer stands."

"You're making Allison an offer? You might need legal counsel for that."

I turned and, of course, smiled too eagerly at Kade who was emerging from the kitchen with three plates of tiramisu balanced up his arm.

"You ever work as a waiter?" Bonner said.

"All through law school. I made more in tips then than I'm making now."

Bonner took a plate from him and moved with typical tact toward the door. "The apple doesn't fall far from the tree. You're both going to pro bono yourselves straight into heaven."

He let the door close behind him, leaving Kade and me examining our mascarpone. I thought I should sit down but I was afraid he wouldn't.

"Nice ceremony," he said.

"Uh-huh," I said. Eloquently. "I liked what you said about getting Desmond through math for the rest of his academic career. I'm a complete liability to him in that area."

I then shoveled a hunk of Hank's liqueur-and-lady-fingers into my mouth so I wouldn't say that I now had two sons or that what I really wanted was for them to be brothers. Or ask if witnessing an adoption made him feel … something … I didn't know what. I stuck another mouthful in on top of the other one, though none of it was going anywhere. My esophagus was in a square knot.

"I'm buying a house," Kade said. "Up at Ponte Vedra Beach."

"Duh tha me yo s'aying?" I said.

His clear blue eyes danced. "Say again?"

I swallowed, which gave me time *not* to repeat, *Does that mean you're staying?*

"That's wonderful," I said instead. "Tell me."

I mean, if you want to. You don't have to. I don't want to be pushy.

I all but rolled my eyes at myself. Any time God wanted to intervene would be great. Except that God seldom did when it came to things I could figure out for myself if I weren't such a basket case.

"It doesn't look like much now," Kade said. "Matter of fact the bank wouldn't finance it so I had to get a loan from my father."

"Great—"

"My real father. Not my biological father."

I put the fork down. "You don't have to make that distinction with me, Kade. We don't ever even have to discuss Troy. For any reason."

"Good luck with that."

Kade abandoned his still half-full plate to the arm of one of the Adirondack chairs and perched on the edge of the porch railing, hands jammed into his pockets.

"He's part of the reason I'm staying," he said.

Early-evening shadows fell across his face and across my heart. So this had nothing to do with us having a relationship.

"I won't just sit around and watch him get away with what he did."

"You haven't exactly been sitting around," I said. "What about all those editorials in the paper?"

"What about all those rebuttals? My dad's piece in *Fortune* didn't even faze anybody." Kade looked at me, face struggling. "The DA can let him off. Everybody else can just go back to business as usual with him, but I can't. I don't see how you can either."

"All I can do is work at what I'm given to do, and I'm not getting that taking down Troy Irwin is it."

"How do you know this isn't what *I'm* given to do?"

"Because God doesn't give anybody revenge as a job. Justice, yes, but—"

"Justice. Are you serious? Justice went down the tubes when nobody forced Irwin to give a DNA sample—even though we had an eyewitness. Hey, maybe *I* should become a prosecutor." Sarcasm laced his voice. "Oh, wait, I can't do that here. I'm not a good ol' boy."

I smeared my palms, now oozing sweat, across my thighs. This would be a good time to measure out the words with a teaspoon and maybe *not* alienate him any further.

"I'm not trying to tell you how to feel about this," I said. "I would just hate to see you turn into what Troy Irwin is."

I could almost see that sentence bristling up the back of his neck. "Because it's in my genes?"

"It's not in your soul. That's all I know."

I bit at my lip. If he said I knew nothing about his soul I might have to rip my own larynx out.

"It's not just about me," he said finally. "What about Ophelia? Don't you want her to have closure?"

"That would be great. But even without it, what we really want is for her to heal, and she's doing that—"

"And how about the damage he's done to West King Street?"

"At this point I think he's done all the harm he's going to do down there. His investors have all pulled out."

"And made it worse than it was before he got his hands on it. That tattoo parlor he shut down has about six guys living in it now. The only two things left going are C.A.R.S. and that one bar."

"So we fix it. One person at a time." I could hear my voice going thin, and with it my hope that this conversation could end well.

"What makes you think Irwin will let us?" Kade said. "As long as he's CEO of Chamberlain Enterprises and owns the majority of the stock, he can obviously still take apart everything we try to do."

"How do you know he hasn't given up fighting us?" I said. "He's obviously got the whole police department in his pocket, except for Nick Kent. But he did confess to *us*, Kade. He knows that we know."

"You don't really believe that's going to stop him."

"I haven't heard from him in two months. Have you?"

"No." Kade slid off the porch railing and reached for his plate. "But it's not over with him, and I'm not letting him have the last word." He paused en route to the door. "Congratulations on Desmond. I'm happy for you."

As soon as the door closed behind him, I crossed to the other side of the porch and dug my fingernails into the railing he'd just left. I had sidestepped Ms. Willa when she tried to steer me to the subject of Troy, only because it was easy to imagine myself not trying to take him down financially. International business tycoons had tried, to their eternal regret. I couldn't even get Desmond through eighth-grade algebra.

But Kade had dragged me right where I hated to be: the place where my insides twisted and my mind conjured equally contorted scenarios and my soul rebelled against everything I was supposed to be now.

I looked down at my hands, still straining to strangle the railing with sweaty palms. Ten minutes before I'd been so sure I could handle anything that landed on my pile of life, now that Desmond was mine and hope was so clear. Hope could hold up the Sisters and Sacrament House and even my shriveling bank account.

But at this point, all I could see was Troy Irwin sitting astride that hope, laughing the laugh that had long since lost its mirth and threatening to pull it down completely.

"Except you can't," I said. Out loud. Because there was more hope than there was Troy. There had to be.

No one ever seemed to want to leave Palm Row once invited in. I believed that was partly the spirit of Sylvia, the nanny who had raised me in that house, inherited it from my parents, and then left it to me. She'd embodied Jesus there. She'd died there. And I knew she still lived there, continually erasing the scuffs of my childhood and making room for an even holier Spirit. People cleaned up their language when they were in that living room and relished their food more in that kitchen and saw the Christ in down-and-outers who'd been given up for godless right there on that side porch.

Normally I was more than fine with that. But that night I wished the Spirit would usher the lingerers toward the door. Even after the moon nosed its glow through the trees, I still hadn't had a moment alone with Chief, and now that I'd talked to Kade, I needed more than the resolution of a hug. I had to feel like I could get my balance again.

I piled the last of the empty baking pans into Hank's arms and sent Desmond off to bed wearing his leather jacket with his T-shirt and boxers and was poking in the refrigerator for the piece of lasagna Hank had salvaged when a pair of arms came around me and pulled me close to a warm chest. A strong leg shut the fridge door.

"You forgot to pencil me in," Chief said.

"Pencil?" I said. "I used a big ol' honkin' Magic Marker, but no one could read it."

"You think everybody's gone?"

"Yeah."

His arms tightened, though I didn't need that to leave me completely helpless. "You sure? You checked the closets?"

"Y'know what?" I said. "I don't care if they're all standing outside with binoculars."

I twisted to face him and looped my arms around his neck. I wanted a kiss more than I wanted to breathe, but even more than that I wanted to watch him look at me. His eyes turned downward, searching my face as if he were discovering yet another layer under my skin. It was a prelude I never got tired of.

The only thing worth ending it for was the kiss itself, which Chief knew just when and how to bring me to. Where I wanted him to bring me was away from the careening stack of issues. Just until I could steady it once more.

He pulled back to look at me again, eyes sizzling. Yes. A subject I was clear on.

"I can't," I said.

"I know."

"Then why are you asking me?"

"I'm not."

Chief took my face in his hands and kissed my forehead and smiled with only half his mouth.

"I thought us sleeping together wasn't up for discussion," he said.

"It's not."

"Then why are we having this conversation?"

He wrapped his arms around me, lifting my feet off the floor, and nuzzled his face in my hair. When he let me go he was still wearing the semismile.

"You've set the boundaries, Classic. I'm not going to cross them."

"I know you're not."

"So do me a favor, would you?"

"Yeah?"

He brought his face close to mine. "Quit bringing it up."

I wriggled happily away. This was the center I was looking for. He was so grounded he was practically gravity itself.

"You want coffee?" I said.

He tilted his head at me.

"Tea?"

"What I want is to know is what's going on with you. Today should have lifted the weight of the world off your shoulders."

"It did."

"I'm still seeing it in your eyes."

I shut them. And then I felt his fingers on my chin.

"What are we doing here, Classic?"

There was no point in not looking at him. His raptor eyes were already seeing into me anyway.

"Are we in this or aren't we?"

"We're in."

"To me, *in* means you don't shut down when there's something on your mind."

"I hate it that you know everything," I said.

He didn't smile.

I sighed. "It's Kade."

"Keep going."

I turned to the stove and switched on the burner under the teakettle. "I feel like one of Desmond's little middle-school chickies when I'm around him. I don't want whatever relationship we're going have to be based on my desperation."

"I've watched you form a bond with one son, Classic, and he was a much tougher case. You'll work this through with Kade."

"I don't want to work it through." I rummaged in the canister of tea bags. "I want to go straight to making up for the twenty-six years I've missed."

"Not gonna happen that way."

I considered a bag of Darjeeling and dropped it back in. "It's just so painfully ironic that I have a deeper relationship with Desmond than I do with my own flesh and blood."

"You looking for some bag in particular?"

I turned to him to find the half-smile crinkling his eyes.

"I don't know what I'm looking for."

"Yeah, you do." He put his arms around me. "And you'll find it. There's nothing standing between you and Kade but time."

"And Troy Irwin."

Chief pulled back to look at me again. "That's where this is coming from."

"It's like Kade's obsessed with taking him down."

"You can't really blame him. Kade could be rotting in prison right now because of him."

"I get that. But we're talking hatred here. And what *I* hate is seeing *him* hate."

Chief's eyes crinkled again. "You hate hate."

"Yeah. With everything that's in me."

"And that's what I love about you."

"You love that I hate?"

"Classic," Chief said, "shut up, willya?"

He pulled me into a kiss, and I didn't want it to end. Which was the very reason he set me solidly against the sink and held up one finger before he crossed the room to the door.

"Gotta go," he said.

"I know."

"Gotta go now."

"Yes, you do."

"You okay?"

"I'm better. Thank you."

"Good. Going."

"Yeah."

He stopped, hand on the doorknob. "I want to take you to dinner on Friday the eighth."

"What's the occasion?"

"Our anniversary."

"Our anniversary." I did a mental index, and then realized I was doing it with my brow pinched and my mouth hanging open. Very attractive.

"You're a hopeless romantic, Classic," he said. "We met one year ago. Exactly."

"Only a year?" I said. "I thought I'd been putting up with you for longer than that."

"World *class* hopeless romantic."

"I thought you were going."

"I am." But he still stood there, and his eyes grew solemn. "You and God going to have a talk?"

"Oh, yeah," I said.

"Let me know how it goes," he said.

I watched through the window in the kitchen door as he strode across quiet Palm Row to the garage where his Road King waited in the shadows.

"God, I love everything about him," I said. "How about I just go another mile with *him* and you take care of the rest of it?"

I could almost feel God patting me on the head.

Silly woman.

So yeah, I took care of the "rest of it" at the customary speed of a freight train over the next two days—taking the new Sisters to various doctors' appointments, making the weekly Costco run, arranging rides to NA meetings. So it was Thursday before I had a chance to find out what was going on down at C.A.R.S.

As I cruised the Classic down West King Street, I had to admit Kade was right. As much as I despised the places where I'd found Jasmine and Mercedes and Geneveve a year ago, at least back then some people had been making a living at Titus Tattoos and the greasy-windowed laundromat and the bar that used to sell an affordable lunch. Now all the spaces were gutted in hopeless anticipation of re-dos by investors who had turned away in disgust when the promises made by Chamberlain Enterprises had disintegrated. Yet the hookers still hawked themselves up and down the block at night, and the drug deals still went down in the back alleys. It truly was worse than it had been before Troy Irwin tried to redline it.

Except for C.A.R.S. Old Maharry was still hanging in there, keeping at least two of the Sisters working decent jobs. But according to Zelda, even that wasn't going so well. Time to head for the proverbial horse's mouth.

Maharry was alone in the "showroom" of Choice Auto Repair Service when I arrived, frowning at a stack of tires out of tiny eyes squinted to near extinction behind their thick glasses.

"I'm glad I caught you alone," I said.

"Why?" he said. "You need tires?"

"Nope. The ones you put on the van are still holding up fine. It's about Zelda."

His face puckered. One more wrinkle and it, too, would disappear. "Who?" he said.

"Zelda. The young woman you've got working here?" I glanced around uneasily. Had he fired her?

"Sherry Lynn's friend," he said. "What about her?"

"Is she working out okay for you?"

Maharry shuffled around the stack of tires and, from what I could hear, down the next aisle. Sherry hadn't mentioned anything about senility setting in …

"You want an answer or not?"

"Yes," I said.

"Well, come over here, then."

I followed his trail around the stack to find the old man pointing to a display of hubcaps. The shine nearly blinded me and it took me a minute to realize I had never seen sunlight coming through this window before. As a matter of fact I wasn't sure I'd known there *was* a window.

"She did this," Maharry said. "Imelda."

"Zelda?"

"Whoever you came in here asking me about. She set this all up."

I blinked. In addition to the pyramid of wire wheel covers and gunmetal rims, there were neatly printed signs declaring that the biggest sale in wheel history was taking place inside.

"This is great," I said. "Isn't it?"

"You tell me."

Maharry stared at me from within the countless folds of skin as if he were waiting for me to do just that.

"I guess it depends on whether you've sold any," I said.

"I have."

"So there's no problem."

"Not yet."

I crossed my arms. "Maharry, you're going to have to work with me here. I'm not following."

He pulled a knotted hand from behind his back and jabbed it toward me. The thought struck me that he was a far better match for Ms. Willa than Owen Schatz was.

"You mark my words," he said. "Before you know it she's going to want a commission on these."

"I'm not sure Zelda even knows what a commission is."

"See, there's your trouble. All of you."

Again he waited. He was as bad as Judge Atwell.

"What trouble?" I said.

"She's made you all think she's dumb as a post and she's not. She's smart, that one. Too smart."

I let out a long breath of relieved air. "I gotta tell ya, Maharry, I never heard an employer complain that his employee was 'too smart.'"

He stopped midway into wiping saliva from his weedy moustache. "She complain about me? She did, I can see it on your face."

"She did say you fussed at her."

"I just want her to know she might be smart but she's not smarter than old Maharry. Not when it comes to the car repair business."

He poked his thumb in the general direction of the window that separated the repair bay from the front of the shop.

"You know what I got back there right now?"

I tried to see through the glass but as yellowed and wavy as it was I could only make out the vague shape of a black vehicle. Or it could have been a beached yacht. Hard to tell.

Maharry smacked his lips. "Big fancy Lincoln."

"Owen Schatz's car?" It was a ridiculous question. Owen's car was brand new, although I wouldn't put it past him to bring it in for repairs it didn't need just to keep Sherry and Zelda working.

Maharry waved me off. "This is a special job. Guy said nobody else could figure out why it keeps breaking down, even over at the dealership. That's because these new mechanics, all they can do is rely on computers." He hammered the side of his hand into his chest. "Maharry isn't afraid to get his hands dirty."

That was obvious. I was sure those old digits hadn't been clean since he first learned to use a crescent wrench.

"Daddy?"

Sherry marched around the end of the hubcap aisle. She skidded when she saw me.

"Is everything okay, Miss Angel?" she said.

"Actually, it is. Your dad just gave me a good report on Zelda."

Her eyes popped slightly, but she nodded and turned to her father. "You didn't take your pills this morning, Daddy."

"I'm not taking those things. I'm not sick."

"You will be if you don't. I put them on the counter with a glass of water."

Maharry scowled so deeply the only thing left visible was his nose. "I got to get some men in here. You women are driving me crazy."

I held back a smile until he'd muttered himself out of sight across the shop. Sherry, however, was far from a grin.

"Is he okay?" I said.

"Blood pressure. You need anything else, Miss Angel? Because I need to go make sure he takes those meds."

"I just need to know if you and *I* are okay. After our conversation the other day."

She shifted her eyes to a wire wheel. "What conversation?"

"About Sultan. You left upset."

"Because I want you to let it go and you won't."

"That's hard to do when you're the one who brings it up. Maybe not verbally, but you were thinking it."

Sherry's gaze moved from the shiny chrome to the ceiling. "Only because I know he's not coming back."

"You've heard from him?"

"No!"

"Then we don't know—"

"That's what I was trying to say to you. He's got no reason to come back. Geneveve's gone. Desmond is yours now. We're all of us off the streets. He's done."

"Except for the revenge he obviously wanted last spring and didn't get."

Sherry tried to look at me, but once again her eyes darted, this time to some place beyond us both. "He knows if he comes back here that detective will be all over him."

"Detective Kylie."

"And Sultan knows he doesn't have it like he used to."

"What does that mean?"

"You told me he's all deformed since he was shot. No girl is gonna work for him now. He can't even drive a car. I'm telling you, he's done."

"I want to believe that. But for me he's not done until I see him serving a life sentence. That's the only way I'll ever know Desmond is protected. I'm going to ask you this again: Do you know something—?"

She whirled to face me. "I just know, the same way you know things. But I can't prove it so there's no point in us discussing it anymore."

I couldn't answer. The thing that was strangling her had its fingers around my throat as well.

She straightened her ghostly shoulders. "So to answer your question, you and I are okay. We through here?"

Before I could answer she crossed the shop, once again calling, "Daddy?"

Sure. We were done. Until the next time I had reason to believe Jude Sultan Lowery was nearby. It was clear Sherry and I both hoped next time would never come. But in Sherry's case, I still didn't know why.

CHAPTER THREE

Friday mornings I always met with Hank, who invariably helped me put the piles on hold for an hour so I could focus on my own stuff. And I knew exactly what I wanted to put on the café table for discussion.

After I delivered Desmond at school on the bike—so his prepubescent "women" could be impressed by his arrival on a "bad-butt Harley"—I parked it at Palm Row and walked to St. George Street. I wanted to take advantage of the rare morning breeze that would seem like a figment of our imaginations by eleven o'clock. The start of a Florida September was infuriating that way. Besides, I only had to walk two blocks to where St. George was closed off from traffic so pedestrians could wander freely in the heart of St. Augustine's historic district.

When I stopped to let a family of sulky kids pass so I could cross to the coffee shop I took a long look at the building Ms. Willa had bought for us. As she never tired of pointing out to me, it was a coveted piece of real estate just by virtue of its location. But our guys had made it even more enviable than it was when the Monk's Vineyard owned it.

One of the HOG members was a contractor and had headed up a crew that built an outside stairway and shored up the balcony on the second story so Jasmine could set her plants out there, and widened the porch below to accommodate more tables. Inside Stan, a finish carpenter, had replaced the wine bar and the shelves with a counter and booths for Patrice's Sacred Grounds customers.

Upstairs the dark apartment that had housed Ophelia's former life was now a bright secondhand boutique, hung with castoffs donated by India's customers, Ms. Willa's wealthy friends, and, of course, Miss All-Hair. The rent Patrice paid us for the coffee shop on the lower level went straight to Sacrament House. Income from Second Chances Boutique hopefully would as well. Hopefully being the operative word.

Hank was sitting at our usual table on the porch, hair still in a red bandana. She'd shed her jacket, but she apparently wasn't too hot for a caramel and hazelnut coffee. We'd have to be on the equator for her to turn that down.

She slid a menu across the table as I sat down. "Patrice has added some new items. The woman has the ministry of carbohydrates."

I scanned the menu and groaned. "White chocolate and amaretto? Dark chocolate and banana? This is way more over the top than when she had the Spanish Galleon."

"That's because you give her a decent rate on the rent."

"Toffee nut coffee? I can*not* bring Desmond here anymore. His teeth will decay just reading this."

Patrice appeared on the porch, her long hippie hair lifting as she made her way toward us with an order of eggs Benedict. "What are you having, Miss Allison?" she said as she set the plate in front of Hank, who was virtually salivating.

"Café latte, Patrice," I said.

She shook her bohemian head at Hank. "She's so boring."

"Give her two shots of espresso," Hank said.

I stared at her as Patrice left us murmuring that her white chocolate raspberry truffle in a cup would be wasted on me anyway.

"What?" Hank said.

"Two shots?"

"I hope that's going to be enough."

"For?"

"For whatever you're fighting with. Bring it."

"Miss Angel!"

"Or not," Hank said.

I didn't have to turn around to know that Jasmine was on the outside stairs and that she was close to tears. Her voice was so shrill she momentarily chased off a grackle picking at cracker crumbs on the porch railing. He returned, disgruntled, after Jasmine hoisted over it to join us. If India had been there, she'd be having a litter of kittens about now.

"I'm going to go see about that latte," Hank said.

She patted the chair she was vacating and nodded Jasmine into it before she disappeared into the shop with her plate in her hand. I watched Jasmine drag her palms over her eyes, which did little to stop the stream. I wasn't worried yet. Tears could mean she'd witnessed a stabbing in the alley or that she was merely mourning a dead geranium. Her chin was the litmus test. If it wasn't quivering we were probably okay. I used to think her jitters were drug-induced, but she'd been clean for nearly a year and she still looked at times like she was suffering from hypothermia.

Only her lower lip was trembling so I said lightly, "What's up, Jazz?"

"Can we get fired?" she said.

"Who?"

"Me and Ophelia and Mercedes. Can we get fired from the boutique?"

"Tell me some more."

She plastered her hands over her caramel-colored face. "We failin', Miss Angel."

"Jasmine," I said. "Look at me."

She lowered her hands, but her large liquid eyes stayed glued to the table top. Close enough.

"Did somebody say you were failing?"

"Didn't nobody have to. We ain't sold nothin' in days."

"Have you had customers?"

"We got people comin' in, but don't nobody buy nothin'."

"Jasmine, what are you doin'?"

Even I jumped. The grackle took off for good, leaving the biggest of the crumbs for his fellow scavengers. Mercedes took the bottom three steps in one long, annoyed stride.

"I saw Miss Angel down here," Jasmine said, "and I just—"

"You just botherin' her with stuff she don't—doesn't—need to be bothered with."

"Who else I'm gon' bother with it, then?"

"Your own self, that's who. *We* got to work this out."

"We can't!"

"Maybe *you* can't—"

"Ladies." I put up both hands and simultaneously smiled at an elderly couple below us who had been startled from their study of the tour map. India would be having more than the aforementioned litter by now.

"How about we discuss it over coffee?" I said.

Mercedes pulled her eyebrows so close together they nearly traded places in her forehead. "We ain't—we don't have time for no coffee. We got to get up there and fix this."

I took the latte Patrice put in my hand and turned it over to Jasmine. "We'll have another one of those, Patrice. You want sugar, Mercedes?"

She shook her head, deposited a glare into Jasmine, and headed back up the steps, leaving a wake of muttering behind her. Jasmine stared miserably at the foam in the cup.

"We're fine," I said to Patrice.

"If everybody was like y'all I'd go out of business," she said.

When the door closed behind her I touched Jasmine's arm.

"Mercedes, she says we got to do this," she said, "and I'm so scared we can't. Maybe we wasn't ready after all, Miss Angel."

She was retreating toward the railing and I was already imagining her vaulting back over it and landing on the ground in a puddle of hot milk and tears.

"Not to worry," I said. "We'll figure something out. And Jazz?"

"Ma'am?"

"Use the gate, babe."

She flung both arms around my neck, barely missing the returning Hank with a waterfall of coffee.

"Business slow?" Hank said when Jasmine was gone.

"Slow?" I took the cup she handed me and paused until she sat with her still unfinished eggs dish. "It has apparently come to a complete halt. Not that that's the total point of the shop. All I really want is for them to learn how to get to work on time and not dress in hooker wear."

"That part seems to be working."

I took a sip of the latte. "Patrice snuck chocolate in here."

Hank waited.

"They need to feel productive and successful," I said. "And apparently *that's* not happening."

"Trust India. This is her baby."

"You're right," I said. "Absolutely. I can leave it to her."

"Then why are you about to squeeze that cup in half? Sit."

I did, and watched Hank neatly pile her fingers into a fold on the table between us. "We were about to talk about why this is a two-shot day."

I took a gear-shifting breath. "Okay. This isn't exactly spiritual. Well, I mean it is, but it doesn't have anything to do with my work for God, but then I guess everything does, except when God doesn't tell me what the Sam Hill to do——"

"You're killin' me, Al," Hank said. "Let's just cut to the chase: this is about Chief."

"OhdearGod yes."

Hank gave me a rare full-blown smile. "I love young love. Or in this case I guess it's middle-aged love."

"He's taking me out for our 'anniversary' next Friday."

"It's been a year since you met."

"Why am I the only one who didn't remember that?"

"Because you're scared spitless."

I had to grin at her. "Yes, why *don't* we cut to the chase?"

"Are you afraid he's going to propose?"

"Is he? Did he tell you?"

She stopped with her fork halfway to her mouth. "Have you met the man?"

"Okay, yeah, I'm afraid he will. And I'm afraid he won't."

"Guess that kind of puts you in a hurt locker."

"Whatever that is, yes, I think I'm in it."

"I know why you're afraid he *won't* propose. You're nuts about the guy."

"I never thought I could love any man the way I love him."

She nodded and went for the bacon. "So why are you afraid he *will* ask?"

"Because I want to make sure I can say yes."

"Because of God."

I closed my eyes. "Thank you for not making me explain that to you."

"You don't have to explain it to *me*. You have to explain it to yourself. I'm just the sounding board."

She popped in a mouthful and looked at me while she chewed.

"It's the one thing that keeps *me* from proposing to *him*. He's come a long way. At first he didn't even believe in God."

"Or so he said. Personally I think it was more that he didn't believe in the God he'd been introduced to by organized religion." She shrugged the stocky shoulders. "I don't believe in that one either. Neither do you."

"At the Sisters' baptism, on Easter, he said he wanted to believe what I believe, and it seemed like that was enough."

"Enough for who?"

"For God. God's not coming right out and saying it, but what I feel for Chief is different than just 'this man is hot.'" I glanced around at the still empty nearby tables. "Chief respects that I try to be obedient to God. We agreed, Chief and me, not to . . ."

Hank leaned in, eyes sparkling, and lowered her voice to a hoarse whisper. "Have sex?"

"I don't even like to say it like that. I don't want to just 'have sex' with Chief. Not that I don't *want* him. I'm dyin' here."

"I suspect he is too. You're a bit of a hot mama yourself."

"But it's more than that. I don't know, it's surreal."

"I think what you're feeling is joy. You haven't had a lot of it in your life so it would be hard to pinpoint." She set the fork down and folded her hands again. "It's like when you experience serious pain for the first time. Or panic. It doesn't seem real. Or maybe it's a little too real."

"So—"

"So marry him. You said God appears to be fine with it."

"What I'm getting from God is 'go another mile,' and I don't know if that even applies to Chief or if it's about something else. And if it is about Chief, does it mean go ahead and marry him even if I'm not totally sure we're on the same spiritual page? Or go another mile until I find out ..." I swallowed as if I were the one downing a six hundred–calorie breakfast. "I just keep going deeper and deeper with God and I want to make sure that's not too much for Chief."

"Have you talked to him about it?"

I raked my hands through my hair.

"You're afraid to do that, too."

"I'm terrified."

Hank pushed the plate aside. "One thing I've learned in my marriage to Joe: if you can't talk about everything with your partner without being afraid, you aren't going to make it. You've faced thugs in dark alleys and dragged prostitutes out of darker ones, and yet you're afraid to talk to the man who is so crazy about you he'd cut off that ponytail if you asked him to."

"I'm a mess."

"We all are. But you less than most because you get the big time Nudges." She patted her mouth with a napkin. "I want to go back to 'go another mile.'"

"Anywhere, as long as it takes me someplace," I said.

"You know where that expression 'go the extra mile' comes from?"

"The Sermon on the Mount."

"'If somebody asks you to go one mile, go the next mile too.' I'm paraphrasing, but that's basically it."

"Why didn't I even think to look that up?"

"Oh, I don't know. Because you're trying to do about sixteen things at once."

I glanced at my watch. "Aw, man, I'm supposed to be meeting with Chief right now."

"Perfect timing."

"I don't know about that. We're going to talk about my personal finances."

Hank's eyes bulged. "Whose idea was that?"

"Bonner's." I put up both hands. "I'm not asking Chief to handle them. I'm just hoping he'll know somebody who can."

Hank waited again.

"Okay," I said, "and then I'll be less strung out and I can look this up and talk to Chief and stop freaking out."

"You're killin' me, Al," she said. "You're killin' me."

Between Sacred Grounds and the Wells Fargo Building around the corner there wasn't a whole lot of time to contemplate the Sermon on the Mount. If anything, I needed a Sermon on the *A*mount. The morning heat hadn't picked up enough to account for the fact that I was sweating like Miss Piggy. Just the thought of dealing with money did that to me.

The ground floor of the building was occupied by the Wells Fargo Bank, spacious and high-ceilinged and reeking wealth. The first thing visible as I passed through the heavy glass doors off the sidewalk was the massive vault, trimmed in conservative brass with just the right amount of intricacy in its hardware. My father always said having the vault in the front showed the bank as an institution of integrity and trust. I'd once told him I wasn't sure he'd have known those two things if they bit him in the behind. One of the many reasons he left me out of his will.

Chief's office suite was on the third floor facing the long, rectangular park known as the Plaza that stretched between the two one-way streets, Cathedral Place and the "good" end of King Street. This office had a higher class factor than his previous digs. When he invited Kade in they'd needed more space as well as better visibility, although the modest sign on the door that said simply "Ellington and Capelli, Attorneys at Law" wasn't exactly a billboard.

Inside, their secretary, Tia Davies, continued the understated tone. She was only in her early fifties, but she carried on the pre-Baby Boomer traditions of having her graying hair washed, set, teased, and sprayed into a helmet every Monday afternoon and wearing panty hose even in the summer. I could always count on Tia to have Kleenex, breath mints, and a double dose of decorum.

"Mr. Ellington is just about ready for you, Ms. Chamberlain," she said when I entered the outer office.

She offered me coffee, which I turned down, and a tweed and leather chair, which I accepted, and looked at me with perfectly poised hazel eyes.

"I understand congratulations are in order," she said. "You have to be so happy."

"Do you know something I don't, Tia?" I said.

"She's talking about the adoption."

Chief was framing the doorway to the back hall, making no attempt to hide a grin. The beast. Now I was sweaty *and* blotchy-faced: the perfect combination for romance.

"I knew that," I said.

Tia nodded without moving a single hair.

"We'll need about an hour, Tia," Chief said.

"Yes, sir."

It was my turn to grin. He'd told me no less than sixty times how much he wished she wouldn't call him sir. But she would probably rather come to work without her pumps than address him as Chief. I was glad there were people like her in the world. It made up for there being people like me.

Chief led me into his office, which was as streamlined and masculine as the man himself. It was all I could do not to pull him onto the leather couch and, as India so often put it, get a little neck sugar. I made a deliberate beeline for one of the high-backed chairs in front of his desk, but he curled his fingers around my upper arm and pulled me in for a quick kiss.

"I came here to talk business, Mr. Ellington, sir," I said.

"Just greeting my client," he said close to my mouth.

He let me go so I could sit before my knees jellied completely. I was already saying, "So we've agreed I can't be your client when it comes to my personal finances."

"Your personal shambles," he said.

"My point exactly. So you have any ideas?"

"I have one thought." He was clearly all contracts and depositions again. "But I really want you to think about it before you decide."

"Do you think I'm going to hate it?"

"Not at all. Just the opposite."

Chief tilted his head. "Would you consider Kade?"

I stared. "Do you think he'd do it?"

"He seemed okay with it."

"You already asked him?"

"I told him I wanted to mention it to you."

"And he was all right with it?"

I stopped before I completely turned into a forty-three-year-old rendition of a tween with a crush on Justin Bieber.

"He believes in what you're doing. He wants to help." Chief leaned forward, forearms on his thighs. "I think more to the point, Classic, is whether *you* are all right with it."

"Why wouldn't I be?"

He shrugged one shoulder. "He's going to be smack in the middle of your personal affairs."

"You mean he's going to know that I'm hopeless with money."

"There's that."

"You could have at least pretended to argue with me there." I shook my head. "I don't think that's a secret to anybody. I've got nothing to hide. What's the other thing?"

"This is going to mean spending some time with him."

"I want that. You know I want that."

"I do. Just be aware that he's probably going to be strictly professional about it."

"So I shouldn't count on a mother-son bonding experience."

Chief's eyes softened. "Maybe not. But who knows?"

"Certainly not me." I sank back in the chair and felt my wet back adhere to the leather.

"I don't suggest him just because it would give you a chance to get through some of this," Chief said. "But if it helps ..."

"Okay," I said, "I'll make an appointment with him. How weird is that?"

His eyes crinkled. "No weirder than anything else about your life, Classic."

After the three-day Labor Day weekend, I was only able to get Desmond vertical and out of his room to go to school by promising I would take him to school on the Harley. Then the only obstacle was making him actually get dressed before he donned what he was now calling his D.C. jacket.

"That stays with me when we get there," I called to him the second time I sent him back to his room to get out of the T-shirt he'd slept in.

"Ain't nobody gonna gank it," he called back. "Imma keep a eye on it."

"What exactly does that mean, Clarence?"

"Nobody gonna jack it."

"Really?"

"You got to get hip, Big Al. Means Imma make sure nobody steals it."

"Oh. I'm not worried about that."

I dropped the second p.b.-and-pickle sandwich into his lunch bag and surveyed him as he emerged. The shirt he'd chosen was wrinkled from spending two days in the dryer, but at least I couldn't smell it.

"What I'm concerned about," I said, "is the jacket becoming the focal point in every one of your classes."

"What's a focal point?"

"It's the center of attention."

He grinned. "I gotta get me one of those."

"You *are* one of those. The jacket stays with me."

Go another mile.

The Nudge was so out-of-nowhere I stood there, head cocked.

"I'm seein' a 'but,'" Desmond said. "Is it a good 'but' or a bad 'but'?"

Go.

"It's an if-you-hurry-up-we'll-go-a-long-way-to-school but," I said.

"Dude, Big Al, I was ready *yesterday*."

He was out in the garage putting on his helmet before I could locate the keys and the cell phone and the list of fifty things on the pile that I had to do that day, all the while considering this latest Nudge. It was actually more like a Shove. There was an urgency to it that didn't match just taking Desmond for a longer ride to pull him out of his school funk. It was a physical jolt I couldn't ignore.

Desmond wasn't about to ignore it either. When I joined him in the garage across the lane every rule had been followed, right down to the fact that he hadn't climbed on the bike without me there.

As I threaded the Classic through the back streets, he showed the proper amount of appreciation by yelling, "Yeah, baby!" at every bump in the bricks. At the corner of Bridge and Aviles I reminded him that it was 7:00 a.m. and some people were lucky enough to still be in bed. He ratcheted his voice down to a husky whisper that still made the otherwise bold, indulged squirrels run for the magnolia trees.

Aviles was even narrower than most of the historic streets and was lined on one side with park benches and pots of impatiens. Though it hosted several small cafés on the other side, it had escaped the souvenir-shop mentality and largely remained true to the past St. Augustine was so proud of.

Most of the block we were on was taken up with the old Spanish Military Hospital, which in its day was known for amputations. The solution to every ill back then was to cut off the associated limb. When I was a carriage driver, in my life before Sacrament House and Nudges and Harleys, I used to tell my customers that no one ever went in there complaining of a headache.

The umbrellas on the tables outside La Herencia Café made it hard to see anyone who might be coming out of a doorway, so I slowed down. I could never understand how anybody could eat

Mexican food at this hour of the morning, but a figure did indeed emerge from behind the red canvas and step right into our path.

The thought, *You couldn't hear us coming, pal?* hadn't fully formed in my head before I realized who it was. It was quickly followed by: *You had me go another mile for* this?

There was no doubt it was Troy Irwin. The stylishly mussed hair and the high-end summer suit could have belonged to any fit middle-aged CEO with an American Express Platinum card and a Caribbean tan, but not the body language. The entitled pulling in of the chin, the hubris-filled lifting of the eyebrows, the arrogant raising of the commanding hand to stop the progress of an eight hundred–pound vehicle—that could belong to none other than Troy Allan Irwin, Esq. Only because I had Desmond with me did I not attempt to pop a wheelie in the hope that the man would wet his pants.

I stopped and dropped my feet to the ground on either side of the bike and waited for him to cross. No such good fortune. While the Classic idled indignantly under its rumbling breath, Troy strode over to my side, tucking his sunglasses into a silk-blend pocket. I was tempted to at least give the throttle a twist as he approached, but it wouldn't have fazed him. I knew that walk. He had something to say, and he was going to say it even if I dumped the bike over on him. He wasn't worth the damage to the paint job, or the dent in my firm resolve not to let Troy Irwin make me hate him.

"You know this dude, Big Al?" Desmond said between his teeth.

"Unfortunately," I said.

I could feel him stiffening against my back. "You want me to take care of him for ya?"

"I think I can handle it. Just—"

"I know: let you do the talkin'."

Troy was now standing no more than two feet away, one hand parked in his slacks pocket, the other dangling casually at his side. I had often wondered if he stood in front of a full-length mirror perfecting that pose. Half of my last cup of coffee rose in my throat.

"Good morning," he said.

This was another of those moments when it would be good of God to put words in my head. If any were there, they were stuck in some crevice I couldn't get to, not with Troy turning his arrogant gaze on Desmond.

"Is this your son?" he said. "I don't think we've met."

"Nor do you need to," I said. "Listen, we're in a hurry."

"I can see that. You almost took me out." He cocked a sandy eyebrow. "I guess when you have a nice young police officer kissing your feet you can get away with driving any way you want to."

I thought I'd stopped being shocked by his shamelessness. Apparently not. All I could do was look at him with my jaw heading for my chest. He put out his hand to Desmond.

"Troy Irwin. I'm an old friend of your mother's."

I'd never put it together that Desmond hadn't met Troy, and the thought of it now brought the rest of that coffee into my throat. I tilted my head back to tap my helmet against Desmond's but he didn't need the reminder. He looked in the opposite direction, leaving Troy with his hand stuck out.

"I see you've told him your side of the story," Troy said to me.

He was still wearing the plastic smile that reminded me of something out of a Mr. Potato Head kit. So did his eyes for that matter. I wished my heart had some of that same plastic quality, but it clenched like a fist in my chest.

"As a matter of fact," I said, "it never occurred to me to mention you to him." I nodded toward Desmond. "He's obviously rather good at judging people for himself."

The synthetic smirk didn't waver. "When I saw you coming I just wanted to congratulate you. You've gotten everything you wanted. I, on the other hand, have not. But I will. You know that, Ally."

I was abruptly thrust forward, straight into my next words. "Do what you have to do, Troy. But you can't hurt us."

That was what I said. What I thought was, *Are you serious, God? He* can. *He so* can!

Troy just watched me until I was very close to throwing up on his shoes. But as I watched back, I saw something in his eyes, something that bent a slat in the blinds he kept firmly pulled down over them, something that peered out in an instant of desperation before the slat snapped back into place.

I went cold. Arrogant Troy. Infuriating Troy. Even Angry Troy—those versions of the boy I grew up with didn't push me to rage anymore.

But Desperate Troy was unfamiliar territory. He had never been backed to the wall in his life, and I had no idea what he would do with that. The possibility that it might be worse than what he had already done froze my fingers to the handlebars.

"Well," Troy said, "nice meeting you, Desi."

"Right back at ya, Roy," Desmond said.

I took that as my cue to rev the engine. Troy stepped back and I pulled away far more slowly than I wanted to. It was as if I was being held back by the same force that had catapulted me there ten minutes before, right to a place I went to great lengths to stay out of. I never drove Desmond to school that way. There was no way Troy could have known I'd be going by.

What are we doing here, God?

Go another mile, was the answer.

We pulled up to the stop sign at Charlotte and King Street and Desmond leaned in to shout over the engine's growl.

"That dude really a ol' friend of yours, Big Al?"

I barely trusted myself to speak, but I managed to say over my shoulder, "We used to be friends a long time ago. Not anymore."

"I know that thing, now. Ain't no way you be friends with some-body look at you like that."

"Like what?"

"Like he 'bout to gank everything you got. You coulda took him out. He look like a wussy."

The car horn behind us blasted and someone yelled, "Whatta ya waitin' for, Harley?"

I opened the throttle and shot out into King. To my left, tires screamed. I could feel the heat from the hood of an SUV as I leaned to the right to miss and over-corrected to the left, into the path of a Mini Cooper. Between it and the pickup truck in the far lane was a narrow opening I squeezed through with no room to breathe. We left so much squealing and honking behind us it sounded like a scene from *The Blues Brothers.*

With Desmond yelling, "Yeah, ba-*bee!*" on the seat behind me I let off on the throttle and kept the handle bars straight until I could ease into the no-parking zone next to the tourist train stop. He and

Classic seemed to have had a fabulous time, but I shook my heart right up into my throat.

Or was it the answer I hadn't given Desmond that was stuck there? *I have nothing left he can steal, son,* I wanted to say.

But the image of Troy peering desperately from a slit in his facade made me far less than sure of the truth in that.

PleaseGodpleaseGodplease show me what we're doing.

The warning bell had already rung by the time we got to Muldoon Middle School, so none of Desmond's gaggle of girls was there to be impressed. The only person at the curb was a tall, lean woman with short spiky hair and sunglasses as big as windshields.

"This ain't good," Desmond murmured to me as I slowed for the curve.

"Why?"

"That's the Mosquito."

I'd heard him refer to his PE teacher, Miss Skeeter Iseley, as that before, but I hadn't met her. Currently she wore spandex shorts and a whistle on a lanyard in black and gold school colors that matched her tight T-shirt. There was so little fat on her I could see the bones in her sternum.

Yeah. I'd probably have come up with that nickname myself.

I prayed heavily Desmond hadn't called her that to her face, although from the pointed way she stared at us as I slowed to a stop I couldn't count on that being the case.

"Ms. Chamberlain?" she said when I'd turned off the engine.

Her voice whined, replacing all the other reasons for naming her after an annoying insect.

"Skeeter Iseley," she said. "I'm Desmond's PE teacher."

"Yes, ma'am," I said. How else did you respond to a woman who looked and sounded like she could raise welts on you?

"Hey, Coach," Desmond said as he climbed off the bike. "I'm only late 'cause—"

"You still have five minutes to get to first period."

He started to take off, but I caught him by the sleeve.

"Jacket," I said.

He gave us both a toothy grin and wriggled out of his leather. "I can't get away with nothin' with you women." He gave the top of my helmet a juicy kiss and once again headed for the front door.

"A motorcycle," the Mosquito said. "A Harley."

Desmond stopped behind her and formed the word *Du-uh* with his lips.

"Yes, ma'am," I said again. "Is there a problem?"

"No," she said. "Not yet."

She zipped her head around to find Desmond, who, fortunately, was now forming nothing on his lips. They were firmly plastered together.

"I'm just trying to *forestall* a problem," she said. "Just trying to be proactive."

I leaned around her and once again looked at Desmond. "Have you done something to make the—Coach Iseley think there might be a problem?"

"No," Desmond said. "Ma'am."

"He knows what I'm talking about," the coach said. "He knows."

"Then let's include him in the conversation," I said.

She looked as if that thought hadn't occurred to her.

"What's she talking about, Desmond?" I said.

"You got me, Big Al. Only thing she ever said to me was, 'Leave those girls alone. Give me five.'"

"Five ...?"

"Push-ups," the Mosquito said. "I'd give him more than that, but that's all he can do. All."

"Desmond," I said, "are you acting inappropriately with the girls in your class?"

He looked stung. "I don't act inapproprimately with girls *any-time*. Me and Mr. Chief talked about that, now."

"Desmond, get on to class," Miss Iseley said. "Go."

I wondered vaguely if anyone had ever told her she repeated everything with a synonym. I felt like reaching for a flyswatter.

Desmond was still looking at me.

"Go on," I said. "We'll talk later."

I waited until he was inside before I turned to the woman who appeared to be sharpening her stinger.

"I hope you have a minute," she said. "Just one."

I pulled off my helmet. "Where Desmond is concerned I have all the minutes you need. But just so we're clear, whatever you have to say about Desmond can be said in front of him. He's old enough to be involved in discussions about his welfare." I lowered my chin. "I assume this is about his welfare."

"Not entirely his. It's about the welfare of his classmates, too. Particularly his harem."

"His *what?*"

"The girls who follow him around like he's the sheik."

She wasn't telling me anything I wasn't aware of, but her tone zinged its way right between my shoulder blades.

"Has someone claimed harassment?" I said.

"No," she said. "If there were harassment, he would already be on in-school suspension."

There was no mistaking the disappointment.

"Then what is the problem?" I said.

"There isn't one. Yet. As I said, I'm trying to be proactive."

"About what?"

She planted her hands on hips so narrow they barely existed. "There is one girl who is obviously having issues. Crying. Withdrawing. Like every other girl in the eighth grade, depending on her hormone levels."

"You're saying Desmond is the cause of that?"

"No. On the contrary. Just the opposite. He sits next to her constantly and talks to her like he's Dr. Phil."

Which is he, Mosquito Lady? I wanted to say. *Dr. Phil or the sheik?*

"As I see it," she went on, "he is making this girl dependent on him for emotional support so that … may I be blunt?"

"I think that ship has sailed," I said.

"I've seen it before, though never quite this blatant. He's setting himself up as her comforter so he can prey on her sexually."

My leg swung over the bike almost of its own accord. I had my face in hers before Classic's weight even balanced on the kickstand.

"Has my son ever touched that girl in your class?" I said.

"I didn't say he had."

"No. You just said he was trying to get her in the sack. That is a very serious accusation."

I had to hand it to her: she was not visibly cowed by the fact that I was all but breathing fire from my nostrils. "As I've *said*, I'm trying to ward off a problem before it starts."

"You have no reason to think *that* problem is ever *going* to start."

"Really. Because in my experience, children aspire to what's celebrated in their community. If drug dealers are making the big money, all the kids want to be one. In this case—"

"In this case what's celebrated in Desmond's community is love and acceptance and healing."

The woman looked at me as if I were five years old. "I'm talking about his community of *origin*, Ms. Chamberlain. I admire what you've done in adopting this boy, but you have to understand: the pimp was glamorized in his formative years, and you're going to be hard put to erase that at this age."

Pleasegodpleasegodpleasegod do not let me hit this woman over the head with my helmet and leave her for dead.

I pulled back and straightened my fingers as far from fists as I could get them. Just to be on the safe side.

"Ma'am," I said. "You are out of line."

"And you are in denial. Head in the sand—"

"No. I have never been clearer on an issue in my life. And here is how we're going to deal with it."

For the first time, she looked as if this was not the next line in her script.

"*We* will handle what, if anything, needs to be handled at home," I said. "And I advise *you* to refrain from applying your sidewalk sociology to my son. He is in your class to do push-ups, apparently. His physical fitness is your only concern. Leave the rest to me. Now if you'll excuse me, I think we've gone beyond a minute."

At least she had the good sense not to try to argue further. I think that was mostly due to my jamming my helmet back on my head and letting Classic have the last growling word with her pipes.

I only drove as far as the parking lot at the Oldest House Museum before I stopped and let both the engine and my heartbeat idle. I sat staring at the line of school children forming for their field trip tour.

There was no doubt the malaria-carrying creature didn't know Desmond. At all. In the first place Chief had talked to Desmond on more than one occasion about the disrespect in considering the adoring group of pubescent females to be "his." And the minute Desmond's thirteen-year-old voice had started to deepen and those first tiny hairs had appeared on his young chin, Chief had the "talk" with him, which I gathered had not been the typical birds-and-bees conversation.

In the second place we didn't glamorize anything in our community. It was all so real and raw the Mosquito wouldn't last through the first hour of watching a woman howl her way into withdrawal.

Still, something poked at me. I pulled off my helmet and wiped my face with my denim sleeve. I knew my Desmond, but I didn't know young girls with angst. I'd never been one. What if one of them *wanted* to show her appreciation for his comfort with more than a peck on the cheek?

Wow. I was thinking like a mother. Not *my* mother but one who actually cared whether her child's life was twisted by adolescent sex.

I put my helmet back on and went easier on the throttle as I restarted the Classic. It wouldn't hurt for Desmond to have another talk. I would put Chief right on it.

CHAPTER FOUR

I wanted to fill Chief in that night before the board meeting, but India got to me first and pulled me aside, eyes full of news. That could have been anything from a reminder that my roots needed touching up to her opinion that Second Chances was never going to get off the ground. It was neither.

"I have news about Reverend Howard," she said. "I thought you'd want to know."

I almost asked her why on earth she'd think that. Garry Howard and I hadn't spoken in months, not since I'd offered my condolences for his being asked to leave the church he'd led for twenty-five years. Even then he just didn't get why I'd left before him, of my own volition.

"He's in hospice care now," India said. "I think he was a perfect snake, treating you like he did, but still …"

She waited, her almost-violet eyes wide.

"Still what?" I said.

"Well, don't you think the whole congregation turning on him because he took Troy Irwin's money for building that school is what's killing him?"

"I don't even want to go there," I said.

Where I did want to go was after Hank, who had just passed us with a plate of bruschetta saying, "Last call."

India gave my arm a squeeze. "I just thought you'd want to know."

She whispered her lips across my cheek and followed Hank into the living room. Chief passed her on the way toward me. It was starting to look like a Marx Brothers comedy.

"You coming?" he said.

I nodded him into the foyer, where I only had time to whisper the Skeeter Iseley highlights to him. All I actually got out was, "Would you talk to Desmond again about the girl situation? The Mosquito thinks he's trying to bed one down by doing therapy with her."

"You're going to explain that to me, right?" he said.

"After the meeting."

I started for the living room, but he pulled me back and put his face achingly near. "Just tell me you're not seeing talking insects."

When we joined the rest of the group, Hank, Bonner, and India were focusing too intently on the hors d'oeuvres, even for a D'Angelo special. Lips were fighting smiles and knowing glances were being furtively exchanged. They were all but blurting, "Aw, aren't they *cute?*"

"These are fresh tomatoes, aren't they, Hank?" India schmoozed.

"Right out of the garden at Sacrament House. Owen said they had more than he could can for them so he gave me the overflow."

"God bless him," Bonner said, mouth stuffed.

"Oh, here they are!" India tossed back her luscious hair and wafted a silk-draped arm as if she *hadn't* had one eye and ear pointed in our direction the whole time Chief and I were in the foyer. "Y'all are missin' it. I am holding Hank personally responsible for the size of my thighs right now."

"Responsibility not accepted," Hank said. "Is this meeting officially in session?"

"As official as it's ever going to get." Bonner waved the leather book he always took notes in. "Go for it."

"Good, then," India said, "because I would like to start with the boutique."

"It's tanking, isn't it?" I said.

She looked at Chief.

"Not yet," he said. "Ms. Willa gave us enough seed money to keep us afloat for a while."

"Which takes the pressure off the Sisters." Hank slid the bruschetta toward me. "They can develop their skills like you want them to—"

"But not their confidence," I said. "Jasmine and Mercedes are convinced they're failures because they're not selling much. I don't know about Ophelia."

We all turned to India, who pressed her fingertips together on her chin. "How can I put this?"

"You could just say it," Hank said.

Bonner gave a soft snort. "No, she couldn't."

"I don't want to look that ol' gift horse in the mouth," India said, each word carefully formed. "Ophelia and I just think that the concept is wonderful and people are drawn to it, but, and again, I don't want to sound ungrateful, because Erin and Ms. Willa and Leighanne and Nita have been so great about collecting clothes for us—"

"Mercy, India," Bonner said.

"Most of the garments are top quality and yet, shall we say, less than stylish."

Hank gave a grunt. "No, we should say they're downright dowdy. I tried on everything they had in my size and I looked like a frump. I bought a couple of things and then gave them to Goodwill."

"Tourists aren't going to do that," I said.

"And neither are the townies," India said. "Now, hear me, the Sisters have done a fabulous job with the displays, and they do everything except kiss the customers' feet when they come in, but those shoppers take one look at the things we've got hanging on the racks and ..." She shrugged.

I glanced at Chief, who was gazing at Bonner. Although Bonner could easily have made it to the cover of *GQ*, his eyes were beginning to glaze over as well.

"I'm no help whatsoever with this," I said.

India patted my knee. "You have other gifts, darlin'."

"So ... suggestions?" Hank said.

"Well, now that we know what the problem is," India said, "we can focus on it. Meanwhile let's not encourage any more donations from anyone over forty until we get a handle on this."

Erin O'Hare with her garbage bags flickered through my mind, but I turned to Bonner. "Any property issues?"

He glanced at a set of notes resting on the arm of his chair. "Both houses are in good shape right now thanks to the HOGs, but we need to have some funds in reserve.

"Owen's got the Sisters working the gardens. Some of them. Not so much with Zelda and Gigi."

"Yeah but Zelda's tearin' it up over at C.A.R.S.," I said. "Gigi's too new for us to know where she can fit in."

"We have room for one more in Sacrament One," Bonner said. "There are still women on the street, right?"

My turn.

"There are," I said. "Probably more now than ever. Instead of, 'I came here for a few beers and oh, look, I can get an hour with a hooker,' it's 'I came here specifically to get a quickie in the alley because this is the Whore Mall.'"

"Allison, honey, that's a little graphic," India said.

Hank gave a soft grunt. "I think she cleaned it up a little for your benefit."

I moved to the edge of the chair. "Even if they all came in and we had a fourteen-room facility, the real problem is we really need someone to help me oversee the houses. I mean, we want the Sisters to live on their own without somebody in there telling them what to do, but with me being the only one who can afford to do this full time …"

"And that isn't going to last forever," Bonner said, looking directly at me. "Anyway, it's something to pray about."

"Then the Lord be with you," Hank said.

When everyone left I saw Chief edging toward the door himself. And I knew why.

"Desmond," I said, eyes drilling into Chief, "would you come out here, please? Chief wants to talk to you."

"You're shameless," Chief said as he headed across the kitchen for Desmond's room. "I'll go in there. We don't need an audience."

"Fine with me," I said.

But I continued to hang out in the kitchen and, yes, shamelessly listened for snatches coming out under the door. From what I could piece together it went something like:

"We gon' have the sex talk again, Mr. Chief?"

"Do we *need* to have the sex talk again?"

"I know everything I need to know."

"I understand that. Knowing isn't the same as not doing, though."

"Ain't doin', Mr. Chief."

"Just so you know, it's harder not to when they find out you get them. Women like it when you get them."

"I know that thing, now. They can see I feel it when they get all emo. Is that what you're sayin'?"

"That's what I'm sayin'."

"It's all good, Mr. Chief. I got me a female philosophy. You wanna hear it?"

"I can use all the female philosophy I can get."

The sound of hand slapping.

"See, I make myself available to *all* my … wait, no … *the* women, whenever one of 'em needs me. That way don't nobody think I'm gettin' serious with anybody and I can be a friend with all of 'em, and that's the Jesus-thing. You pickin' up what I'm puttin' down, Mr. Chief?"

"Pickin' it up, Desmond."

"We good?"

"We're good."

More prolonged hand slapping.

I shifted my face into neutral just in time for Chief to emerge and close the door behind him. I nodded him into the dining room.

"Was that what you wanted?" he said.

I leaned against the table. "I didn't hear a thing. Did *you* feel like it went well?"

Chief leaned beside me. "If you mean do I think he's playing Father Confessor so he can seduce them, no."

"You think he respects them, though?"

"Does he have a choice?" He pressed his elbow against me. "You'd put his helmet down the garbage disposal if he didn't."

"Yeah, but that whole 'Female Philosophy' thing."

"I thought you said you didn't hear a thing."

"I lied."

Chief shrugged. "Every thirteen-year-old boy has a plan for getting girls to notice him."

"Notice him? He wants them 'right here.'" I pointed into the palm of my hand.

"That's his shtick." He squinted at me. "What's really bothering you about this, Classic?"

"Am I in denial about him?"

"Define denial," he said.

I rubbed my palms together. "I've always thought the healing he saw in his mother the few months she was at Sacrament House had wiped out everything he lived with in the years before that."

"He remembers she was a prostitute and an addict," Chief said.

"That's not what I mean. I'm talking about the influence. I want to believe what we're doing is more powerful in him than that was. I want to keep thinking that he wants to be the kind of man you are. But am I being realistic?"

"Where's this coming from?" Chief nudged at my forehead with his. "The Mosquito?"

"Yes. But no."

"That's clear."

I pulled away from him.

"What, Classic?"

"What if nature is stronger than nurture? I've only had him for a year."

"A year during which you fought for him like a mother bear and took down anybody who tried to get to him. Including Sultan."

"That's just it, Chief. I didn't take Sultan down. He's still out there."

"I don't think you have to worry about that. Detective Kylie is obsessed with catching him. Sultan gets a hangnail and Kylie knows about it."

"What if Kylie isn't telling *me* about it?"

"He told you he would. And what about Nick Kent? You know he passes on everything he finds out, and he says the coast is still clear."

"What about the Sultan that's in Desmond's genes?" I said. "It's the same thing that eats at Kade. He's afraid he's like Troy whether he wants to be or not, and he hates the man."

"So where does God come in?"

My head came up.

"You talk about hope for the Sisters." Chief shrugged the big shoulders again. "Doesn't it apply to Desmond?"

"I didn't say I didn't have hope. I wouldn't have adopted him if I didn't hope I could give him a better life than he was going to have otherwise."

"So ..."

"I don't know."

"Hey." Chief lifted my chin with the tips of his fingers. "How many times do we have to go through this? If you don't trust me with what's going on in there—"

"I do."

"Up to a point."

"What point?"

"The point where you think I'm going to say 'enough.'"

"Enough … God?"

"*Do* you think I'm going to say that?"

I was tempted to ask him if he'd been talking to Hank. The point was, *I* had been talking to Hank. And I was in prime position to do what she said I needed to do.

"Okay," I said. "I just have to keep hoping that God the Father will replace Sultan the Mack Daddy in Desmond's mind."

Chief's face went so soft I had to touch it to make sure it was still his. He caught my hand and kissed my sweaty palm.

"I can hope that too," he said.

The moment was so stunning I almost missed the next one.

"We still on for Friday night? I made a reservation at Columbia."

"My, my," I said, scrambling to recover. "Should I go with a sequined gown, then?"

"I'm picking you up on the bike." He gave me the long prekiss look, sucking all the air out of the room. "Just one thing, Classic."

"Yeah?"

"No shoptalk. This is going to be about you and me."

"I can do you and me," I said.

He left via the front door, and I watched through its tiny window as he eased himself onto the Road King and made it rumble the way his voice did. Longing. That was the only word for the push to run after him and beg him to stay.

I sat on the pew among the pillows and looked up at Desmond's drawings. I'd found time to put the latest one of the two of us in a frame and as I dwelt on it now I decided it outshone all the rest. But even at that, I wanted one more, one that would make the picture of our life complete.

"Yeah, Chief," I whispered. "I can do you and me and Desmond. In a heartbeat I can do that."

The next morning, Wednesday, as I headed out on the Harley to Sacrament One for communion I decided to take God at his go-another-mile word and drive a longer route. Instead of going straight down West King, Classic II and I took a back way around Oyster Creek with its clusters of shellfish gaping from their beds.

Once we made the curve on Davis, I let the throttle out a little. I always found it ironic that the moss-hung streets in the weary West King area made for better riding than the ones everybody wanted to live on. Classic seemed to like the freedom to make wide, sweeping turns, the kind we could lean into like one being, purring all the way. As Desmond would say, "Yeah, baby." My mood improved by several degrees.

Until I made the turn from Moultrie onto San Luis and remembered why I made a point never to come this way.

The forgotten framework of Flagler Church's partially built school was on that corner. It looked little different than it had four months ago when I'd last let myself look at it. The only new addition was the mounds of Johnson grass that grew wherever the bulldozers hadn't completely killed the earth. My mind said, *Don't look at it. Keep going. You'll be late.* But something else pulled me to a heavy stop. I planted my feet and let the Harley rumble impatiently.

The naked, hulking frame was as far as Troy Irwin's money had taken the church's project before he teetered on the edge of disgrace. At least the Reverend Howard had the integrity to part company with him.

Yet apparently not enough for his congregation. Being unforgiven could kill a man like Garry Howard.

"Your school was a terrible idea, Reverend," I whispered. But the skeleton of a dead hope was worse.

Hank's Sportster wasn't parked in front of Sacrament House I when I pulled up, which meant I'd have a few minutes with the Sisters before she arrived. As I walked toward the front porch it occurred to me that this first house looked like a wise older sister to Sacrament Two across the street. The two pecan trees Owen had supervised the planting of were gaining some heft as if the yard were growing toward a maturity the second house hadn't caught up to yet.

When I peered through the screen, Jasmine peered back and whispered, "I am *so* glad to see you, Miss Angel."

The chin was in full-quiver. I took a deep breath and slid through the mere crack she made for me as she opened the door.

"What's going on?" I said.

Mercedes's deep voice answered from the direction of the couch. "Just so you know, Miss Angel, I told them we shoulda called you last night."

"I didn't want to be wakin' you up at midnight," Jasmine said.

"More like two a.m." That came from Sherry who approached me with a steaming mug. "You're gonna need this."

"Why?"

The three of them eyeballed each other like siblings with a joint confession they each thought the other should make. Stocky Rochelle didn't even grunt from her position against the wall that led to the hallway. She just leaned there, arms folded, revealing part of the tattoo sleeve that depicted what appeared to be the complete Battle of Gettysburg. Only Ophelia seemed unruffled, although she was probably still half asleep and had no clue what this was all about. She gazed at my coffee mug.

"Somebody," I said as I handed the coffee to Ophelia. "Anybody."

"What are y'all waitin' for?" Zelda strode in from the hall and bounced off of Rochelle's hefty arm as she passed her. "It ain't like we done somethin' wrong. We just doin' the Jesus thing."

"That's what I told them, Miss Angel," Jasmine said.

"So how about telling *me*?"

"Foxy." Zelda's voice was reminiscent of heavy-grade sandpaper as she craned her neck to look down the hall. "Come out here and meet Miss Angel. She don't bite."

No. But I wasn't sure I could say the same about the person who appeared beside Rochelle. Her face took a piece right out of my soul.

She was a waif of a thing, even shorter than the diminutive Ophelia, thinner than Zelda, and with bigger eyes than Gigi. Her skin might be fairer than Sherry's near translucence, although it was hard to tell with the makeup she'd apparently applied to lips, face, and eyes with a trowel. No one in the room had hair like hers—auburn and thick and curly—nor could any of them rival her for the stubborn set of her chiseled chin. Not Rochelle. Not even Mercedes.

"So, what?" this slip of a redheaded person said. "Do I have a booger hanging out of my nose?"

"I apologize," I said. "I'm Allison Chamberlain. And you are?"

"Foxy." A cute-husky voice bore no resemblance to the disdain that claimed the rest of her. "And don't ask me for my last name because I don't give out that information."

Mercedes obviously couldn't hold back an "Mmm-*mm.*"

It wasn't as if we hadn't seen attitude here before. It was the habit most of *them* had worn until they could believe we, and God, loved them enough to want them whole. But none of them had looked like they were concealing a weapon under it. Something had nudged them to come in. This one looked like she'd been forced at gunpoint.

"Why don't we all sit down?" I said. "Have some coffee—"

"I don't drink coffee."

"Anybody else?"

"I got it handled." Sherry nodded at Rochelle who grunted and followed her into the kitchen.

"Join us," I said to Foxy.

We all took our customary places on the couch and the two chairs covered with afghans to hide their bald spots and on the big floor pillows that had once lived at India's house. Jasmine smiled at Foxy and patted a spot next to her on the couch, which Ophelia had graciously given up. Of course, we could probably have parked Ophelia on the front porch and she wouldn't have noticed until her second cup of caffeine.

Foxy watched that all happen and then straddled the arm of the sofa near a now scowling Zelda. Our Zelda *could* give her a run for her money when it came to out-and-out glowering, but Foxy looked unaffected.

I took a beaded turquoise pillow on the floor next to Mercedes's chair and said, "So how did you find us, Foxy?"

"I didn't. They found me."

I waited, but further elaboration was apparently unnecessary in her view. Or something had dried out her mouth and she wasn't owning it.

"Who are they?" I said.

"Me and Sherry," Zelda said. "We was lockin' up at C.A.R.S. last night, and it was late 'cause Sherry was doin' the books 'cause ol' Maharry messed 'em up, but you didn't hear that from me."

She glanced warily at Sherry who was entering with a tray of mismatched mugs. Rochelle followed with the coffee pot.

"Go on," I said.

"And we seen this one—Foxy—back in the alley with some dude, 'bout to … well, they was fixin' to get it on."

"Which was none of your business," Foxy said.

Sherry paused midway into handing Jasmine a cup. "When some man slaps a woman across the face and I see it, that is my business."

I sat straighter on the cushion and watched Foxy. She picked at a hole in the upholstery between her thighs.

"When we saw he was gettin' ready to hit her again," Zelda said, "we both just took off down the alley toward 'em."

"Never mind that he coulda been carryin'," Mercedes said.

Zelda's voice pitched upward. "You sayin' you wouldn't a done the same thing if you saw somebody bein' abused?"

"Who said I was being abused?"

We all looked at Foxy.

"He just wanted it rough."

Sherry leaned over to get her face closer to Foxy's. "Maybe so, but you didn't."

Foxy looked right back at her. "Since when does it matter what I want?"

A chill rippled up my backbone.

"Since right now," Sherry said. "All you got to do is say you don't want that kind of life anymore, and we'll help you find a real way to live."

"Like this?" Foxy looked around the room as if she smelled something foul.

"Yeah, like this," Mercedes said. "With a future."

"Working in a car place?"

"Turning tricks in an alley?" Jasmine came off the couch, eyes shimmering, and knelt in front of Foxy. "You can try to tell us you like starvin' half to death but we ain't gon' believe it any more than we believed it when we said it our own self."

"I wasn't starving."

"You fainted before we even ran off your john." Sherry looked at me. "Zelda and I had to carry her here."

"And she about ate the plate when Mercedes scrambled her some eggs," Jasmine said.

Rochelle motioned to me with the coffee pot but I shook my head, eyes still on Foxy. It had taken me until then to realize what else was different about this one: she clearly wasn't an addict. I didn't even see any evidence that she was an alcoholic. The ghostly look of her skin and the dried stuff on her lips might have been the result of dehydration, but it wasn't from drugs or booze.

"Why do you keep staring at me like that?" Foxy said to me.

"Miss Angel ain't bein' rude." Jasmine still knelt in front of Foxy, who was plucking stuffing from the hole in the sofa arm. "She lookin' to see if you want what we got to offer you."

"Mm-hmm," one of them said, followed by a "That's right, now." The Sisters were finding their rhythm.

Foxy shrugged the negligible shoulders. "I hit the wall, okay? I guess I don't have any choice but to stay."

"Oh, you always got choices," Mercedes said. "You done made some already. If you want, we can show you how to make better ones. Us and God."

That was the philosophy Sacrament House was built on, only, something about it didn't seem to fit Foxy the way it had the women before her who had been so far down when they came in, they weren't even sure of their own names. Yes, she was terrified to the marrow and masked it with a ferocity none of them had had the energy for.

I just wasn't seeing the wall she said she'd hit.

"What do I have to do?"

Foxy was looking at me, but I deferred to Ophelia, who set down her second cup of coffee and smiled at Foxy. Her soft eloquence made her the designated explainer to new initiates. I mentally thanked India for that training because I wasn't sure anyone else had her heart in it right now. I obviously wasn't the only one who found Foxy a little less than eager to be part of the family.

"You'd be in the Initiate Phase for eighteen days," Ophelia said. "You'd still be considered one of the Sisters—"

"Is it like being a nun or something? Because I'm not Catholic anymore."

She gave the magnificent red hair a toss. She looked less like a candidate for a convent than Lady Gaga.

"I heard you all talking about God ever since I got here and just so you know, I don't need church."

I didn't have to say a word. Every single body in the room tilted toward her. Mercedes grabbed the floor first.

"We don't just do church," she said. "We do the Jesus thing."

"What—walk on water?"

At least she'd actually heard of Jesus. That reference would have been lost on most of these women in the beginning.

"You're gon' *see* more about God and Jesus than you're gon' *hear* about it." Jasmine put her hand on Foxy's sleeve, and I realized Foxy was wearing the silky yellow pajamas I'd given Jasmine for her birthday. Foxy could have fit Zelda and Gigi in there with her and had room to spare.

"Mmm-hmm," Mercedes said. "I was the same way as you when I first come here: all thinkin' I didn't need no help from God."

She let the "mmm-hmm's" and the "I know that, now," gently rock the room before she went on to, "But didn't nobody push me. I just got it."

"Got *what?*"

"That I couldn't save my own life."

Somewhere in the silent wonder of these women I heard Hank's Sportster pull up and sensed her coming through the screen door. But I kept my gaze on Mercedes and savored the hope she exuded like musk.

"So I don't have to go to confession," Foxy said.

"Oh, they be plenty of confessin'."

"But not the kind you're thinking of," I said.

Zelda frowned. "What kind's she thinking of?"

"Any kind." Foxy gave the hair an expressive toss, which made me suspect she wouldn't be able to talk if her head were shaved. "I just want to leave the past behind and move on. Without anybody shoving church down my throat."

"You don't have to worry 'bout that," Mercedes told her. "God doesn't get into a person that way."

By then Hank had squatted beside me, and the divine aroma of communion bread was wafting from the bag over her shoulder. I nodded for her to join me in the kitchen.

"Are you hearing this?" I said, motioning in the direction of the living room.

"Ya gotta love it when God does God's thing, don'tcha?"

"But I just don't get the feeling that this one is totally ready."

"What's her name?"

"Foxy."

Hank set the bag on the counter. "You're buying that?"

"No, but that's all she's telling right now. I mean, who knows? Is Gigi's real name Gigi?"

"I hope not. It sounds like a poodle." Hank pulled off her do-rag and wiped her damp forehead with it. "You going to let Foxy give it a shot?"

"I'm letting the Sisters decide that for now. It just sort of played out that way."

"Then I guess we'd better get a basin of water."

Jasmine and Zelda were ahead of us there. When we carried out the still-warm loaf and the chalice of grape juice—in deference to the recovering ones among us—they'd already filled our traditional basin and provided a stack of towels Mercedes had undoubtedly bleached to within an inch of their terry-cloth lives. Ophelia was explaining that a footwashing was our official welcome into Sacrament House, and Foxy, though she pulled her chin practically into her larynx, was rolling up the pajama pants. The legs underneath were approximately the size of curtain rods. And hairless as pears. Huh. Most street girls didn't have the means to shave their legs.

We each took a turn bathing Foxy's baby soft feet and telling her what we would offer her as Sisters. Nourishment. Attention to her physical needs. Support. Encouragement. Hope. Some space.

She endured it all without comment until that last one. "Do I get a room to myself?"

"For the first eighteen days you will," I said. "At my house. Then if you decide to stay, you'll move in here and Rochelle will be your roommate."

"I slept in there last night. She snores. What else ya got?"

"Mmm-*mm*," Mercedes said.

"So are we going there now?" Foxy said to me. "To your place?"

"We haven't had communion yet."

Jasmine pointed toward the dining room where Hank and Rochelle had set out the bread and juice and covered both with snowy cloths embroidered by Ophelia with red crosses.

"We do it every Wednesday morning," Jasmine said.

"Why?"

The question was more an insult than a genuine query, one Mercedes looked primed to address until the door banged open and Gigi rushed in, hair askew and gaze bleary. She was as narrow as Rochelle was wide with the exception of her eyes, which always seemed too large for their sockets. Their constant bulge made me suspect she had a thyroid problem, but the people at the clinic dismissed it as "stress." Of course, if one of the Sisters were hemorrhaging they'd say the same thing.

"You know what, Gigi?" Mercedes said, "you can't be showin' up for Eucharist late with your mind and your heart someplace else. Preparation's been done for you, and you ain't prepared *yourself*."

Gigi's glare said, *Get off me,* but her mouth mumbled, "I'll do better."

"The Lord be with you," Hank said quickly.

"And also wichoo," was the group reply.

Except from Foxy, who was watching us all from behind a curtain of red hair and caution. I felt a Nudge, a hard one. A deep one. One that pushed until it bruised me with a pain I'd come to recognize as God's.

I know. Go another mile.

I felt like I'd gone a hundred already, and it was only eight thirty a.m.

We shared communion, all but Foxy, who refused the elements, though she did watch the faces of the Sisters as they relished every sip and morsel with their eyes closed. I wondered if she got that this was church. I was fairly certain it didn't matter to her. As eager as she was to move on to the next thing, her only goal was clearly to stay away from herself. I found it shocking that she *wasn't* strung out on something.

Afterward, Hank cleaned up, and the others all went off to their jobs except Gigi and Rochelle, who were scheduled to work in the Sacrament One garden with Owen that morning. He showed up clad in plaid Bermuda shorts and white socks pulled up to his knobular knees, with a floppy sunhat for each of them. Rochelle grunted and put hers on without further comment. Gigi looked at me, bug eyes pleading.

"Do I got to work in the garden?" she said, out of a small hole she formed with the sides of her lips. "I promised I'd do better, but does it got to be this?"

Although I was sure Owen didn't hear her, his timing was precise. "Come along, ladies," he said. "We have to toil in the soil before anything's going to grow. If we stand and weep, we will not reap."

"If I work with this *guy,* I'm gonna *die,*" Gigi muttered.

"I like the similes better than the poetry," Hank said when Gigi and Rochelle had followed him out the back door.

"Will you watch to make sure Gigi doesn't go after him with a hoe or something?"

I left Hank in the kitchen and found Foxy stretched full length on the couch, legs extended straight up. She was in the process of pulling her feet toward her forehead when I sat on the table to face her.

"Impressive," I said. "Have you studied yoga?"

"No." She let her legs flop to the cushions. "But don't try to trick me into telling you things about myself. Not gonna happen."

"No tricks. No games." I exposed my wrists. "Nothing up my sleeves."

She appraised my denim jacket. "Why are you dressed like that, anyway? Aren't you hot?"

"I always dress like this when I ride my Harley. You're going to need a jacket. Do you have one here?"

"Why do I need one?"

"Because that's how we're getting to my house."

"On a motorcycle?"

Her eyes bulged out further than Gigi's could ever hope to, a feat I hadn't thought possible with that amount of eyeliner and mascara. It was the first sign of fear this woman had shown that was visible to the naked eye. I could almost hear her pulse go into high gear.

"That doesn't sound like fun to you?" I said.

"No. It sounds like you're trying to get me killed."

"Never killed anybody yet. Seriously, are you scared? We can always take the van and I can come back for my bike later."

"Mercedes and Jasmine took the van," Hank called from the kitchen. "They had to pick up some stuff Erin dropped off at India's."

Foxy jerked her head in Hank's direction. "Can't she take me?"

"She rides a Harley too."

"What is *wrong* with you people?"

"We're crazy," I said. "But it's the good kind of crazy. I peeled off my jacket and handed it to her. "I have an extra helmet. It's my son's, but I swear he doesn't have head lice. We'll use the back roads, and I absolutely will not freak you out."

She stuck out her china chin. "I don't get freaked out."

"Good," I said.

At least now I knew one thing about her. She was a really rotten liar.

CHAPTER FIVE

Foxy was like her predecessors in one respect. Once I got her settled into the room at my house that had been occupied by Geneveve, Zelda, Ophelia, and Gigi before her, she went into a virtual coma. But there all similarities ceased.

Before that she did take the suggested bath, but she didn't need my help. She also didn't luxuriate in it nor did she wash the makeup from her face as far as I could tell. I was going to have to replace the pillowcases.

None of the sleep pants and tops we had on hand would fit her, and she didn't hug the smallish T-shirt I unearthed as if it were from Abercrombie and Fitch the way the others had done just because they had something clean to put on their bodies. She examined it with lip curled and asked if she could just sleep in her underwear.

"You can sleep however you want," I said. "As long as you're not under the influence. That's the one thing we do insist—"

"Under the influence of what?"

"Illegal drugs. Alcohol. Any controlled substances."

"I tried pot once and I hated it. I don't like not being in control."

Imagine that.

I didn't say anything, though, because her lips were now clamped together so hard the space under her nose went white. She obviously hadn't intended for that much to escape and she was making sure it didn't happen again.

She conked out until after I got back from picking Desmond up at school. By the time he and I heard her on the second floor getting up from the sleep of the thoroughly exhausted we were sitting at the bistro table in the kitchen finishing up my prelude to his meeting this new addition to the household.

"I done this 'bout a hundred times before, Big Al," he said, as he slyly palmed his third Oreo from the plate between us. "I know I got to give her space and don't ask questions and don't go poppin' my eyes out if she look like she just done crawled outta the gutter."

"You don't have to worry about that part. She's not an addict."

"Then how come she was hookin'?" he said.

I felt the pang I always felt when my thirteen-year-old came out with something he'd learned from living in the gutter himself. Only this time the Mosquito came to mind, buzzing about his community of origin.

"'S wrong, Big Al?"

I pulled the lid off of my second Oreo and lied, "I was just thinking that that's a good question."

"And I ain't supposed to ask it 'cause itta come out when she ready. What's her name again?"

"Her street name is Foxy."

His brow puckered. "What kinda name is that?"

"You don't know the expression *foxy*? Like foxy lady."

"That some ol' tired thing they use to say in the old days?"

"It wasn't tired then. It meant the person was very attractive."

"Like hot." The irrepressible grin swallowed his face. "Then they musta called you that back then. Imma start callin' you—"

"No, you're not. So look, it's just business as usual with Foxy. Love and respect."

"Got it."

"Even if she doesn't show us any."

"We got to be the model."

"Right."

The door from the dining room swung open and Foxy appeared wearing the T-shirt. That was it. It came down just to the top of her thighs, which was right where Desmond's eyes went.

"Des," I said, "go grab a pair of your hanging-out pants from the clean laundry basket I put in your room."

"Huh?" he said.

"Go," I said.

He fell more than climbed out of the bistro chair and walked backward to his room. The pot rack and the kitchen trash can tottered in his wake.

"That was your son?" Foxy said. "Were you married to a black guy?"

"No," I said. "He's adopted."

"How old is he?"

"Just turned thirteen."

"What grade is he in?"

"Eighth." I crossed my arms. "Y'know, for somebody who doesn't want to divulge anything about herself, you sure ask a lot of questions about other people."

She shrugged her hair back. "Other people don't have to be on their guard every single minute."

It struck me how articulate this young woman was. The fact that she knew what the word *divulge* meant once again set her apart from the newcomers we were used to. She might actually have gone to high school.

"Desmond's going to bring you a pair of pants to wear until we can get you some of your own. While you're here, buns, breasts, and navels need to be covered."

"Why?" Her eyes challenged me. "You think your kid might want to jump me?"

"I think you expect him to want to jump you. I think that's how you define yourself."

I turned an ear toward Desmond's door but he still sounded like he was ransacking every drawer and cubbyhole. Even so, I lowered my voice.

"We'll help you develop some self-respect here, God-respect actually, so you can discover a new definition. Meanwhile we're going to go through the motions."

Desmond appeared before she could answer, carrying no less than four choices for Foxy. Among them were the cotton sleep pants with the Harley-Davidson logo printed on them. If he was offering her those we were already in trouble.

Not surprisingly she passed them up. On our earlier ride on the Harley from Sacrament House she had latched herself to me and shaken like a Chihuahua until we pulled into the garage.

"You can have all of 'em," Desmond said when she'd selected a plain black pair.

"That's okay, Des," I said. "We'll go shopping later."

"When?" Foxy said. "And where? I don't want to go to a mall. Too many … I just don't like crowds."

Desmond stared at her as if only a crazy person would not want to go to the mall. He had a point. Most of the women before Foxy had said their first excursion there was like going to Disneyland. And none of them had been ready for it for several weeks, after they had learned how to lie down and sleep, feed themselves, brush their teeth, and do anything without either looking for the next fix or watching for the person who was going to take it away from them.

That did not describe this person, who was about to don the pants right there in the middle of the kitchen until I nodded for her to go into Desmond's room to do it. I took the opportunity to pull Desmond in by the back of his neck and get directly into his face.

"She has zero self-respect, Des," I said. "That means—"

"I know." His voice teetered momentarily out of man-range. "You gon' be impressed with the kinda respect Imma show Miss Foxy Lady."

"Yeah, well, start by finding another nickname for her."

"I can't call her Miss Foxy Lady?"

"No."

Foxy reappeared wearing the black pants. I could tell from the bulge under the shirt that she had them rolled down to her navel, but I let that go. One baby step at a time.

"Do you have Wi-Fi?" she said.

"Oh, *yeah*," Desmond said, brows pointed down. "We only got one computer, though, and you got to ask Big Al can you use it."

Foxy pulled her hair back with both hands as if she were annoyed with it. "Actually I'd rather use my cell phone."

"You have a cell phone?" Desmond and I said in unison.

"It's an iPhone. My next question is, do you have a charger for one? I had to leave mine—I lost it."

I was astonished that she ever had it, or the phone. She must have been handled by a high-end pimp to have mobile service. The chill made its way up my backbone again.

"Desmond," I said, "will you excuse us?"

He looked about to protest.

"Take the rest of the Oreos with you."

Even that didn't have its usual effect. He couldn't seem to take his eyes off of the tiny woman who was currently fishing something out of her bra. When she produced the cell phone in question, I just handed him the cookie package and gave him a shove toward the door. He stiffened under my hand but he went.

"Let's talk in the living room," I said.

"But do you have a charger?"

"Living room."

She rolled her eyes, but she followed me and parked herself with a huff in the red chair-and-a-half. I could just hear Sylvia now, telling her to, one, get her smart little butt out of her chair, and, two, to roll those eyes again and see if she didn't roll her head. I had tried that once as a teenager. She basically did roll my head.

"If you're going to stay with us," I said as I sat on the edge of the half part of the chair, "I do need a few pieces of information."

"I'm not telling you my last name."

"I'm not asking for your last name. But I do need to know if you think you're in any kind of danger."

"From who?" she said, too quickly.

"Your pimp maybe?"

"I do not *have* a pimp. I work alone."

"And you make enough to pay for a cell phone."

"Clearly."

"But not enough to feed yourself."

She tried a smile on me. "I have my priorities."

I smiled back. "My other question is: How old are you?"

"Why?" she said.

"Because if you're underage—"

"I'm eighteen. I was born in 1994." She brushed a curly tendril away from her face. "Why would you even ask that?"

I gave her a long look. I wanted to say, *Because you're acting like you're about sixteen,* but that wasn't the way we ordinarily approached a potential Sister's attitude. The bristlier the 'tude, the softer the touch required. It was one of those times when I wondered why on *earth* I had been selected for this. Soft was not my strong suit.

"You have the distinct advantage of looking really young," I said.

"I'm not. I've seen more life than most people twice my age."

"I'm sure you have, and I'm sorry for that."

"I don't want anybody feeling sorry for me."

"I'm not sorry *for* you. I'm just sorry about whatever it is that got you in this position."

"You didn't do it," she said, once again with the *That was, like, the stupidest thing I've ever heard* flounce of the hair.

"I might not be guilty," I said. "But I'm responsible. Every person who lives in this sick society is responsible for healing it. That's why we're here."

"I'm not sick. I told you, I haven't ever done drugs."

"Then you're way ahead." This wasn't the time to tell her she had about the sickest little soul I'd met up with in months.

"So can I charge my phone?" she said.

"I don't have an iPhone charger. My phone's a Droid."

"Does anybody else over there at Sacrifice House have one?"

"The Sisters at *Sacrament* House don't have cell phones."

"You seriously don't let them?"

"They could have them if they could afford them. Once they start making a real living they can spend their money however they want. We have a guy named Kade who advises them on that."

"So when do I start working? I need my cell phone."

"For?"

She stared at me. I was obviously beyond moronic at this point.

"To text people, for one thing."

I rubbed at my temples with my fingertips. "Okay, here's the deal. The reason you're here is because you want to leave your old life behind and enter into a new way of being. So why would you want to contact any of the people who helped get you here? If you have family you need to get in touch with, we can help you with that."

"No." I could almost hear her backbone calcifying.

"If you're going to keep one foot in your old life and one here," I said, "you aren't going to make it. That's a decision you need to make today. Just today. Tomorrow you'll need to make it again. And the day after."

"Who lives like that?"

"I do. Some days I have to do it every hour."

Faint interest flickered in her eyes. "You were a hooker once?"

"No. And by the way, we don't call the Sisters hookers, and we won't call you that. That isn't God's name for you."

"Whatev. So why do you have to keep giving up your old life?"

"It was a life I'm not proud of. I gave up who I was for ... someone else."

"Who?"

"You going to tell me who you've given yours up for?"

"See? You're trying to trick me."

"No. Just playing fair."

"So if I tell you, you'll tell me."

"If it seems like it would help us, yeah."

She made a sound in her throat that was something between a Rochelle grunt and a Bonner hairball. "I was right. You people *are* weird."

"So, what's it going to be today? This life or the old one?"

Foxy looked down at the dead cell phone in her lap. "What do I have to do in the new one?"

"What do you want to do? Really. Deep down."

As she looked up at me even the makeup seemed to drain of color. Deep down was clearly a place she hadn't visited in a long time. Maybe never.

"Think about it," I said. "And meanwhile, let's get you into a healthy routine."

"I hate schedules."

"Me, too. It's not a schedule, it's a rhythm."

And for at least the hundredth time she said, "I don't get it."

Foxy definitely *didn't* get rhythm. For the next twenty-four hours everything I suggested that even remotely smacked of settling in resulted in her looking more and more like the poster child for ADHD.

She was up when I got back from taking Desmond to school the next morning, so I recommended breakfast and some quiet time on the side porch before the day turned into a steam bath. She walked around out there with a bowl of cornflakes until Owen came over and said Miz Vernell, my neighbor on the porch side, had called him to tell him that a girl was locked out of my house and needed a bathroom.

When I offered Foxy my laptop to write down some of her thoughts she lasted about ten minutes and then proceeded to pace around the house, peeking out the windows and closing the blinds. The place was a veritable tomb by noon.

Despite my shriveled entertainment budget, I even suggested we take a walk down to O. C. White's and have lunch. After an interrogation about where it was (two blocks away) and who was likely to be there (tourists and business people), she declined. We had turkey sandwiches at the bistro table and she talked nonstop about nothing. I felt like I was in an episode of *Seinfeld*.

By the time I left to pick up Desmond, I was sure of only one thing: Foxy couldn't stand to be alone with herself. It was time to stop trying to relieve the symptoms and get to the root. And the sooner the better, because the further I went with this one, the further God kept telling me to go, in one-mile increments. I had the undeniable urge to Nudge back.

When I pulled up to the curb at the school, Desmond was not accompanied by his—what did that Mosquito woman call it? His harem? He just shrugged on his jacket and said, "How's Foxy?"

"Antsy," I said.

"She still at our house?"

"Uh-huh."

And now that he was going to be there, too, I had no idea what I was going to do with her. It wasn't like I could call Leighanne or Nita and get her started in NA.

To my surprise Foxy had a plan when we got back to Palm Row.

"There's an art fair going on," she said, in lieu of hello.

"You talkin' 'bout my work on the walls?" Desmond said, chest puffing. "That ain't no art fair. It's there all the time. I'm thinking a addin' more. I could even do one of—"

"What are you talking about?" she said. "I meant the one going on down by the Information Center. I got bored so I turned on the radio and they were advertising it." She shook her hair back. "You said I should think about what I wanted to do and that's it."

I put aside the urge to smack her for deflating Desmond like yesterday's party balloon and said, "All right then. But first there's the matter of what you're going to wear. Not so much with the pajamas down on St. George Street."

"Where are the clothes I had on when I came?"

I hadn't seen the attire Zelda and Sherry had found her in but I suspected Mercedes had probably disposed of them by now. She was in charge of doing away with the working girl uniform soon after an initiate's arrival. Foxy could make a pair of sweat pants look seductive. I hated to think what she looked like when she was dressed for work.

"Let's go with one of my tops and a belt for now. I know we have flip-flops in your size."

"Are you *serious*?"

"We'll get you something else first thing."

I secretly hoped Ophelia was around when we hit Second Chances. I'd give her a hundred bucks and tell her to take Foxy and go for it. I could hear my bank account circling the drain.

The scowl on Foxy's face when she'd donned the outfit was so deep Owen could have planted potatoes in the furrows of her brow. I didn't have to look at it for long. She requested sunglasses and a hat that covered not only the disgusted expression, but her mane of curls as well. We had to drop Gigi and Rochelle off at an NA meeting first, and I asked Rochelle to sit up front with me in the van so I could make my twenty-fifth attempt at having a conversation with her.

"How's everything going?" I said.

"Okay."

"Just okay?"

A nod in my peripheral vision.

"I guess that's better than horrible, huh?"

Another nod.

"Have you spoken during any of your meetings at all?"

"Hi, I'm Rochelle, and I'm a recovering addict."

Hope lived. That was the most I'd ever heard her say at one time.

"Found anybody you want for a sponsor?"

Head shake, punctuated with a hiss from Gigi in the seat behind me.

"What was that, Geege?" I said.

"We already been turned down by two women and a dog."

"A dog?"

"That's what he look like. All smellin' and slobberin'."

"He wearin' a collar too?" Desmond said.

I caught his grin in the rearview mirror, but Gigi was miles from a smile. When I pulled up to Grace Methodist Church, Rochelle grunted getting out of the van and Gigi climbed unceremoniously

over Desmond and slammed the sliding door behind her. I jumped
when her face appeared in the open passenger side window.

"Some of them people stole from they own mama to buy drugs,"
she said. "But I guess sellin' your body is a worse sin." She shrugged
the shrug of the disheartened and followed Rochelle up the walkway
lined with rosebushes.

I felt pretty disheartened myself and added a sponsor crisis to the
Things I Have To Take Care Of pile. Although when I was going to
get back to that was anybody's guess. I'd only had Foxy for twenty-
four hours and already it felt like she'd siphoned about a year out of
me.

"You know *I* don't need to go to a twelve-step program, right?"
Foxy said as we drove toward the Visitor Center.

"You talkin' 'bout NA," Desmond said.

I caught a glimpse in the mirror of Foxy lifting her lip at him.
"You're pure genius. Yes, I'm talking about NA. And since I'm not a
junkie, I don't need it."

"We don't usually refer to it as a twelve-step program," I said.
"That's why he didn't know."

Desmond didn't say anything. At least, not until we got out of
the van in the parking lot and he muttered between his molars, "Big
Al, you don't got to be speakin' for me."

"Did I do that?" I said, although I knew perfectly well that I had.
Little Miss Foxy-ness could act like *I* was a moron, but she wasn't
getting away with it with my kid.

I watched as the kid in question loped off and caught up with the
girl who had just treated him like an insufferable boy creature. She
didn't look at him as she reached up to tuck some escaped curls back

under the hat. Her lifted arms raised the top-turned-dress almost to the bottom of her black underwear.

"Second Chances, Desmond," I called out.

"That's not the art show," Foxy said.

"I know," I said. We were going to stop the show *she* was putting on first.

I hoped Ophelia would be there, but we were greeted instead by India. Even better. She took one look at Foxy and simply said, "Oh, my." I could see the possibilities going down the runway in her mind.

"She made me dress like this," Foxy said, pointing to me.

Desmond nodded soberly. "That's true, Miss Indiana."

It struck me as he followed Foxy down the skirt aisle that there had been a definite shift in loyalty.

"I don't think we have anything here for you," India said, exchanging a significant big-eyed glance with me.

"No doubt," Foxy said from the other side of the rack. "My mother wouldn't even shop here."

The air went dead.

Her mother? India mouthed.

"She's, like, forty," Foxy said.

"She old, then." I had never heard that voice come out of Desmond's vocal cords. It sounded like a male version of hers.

India widened her eyes at me one more time. "So, Foxy, is it?"

"*Yes.*"

"Let's do this. I'll go down to my other shop and pick up a few things that will do you until we can get you to Old Navy."

"Is it at the mall?" Foxy said, still from the other side of the skirt rack.

"Foxy don't like the mall, now," Desmond said.

A hanger scraped the pole. "Look at this. Who wears this?"

"Somebody grandma."

"If she's going on *Biggest Loser*, yeah."

Desmond gave an unnatural laugh. I was hung up on the fact that Foxy had access to TV as well as cell phone and English class.

"I'll be back," India said to me as she positioned an enormous sun hat on her head. It was her summer signature. She could be seen all the way down Cathedral Place in that thing. "Mercedes should be done with her break. I'll send her up." Then she added in a whisper, "Are you sure about this one?"

I didn't answer because in truth I wasn't. God was peculiarly silent at the moment. Foxy was not.

As soon as India was gone Foxy poked her head around the end of the rack and pulled in an incredulous chin. "She looks way too hip to be running a shop like this."

"She got another real shop," Desmond said.

I waited for him to explain about *this* shop, but he didn't. None of his usual Sister pride expanded his chest. All he seemed to be able to do was look at Foxy like a puppy and wait for her next nonverbal command. I wanted to pick him up by the scruff of the neck and shake him.

I might have if Mercedes hadn't come in. She had a smile and a hug for me, a coldly courteous nod for Foxy. She started to wrap her arm around Desmond's neck but he sidestepped her and joined Foxy at the scarf table.

"*Great* grandmother," Foxy said to him, holding up a shades-of-purple one I'd seen on Ms. Willa.

"You got that right," Desmond said.

Mercedes pulled her head almost to the ceiling. "Boy? You too good for a hug from me, I'm too good for a batch of biscuits next time you come around beggin'."

Desmond looked at Foxy. She continued to smirk at the scarf collection. Only then did he sneak a grin at Mercedes.

"Mmm-*mm*," Mercedes said.

She gave Foxy's back a long look and motioned me with her head toward the tiny dressing room. We both squeezed in with the door shut, which gave me a close-up view of Mercedes's nose hairs.

"I'm going to get these two out of here," I whispered. "Will you have India call me on my cell when she gets back? She went to get some clothes for Foxy."

"She gon' get her a muzzle too?"

I stifled a guffaw.

"That girl got a mouth on her."

"She's covering up her stuff, Merc, you know that. It's only been a day."

"Mmm-hmmm."

I nodded and twisted to face the door, which was no easy task. No wonder nobody tried anything on up here. You had to be Foxy's size just to move around in the fitting room.

I finally managed to get the door open, already saying, "Okay, let's check out that art fair."

That was met with a guilty silence.

"Desmond?" I said.

Nothing.

"Foxy?"

By then Mercedes had squeezed out behind me and was charging through the shop shaking her head.

"They gone, Miss Angel."

I pointed down. "Three guesses where. Desmond could probably taste the sugar through the floorboards. You okay here by yourself?"

"I think I can handle all these customers."

The sarcasm in her voice was a thin veil for the defeat in her shoulders, and it sent the pile into a precarious lean.

I made a promise to … somebody … to deal with it all as soon as I located my son and his nemesis and took the stairs two at a time. Desmond and Foxy weren't on the porch of Sacred Grounds, which meant Desmond was currently trying to talk Patrice into putting a couple of whitechocolateamorettomacadamianut coffees on his tab, which didn't exist.

"What has he talked you out of, Patrice?" I said as I pushed through the door into the coffee shop.

She raised her hippie-esque head from a table across the crowded room and look at me blankly. "Who?"

"Desmond."

"He didn't come in. He was standing on the porch with some girl so I got out the whipped cream, but then I looked up and they were gone."

"Did you see which way—"

She shook her head.

There was no reason for the panic already squeezing my insides as I burst through the door and leaned out over the porch railing to look first up St. George and then down. The air was too hot for any but the heartiest of postseason tourists so the crowd was thin. I saw three girls, who weren't Foxy but could have been, wearing the shortest shorts they could get away with, hair pulled up off their necks, looking as if the sun were a personal affront. A large family passed with two high-maintenance teenage daughters walking with their hands on their hips. Foxy would have fit right in with them, too. But she and my son were nowhere to be seen.

I took off to the north, the dew on my skin quickly turning to downward-running streams of sweat. I darted into one of the shady piazzas and called out to Desmond, but only the cicadas answered. I stopped in front of Pizza Tyme and asked the old guy hawking pepperoni by the slice if he'd seen a mocha-skinned boy and a redhaired girl. He just looked at me like I was delirious, or maybe he was. Incense wafted from one open doorway, Celtic music from another, but none produced Desmond or Foxy. I fought back the fear and focused on being justifiably ticked off.

I tried the Bunnery, although as far as I knew neither of them had any money. I was headed for the Harley Davidson shop, certain Desmond had lured her there to impress her with his knowledge of all things motorcycle, before I remembered that was the last place where Foxy would darken a door.

I was fighting back the urge to call Nicholas Kent when my phone rang and jangled my nerves up ten more notches. It was India.

"Forget the clothes," I said. "I can't find Desmond and Foxy."

"I know, honey. They're here."

"At the shop?"

"Downstairs, and darlin', I think you'd better come right quick."

I didn't bother to end the call on my phone. Nearly taking out a cranky toddler in a stroller, I ran against the foot traffic back to Sacred Grounds. Rehearsals of the various ways I could approach Desmond played out in my head, until I found them both on the outside steps. Foxy was sobbing in Desmond's arms. He barely glanced at me when I joined them and crouched on the step below.

"What's happening?" I said.

Foxy dug her fingers into Desmond's bare arms and buried her face in his chest. He was about to lower his own face to the top of her hat when I took him firmly by the prickly chin.

"Desmond," I said, "tell me what's going on."

"We was down at—"

"Don't tell her!"

Foxy lifted her head and shook it until the hat slid off and they were both smothered in red hair. I took her by the shoulders and pulled her toward me, away from Desmond. He had the good sense to at least let one hand go.

"We don't keep secrets around here," I said. "Look at me."

She dropped her head.

"Look at me."

This time she did.

"Shades off," I said, and then raised an eyebrow at Desmond, who released his other hand. His face showed him somewhere between resentful and it's-a-good-thing-you-came-along-'cause-I-was-outta-ideas.

"Are you hurt?" I said to Foxy.

"No."

"Are you having a flashback?"

She blinked what I could now see were swollen eyelids.

"I don't think so, Big Al," Desmond said. "'Cause it just happened."

"Shut *up,*" Foxy said.

"Then *you* tell me," I said to her. "It doesn't have to be here. We can go back to my house, or we can go inside the coffee shop—"

"I just got freaked out, okay?"

I didn't remind her that she'd assured me just the day before she didn't get freaked out.

"I thought I saw somebody I knew and I started to lose it. That's all."

I looked quickly at Desmond. He was an even worse liar than she was, and he didn't even have to open his mouth to do it.

"You want to try that again?" I said.

"It's the truth!"

"Look, if it's just your stuff you can tell me or not tell me depending on how fast you want to get healed. But when it involves my son I need the whole story."

"It's all good, Big Al." Desmond's voice was low and completely without charm. "I can handle it."

"I can't," I said. And then I prayed from the pit of myself because I knew in that moment that Oreos and motorcycle privileges no longer provided leverage.

"Okay." Foxy tossed her hair back and smeared at her cheeks with the backs of her hands. The two-day-old makeup trailed from the corners of her eyes and into her hairline.

"I wanted to find somebody with an iPhone so I could borrow their charger. We went into this one shop where they had T-shirts and I saw the guy behind the counter talking on one, so when he hung up I just asked him if I could use his charger." Her voice wavered. "And he just started yelling at us, saying we were trying to distract him so we could shoplift."

"We tol' him we didn't want any of his ol' tired T-shirts," Desmond said. "They had drawings like stick figures on 'em. I could do a *whole* lot better than that, now."

He was sounding enough like himself again that I nodded him on.

"Then he said he was gon' call the cops and I tol' him to go on ahead, now, because we ain't done nothin' against the law." Desmond swallowed, always easy to see with his adolescent Adam's apple in prominence. "That's when Foxy, she got *up-set*."

By now Foxy had recovered enough bravado to shake her hair back and regard me with faux self-assurance. The darting eyes, however, were a dead giveaway.

"I hate cops," she said.

"You don't need to hate 'em when you ain't guilty a nothin'," Desmond said.

"Did the guy in the store actually call the police?" I said.

Foxy shook her head. "Don't know. I just took off running and Desmond caught me and brought me back here."

"Good call, Des."

"And we didn't take anything." Foxy curled her lip all the way into her nostrils. "Desmond is right: it looked like some little kid drew on those shirts. We could *both* make better stuff than that." She nodded up the stairs, her contempt safely back in place. "We could even make some of those dumpy-looking clothes up there look cool."

"Really," I said.

"*I'm* still not going to wear them," she said quickly.

"You don't have to. I brought you a few things."

India floated toward us down the steps with a handled shopping bag, wearing the expectant smile even Foxy couldn't continue to glower at.

"Thank you," she said. "I guess you really didn't have to do that."

"I guess I did," India said. "It's the Jesus-thing."

Foxy didn't inspect the contents of the bag or inform India that she wasn't into Jesus or do any of the other things I expected her to do. She just murmured another thank-you, eyes pointed toward her lap.

"All right, then," India said, and floated back up the stairs. She stopped at the landing, though, and looked back at Foxy. "If you want to try your hand at modifying some of our clothes, I'll bring some things by Miss Angel's for you to experiment with. I'd like to see your work."

Foxy nodded.

I stared up at India and wondered just who the angel really was.

The next morning, Friday, was cloudy and the bay was a study in confusion when I set out to meet Hank. It couldn't seem to decide whether to be green or gray, and it dared me to try to figure it out. So what else was new? I was feeling more Shoved than Nudged, and I couldn't even tell what direction I was moving in.

"Did you find your kids?" Patrice said when I arrived at Sacred Grounds.

"Yeah. I'll have my usual. I know, Patrice. I'm drop-dead boring."

"Your kids?" Hank said when she was gone. "Plural?"

"She was talking about Desmond and Foxy. It was a whole thing yesterday."

I filled her in. When I was through she folded her hands neatly on the table like she always did when I was about to be prodded toward something I didn't want to look at.

"How old do you think 'Foxy' really is?" she said.

"She says she's eighteen."

"I didn't ask what *she* said. Seriously, without the makeup, how old does she look?"

"I haven't seen her without makeup. She didn't wash her face for two days, and when she cried the stuff off, she evidently had more in her bag and started all over again."

"You think she's trying to cover up her age?"

"She's trying to cover up something. But didn't they all at first?"

"True. You feel like telling me what *you're* covering up?"

I took the cup Patrice handed me and waited while she laid out the usual buffet in front of Hank.

"Shall I bring an extra plate?" Patrice said.

"No, I'll just gain ten pounds looking at this," I said, and she was off.

India chose that perfect moment to waft down the steps, sun hat shading her upper body, another shopping bag in hand.

"Allison, honey, I'm glad I caught you. Hey, Hank."

"Can I get you a coffee?" Hank glanced at me. "Something a little more interesting than a latte?"

India peeked out from under the brim. "No, I just wanted to give these to Allison for Foxy to play around with. See what she comes up with."

"If we're talking clothes, I hope they at least cover her backside," Hank said. "And speaking of wardrobe, what are you putting Al in for tonight?"

"What's tonight?" India said.

"Big date with Chief."

"Well, do tell." India sank into the third chair at the table and whipped off the hat.

"You two done talking like I'm not sitting right here?" I said.

India put a hand on my arm. "Where's he taking you, honey?"

"Columbia."

"Then I think we're talking something with a little Latino flair."

"I have to be able to wear it on the back of a motorcycle."

India closed her eyes. "I just completely give up."

"Who's staying with Desmond?" Hank said.

I shook my head. "Nobody. We talked about since he's thirteen now, he's old enough to stay alone ..."

I let my voice drift off.

"He won't be alone," Hank said.

"I know. I just realized that."

"It's just going to be Desmond and the Foxette?" India's voice went falsetto. "Ophelia told me about her. Now I'm not one to say how you should raise your son, honey, but I don't *think* so."

"I don't either. I can always ask Owen but I think Desmond's outgrowing him." I felt my eyes roll. "Just since yesterday."

"We've got to get Little Miss Thang out of your house, Allison," India said. "When do you think she'll be ready for Sacrament One?"

"I think it's more a matter of when they're going to be ready for *her.*"

Hank gave a grunt that would have impressed Rochelle.

India narrowed her eyes. "I have a life-size picture of Jasmine dealing with her. Foxy'll walk on her like she's the bathroom rug."

I glanced at my watch. "I'm due at Ms. Willa's."

"And after that you just focus on Chief today." India winked at Hank and smiled back at me. "If you want to come by Secrets today, I'll fix you up with some black satin pants and maybe a silver lamé tunic—"

"India," I said, "this is me we're talking about. "

I left them there, though I could hear Hank howling and India saying, "What? What did I say?" all the way to the parking lot.

The only problem with riding the Harley to Ms. Willa's was that I had to park on Toques Place, the alley that ran along the side of her house. Every time I rode back there I expected Sultan to screech up in his Lincoln Town Car and try to smash me into the line of trashcans I'd had more than one run-in with in my motorcycle riding life. Even in the oppressive prestorm stillness, I shivered.

But no parking was allowed out front on Cuna Street. There was barely room for one car to pass, not to mention the folks poking around in the candle shops and art galleries that bordered the road. Ms. Willa was one of the few who had refused to sell her property to a commercial buyer and remained a resident in her venerable three-story Victorian. I was sure not too many had argued the point with her, though they were probably watching the obituaries daily.

Owen answered when I rang the doorbell. He was incongruous with the gold brocade wallpaper and the crystal chandeliers that rivaled the one in *Phantom of the Opera*.

"She's been expecting you," he whispered.

"And what should *I* be expecting?" I whispered back.

"She's crankier than a mother bear. Grumpy as a—"

"Got it. Is she in there?"

Owen continued to mutter "—as a hungover hornet," as I followed him into what I was certain was the last parlor left in America. Ms. Willa was enthroned as usual in her green velvet high-backed chair, though it was hard to detect her there dressed as she was in a matching shade that covered everything but, fortunately, her hair, which tended more toward aqua. Her bark, however, left no doubt about her presence.

Or her mood.

"Where have you been?"

"Nice to see you, too, Ms. Willa."

"No, it isn't. I'm not fit for human company today."

I couldn't hide a grin. "Then I guess I better go out the way I came."

"You'll do nothing of the kind. I need you to straighten these people out."

It took me a minute to realize that "these people" just meant Owen, who had retreated to the glass-fronted china cabinet where

Ms. Willa kept her Lladro figures like specimens in a zoo. I sat on the ottoman facing her.

"If *you* can't straighten them out, I don't think I have much chance."

She narrowed the small dark eyes at me, until all I could see were the fragile wrinkles that framed them. "Since when did you start flattering me?"

"That wasn't a compliment."

"That's more like it. I don't like to go by way of Cape Horn."

"Then let's get to the point."

"I'll tell you the point," Owen said. "She's stubborn as a confounded mule. I've met bulldogs would let go of a thing easier than she does—"

"Hush up, old man!" Ms. Willa said.

"She's sick."

"I said hush!"

He hushed so hard I heard his dentures clack.

"I am not sick," Ms. Willa said to me. "I'm just old. Isn't a woman allowed to age with some dignity?"

I didn't point out that there was really nothing dignified about a snarling fox terrier, no matter how old it was. I merely nodded even as I took a closer look at her.

She did appear to have more of a pallor than usual, though I'd attributed that to the pea soup motif she was practically smothered in. The gnarled finger she currently poked first at one of us and then the other trembled in a way I hadn't noticed before. But it was the tenor of the whole scene that made me think Owen might be right. In the seven months I'd known her, wrinkly, wobbly, shriveled Willa Livengood had never once described herself as old.

"So what do you want me to do, Ms. Willa?" I said. "Throw him out?"

"Just tell him I do not need a doctor. I'm as healthy as an eighty-year-old woman has a right to be."

I forced a smile. "I'm sure you've told him that in no uncertain terms."

Owen sniffed.

"I have."

"Then I don't see what the problem is."

She set her face as firmly as one of that vintage could set. "I want him to hear it from you. Everyone listens to you."

"Except you."

She flapped her hand at me, and I noticed for the first time the purple bruises that blotched her tissue-y skin.

"All right," I said. "Owen, back off Ms. Willa. She's perfectly capable of knowing when she needs medical attention."

Ms. Willa looked at him, literally growling under her breath. I looked at him, too, hoping he was, as Desmond would say, picking up what I was putting down.

Owen nodded slowly. "Clear as glass, Ally. A sheet of cellophane couldn't be clearer."

"There you go," I said to Ms. Willa. "Now am I going to get some tea for my trouble?"

"Yes. And I want you to tell me about this new girl you've got over there at the sorority."

Ms. Willa had her own concept of what the Sisterhood was all about. We'd all stopped correcting her.

"Right now we know her as Foxy," I said. "She's—"

"When are you going to bring her around? I want to know who's reaping the benefits of our enterprise."

There was so much wrong with that statement I didn't even know where to begin. I was about to start with the word *enterprise* when I felt a Nudge. An amused Nudge.

Oh, come on, God. Foxy and Ms. Willa? You can't be serious.

But I said, "I'll bring her by."

It was the first reason to chuckle I'd had in days.

CHAPTER SIX

I had one more errand to run, and as I headed for the Wells Fargo Bank building I repeated the mantra I'd made up for myself while staring out the window at four o'clock that morning.

This is strictly business with Kade. It's not mother-and-son bonding. Don't expect too much.

For once I was sorry I didn't hear *Go another mile.* I'd have run a marathon, barefoot, if it meant I could have what I wanted with my son. Something that didn't include pointless discussions about Troy Irwin.

It helped to be greeted by Tia, who had strictly business down to an art form. I didn't know if she was aware of my biological relationship with Kade. She just ushered me into his office like I was any other client.

Kade leaped up from his desk chair like a second string player suddenly being called onto the field.

Was he that eager to see me? Or was it just because he was young? Didn't he always move as if everything was an opportunity to shine?

Stop, Allison. Just. Stop.

"You've never seen my new office, have you?" he said.

"Oh! No!"

I looked around at the black and metal motif, accented by sepia photos in silver frames—one of Kade in a sailboat cutting through New England waters and looking like one of the Kennedys, another of him shaking hands with Chief the day their partnership became official, still another of a handsome gray-templed Italian. That had to be Anthony Capelli. His "real" father.

"The place is you," I said. "I mean, as much as I know about you … you know, in the short time we've … y'know, known each other. I guess."

"It's getting there. Please, sit down. Can I get you anything to drink?"

He was either utterly clueless or incredibly smooth. The former he would have inherited from me, the latter from Troy. I made up my mind he was just diplomatic and sank into a chair.

"I'm good," I said.

"Good."

Kade sat to face me and looked blankly at my hands. "Did you bring your files?"

"My files?"

"Your financial records." He rubbed at his smooth jaw. "Tell me you actually have some."

"Does a basket full of bills and receipts counts as 'records?'"

"One basket doesn't sound that bad."

"Actually, it's two. Three. Maybe four. I don't really know. They're covered with afghans so I don't have to look at them."

"You're serious."

"As a triple bypass."

A long, slow smile spread over his face and into eyes so clear even Owen didn't have enough metaphors for them.

"So what you're saying is I better bring my laptop over to your place. You got tonight free?"

"Yes. No."

"Okay."

The dimples were fully engaged. He must have been adorable when he was a little boy.

"I have a date with Chief," I said.

"Then you are definitely not free." He shrugged. "What's Desmond up to tonight? I could hang out with him and get started on those baskets."

I tried not to let my own jaw drop. "He'd love that. Only, we have a new Sister staying with us right now."

"I've heard about Foxy. Is there a rule about her being around guys? I don't mind if *she* doesn't."

I leaned back in the chair. "I don't know, Kade. She's a pistol, and Desmond's got a thing for her."

"You're kidding."

"She's only eighteen. And cute. Hot, actually. And she's not an addict."

Kade nodded, eyes squinted. "So what you really need is a chaperone for the evening."

"Yeah. But I'm not asking you to do that."

"I'm volunteering. I dig Desmond. And how much of a—what did you call her?"

"Pistol," I said. "Twenty-two caliber."

His grin faded. "You know you can trust me, right?"

"Of course. She's the one I don't trust. I'm not sure she's all that ready to give up the life. I just don't want to put you in an uncomfortable position."

Kade leaned forward, hands on his knees. "I'm not going to encourage her. And if she comes on to me, I know what to do."

"I never thought—"

"So what time?"

I opened my mouth to answer, and my cell phone rang.

"You need to get that?" Kade said.

"I wouldn't, but you know how things are—"

"Go for it. I'll get us a soda."

He stepped discreetly out of the room and I looked at my phone. Nicholas Kent's name looked back at me. I answered with my heart already pounding.

"Nick. What's up?"

"We have a little issue down here on Palm Row, Miss Allison."

"What kind of issue?"

"Her name is Foxy."

"I'll be right there."

"Yeah," Nick said. "That would be good."

It only took eight minutes to get from Kade's office to my house, but I was able to come up with at least fifteen scenarios for what I was going to find when I got there, everything from Foxy soliciting from the side porch and being outed by Miz Vernell, to the pimp she said she didn't have showing up and dragging her by that red hair down Palm Row.

None of them even came close. It wasn't Foxy I saw straddling the railing on the porch. It was Desmond, with Nicholas Kent standing between him and the back door, hands on his hips. The only thing that kept me from dumping the bike in front of the garage was the fact that Nick didn't have his Glock drawn.

"She's okay, Big Al," Desmond said when he saw me running across the lawn. "I took care of it."

"Took care of what?"

I was looking at Officer Kent, who didn't seem to think anything was okay at the moment. Even his freckles looked grim as he nodded toward the door. "She's inside."

I pointed at Desmond. "Don't go anywhere."

"Not a problem," Nick said.

"You want somethin' to drink while we waitin'?" Desmond said to him.

I heard Nick answer, "Dude, are you serious?" before I stepped into the kitchen.

Foxy was curled up on the floor in the corner next to the refrigerator, face pressed into her knees. She did not look "taken care of."

"Hey," I said.

She didn't look up. If anything, she sank her head further into her thighs. I sat beside her and pulled my own knees up with about half the flexibility.

"Are you hurt?" I said. "Physically, I mean."

She shook her head.

"Has someone threatened you?"

"No."

"So you're not in any immediate physical danger."

"No."

That was the last of the screening questions we always asked a Sister when she was melting down. I had a feeling the melting had already happened and Foxy was sitting in a pool of her own stuff.

"How about if we try some eye contact?" I said. "That usually helps."

"I don't want you to see me."

"Trust me, whatever you look like right now, I've seen worse."

"Worse than this?"

Foxy lifted her face. One eye was fiery and swelling even as I looked at it. Blood had left a dried track from her nostril to her split upper lip. But that wasn't why I caught my breath in the back of my throat. I wasn't lying to her; I had seen worse. What I hadn't seen in one of our Sisters was a face that could not have been older than fifteen.

There was no makeup today, nothing to hide the flawless baby skin, the rounded little girl cheeks, the one eye as innocent as the child she had once been.

"Okay," I forced myself to say, "let's put some ice on that."

Foxy reached into the corner and pulled out a dripping sandwich bag. "Desi fixed me up."

Everything in me wanted to ask how *Desi* came to be involved in this, but I put that in the growing pile of things he and I were going to deal with later.

"Why don't you put it back on your eye for now?"

To my surprise she did, without argument.

"Have you told Officer Kent what happened?" I said.

"That cop out there?" Foxy shook her head, and then winced. "He shined a flashlight in my eyes to make sure I didn't have a concussion. Then I told him to leave me alone." She appeared to be trying to roll her good eye. "He didn't have to call you. Desi and I had it handled."

"Desmond is thirteen years old. He doesn't handle assault cases."

"I don't trust the police."

"How about me? You trust me?"

Her face startled, which was understandable. I saved that particular tone for the hard-core situations. And yet still she said, "I don't even trust my own mother."

"I'm not *your* mother," I said. "But I am a mom, and I think you can surmise from the fact that Desmond is vertical at this moment and still has all his teeth that I'm the kind who can be trusted."

"You're the kind who has cops for friends and obeys the rules."

"Actually, the rules I follow at times like this are God's. The rest I kind of make up as I go along."

She tried to curl the lip. Both of us cringed.

"I didn't turn the other cheek," she said. "Isn't that one of God's rules?"

"So I should worry about what the other guy looks like about now?"

"Girl."

"Excuse me?"

"It was a girl. And she hit me first."

"Because ..."

"Because she thought I was trying to cut in on her territory."

If I'd been a swearing woman, I would have spewed an explitive. I tried not to make it sound like one as I said, carefully, "You went back to West King."

"You mean where Jasmine and that other woman busted me?"

"Where Jasmine and Sherry saved your hide, yes."

"No. That place is a complete hole."

I held back a relieved sigh. "Then what territory are we talking about?

I didn't bring up the fact that it was the middle of the day, or that the only place I knew about for turning tricks in St. Augustine was the hole she was referring to.

Foxy struggled to lift her chin. I couldn't imagine there was a spot on her head that wasn't throbbing.

"I wasn't there to take away her business. I went there to help."

"How were you planning to go about that?"

"I told her she needed to run, but she didn't exactly want my advice."

I pulled in air through my nose and hoped some wisdom would come in with it. All I came up with to say was, "Should I be concerned about her physical condition right now?"

Foxy shrugged.

"Seriously. Do I need to worry about you being arrested for assault and battery?"

"She's not going to press charges. She hates cops worse than I do."

I leaned in. "Just so you know: that cop out there *is* a friend of ours. If it does turn out she tries to take legal action, he needs to know what went down."

"Like file a report? No freakin' way."

Foxy tried to get up but I put my hand on her arm and my face close to hers.

"None of us can help you if you don't tell us the truth. Every woman who comes to Sacrament House learns that."

I was sure it was a blend of sheer stubbornness and full-out fear that kept her one-eyed gaze riveted to mine for the next ten seconds.

For the second ten, she searched my face. Whatever she saw looking back at her made her press herself against the refrigerator and nod for another ten. That meant thirty seconds of the Pathetic Pleading Prayer from me: *pleaseGodpleaseGodpleaseGod.*

I could handle women flipping out on speedballs and crawling across the floor because withdrawal wouldn't let them walk and spitting at me across a jailhouse table. But I had no idea what to do with a teenage girl who was perfectly sober. And perfectly lost. *PleaseGodpleaseGodpleaseGod* was all I could think of. The answer was a deep patience I could never have manufactured on my own.

"What do you want to know?" she said.

"Let's start with your real name."

"How do you know Foxy's not—"

"Because I'm not an idiot."

She licked at the torn place in her lip. "Flannery."

I waited.

"Donohue. And I'm not making that up."

"If you did, nicely done. It's a beautiful name."

"It's Irish."

"How old are you, Flannery?"

She shrugged again and stared at her knees. "I lied before. I'm younger than eighteen."

"How much younger?"

"I'm sixteen."

"I thought we were going for honesty here."

"What difference does it make? Underage is underage."

"And the truth is the truth."

She tilted her head back to give the ceiling a cyclopic search. "Fifteen?"

"You tell *me*."

I heard myself sounding calm, but my mind screamed, *She's younger than* fifteen?

"I'm fourteen," she said. "And that *is* the truth."

I started another pile: Things To Weep Over Later.

A thousand questions raised their frantic hands in my head, but I ignored them all for now. The one *answer* I had was that this child was a runaway, and the wrong query could set her right back out on the path she ran in on.

"Thanks for that," I said. "Now, let's go back to the beginning and walk through what happened today."

Flannery squared her shoulders. I could see her pulling up the you-can't-get-to-me attitude, despite the tremor around her lips. I had to work fast.

"I want Officer Kent in here," I said. "Strictly off the record."

"I don't have a record. And I want to keep it that way."

I didn't inform her that the minute she ran away from the mother who didn't wear frumpy clothes, she earned herself a juvenile rap sheet. Instead, I said, "I'm just trying to give you the best possible protection from the chick who tried to take you out."

And anybody else who might be after her.

Whether that came from God or me, I didn't take time to figure out. Not with Flannery saying, "Can Desmond be here too?"

I hesitated. Not having him there could be a deal-breaker for her. I would just have to make it clear to him later that this was his final act as Flannery's caretaker.

"I'll get him," I said. "Why don't you get comfortable in the red chair in the living room? And I suggest you take the ice bag with you."

The fine white skin over the unpunched brow puckered slightly, but Flannery nodded and let me help her up so she could hobble toward the door. I definitely did not want to know what kind of shape the other girl was in if she really had taken it heavier than this.

Nick Kent was sitting on the railing *with* Desmond when I returned to the side porch. Both of them were turned toward the steps where Chief stood with his eagle gaze piercing Desmond. I got there in time to hear him say, "Desmond, what were you *thinking*?"

That alone was grounds for marrying the man.

"All right, gentlemen," I said, "Flannery has agreed to an audience."

"Flannery," Chief said.

"Foxy just her street name," Desmond said. "I knew that thing."

Nick Kent slid off the rail. "What else did you find out, Miss Allison?"

"That she's ready to talk."

Desmond pointed to his own chest, the expected question in his eyes.

"Yes," I said. "This time."

He bolted for the door, taking out an Adirondack with one big foot. Chief didn't even have to look at me to know to follow him.

The screen was barely closed after them before Nick Kent said, "She's underage, isn't she?"

"Oh, yeah."

"Fifteen?"

"Fourteen."

He let out a long, slow whistle. I put my hand up.

"I know we can't approach this the way we do with the women," I said. "But just so you know, I'm not ready to turn her in to whoever it is I'm supposed to turn her in to until I find out what kind of situation she came from. If that puts you in a bad spot, I understand. Do what you have to do. I just want her protected."

"I'm off duty."

"You are a lying sack of cow manure."

He gave me half of his boyish grin.

"And besides," I said, "I know not being on duty doesn't change your responsibility."

Nick put up both hands. "I just happened on a situation where two youths appeared to be in distress, but a parent arrived and my services were no longer needed." He pulled his sunglasses down his freckled nose. "Whatever I don't hear for myself I can't report. Call me if you need me."

"You are an angel from heaven."

"Just promise me you won't get yourself in trouble."

"Nick," I said. "When have you ever known me not to be in trouble?"

The teakettle was steaming on the stove as I passed through the kitchen, probably Chief's doing. Desmond would have sent out to Sacred Grounds for a triple mocha peanut butter something.

I was actually surprised to find Flannery in the red chair with the ice bag positioned on her eye. Desmond was sitting as close to her as he could manage, and it did *not* surprise me that I had to jerk my head at him twice to get him to move elsewhere. Chief coaxed him by the sleeve into the green striped chair and perched himself on the arm. I pulled an ottoman up next to Flannery and tucked the Harley Davidson throw around her legs, just as I'd done for so many frightened, wounded women before her. Except that my initial instincts about her had been right: she was nothing like any of them. She was in far worse trouble.

PleaseGodpleaseGodpleaseGod.

"Here's the deal," I said. "All we're here to do is find out what happened today. Nobody's going to be punished—"

"That's good, Big Al," Desmond put in, "'cause didn't nobody do nothin' wrong. 'Cept that jackal-woman hit Flannery."

"As your attorney, Desmond," Chief said, "I advise you to zip it until you're asked a direct question."

"He has an attorney?" Flannery said. "Do I need one?"

"Chief's your attorney, too, as of now," I said. "Okay?"

She shrugged, but the pucker left her brow.

I tapped the arm of her chair. "Let's start with you. What made you go out looking for …?"

I waited for her to supply a name but she wasn't forthcoming. Desmond muttered, "Jackal-woman."

"All I wanted to do was tell her she needed to get out of town." Flannery narrowed her good eye at me. "I would have just called her, but nobody has a charger for my phone."

"So she obviously has a cell phone too," I said.

"Seriously, who doesn't?"

Desmond raised his hand. Chief gently lowered it for him.

"And you knew where to find her," I said.

She turned to Desmond and gave him a warning look that very obviously thrust him into an interior wrestling match. He bugged his eyes at her. Stretched his neck in three directions. Gave the Adam's apple a complete workout. Finally Chief pressed Desmond's shoulder with his elbow.

"Now you can talk, Des."

Desmond still looked at Flannery, his eyes full of apology, before he said, "She didn't know till I tol' her where the Hot Spot was."

"The what?" I said.

"It's just a place where kids meet," Flannery said.

"To do what, exactly?"

She went through as many gyrations as Desmond had: eye rolling, nostrils flaring, lip attempting to curl. We all waited, Desmond the least patiently. He screwed up his face as if he were in pain.

"To get hooked up," she said. "It's how she makes extra money." I wasn't sure just *she* was the right pronoun, but I let that pass for the moment. We could go down so many bunny trails in this conversation we might not find our way out before she and Desmond were both of age.

"So Desmond told you where the Hot Spot is." I looked at him. "Which you and I will discuss later."

"We can discuss it right here," he said, his pitch rising. "I ain't gon' let Flannery do this all on her own, now."

"That's very noble of you, buddy," Chief said. "We'll get back to you."

"I got the information from Desmond," Flannery said. "I went down there."

"Even though you don't like crowds," I said.

"I didn't have any choice. I had to go down there and tell her she needed to get away from here as soon as she had the money—and she accused me of trying to cut in on her business and then she punched me, right in the face, like three times. I wasn't going to just stand there."

"So after you hit her, you came back here?"

"One question," Chief said. "Was she conscious when you left her?"

"Ya think? She was screaming every cuss word in life at me."

"Was somebody there to help her?" I said.

"When we first started arguing everybody else left. I tried to grab her and make her come back here with me but she just ran."

I looked at Chief.

A little help here? I said with my eyes.

You have opened a gigantic can of worms, Classic, he said with his. But he turned to Flannery.

"What is this girl's name?"

"Why?"

"Because we have a responsibility to make sure she's okay. Does she live here in town?"

"No. And I don't know her real name. We never told each other."

"How about her street name?"

"Tango. Actually, Tango in Paris. After some old movie or something."

"So you have no idea where she might have gone?" I said.

"No."

"Did you tell her where you could be contacted?" Chief said.

Flannery shook her head. "She has my cell phone number, but a lot of good that's going to do her."

"Maybe she gon' go back to the Hot Spot," Desmond said.

The glare Flannery gave him couldn't have been more pointed if she'd done it with two eyes.

"Just sayin'," he muttered.

There was no point in asking her where said Hot Spot was. That was another item I'd have to get out of Desmond later. Along with about seventeen other things.

"So you came back here …" I said.

"I was trying to. I was, like, right at the corner out there when that cop pulled over and asked me if I was all right. I told him yes and just to please leave me alone and I guess my voice got loud because Desmond heard me."

"Where were you?" Chief said to him.

"I was watchin' from the bushes 'side the house."

Chief's eyebrows twisted. "The bushes?"

"I was gon' wait on the porch but I knew Miz Vernell would see me. Or Mr. Schatzie maybe." Desmond straightened in the chair. "I wasn't bein' a coward or nothin'. I tol' Flannery I should go with her but she said she need to do this by herself, and I know not to mess with a woman when she get that look in her eye. You know what I'm sayin', Mr. Chief."

"Go on," Chief said.

"I seen Officer Kent talkin' to her so I went on down there and tol' him she one of the Sisters and I could take it from there." Desmond's voice teetered upward again. "I got no problem with Officer Kent most of the time, but he jus' got all up in my grill work, now, and said he had to wait with us till you got there. Then we come up here and he's all shinin' that light in Flannery's eyes and she just took off in here and act like she wanna climb right in the refrigerator." He thumbed his chest. "*I* got her ice and then I left her alone like she *said* she wanted to be."

He looked up at Chief as if he expected a high-five. He got an eagle-eyed stare instead.

"My head hurts," Flannery said.

"I imagine it does," I said.

It occurred to me that the kettle had been whistling for the last five minutes. I stood up and nodded to Chief.

"Let's go fix some tea. Desmond, go upstairs, please, and get some more blankets, would you?"

"On it, Big Al."

"And some Advil."

He started for the steps.

"And a couple of pillows."

"Imma be back in—"

"Take your time," I said.

He gave me a look of innocence that was almost convincing. Almost. I gave him one that said, *I'm not done with you yet.*

He took the steps at half speed.

That would still only give me about three minutes to have a conversation with Chief. I found him in the kitchen already pouring me tea so strong it could have poured itself.

I went right to his elbow and talked with a bare minimum of lip movement. "Okay, how bad is it?"

"Not that bad, if you don't count the part where we've been harboring an underage runaway who's guilty of prostitution and assault of a minor."

I pressed one hand to my temple and took the cup he offered me with the other. "What are my options?"

"Call Liz Doyle."

"What are my other options?"

"Call Liz Doyle right now."

I gave up trying to drink and settled for warming my hands around the mug. It might have been eighty-eight degrees outside, but I was suddenly shivering.

"I can't bring Liz in on this for the same reason I sent Nick Kent away. We'd be putting her in a really tough place."

"Meaning?"

"As a social worker, she'd have to report Flannery, wouldn't she?"

Chief stuck his head into the refrigerator and came out with a carton of half-and-half. "Why don't we just ask Liz some legal questions? She'd be under no obligation to take action based on that."

"Except that she would know who and what we were talking about."

Chief set the carton on the tea tray. "I don't see that we have another viable plan right now, Classic. And I think we're going to have a harder time dealing with Desmond than we are with her."

The word *we* had never had a sweeter sound.

"I'll call her," I said. "Okay, that's him coming down the steps."

"You go chaperone that action. I'll call Liz."

"And call Kade, would you? He was going to come over and babysit tonight while we went out, which now—"

"I'm on it."

I made my way to the living room with the tray wondering how I was going to deal with a teenage girl. I had spent my entire adult life trying to forget I ever was one, and I had no idea what to do with this one.

Desmond had no such issue. He was spreading a second blanket over a shaking Flannery. I took it from him and finished the job.

"Imma get some snacks to go with that tea," he said.

"Actually, you need to get ready to go back to school. One of us will take you."

For the first time, Desmond looked truly cowed. I pressed a cup into Flannery's hand and steered him into the dining room, where he looked everywhere but at me.

"Whose class are you missing right now?" I said.

"I'm only a little bit late—"

"Desmond."

"Coach Mosquito."

"Wonderful. Exquisite, in fact."

"I missed Miss All-Hair's, too, only she won't count it once you tell her I was on a mission."

"*I'm* not going to tell her anything. Or Coach Iseley."

Desmond's Adam's apple ground into gear. "I hadda be here for Flannery, Big Al—now, you know that thing."

"No, that's *my* job."

"How was you gon' find out where the Hot Spot was for her?"

"How did *you* know where it was? Not only that, how did you even know about it to *find* that out in the first place?"

He toed the rug. "We been talkin'."

"You and Flannery."

"She was about flippin' all the way out 'cause she couldn't call that Tango girl, and Flannery said if she jus' knew where they was a Hot Spot, she could jus' go talk to her, 'cause she was sure Tango woulda figured it out by now. So I tol' her I could find out."

"I'm afraid to ask how you came by that information."

"I jus' asked one a my—one of the girls at school. She was cryin' one day, and I made her tell me what was goin' down and she said she was in some trouble with some boys that wouldn't pay her what they owe her." Desmond knifed the air with his hand as if he were talking to the girl in question right then. "I tol' her she need to have some *respect* for *herself* and she need to be talkin' to God 'cause that business she in ain't gon' take her nowhere she want to be."

"We'll come back to that," I said. "Des, Flannery could've ended up a whole lot worse than she did by going wherever it was she went."

I paused, but he didn't offer an address. Another thing we'd come back to later.

"I know you just wanted to help her."

"'S'what we do. I got the gift of gettin' women to open up to me."

"And sometimes that serves you well, and sometimes it doesn't. This is one of the times when it didn't."

He set his jaw. "I kep' her from bein' throwed in the jail by Officer Kent."

"As soon as she told him she lived here he would have called me anyway." I cupped his chin before it could fall. "Here's what should have happened, and what's going to happen next time, so listen up."

Desmond pulled his head away but he nodded.

"When Flannery told you about the Hot Spot, you should have brought her to me. Period. Because you didn't, you now have to face two teachers and tell them you cut their classes without my permission, and you have to take the consequences."

"You seriously gon' make me do that, Big Al?"

"What other choice do I have?"

"That ain't right. I'm tryin' to help somebody and I'm the one gets in trouble."

I looked him in the eye until he had to hook his gaze onto mine. "How many times have you seen that happen to me? The difference here is that you have a parent whose job it is to show you when what looks like helping really isn't."

"You gon' make me tell you where that Hot Spot is?" he said.

I wanted to say, *Yes, even I have to slide bamboo shoots under your fingernails.* But my response came from that same deep patience God was giving me on loan.

"Here's what I'm thinking," I said. "I'm thinking if the time comes when I need to know that, I won't have to force it out of you. You'll know telling me is the right thing to do."

"I'll prob'ly forget by then. I think I already did."

"It's been a long time since you lied to me," I said. "I'd almost forgotten what it sounded like."

The Adam's apple rose and fell so sharply I was sure he would bleed.

"Think about it," I said. "And pray. That's all I can say."

The door from the kitchen swung open and Liz appeared. In spite of her damp, disheveled state, she reached for Desmond's neck for a hug. He dodged and headed for the kitchen. The door swung back like a slap.

"Not good," she said to me.

"Did Chief tell you what's going on?"

She nodded. "Where is she?"

"Living room."

"Let's you and I talk on the porch then."

"I'll take Desmond back to school," Chief said as we passed through the kitchen. "You want to write him a note or anything?"

"Absolutely not."

His eyes crinkled. "Busted."

"You have no idea. You might want to stay and make sure the Mosquito doesn't put him in the stocks or something."

"On it."

The wind had picked up while we were inside and an eerie darkness was settling over the afternoon. Liz barely gave the glowering sky a glance and merely batted her hair from her face as she parked on the swing and motioned for me to join her.

"Do I have to turn her in to the police?" I said.

Liz craned her neck toward me. "Who?"

"Fl—"

"Stick to hypothetical questions."

I watched Chief and Desmond cross the front lawn to Chief's Road King. I'd seldom seen Desmond that reluctant to get on a motorcycle.

"I don't even know what to ask, Liz," I said. "Just give me the options."

"If a minor of, say, fourteen were to come to you and you had reason to believe that she was a runaway and that she had been soliciting and that she had been involved in an altercation with another minor resulting in an injury, you would be obligated to report all of the above to the juvenile authorities. They would put her in custody and notify a parent or guardian. If running away were her only offense, she would probably be returned to them. With the other allegations on the books, however, she would have to appear with her parents before a juvenile judge who would determine the next step."

"Like, put her in some kind of program."

"No, like sentence her to incarceration for a designated period of time. She would have a juvenile record but that would remain sealed."

"What about helping her?"

"That would be optimum but there is no such program. She's committed several crimes."

"And ya gotta wonder why," I said.

All the patience I'd kept with Desmond and Flannery was whipped away with the wind. The thunder that rolled in the distance was no more ominous than the sound of my voice.

"A kid doesn't just run away for the heck of it," I said.

"That's true—"

"And she doesn't sell herself unless she's really hungry and doesn't know what else to do. Especially a girl like that. She's bright. She has a better vocabulary than I do, for Pete's sake. "

"I'm just telling you how the system works."

"I hate the system."

"The system that let you keep Desmond as a foster child? That system?"

"That wasn't the system. That was you. But what can you possibly do about this situation? You just said yourself—"

"I haven't really said anything yet, because you won't listen to me."

I stared at her, my last words still hanging on my lips. "I'm sorry, Liz. I'm just losing it here."

"I have a couple of suggestions if you want them."

"Please."

Behind Liz a three-pronged fork stabbed the sky and an angry clap of thunder followed it. She pushed her hair out of her face again and watched me, eyes full.

"First, it would help if you found out what was going on at home that made her think she had to run away. If there was abuse, she'll be placed in foster care, not detention."

"What about the other charges?"

"Have any been pressed over this catfight thing?"

"*Cat*fight? We're talking dadgum WWE, Liz. And no, I don't think there will be. That girl is evidently one of Foxy's coworkers."

"Then we won't worry about that one." The first fat drops of rain pelted her face. She slapped them away. "Has anyone actually witnessed your girl soliciting?"

"Jasmine and Sherry saw her with a guy in an alley."

"Would they testify in court?"

"If somebody put a gun to their heads, yeah."

"Then I don't see us running into a problem there either. Not unless she's been picked up before."

"She says she doesn't have a record."

"You believe her?"

The wind snapped the border of the swing's awning, and lightning jabbed angry tines from the sky. I took Liz by the arm and nodded toward the door. I could see the rain coming down in a sheet that was headed for us at a slant across Palm Row. We stepped inside the kitchen just before the screen door slammed at the hands of the gale behind us.

"The girl is more about lies of omission," I said. "So, yes, I think I do believe her."

Liz shook her hair, looking every bit like an indignant Yorkie, and tried to slide the dampness from her arms with her hands. "Just find out what you can. I'll check the National Center website and see what I can come up with there. What's her last name?"

"Donohue."

"Doesn't ring a bell, which might be a good thing. It could mean this is a first offense."

"So running away is an offense," I said, as I handed her a dish towel. "Sounds more like self-*de*fense to me."

"That's what you need to find out," she said. "Until then, you and I did not have this conversation."

I nodded, but she didn't see me. She was burying her face in the towel.

Chief returned right after Liz left. I was in the living room watching Flannery sleep. When I heard him close the back door behind him I joined him in the kitchen.

"She looks even younger when she's asleep," I said.

"How much younger can she look? Did we just miss that because we didn't want to see it?"

"Desmond obviously saw it or he wouldn't have been so attracted to her. She was pretty much like his 'women' at school."

Chief put my cup of now cold tea in the microwave and prodded me by the elbow to the bistro table. "He told me he's given up the women so he can concentrate on Flannery."

"Oh, *man*. What did you say to him?"

"I didn't have a chance to say anything yet. He's telling me this as we're walking into the school, and that coach is standing right there in the office." The corner of his mouth tweaked. "She does look like a wasp."

"Mosquito."

"Nah. I have her for a wasp."

"So what happened?"

"There was some testimony from her. Said everything twice. Desmond refused to take the stand. Then the judge came out—vice principal? Looks like a Labradoodle?"

"I just know her as Vice Principal Foo-Foo. What was the verdict?"

"Guilty. The sentence is three days of ISS, whatever that is."

"In-School Suspension," I said. "Coach Iseley has been licking her chops to make that happen ever since the semester started. At least *she'll* be happy to know he's given up the women."

Chief retrieved the tea from the microwave and set it in front of me. "Drink it this time. So I take it you aren't happy about that?"

"I do think three days is a little excessive."

"No, I'm talking about the women."

"Oh. No, what I'm not happy about is Desmond wanting to concentrate on Flannery. I just got through telling him that wasn't his job."

"And you think that's going to switch off his feelings?"

I let my forehead drop into my hands. "Yikes, we *are* talking about feelings, aren't we?"

"Affairs of the heart, Classic. Complicated stuff even when you're thirteen."

I looked up and was surprised at the lack of crinkle around his eyes. "Could you talk to him about it? He's obviously going to trust you more than me on this. You were a boy once, right?"

Chief moved the cup aside and smothered both of my hands with his on the tabletop. "I can talk, and he might even listen. But there is nothing logical about this. You feel what you feel, no matter what anybody tells you, or even what you tell yourself."

I was unsure whether we were still talking about Desmond.

"You think we should just let him fall all over himself with Flannery?"

His phone rang. Chief glanced at the screen and then looked back at me. "It's Kade, returning my call."

I motioned for him to get it and stared into my tea. *It wasn't complicated enough, God? Really?*

Go—

"He wants to talk to you," Chief said.

I took the phone but Kade gave me no time for hello.

"You still have to go out tonight," he said.

"We can go another time, Kade. When things settle in—"

He actually laughed. "I don't see that happening, ever. You think I can't handle two kids? My younger brother and sister were like Bonnie and Clyde, but they never got a thing past me. So—you want me to bring pizza? A movie?"

"I don't know—"

"I can always call you if it gets out of control."

I looked at Chief who was testing my tea with his upper lip and frowning.

Kade lowered his voice to a husky whisper. "Just trust me on this. You need to go out with Chief tonight."

"Okay," I said.

"And don't forget to uncover those baskets."

"What ba—oh, yeah."

"Later."

I stared at the phone until Chief took it from me.

"Did you know he had younger siblings?" I said.

"He mentioned it once." Chief caught me with his eyes. "Don't go there."

"Don't go where?"

"Where you were headed."

"How do you know where I was headed?"

"It's just like riding a Harley, Classic."

I couldn't stop a grin. "Of course it is. Go ahead. Explain."

"You can tell where a rider's going to go by the direction her head's pointed."

"*What?*"

"Hello! Anybody home?"

"Come in, India," I said, eyes still on Chief. "To be continued."

"Over dinner," he said. "I'll pick you up at six."

India gave him the customary holy kiss on his way out the door and watched through the screen as he dashed through the rain to his bike. She herself was unblemished by the storm. I had to get me one of those sunhats.

"Is he still picking you up on the Harley?" she said, floating said sunhat to the counter.

"This is supposed to pass over," I said.

"Fabulous, because I have brought you the perfect outfit, and honey, I do mean perfect … Allison, darlin', what is it?"

I closed my eyes. "Is it that obvious?"

"It's practically written all over your face in Sharpie. What is going on?"

I told her, and swore her to secrecy.

"And Kade is going to stay here and chaperone those two children by himself?" she said when I wound down. "I do not believe so."

"He—"

"No, honey, he is gon' need backup. I'll be here and work with Flannery on those clothes I gave her to look at. That will keep her busy while Kade amuses Desmond. Now *that* I wouldn't take on."

"You don't have to do that, India."

"Why is everyone always telling what I do not have to do when I know perfectly well what Jesus wants from me?" She pushed a shopping bag into my arms. "Now, you just go up and try this on and come down and model for me. I'll figure out what we can order out for supper."

"Kade's bringing pizza."

India shuddered and waved me out of the kitchen.

When I came down fifteen minutes later, clad in an ensemble of ice blue flowing pants and tunic that admittedly was pretty stunning, India was on the phone with Hank, "ordering out."

"Joe is out of town for the weekend," India said to me, hand covering the phone, "so she was gon' be alone anyway."

There was no point in telling her a cast of thousands was unnecessary. She would probably have Bonner over there, too, if it weren't for the fact that Liz couldn't be around Flannery.

By then India was surveying the contents of the refrigerator. "Yes, she has sour cream," she said into the phone. "And wait until you *see* Miss Allison. Honey, she is a dish. Chief is just going to want to eat her up with a *spoon*."

She hung up and flipped the long silk scarf around my neck and over my shoulder. "You want some help with your hair?" she said.

"It's going to end up under a helmet."

India shook her marvelous head at me. "Oh ye of little faith," she said.

CHAPTER SEVEN

In typical Florida fashion, the storm did pass, leaving the early evening air breezy and new-feeling when Chief picked me up at six. The brick streets were still slick as we left the group of people at my house who, with the exception of Desmond and Flannery, looked like they were sending their kids off to the prom.

I had never actually been to a prom, only because it was expected by my parents and Troy's that we would go. If I recalled correctly, he and I had spent that evening in the back stairwell at Chamberlain Enterprises making out. I tried never to recall that, actually.

But as Chief and I walked hand and hand into the Cuban restaurant known simply as Columbia I thought that the senior prom magic I'd heard of might be something like this, because it mystically evaporated everything in those piles I'd been building.

The bright Spanish tile took care of my concern for Ms. Willa, and the mermaid fountain washed away the baskets Kade was facing. One brush with the indoor palms in their hand-painted pots, and In School Suspension and the floundering Second Chances were a laughing matter. The gap between Kade and me was closed by the guitar-heavy salsa music, and the complications wrought by Flannery on Desmond were at least temporarily wafted away by the sumptuous aroma of the Cuban bread carried on trays larger than my bistro table. By the time I sat across from Chief on the balcony overlooking the diners below, I felt somehow above it all. If it only lasted for an hour, so be it. I let the surreal joy fill me.

Chief ordered a selection of tapas, while I watched with fascination as the server mixed sangria at the next table over and poured it from a painted pitcher.

"You want some?" Chief said when our own server was gone.

I shook my head. "I'm intoxicated enough right now." I felt a strange shyness. "Chief," I said. "I love you."

His face softened. "I can make a pretty good case for loving you more."

Go ...

Go? Really? The Whisper had all the clarity of a Nudge. But most of God's pokes, and lately shoves, pushed me someplace I didn't want to go. This could take me right where I wanted to be, where I longed to be.

Go ...

Still I took a breath. And then several more until Chief's brows drew together.

"It's time for me to trust you," I said, "with—how did you put it?" I pressed my hand to my chest. "With what's going on in here."

"I hoped this night would be about you and me."

"It is. That's what I'm talking about."

"Then talk to me."

The tapas arrived on a three-tiered plate, which gave me a moment to catch up to wherever God was taking me. There was no doubt that I had ceased to call the shots. This was definitely more than a Nudge. I was being pulled with an urgency I'd never felt where Chief was concerned.

"Cakes *de crangrejo*," the server was saying, "Scallops *casmiro, coca de langosta*, and of course, the *al bondigas*."

"Meatballs?" I said.

"Those are essential," Chief said, "for dipping your bread into."

My interest, however, was in the hard round crackers the server set beside me like an afterthought. The sight of them crowded together in the bowl made my throat thicken.

"You okay, Classic?" Chief said as the guy hurried off for more bread.

I scooped up a handful of crackers and brought them to my nose.

"All this great food and you're into the saltines."

"These are Sylvia crackers. She used to come here and buy them for me just to put in my soup. I haven't had them in years."

"Now there's a woman I would have liked to have met. Only person I've ever heard you talk about who's had any real influence over you whatsoever."

"Until you," I said.

Because with the smooth, powdery feel of those crackers in my palm, I could practically hear Sylvia, saying, *Oh, for crying in six or eight buckets, Allison, what do you want—a lightning bolt? Tell the man, already.*

As if that weren't enough, I heard the whisper again. *Go ...*

"You know about the Nudges," I said.

"Wouldn't have met you without them."

"And you know that's how I live my life now."

"I'm privy to that, yes."

"I know sometimes that drives you nuts."

"Doesn't matter now. I'm already there."

"You're enjoying this, aren't you?"

"Absolutely." Chief reached a hand around the candle in the middle of the table and curled his fingers about my wrist. "I don't think you can tell me anything that's going to drive me away, Classic."

Yet another long draw of breath. Yet another *Go*.

"It hasn't been just Nudges for a while now," I said. "I've discovered that I feel what God is … probably … feeling when it comes to people's pain. And it's taking over more and more."

"What will you do about that?"

"It's not like I can be cured."

Chief shook his head. "Why would you go right there?"

"Right where?"

"To the conclusion that I think that's somehow sick. I'm asking what you'll do with what you're feeling."

"Really?" I heard the tears in my voice before I knew they were there. "That's really what you're saying?"

"Have I given you reason to doubt that? Haven't I always supported you?" He gave me half the smile. "Eventually?"

"Yeah, you have."

He nodded at the server who brought the bread, and then he leaned across the table, shutting out everything else with his shoulders. "Who could be in this community you and God have created and not know he's real?"

I swallowed hard. "That's all I need to hear."

"You sure?"

I sat with it. Stroked the back of his hand and watched his eyes and waited for the whisper. And it was there.

Go. Go …

"I'm sure," I said.

His smile was full-blown. "Then let's eat, because we have places to go."

"Where?"

"Surprise."

Yeah. I was certain the senior prom I'd missed was nothing whatsoever like this.

We laughed at each other over the *casmiro* and the *langosta* and the crusty bread that never seemed to run out. We talked about my Sylvia and his first Harley and all the other things that made the world seem faultless. At one point he said to me, "You look good tonight, by the way."

"You can thank India for that."

He shook his head, ponytail swishing between his shoulder blades. "I beg to differ. You could be wearing a garbage bag and you would still be fabulous right now."

I smiled. "I'll be sure to pass that on to her. Are we doing dessert?"

"Depends."

"On …?"

His eyebrows lifted only enough to be the single sexiest piece of body language I'd ever seen. "On how fast you want to get out of here."

"Check, please," I said.

His hand was in the air, hailing the server, before I got the last syllable out. *ThankyouGodthankyouGodthankyouGod.*

It was all right. I knew that as we left the table and made our way down the wide staircase to the crowded dining area below. Whatever happened back in the world we had put on hold for the night, it would always be all right with Chief there believing in me. Believing in God. I wasn't sure what to do with that kind of—what had Hank called it?—surreal security. Oh, but I could learn.

When we reached the first floor Chief said, "Do you need to powder your nose before we head out?"

"I've never powdered my nose in my life," I said. "Do you need to powder yours?"

He grinned and kissed the top of my head and strolled down the hallway to the restroom with that John Wayne–halting gait that turned me to whipped butter. I sat on a low tiled wall that separated the private dining rooms from the main area and crossed my ankles, more to keep myself from doing the happy dance than out of an attempt to be a lady. Still, Ms. Willa would approve—

I was knocked from that thought by a voice jarring from the private room straight ahead of me.

"You people cannot be serious," the man said.

The man being Troy Irwin.

I couldn't will myself to look away. He stood in the arched opening with his back to me but I didn't have to see his face to know it was anger itself, hammered in stone.

But then I did see his face, in my mental vision, minus the graying temples and the mask formed by years of posturing. It was a twenty-five-years-younger-than-now face whose clear blue eyes clouded in a way I'd never seen them do before that instant. I heard the voice that matched it—adolescent, and yet so very much like the voice spewing venom from the dining room. Until that long-ago moment, I had never heard him use that voice: a voice attacking from a corner it had been backed into. I hadn't heard it since. Until now.

"This won't happen," Troy said in the doorway. "It will *not* happen."

The sea of other faces I could see through the opening stiffened and shifted away. I had no idea what he was referring to, but I felt it kicking me in the stomach, knocking my eighteen-year-old self off the path that had seemed so certain an hour before. I had to get out of there now before I returned the shove that had taken away so many years of my life.

I lurched to my feet but there was no time to take a step before Troy marched out of the private dining room, yanking at the bottom of his jacket, and collided with a bread-toting server. The tray twirled in the air like a runaway top and landed with an alarmed clang at my feet. A loaf slid past and bumped over the toes of Troy's Armani's. He kicked it aside, in the process heedlessly kneeing the waiter who dove after it.

And then he saw me.

His eyes glittered as he came close to me, so close I could feel the hot air from his nostrils. It was the second time that evening a man had closed out everything around us. This time I wanted to claw my way out.

I started again for the door, but hard fingers wrapped around my arm as Troy pressed himself to my side.

"Excellent choice," he said into my ear. "Let's take this outside."

I didn't try to wrench myself away as we strode together through the waiting diners who filled the space between us and the outside door. The only time in the last quarter of a century that Troy Irwin had laid a hand on me, it had been with this same entitled grip. I knew his ego wouldn't allow him to have to use physical force for long, just as it hadn't five months ago. Still, the slither of a cotton-mouth across my skin couldn't have repulsed me more than the feel of his flesh against mine. Unless it was the memory of how I had once thrilled to his touch.

As I predicted, he let go as soon as we were on the front patio, inside the shadow of a potted palm. One of his hands went to the sloped ceiling above my head. The other pulled through his hair without disturbing a strand. I could see him snapping the pieces of control into place like Legos.

I wanted to spit.

"I don't know what you heard," he said. "But it won't happen."

"I didn't hear anything except you yelping like a junkyard dog," I said.

He sniffed a laugh, the kind of condescending sound my father used to make, followed by me sneering and being summarily dismissed. "There it is," he said.

"There what is?"

"Everything you were holding back the other day in front of your kid. Come on, let's see it all."

Why was I still standing there? I tried to get past him. He moved in without touching me until my spine hit the tile behind me. Something flashed in my head: the two of us in this same position on the back stairs of Chamberlain Enterprises at seventeen. Wanting and empowered.

"Step back," I said.

"I will. When I'm done with you."

The same words that had thrilled through me then were spoken now with a menace so cold it froze the sweat at my temples.

"I didn't want to say this the other day with your boy there, but I could sue you, and our son, for defamation of character."

"What character?" I said.

"The character that got me where I am and is going to keep me there."

"Stay there. I don't care."

"You'd better start."

"We've had this conversation before. You threaten me. I ignore you. What's the point?"

Once more I attempted to get around him. Troy put himself in my path and backed me again to the wall. I could feel my face hardening.

"I'm not going to sue you," he said.

"Good choice, because I don't have a dime. Nothing left for you to gank."

His brows rose as if he'd rehearsed the move. "Oh, I see you're a tough girl now. Got the lingo down." He pressed closer. "Unfortunately it's too late for that. I'm not offering you any more deals."

"You're breaking my heart."

"See, that's a different story than the one you gave me the last time we spoke."

I groped through my memory.

"You said I couldn't hurt you. Now I'm breaking your heart. Good … because that's exactly what I plan to do."

A cascade of retorts slid through my mind but the look in Troy's eyes slammed into them and sent them crashing into a pile I couldn't get to. It was the desperation I'd seen that day on Aviles Street. Only this time it didn't peek out from behind a bent blind. It hit me full in the face.

"You tried to take away my future a long time ago, Ally." Troy's voice shook at its edges. "You weren't tough enough then and you aren't now, no matter how tight you get with your whores and your Hell's Angels and your little half-breed son—"

"Get—off—me!"

I shoved the heels of both hands into his chest and knocked him backward. He flailed against the palm just long enough for me to hurl myself past him before he grabbed for me. I pulled my arm over my head and tried to whirl away from him. In the swish of silk I heard—

Allison. You must go another mile.

I nearly smacked into the force that held me there, that made me turn and watch Troy Irwin continue to pull the long silver scarf until he held the entire thing in his hands.

"Bring it, Ally," he said. "Show me what you've turned into."

Go—

I CAN'T. I just … can't.

Troy didn't move toward me this time. He simply flipped my scarf around his neck and fingered the fringe, never taking his gaze from me.

"At least you finally admit how you really feel about me." He shook his head. "Now is that any way for a prophet to behave?"

The whisper pulsed in my soul, but something louder and heavier shouted it down. I pushed against the unseen force that tried to hold me back from spitting my own words in his face.

It was the seen force that stopped me. I felt Chief behind me even before he said, "Ease it away from the curb, Mr. Irwin."

Troy slumped his shoulders with exaggerated disappointment. "Too bad your bodyguard had to show up *just* when we were finally making some progress."

Chief's hands came down on my shoulders. Triumph gleamed in Troy's eyes.

"It's still too late," he said. "Even with the Hog here to keep you from making even more of a fool of yourself."

"Is this conversation over?"

Chief said it to me, but Troy answered.

"I've said everything I wanted to say. You, Ally?"

Chief squeezed my shoulders. "If Ms. Chamberlain has anything else to say to you, she'll do it through her attorney."

A chilling smirk formed on Troy's lips. "You mean our son? I'd rethink that, Ally, because Kade's not much of a lawyer. He's definitely failed to take me out—and we all know he wants to." Troy pressed his finger to his nose. "But you know, come to think of it, since you're his mother maybe he'll listen to you. You of all people should be able to convince him that nobody fights me and wins." The smirk faded as he bored his eyes into me. "Nobody."

I didn't answer. The shine of victory had once more been replaced by the cornered prick of desperation. There was nothing I could say to that, and God had stopped competing to be heard.

Chief let go of my shoulders and stepped beside me. "Should a 'fight' become necessary, I am Ms. Chamberlain's attorney, not Mr. Capelli."

Troy leered at me. "A word of advice. Never do business with someone you're sleeping with."

"All right, that's enough." Chief's hand swallowed mine and pulled me with him to the sidewalk. Troy forced an excuse for laughter that still grated my ears raw as Chief continued to haul me around the corner and up Hypolita Street.

Just as we reached the parking lot where we'd left the Road King, I plastered my other palm over my mouth and pulled away from him.

"What are you doing?" he said.

"I think I'm going to throw up," I said.

I stood there, breathing and swallowing so I wouldn't lose the tapas and the marvelous bread and the Sylvia crackers onto the blacktop. What I did want to lose was Troy's touch, his taunting, his fouling of everything I loved. And the anger that pulled through my veins like barbed wire.

But it was all still there when I turned back to Chief.

"I'd ask if you were okay," he said, "but you're obviously not."

"No. I'm not." I dragged my hands through the hair India had so carefully styled. "I thought I was past this."

"This."

"Losing it when he attacks me."

"Mmm."

I folded my arms across my middle, which was still threatening to erupt. "You could at least tell me I really didn't lose it."

"Why start lying to you now?"

Chief put his hand in the center of my back and ushered me toward the Harley. His sudden silence made me anxious.

When he handed me my helmet, I hung it back on the handlebar. "I'm sorry if I embarrassed you."

"You didn't embarrass me."

"Then what's this?"

He didn't ask what this was. He just took my face in his hands. There was no prekiss look.

"I told you earlier that you can tell where a rider's going to go by the direction her head's pointed."

"And you were going to explain that to me."

"Right now yours is pointed backwards, Classic. And that's where you're going to go until you get this thing resolved."

"What thing are we talking about?"

Chief nodded in the direction we'd just walked from. "That thing I just saw between you and Irwin."

"Come on, Chief! There's *nothing* between Troy Irwin and me."

He took both of my wrists in his hands and pulled each of my clenched fists forward so I had to look at them.

"What do you call this?" he said.

"You don't expect me to be angry?"

"That's not what I'm saying."

"So what *are* you saying?"

He let go and took my helmet off the handlebar and handed it to me.

I pushed it away. "We're not going anywhere until you tell me what this is about. You're the one who's always saying, 'tell me what's going on in there—'"

"I don't know, all right?"

Those may have been the most frightening words I'd ever heard. The world I'd magically stepped out of two hours before was crashing back in, because Chief didn't know. And Chief always knew.

"Let's go," he said.

"Where are you taking me?"

"Home," he said.

We rode back to Palm Row in silence. Prom night was over.

The group that greeted me when I walked into the house alone looked like they were about to yell "Surprise!" until they saw the guest of honor wasn't there.

"How did it go, guys?" My voice sounded stiff, even to me.

Nobody answered except Flannery. "We made some killer outfits," she said.

She looked at India, who kept her eyes on me. "We'll show those to Miss Angel later. Have you had a bubble bath lately, Flan?"

Flannery squinted at her like she had two heads, but India's deep-eyed return stare sent her up the steps. Kade wordlessly closed his laptop and Hank picked up her helmet from the counter. India gave me a kiss on the cheek, visibly restraining herself from saying, *Now you sit down right now, honey, and tell me what is going on.* Only Desmond remained motionless, leaning against the refrigerator with dread drawn on his face.

"We'll touch base on your financials later," Kade said.

They all departed as discreetly as diplomats, leaving me to face my fast-deflating son.

"This ain't good, is it, Big Al?" he said.

"I'm not sure, Des."

"I don't see no ring on your finger."

"Were you expecting a ring?"

He swallowed guiltily. India's predictions had clearly been the main topic of conversation in my absence.

"Chief and I just had a little disagreement," I said.

"You want me to talk to him?"

I put my wrist against my mouth and closed my eyes.

"You ain't cryin'? Come on, Big Al—you scarin' me here."

"Don't be scared," I said, although I was. "Listen, I'm tired. We'll talk in the morning, huh?"

"Then we still goin' to Cappuccino's tomorrow?"

"We're going to Kade's?"

"He said he need us all to help him move into his beach house."

"Oh. Sure."

I put up my hand for him to high-five me, but he didn't move.

"I just gotta know one thing, Big Al, or I can't sleep tonight."

"What do you need to know?"

"You and Mr. Chief—you still …?"

His eyes were so big and boyish and frightened, it took every ounce of decency in me not to say, *We'll be fine, Clarence. Just a little spat. Not to worry.*

But the truth was the truth. I couldn't expect it from my kid if he didn't get it from me.

"We have some things to work out," I said.

My voice broke, and the lanky arms were around me.

When he finally went to his room, looking small and sad, I went out to the side porch and leaned on the railing where Chief always propped his feet to wait for me.

It had seemed so clear that God wanted me with him. *Go*, he'd whispered. *Go*. So what was this about?

"Please," I whispered. "I know I shut you out tonight, but what *is* this?"

You'll have to go another mile.

"I'll go anywhere for Chief," I said. Out loud.

The silence that replied was as heavy as the air clinging to my skin. But the push—the push was there. This time, I didn't push back. I didn't know where it was shoving me, but I didn't push back.

A day earlier I would have been ecstatic to be a part of Kade's move into his beach house in Ponte Vedra. But the next morning I could barely haul myself out of the bed. I wanted to pull the covers over my head until Chief came to my bedside and asked me to forget the whole thing and marry him. Sylvia would be saying, *Well, wantin' ain't the same as gettin'.*

So I donned sunglasses to hide my swollen eyes and drank three cups of coffee before I even thought about leaving the house. Flannery actually looked worse than I did. Her swelling had receded, thanks to the ice, but she was a mass of black and blue and it hurt just to look at her lip. We did Neosporin and Advil, and Desmond turned himself inside out trying to coax her out of the sullen place she'd parked herself in.

"I did this for you," he said and presented her with a drawing of an elfin young woman with curls billowing from her head to the sides of the page, wearing a minidress with an unfinished diagonal hem and a collection of buttons following the same flow across the bodice.

When Flannery only gave it an apathetic glance I blundered in with, "You're a fashion designer now, too, Des?"

"Nah. Flannery, she made the dress. Last night." He snapped his fingers. "Took her that long."

"Whatever." Flannery looked at me. "Why are we even going to the beach? It'll probably rain the whole time."

I shook my head. "Storm's over."

"Too bad," Desmond said. "Then we wouldn't have school Monday and you and me could work on our wear-it-on-your-body art some more."

She rolled her good eye at him. "Wearable art."

"They don't close school unless the water's higher than the kindergartners, Des," I said.

That had about as much of a cheering effect on him as he had on her. All three of us were in a funk when we picked up Gigi, Rochelle, Jasmine, and Mercedes on San Luis Street. Sherry and Zelda had to work at C.A.R.S., and Ophelia said she could handle Second Chances by herself. Five minutes into the drive I couldn't deal with the sulky silence any longer.

"Hey," I said to Mercedes, who was riding up front with me, "things are actually looking up for y'all. Flannery and India are onto something with this thing of redoing the stuff that's not selling. Flannery and Desmond painted—"

Mercedes folded her arms and stared at me.

"What?" I said.

"You gon' keep pretendin' you're in a good mood, or you gon' tell us what's goin' on wichoo?"

I felt a huge stab of guilt. I *had* no problems compared to what these women had endured.

"It's nothing," I said.

"Uh-huh. We your family, or not?"

"Hey," Flannery said from the back.

"What?" Mercedes said.

"She broke up with her boyfriend."

Jasmine's hands clutched the seat behind me. "No you did not, Miss Angel! Not you and Mr. Chief."

I glared at Flannery in the rearview mirror, but Desmond was already whispering furiously into her ear.

"We didn't break up," I said.

"You had a big ol' fight, then," Gigi said. "I know that look. Been *there*."

Rochelle grunted.

"I think we better lay off Miss Angel," Mercedes said.

"You brought it up," Jasmine said.

"And I'm bringin' it back down."

After that we rode without talking. Mercedes put her hand on my shoulder and kept it there.

Normally I liked the ride out to the north beaches, through a tunnel of oaks dripping with Spanish moss that led to the low bridge over the marshland. But as we rose above the Tolomato River portion of the Intracoastal Waterway and passed over Comache Island, I felt nothing but the kind of dread I'd seen on Desmond's face the night before.

Passing the entrance to Vilano Beach to our right did nothing to help. It had the potential to be a cute waterside village, but so far no businesses had taken hold. A neon sign proudly announced the Town Center, and a Publix was going up, but there was more false optimism there than anything else.

Nothing, however, looked quite as without hope as the house on Ponte Vedra Boulevard where Kade stood out front waving us in.

"Lordy," Mercedes said. "This where he gon' *live?*"

"Talk about your fixer-uppers," Flannery said.

It in fact gave new meaning to the term. Sandwiched between a respectable elevated A-frame and a proud three-story, Kade's curb appeal consisted of overgrown sawgrass and sea oats that screamed for a machete. The driveway we bounced onto was nothing more than hard-packed sand, the path to the back steps a mere trail of wet leaves. Of course, a box on stilts really didn't require much of a grand entrance.

Kade came to the driver's side window of the van and grinned like he was welcoming us to a McMansion.

"Thanks for doing this, guys," he said. "Come on in—I have breakfast ready."

As the van doors opened and the Sisters and Desmond climbed out, Kade put his lips close to my ear.

"You okay?"

"Fine," I said. "Show me your house."

He gave me a long look before he said, "Okay."

I followed him up a long set of steps to the kitchen at the back of the place where Hank was unpacking a single box of cooking supplies.

"I know what I'm getting you for a housewarming present, Kade," Hank said when we walked in.

"What?"

"Everything." Her lips twitched. "Did that breakfast I smell come from Sacred Grounds?"

Kade grinned and crossed his fingers. "Patrice and I are like this."

Everyone chortled but me. The charm that usually delighted me in Kade was so Troy-like I had to leave the kitchen.

The Sisters were crowding out the sliding glass door that led from the tiny living room onto a deck running the width of the house on the beach side. I stayed inside for a minute to get my bearings both emotionally and literally, seeing how the floor rippled like the ocean itself. One wrong step and I was sure I'd fall through the parquet.

"The shower leaks, and I'm having to stage all-out war with the palmetto bugs," Kade said behind me. "But I got a heck of a deal on the place. Stan said he'd help me shore it up."

I hoped our HOG friend knew how to install a whole new subfloor. But I nodded, attempted to smile, and joined Desmond and the Sisters on the deck, which was in far better shape than anything else I'd seen. It looked practically brand new, in fact, and provided all anyone really needed with a view like that. I told myself I wasn't checking to see if Chief was there, but I wasn't very convincing. He wasn't, and I didn't know whether to be relieved or sad.

While the rest of the group pawed through the bag of Patrice's goodies, I took in the Atlantic, which sparkled no more than a hundred feet away, its tentative early-morning waves ebbing onto the firm sand I'd grown up with. A long plank path led politely to it,

seeming almost apologetic, as if it were sorry to disturb the under-
brush at all, though its very presence kept people from trampling
it down. I could almost hear Owen telling me that sensitive plants
grow by the inch and die by the foot. Sensitive the tall sea grass and
palmettos might be, but they held the sand in place and kept the
beach from disappearing into the sea.

"I say we take a walk before we go to work," Kade said.

"Do we have to go in the water?" Jasmine said. "I can't swim,
Miss Angel."

"No swimming involved, Jazz," Kade said.

"Seriously, you don't know how to swim?" Flannery said. "I
thought everybody did."

I saw Gigi stiffen. "Everybody didn't have a mama that sent them
to swimming lessons."

Mercedes uttered an "Mmm-mm." I was watching Desmond.
He hadn't had a mama who hooked him up with the YMCA either,
and in my year as his new mama other things had taken priority. Like
breaking his petty-theft habit and getting rid of his nightmares and
cleaning up his rainbow of a vocabulary.

Rochelle and Flannery were already down the steps and
Desmond was not to be left behind. When Mercedes and Jasmine
and Gigi all hung back, something occurred to me with a spasm
of sadness.

"You've never seen the ocean before, have you?" I said.

"No, ma'am," Jasmine said.

Gigi scoffed toward the horizon. "I've survived without it."

"Mm-hmm," Mercedes said. "But we ain't—aren't—just about
survivin' here. We're about livin.'" She looked at me, though whether

she saw the sheer awe in my eyes, I couldn't tell. "I think we been missin' out on somethin', Miss Angel."

"You surely have," I said. "Come on. I'll go down with you."

Mercedes nodded, gaze on the sighing ocean below. Jasmine took Gigi's hand—who by some miracle didn't yank herself away—and the three of them somehow managed to get down the stairs and onto the path in tandem. A lump formed in my throat as I followed, but, then, what *wasn't* making me cry that day? Including Kade at the bottom saying, "This will cheer you up."

He strode off down the beach with the wind ruffling the hair that matched the sun. I hadn't seen him step too far out of his lawyerly persona before. Just another stinging reminder of how much I'd missed. He definitely had Troy's outdoorsy-ness, without the ceaseless competition. Troy would have had everybody organized for a boogie board event by now, and who cared if people didn't know how to swim?

The nausea started again.

I focused abruptly on my other son, who was chasing Flannery out ahead of Kade. She'd captured her mane with a hair tie but tendrils danced around her head in a halo as she skittered, plover-like, across the sand. Every time Desmond's endlessly long legs carried him close to her, she darted away with a move my gangly kid could never hope to copy. Still, he laughed, his enormous, handsome grin, even when she neatly dodged him with a series of flips.

"She got gymnastic lessons too," I heard Gigi say.

That was between squeals as the ocean crept over her feet and Jasmine's and splashed past Mercedes's knees. The sheer abandon in their laughter was something I seldom heard, and I stopped to steep myself in it. Although Rochelle didn't make a sound, she did point toward the sea, where a pair of dolphins stitched their way through the top terrace of waves.

It was like watching a family. Mercedes was right: it was *my* family. Once again the joy was beyond real, and I, too, flung my head back to add my laughter to theirs. But the sound caught in my throat.

Ahead, Flannery leapt just out of Desmond's reach and charged headlong into the surf. Desmond stopped short with the water to his shins, and even from where I stood I could see his backbone go rigid. Flannery popped up from the foam, throwing out her arms to wave him in, but he remained frozen on the shore.

I felt Kade's hand on my arm and only then realized I had taken a step forward.

"I'd let him handle it," he said.

"He can't swim. She's humiliating him."

"You'll humiliate him worse if you go over there."

"I can't watch."

"Yeah, I wouldn't."

I looked at Kade, but his face was serious.

"Maybe I'll just … kind of … take a walk the other way," I said.

"Fabulous idea."

"Just don't let him drown."

I went far enough so that I could no longer hear the squeals, or the lack of them, and then I stopped and shaded my eyes to look out over the water. A few breakers lifted to reveal their lacy faces before they curled into themselves. Beyond them the sea had the look of the old-fashioned icing Sylvia used to spread on the cakes she baked for me, all glazed and peaked.

She was the one who had taught me how to love the Atlantic: to dive through its waves and savor its salt and let it carry me, helpless and delighted, toward the shore. While my parents went off to high-class Hawaii and the classy Caribbean, she brought me every summer weekend to this, the middle-class ocean. She always said I had to get some of it on me, which my mother clearly did not do in her Christian Dior swimwear.

Sylvia would point out that the beach looked all the same if you only saw it from the deck of your summer estate. You had to come down here and put yourself in the midst of it to see what was really happening close up. The sand spurs. The horseshoe crab eggs formed into mermaid collars. The cities of shells from the million animals who once lived and thrived in the sea, washed up in a crowd by the surf.

I tore my thoughts from Desmond's inevitable shame at the hands of a child barely a year older than he was, a child I wasn't liking much at the moment, and I watched the sea foam gather on my toes and remembered how I always loved plunging my feet into the sand. The warmth and softness were among the few happy reminders of my childhood, before I knew that I was mostly unloved, before I figured out the emptiness in me was called lonely.

Just like Gigi and Jasmine and Mercedes and probably Flannery, I really was alone as a kid, except for Sylvia.

And Troy.

As hard as the fingers of recent memory clenched around my heart, I couldn't resist the force that sent me beneath it. To the Sunday afternoons when Sylvia shook out the wistful longing for connection with her picnic blanket and sat little Allison and little Troy down to

Yankee coleslaw and baked bean sandwiches and all the other things
we learned to eat from her New York taste. To the shouts of, "You
two go out any further and I'll knock your heads together!" which
Troy and I laughed at as we ventured bravely beyond yet another
set of breakers. To the verses of "I Sing a Song of the Saints of God"
she belted out from the front seat of the enormous Pontiac while we
succumbed to sunburned sleep against each other's shoulders in the
back.

I pulled my hands to my shoulders now and closed my eyes. The
incoming tide splashed me to the thighs, but it couldn't wash away
those memories. Or the pain that usually kept them safely tucked
away in my soul.

A throat cleared softly. I looked up to see Bonner and Liz standing only a few yards away.

"We didn't mean to interrupt your prayers," he said.

"You didn't."

"I thought you might want to know what I found out about
Flannery." Liz put up her hand. "More like what I didn't find out,
although that in itself reveals a lot."

"Let's walk," I said, and looped my arm through hers. I suddenly
had to get moving.

"I checked every list on every website," she said. "No Flannery
Donohue has been reported missing."

"So maybe she's not from around here. She did tell me her friend
Tango wasn't."

Liz shook her head. "These were all national lists, and they
include Canada. Unless she flew in from Europe or something, she'd
be on one of them if she was reported."

"So what does that mean? That her parents don't give a rip that their fourteen-year-old has run away from home?"

"Would you come to that conclusion?" Bonner said to Liz.

She pulled her face into a grimace, not an expression I saw often on those cherubic cheeks. "There are other possibilities. A parent could be looking for her without contacting the police. Maybe they don't want her to have a record."

"They care if she has a record but they don't care that she might be hurt or hungry. Or dead."

"Parental neglect is one of the main reason kids run. If the parents are into drugs or they're serious alcoholics they might not even know she's gone yet."

"They're on one heck of a binge, then, because it's been at least a week, and probably longer judging from the shape she was in the first time I saw her."

I dodged a crab scurrying sideways toward the water. Liz extricated herself from my grip, while Bonner took my elbow on the other side.

"You want to slow down a little, Legs?" he said.

"Sorry." I shoved my hands into the pockets of my shorts. "I would love to get her parents alone in a room."

"That was going to be my next suggestion," Liz said.

I stopped. "Are you serious?"

"Well, not *alone*. You should probably take Chief with you."

Bonner choked as if he'd consumed an entire cat.

"Or Kade." Liz's eyes began to blink.

I shoved the wind-tossed hair out of my face. "You're saying I should actually have a conversation with these people?"

"Off the record. As in, you didn't get this idea from me and I'm not going to be there."

"Tell me some more."

Liz took a step closer to me, as if she were afraid the gulls might overhear and carry the news straight to her superiors.

"If Flannery is more than her parents can handle right now, and they see how you are with her, they might be very open to signing over guardianship to you. *Then* I could step in and handle the legalities for you."

It was my turn to put my hand up. "Whoa. When did I say I wanted to be her foster mother?"

"You didn't. But that's the only way you're going to be sure she isn't going to land in lockdown or with people who could end up being worse than her parents. Or out on the street again."

"There has to be some other alternative."

"Since you've already successfully fostered one child, I can guarantee you they'll give you custody of another one."

I looked at Bonner. "Am I talking to myself here?"

He put up *both* hands.

"You can't blame me for thinking you'd be perfect," Liz said. "But if you want me to, I'll look through the files and see if there might be somebody else ..."

I could feel my eyes narrowing. "But."

"I just don't see anybody else being able to look at that child *like* she's a child once they know that she's had to work as a prostitute. Meanwhile, you need to find out if she was abused at home. Otherwise I have no choice but to report her as a runaway and then she *will* be arrested—"

"But we don't even know who her parents are. How am I supposed to find them?"

"From the only person who knows who they are and where they are."

I looked down the beach where the rest of the group were mere tiny figures against the sun, Flannery among them.

"I seriously doubt that she's going to tell me," I said.

Bonner shrugged. "She told you her name."

"Which could still be an alias. The fact that you can't find her on any list kind of points to that."

He, too, gazed down the beach. "I think the fact that she isn't wearing a string bikini shows you have a pretty strong influence on her already."

"You can do this, Allison," Liz said.

"I'll have to think about how." I dug my hands deeper into my pockets. "What about in the meantime? I'm breaking the law by not turning her over to the authorities."

"Let's just go with the assumption that whoever is supposed to be responsible for her isn't going to care about that." Liz put her hand on my arm. "Just remember—"

"I know. I didn't hear that from you."

Bonner slid his arm around Liz. "We need to get going. I have to look at a house in Vilano that's going on the market. Although I'm not counting on people lining up to buy anything down there."

"You two lovebirds go ahead," I said.

Liz wrinkled her nose at me. Bonner's face went blotchy. They left me longing for that kind of simplicity.

Instead I had about the most complicated life of anybody I could think of. It was enough to make me kick off my sandals and head straight into the surf. I would have if I hadn't sensed someone else approaching from the direction of Kade's house. I didn't have to turn and look to know it was Chief.

"You okay, Classic?" he said.

"No," I said.

"Neither am I."

I had to look then. He was wearing sunglasses so I couldn't see his eyes, but I knew there were no crinkles there. The sad set of his mouth gave that away.

"Did you … have you … are you—" I snapped off that string of eloquence and just looked at him.

"I'm working on it," he said. "I did come up with one answer." He folded his arms across his chest and gazed in the direction of the horizon. "Last night was the first time I ever saw you with Irwin."

"No. Really?"

He gave me a brief glance over the top of his sunglasses. "I would have remembered."

"I wasn't *with* him. He bulldozed himself into the situation. That's his MO. Trust me, I was doing everything I could to get away from him."

"You want to hear this or not?"

"Sorry," I said. "Tell me."

Chief buried his hands in his armpits, eyes still pointed out to sea. "Until I saw you together I always just pictured you in my mind as two people fighting a courtroom battle."

"That's basically what we are."

"No, I saw the connection."

"A *what*? We don't *have* a connection! Okay, we did at one time, when we were kids. And there's Kade, only that definitely does not connect us. Chief, this is absurd. I cannot stand the man. You watched me almost *hurl*, for Pete's sake. What more do I have to do—open a vein?"

He didn't answer. He was silent for so long, the ocean's heartbeat nearly drove me mad. I couldn't tell whether it was God or just pure stubbornness that kept me waiting until he finally spoke.

"I don't see how we can make a commitment to each other when you still have that kind of intense feeling about another man. Even if the feeling is hate." Chief squinted over my head into the sun. "*Especially* if the feeling is hate, because you told me yourself you *hate* hate."

"I guess you do want me to open a vein." I tried to keep the sarcasm out of my voice. "Yes, I hate what Troy's tried to do to our ministry. I hate what he did to Ophelia. I hate that he tried to use interfering with the adoption to get me to give up the houses. It's what he's *done* that I hate. But Troy hasn't won and he's not going to."

"I get that, Classic." Chief said.

"Then *what* is the *problem*?"

He turned to face me, and before I could back away he had his hands on my shoulders. I could feel my anger head for the drain and I couldn't let it, because right now it was the only thing that was making any sense.

"You're not going to make this go away by holding me," I said. "We have to figure it out."

"That's what we're doing. I believe you don't let what Irwin has done make your decisions for you. Otherwise you'd be in Kade's camp."

"Then—"

"The problem is what you *can't* let go of."

"And what would that be? That Troy made it impossible for me to keep our baby and raise him?" I could feel the tears coming into my throat. "I could have. I made the choice not to."

"And you chose not to trust another man for twenty-five years. You chose not to have another relationship—"

"Until now. Until you."

"And what am I to you?"

"Mr. Chief!"

Desmond's voice was shrill on the air, even from the fifty yards left between him and us as he ran toward Chief.

Chief took a step closer to me and held me in place by one shoulder as he talked into my ear. "I love you. But I can't be—"

The rest was lost in the cry, "Hey, Mr. *Chief*!"

A pair of lanky arms came around Chief's waist from behind. I could see Desmond's hands squeezing until the color disappeared from his fingers.

"I'll catch you two later," I said. "I'm going to go see what Kade needs."

I took off running toward the house, but I could still hear the unfinished sentence.

I can't be—

You can't be what? Everything I ever needed? Everything I've missed? The person I have trusted my life with? And Desmond's? After all we've gone through together, you can't be that?

I might have gone on running and asking questions I couldn't answer if Kade hadn't met me between the beach and the steps where Mercedes was leading the Sisters up to the house. I made sure my sunglasses were in place and I put on a smile.

"So what happened with Desmond and Flannery?" I said.

Kade shrugged. "She laughed at him because he wouldn't go in the water. He pretended he didn't care. It's cool."

"How do you know it's cool?"

"Been there."

"Oh?"

"Her name was Ashley," he said, eyes bright. "She made fun of me because I couldn't dance."

"And what did *your* mom say to you when you pretended you didn't care?"

"She didn't say anything. She just put on a CD the next day and started teaching me to waltz."

"*Waltz?* Who waltzes in high school?"

"Who said I was in high school? That was my sophomore year of college." Kade wiggled his sandy eyebrows. "A number of young ladies have fallen under the spell of my waltz."

I didn't doubt it for a minute. I laughed, because I, too, could pretend. Pretend I didn't care that another, probably wiser woman had made Kade Capelli the man he was. This day was falling apart in large chunks.

Mercedes took complete charge of the rest of the unpacking process and had Jasmine organizing Kade's closet and Gigi pairing socks and lining them up in the drawers of the dilapidated dresser he'd obviously hauled out of someone's trash. I heard Chief ask Kade what he was doing with the money he was paying him.

Hank had the kitchen done so she marshaled Desmond and Kade into hosing off deck furniture. Rochelle cleaned the bathrooms without being asked to. I felt a little sorry for the toilets as she all but scrubbed off the porcelain. She was obviously learning *something* from Mercedes.

I started in on the sliding glass doors with a container of Windex and a roll of paper towels, but Hank took both from me, handed them to a less-than-enthusiastic Flannery, and nodded me back toward the beach.

"I've been stuck in here all day," she said. "I need a walk."

I let her coax me all the way to the bottom of the path before I said, "I've never known you to take a walk in your life."

"This is far enough. Let's sit."

She pointed to two low beach chairs tucked just beyond the dunes.

"All we need is Patrice with a couple of lattes," I said as I lowered myself into one of them.

"Is that all you need, Al?" Hank said.

"Please don't make me start crying again."

"I don't think there's much I can do to stop you."

I swallowed until I could talk. "I guess you know."

"That he didn't propose? That was pretty obvious last night."

"Do you know why?"

"No. I take it you do."

"Not really." I told her what I did know, while she sat there with her folded hands and her endless patience. I ended with, "I told God I'll go as many extra miles as I have to."

"With your enemy."

"Huh?"

"I looked up the scripture that comes from. Jesus is referring to your enemy when he says 'If anyone forces you to go one mile—'"

"Chief's not forcing me. It feels like *God* is forcing me, not my enemy."

"Who makes you do *that*?"

"What?"

She pointed to my hands. I could almost see my knucklebones through the skin where I was gripping the arms of the chair.

"Who makes you do that, Al?" she said.

"I only know one person. I think I'm going to throw up."

"Why?"

"Because I don't want to go another mile with Troy Irwin."

I waited for the knowing nod or at least the refolding of the hands, but Hank's gaze drifted over my shoulder. I twisted to see Kade standing there.

"I'm firing up the grill," he said. "A little salmon. Some kabobs. See you in thirty?"

"He heard, didn't he?" I said when he was gone.

"Does it matter?" Hank said.

I watched him disappear onto the deck. "Show me something that doesn't," I said.

CHAPTER EIGHT

Going an extra two *feet* with Troy Irwin wasn't even an option in the next few days. As for finding out the ending to Chief's sentence, there wasn't space for that either.

Monday morning I had to deliver Desmond for his first day of in-school suspension. He was cavalier about it in front of Flannery, but if she was grateful that he was taking a hit for her, she didn't show it.

When we got to the school I had to walk him to the office and sign a document saying I understood that he would be separated from his schedule for three days and would be expected to do his work in a room across from Vice Principal Foo-Foo's office. There were two other boys in there, both of whom looked like they ought to be on a chain gang, and a girl in a hooded sweatshirt with several holes in her nose where rings had obviously been removed for the occasion. Desmond plopped right down beside her, handsome smile fully operational. For once I was relieved. If this girl could take his mind off Flannery, I'd be happy to take *her* in as a foster child.

But Flannery was the one I was Nudged to, and I basically had to drag her everywhere that day. *Drag* is no exaggeration. She didn't want anyone outside our circle seeing her purple face, and that was coupled with her absolute terror of riding on the Harley. I got her out the door by telling her she could wear the pink canvas hat India had given her anytime she didn't have the helmet on—and the sunglasses went without saying. I probably could have used the van, but I hoped a little dependency on me for her safety might open her up.

Our first stop was Ms. Willa's. Fortunately the ride was short, because Flannery very nearly cut off my circulation on the way. When we pulled into Toques Place and I peeled her arms away, she left two handprints of sweat on my denim vest.

"Go ahead and get off," I said to her.

"Gladly." She stood on the pegs to swing her leg around.

"It's pretty obvious you've been on bikes before," I said, "so why are you so scared? Is my driving that bad?"

Flannery pulled off the helmet, releasing the torrent of curls that was now somewhat flattened. "They're obnoxious."

"Watch it now. Classic doesn't like to be insulted."

"It has a name?"

"*She* has a name."

Flannery squinted what she could of her puffy face. "You are so weird."

"A little weirdness can keep you from freaking out."

"I told you—"

"That you don't freak out. But you do, and the sooner you own that, the sooner it'll stop controlling you."

The china chin came up. "I'm never letting anything control me again."

"Then this is a good place to start."

She gave the Harley a long, dubious look like the child she was. The bike was the bogeyman as far as she was concerned, and as she surveyed it fear licked at my own gut. Whether I took this kid on or not, somebody needed to get to the bottom of what brought her here.

Owen greeted us at Ms. Willa's door and, to his credit, did a fine job of masking his initial horror at Flannery's face. She didn't appear to notice the cover-up; she was too busy taking in Ms. Willa's digs. It was obvious she'd never seen brocade wallpaper and velvet drapes, the swimming and gymnastics lessons notwithstanding.

"Is he the butler?" she whispered to me as we followed Owen into the parlor.

"No. He's her boyfriend."

"No stinkin' way!"

Those were the first words Ms. Willa heard out of Flannery's mouth. I almost chewed a hole in the inside of *my* mouth as the bluish mane came back and Flannery was greeted with a squint that outclassed anything she could form.

"Who is this child with the potty mouth?"

"Potty mouth?" Flannery said. "You want potty mouth, I'll give you potty mouth."

"And I'll give you a dose of lye soap. Maria!"

Ms. Willa was yelping like a Jack Russell, and as much as I was enjoying it, I was also struck by the frayed edge on her voice. As Ms. Willa's maid skittered into the room, I said to Owen between my teeth, "Is she getting sicker?"

"She hasn't had any more spells," he whispered back.

"I cannot abide people talking about me while I'm sitting right here," Ms. Willa said, waving a bewildered Maria back out of the room.

"Really?" Flannery said. "Then why do *you* do it?"

"I beg your pardon?"

"You just did it to me. 'Who is this child with the potty mouth?' and I'm, like, two feet away."

Ms. Willa turned to me. "She's been spending far too much time with you."

"See?" Flannery said. "You're doing it again."

Despite the sickly weariness around Ms. Willa's eyes, they took on a gleam. "What's your name, child?"

"Flannery Donohue."

"Are you Catholic?"

"*What?*" I said.

"The Irish are usually Catholic."

"I used to be," Flannery said. "But I got over it."

"What are you now?"

For a moment Flannery was without a sassy reply, until she floored me with, "I'm a Sacrament Sister."

"Did your last customer give you that shiner?"

I thought Owen was going to choke to death, and I wasn't far behind him. Flannery just shook her head and said, "You need another cushion."

"A what?"

"Another cushion. For your neck. You're all scrunched down. I don't see how you can breathe that way."

"I'm breathing just fine," Ms. Willa said, and then succumbed to the red velvet pillow Flannery took from the settee and positioned behind her neck. Some of the color returned around the old woman's lips.

"Why is it that you know what the rest of these people are clueless about?" Ms. Willa said, waving a blue-veined hand at the rest of us.

Flannery flopped herself onto the gold couch. "I used to hang out at a nursing home a lot when I was a kid. This is a weird sofa."

"What I want to know is why you aren't hanging out at school."

Because the authorities would be on me so fast I'd be calling her for bail money.

Ms. Willa jabbed a finger at me. "What's being done about her education?"

"Hey, don't worry about it," Flannery said. "I'm good."

While Ms. Willa went on to set Flannery straight on all the ways she clearly wasn't good, an idea came into view. Homeschooling would be just the thing to keep this young'un focused while I followed up on what Liz said I should be doing.

"What could you teach her, Ms. Willa?" I said.

"Hello!" Flannery said.

Ms. Willa turned the arthritic finger on her. "I would start with penmanship. You young people aren't taught that anymore."

"You mean like writing in cursive?"

"That is exactly what I mean."

Flannery blew air through her lips. "Who needs that when you can text and email?" She shot me a look. "If I ever get my cell phone back."

"Bring her to me tomorrow afternoon, Allison," Ms. Willa said. "Owen will go out and get the necessary supplies and we'll go to work."

"Consider it done," Owen said. "A *fait accompli*. It's history already."

We were barely out the door after the required tea before Flannery was tugging at my arm.

"I will do anything—anything—if you won't make me come here and take penmanship."

"Okay. Let's start with you telling me about your parents."

Her good eye went into a slit. "Give me a pen."

Desmond was far less gallant about going to ISS the next day, Tuesday.

"The Mosquito was in there three periods yesterday," he told me as we were getting the bike ready.

"You're exaggerating."

"Unh-uh. That's parta her *job.*" He shrugged on his leather jacket. "I ain't done nothin' to make her hate me like she does."

"I don't know that she actually hates you—"

"Yes, she does, Big Al. And I think she hates you, too."

I tried to sound casual. "What makes you say that?"

"'Cause I heard her telling Vice-Principal Foo-Foo you be takin' in serial killers next. I 'bout told her—"

"Don't tell her anything, Des. You can't kill hate by feeding it more hate."

"What Imma feed it with then?"

I paused, helmet in hand. "Love, I guess."

Desmond's eyebrows practically folded over his cheekbones. "No, *ma'am,* Big Al. I am *not* gon' love the Mosquito. I won't say nothin' to her, but I am not gon' love her."

He looked like he was about to lose his Cheerios. I figured I could count on him to give the woman a wide berth.

The next thing on the agenda was a scheduled meeting with Hank, Kade, and Chief at Sacred Grounds to form a plan for dealing with Flannery until I could get some information from her, which so far I'd been unable to do. She obviously couldn't be at that gathering, and it was too early to take her to Ms. Willa's, so my only option was to park her upstairs at Second Chances with Mercedes and Jasmine and Ophelia. Flannery wasn't thrilled with that idea, but she admitted it was better than learning how to make fancy *T*s and *S*s over at that rich lady's house.

Getting her out of *my* house, onto the Harley, and finally up the steps to the boutique kept my mind occupied. But as I went back down the stairs to the coffee shop, I could hear Chief's bass underscoring the conversation already in progress and I could no longer evade what I'd been mentally dodging for three days.

I'd seen Chief since the beach. We went on a ride with the HOGs Sunday, but I had the Flannery watch while he stuck with Desmond. Monday he came by to see how Desmond fared at ISS, but he didn't stay long. Even if I'd tried to convince myself he wasn't avoiding being alone with me, Flannery was there to inform me I was in denial.

"You keep saying you guys didn't break up," she said when she was helping me load the dishwasher while Chief and Desmond talked on the porch. "But it sure looks like it to me."

"You have a lot of experience with relationships, do you?" I said.

"I've just seen my mom and her—"

She'd caught herself and gone back to scraping a plate into the trash can.

I steeled myself now for the next hour when I would have to sit near enough to see the beloved creases around Chief's eyes and the twitches in his jaw muscles. When I got there, Hank and Kade had done me no favors; they'd saved the seat next to Chief's just for me. At least Patrice was there taking orders so that when Chief reached over to squeeze my hand I had an excuse not to look at him. Instead of, *Please don't touch me until we get this worked out,* I said, "The usual, Patrice." I looked at Hank and added, "Two shots." Hank gave me the nod.

Kade, bless his heart, kept a banter going until Hank had her typical feast in front of her and the rest of us were supplied with coffee and the chocolate biscotti Kade insisted we had to try because they were "stupid good." When Patrice was finally gone, I filled them in on what Liz had told me.

"Have you made any progress getting her to spill her guts?" Kade said.

"Lovely image," Hank said.

"I know she spent a lot of time at a nursing home," I said. "And her mom has had some relationship ... difficulties."

"We could be talking about a stepfather or a live-in boyfriend," Hank said.

"Or a series thereof," Chief said.

"This is going to take longer than I thought," I said. "She just won't talk to me. Believe it or not, I think she's scared."

"That girl?" Hank said.

"I feel it."

"I don't think we can argue with that."

I looked at Chief, whose eyes were as filled with faith-in-Allison as they always were. So what the—

"In the meantime," Hank said, "what's the plan?"

I told them about the homeschooling idea. They all stared at me for a full fifteen seconds before Kade volunteered to tutor Flannery in math when he worked with Desmond, and Hank suggested I get Owen to teach her botany. Chief just kept looking at me.

"Come on, Big Guy," Kade said to him. "You must have somethin'."

Chief shook his head. "I don't think so. She pretty much steers clear of me."

"Really," Hank said.

"No eye contact. Leaves the room when I come in. Something about me makes her uncomfortable."

When I thought about it, he was right, and yet it was hard for me to believe any female would find Chief anything but—

I pulled my arms across my chest. "I'll try to set that up and let y'all know when I need you. Meanwhile, just pray, will you? I don't know how long I can do this without really getting into legal trouble."

"Oh, you're already there," Chief said.

"Good thing you've got an awesome lawyer." Kade tried a grin, unsuccessfully, on me and turned back to Chief. "Listen, I need to go. Boss, I have to drop some paperwork off, and I'll be back in the office in about thirty minutes."

Hank got up too, and suddenly I didn't want to be left alone with Chief. I couldn't help feeling like anything I said to him was only going to make things worse. He would finish that sentence when he was ready, and not before. That I knew.

Or did I? Did I really know any of the things I thought I knew about him?

That thought alone launched me from the chair and inside to pay my part of the tab with Patrice. I barely had my hand in my pocket before Kade's came over it.

"This is on me, sweetheart," he said to her.

"Sweetheart!" she said. "What do you want now?"

He feigned innocence, dropped a wad of cash on the counter, and steered me toward the door that led to the inside stairs.

"What the Sam Hill?" I said when we were on the other side.

"We're just friends."

"I'm not talking about Patrice. I'm talking about you going all cloak and dagger on me."

Kade ignored that. "So, that was awkward, huh?"

"What was?"

"You and Chief. I swear to you, he hasn't said a word about it to me. I just overheard you and Hank talking at the beach, and I hate it, you know? You guys are good together."

I didn't know how to answer.

"What you said about 'going another mile'—"

"You *didn't* miss much of that conversation, did you?"

"I haven't been able to stop thinking about it."

I felt my eyes widen.

"If you're supposed to go another mile with Troy Irwin, couldn't it possibly mean making that extra effort to seek justice?" Kade put his hand up. "Not revenge. I get that you can't go there. But if you got behind seeing that he pays for what he's done, wouldn't that resolve this whole thing with Chief?"

I searched his face. Even in the dim light of the narrow hallway, I could see it was earnest. I looked for manipulation in those eyes so like Troy's, but I didn't see any. It wasn't son-love that looked back at me, yet something in there cared. The pull to nod with him was strong.

The Nudge, however, was stronger. It backed me a step away so I could look at Kade dead-on and shake my head.

"I'm not going to say it isn't tempting," I said. "In fact, don't even tell me what you have in mind."

"It's not anything illegal." His tone was offended. "I won't stoop to his methods."

"I know that."

Kade let his hands drop to his sides. "Right when I think I get who you are, I find out I'm completely clueless. This just doesn't make any sense to me."

"Then here it is: God won't let me do it. I feel it and I know it and even though I don't understand it any more than you do, I have to go with it."

"Even if it means giving up a chance to get past this whole thing with Chief."

"Taking Troy down isn't going to solve what's going on with Chief and me. That much I know."

And I did know it. It was the first thing about it that made any sense to *me*.

"I'm sorry I can't help you, Kade," I said.

He nodded and disappeared back into the coffee shop. I stayed until the pain stopped pounding before I made my way up to Second Chances.

Even at that it took me a moment after I was inside the boutique to register that Flannery was talking to a customer.

"I wouldn't go with a scarf," she was saying to a gangly girl not much older than she was. "Ophelia can fix you up with a kick-butt necklace, though."

While I continued to gape from the doorway, Ophelia appeared with a selection of neckwear I only partially recognized. I needed another few seconds to realize they'd been put together from several pieces of jewelry that had been sitting there unsold since the day we opened. As for the ensemble the teenager had on, it was one of the skirts and tops Flannery and India had assembled Friday night. I watched as Flannery pulled a belt around the girl's barely existent hips. Even I could tell that Desmond's unmistakable caricatured lips painted at a diagonal across the top made the outfit.

"Can I get it, Mom?" the girl said, revealing an entire mouth full of braces.

A very round woman ducked from behind a rack of elastic-waisted pants and nodded. "I wish you had stuff like that in my size."

"We will," Flannery assured her. "We've only just started our new line."

Ophelia put her hand on the woman's arm. "You tell us what you're looking for and we can maybe work something up for you."

The woman's eyes grew in her plump face. "Really? You do custom clothing?"

Ophelia looked shyly at me.

"Um—we're certainly experimenting with it," I said.

The woman gave a juicy laugh. "I have no problem being a guinea pig."

Ophelia swept her over to the skirts, and Flannery pointed the girl toward the tiny dressing room.

"I'll bring you more stuff," Flannery said to her.

"Can I see that green dress you have hanging out front? Or is that, like, just for display?"

"Oh, you can totally try that on."

Flannery headed for the French doors that led to the narrow balcony, and I followed her. Between the time I'd dropped her off and now, an array of clothes that would have pulled even me into the shop had been arranged on the railings and hung from the awning.

"Wow," I said, "who did this?"

"Me and Ophelia. We need to make more like these because we're going to sell out, like, today."

I couldn't disagree. At that very moment a trio of women was looking up from the street below with that we're-so-goin'-in expression on their faces.

"This'll be cute on her," Flannery said as she pulled a slippery green dress from the railing. "It was, like, mid-calf length and I cut it off. Her mom's gonna say it's too short, but whatever."

"Moms have to do that," I said.

"My mom totally did until …"

Flannery stopped, as if something inside her had startled her.

"Don't start," she said. "I'm working."

She brushed past me into the shop, already telling Ophelia they had three more customers on their way up.

It dawned on me that I hadn't seen Mercedes and Jasmine.

I found them both at the cash register, arms folded against the activity going on beyond them. Jasmine was close to chin-quivering. Mercedes just looked like she wanted to take one of the newly bejeweled flip-flops off the rack and smack somebody with it. Probably Flannery.

"Problem, ladies?" I said.

"Oh no," Ophelia said behind me. "You know what I think is so sweet?"

"I got no idea," Mercedes said.

"Nobody Flannery has waited on has said anything about her bruises."

"Oh, yes, they did." Mercedes's usually deep voice went falsetto. "When that woman that bought that belt with the eyes painted on it? She wanted to know what happened and that child told her she got hurt *bowlin'.*" Her scowl deepened. "You can't believe nothin' comes out of her mouth."

By then Ophelia had gone on to greet the three women. I could hear Flannery's teenager pleading, "Please, Mom. I feel so good in it."

"She has to feel good about herself," Flannery said.

"She's bringing in customers," I said to Mercedes.

"Mm-mmm."

"But we should discuss it, yes?"

"Mmmm-hmmm."

I started to nod her toward the door with a couple of lattes in mind, but my cell phone rang. It was Nicholas Kent.

"I have to take this," I said.

Mercedes nodded and I stepped into the hallway. "Nick. Everything okay?"

"We need to talk," he said. "Can you meet me at Georgie's Diner?"

"Georgie's ... oh, over by the college."

"Yeah. It's on Malaga."

"When?"

"Does now work for you?"

Anxiety went up my backbone. "I'll make it work," I said.

I went back into the shop where Teenager and Mama were checking out with Jasmine. Everything, including the slippery green minidress, was going into the bag.

"I have to go meet somebody," I whispered to Mercedes. "But we'll definitely talk about this later."

"That's fine, Miss Angel," she whispered back. "Just take that child with you."

I agreed, but my mind raced. Nick obviously wanted to talk to me *about* the Flannery situation, so I couldn't exactly have her sitting at the table with us at the diner. But considering the mood Mercedes was in I couldn't leave her here either, and there wasn't time to drop her at Ms. Willa's. It was worse than having a toddler.

I didn't decide what to do until after I'd pried Flannery out of there and was prodding her toward the Harley.

"I don't see why I can't just stay there," she said as I handed her the helmet. "They totally need me."

"I need you too."

"To do what?"

"To sit at a table at Georgie's and have a milkshake while I talk to Officer Kent."

"I told you I hate cops."

She actually looked more suddenly scared than hateful, but I let it pass. "You'll be at a different table," I said.

"Why *can't* I just stay here?"

"Because evidently you ticked somebody off and until I get it sorted out, you're hanging with me."

"I bet it was Mercedes. She doesn't like me."

Neither did I about 90 percent of the time, but I just motioned for her to get on the bike and we took off for Malaga Street.

The diner wasn't a place I frequented. The owners had, in fact, reconfigured the parking lot since the last time I'd been there, before I got the Harley, so it took me a few minutes to find my way into the place. That did not set well with Flannery, who clung to me like a koala cub suffering from separation anxiety until we stopped, and then hurled herself across the lot and in the door before I could set the kickstand. She didn't even take her helmet off until I joined her inside. By then I was such a stew of annoyance and anxiety and just plain somebody-take-this-kid-off-my-hands that I would have missed Kade if he hadn't walked right up to us.

"What are you doing here?" I said. "I'm sorry—I didn't mean to sound—it's none of my business …"

"I had a meeting here," he said. "Just to hand off some paperwork. What's up with you two girls?"

I looked around for Nick and found him craning his neck over a back booth.

"She's meeting that cop," Flannery said. "I'm supposed to sit there with a milkshake and die of boredom."

"Do I bore you?" Kade said.

Flannery's good eye sprang open. "No. You're, like, the coolest person around here."

"So hang with me while Miss Angel does her thing."

I asked every question but "What is the meaning of life?" with my face, but Kade still shooed me toward the back booth.

"Who needs ya, Miss Angel?" he said. "Go. Do."

I mouthed a thank-you.

"So what's this place supposed to be, like the fifties or some-thing?" I heard Flannery say as I hurried to Nick.

That was the idea of the decor, though I didn't pick up many details on my way. I did hear jukebox music, the kind that sounds like having the right steady will render life perfect. As if.

I slid into the booth across from Nick, who pointed to the thick coffee mug he was holding. I shook my head. Between the two-shot latte and my own anxiety, I was already jittery enough to launch right in.

"Okay, look, before you say anything, I want you to know that we're working toward making this whole thing legal with Flannery. I don't even want to know how much trouble I'm going to be in if anybody but you and Liz finds out, so don't tell me. Hopefully we'll get through this before then ..."

Nick was shaking his head. For the first time I noticed that his face was so red I could hardly see the freckles.

"You didn't ask me here to talk about Flannery," I said.

"No. But just so you know, I'm so over the way things are being done in that police department you don't have to worry about *me* turning you in for breaking the rules. I'm sick of their 'rules.'"

The fingers that formed quotations marks were shaking.

"Yikes, Nick," I said. "What's going on?"

He gripped the sides of the mug and leaned into the table.

"I found out this morning that Detective Kylie has probably been sitting on information about … you know."

"Sultan?" I whispered.

"Yeah. He hasn't talked to you, has he?"

I shook my head. My anxiety ratcheted up ten notches.

"Okay—I picked up a guy for drunk driving last night and took him into the station. You remember Marcus Rydell."

My mouth was already turning to sawdust as I nodded. I wouldn't soon forget the heinous hulk who had tried to kidnap Desmond for Sultan.

"He's out of jail?" I said.

"He never actually went to jail. When he was arrested for attacking you and Desmond he got bailed out. Then he jumped bail, and—now don't blow a gasket—Detective Kylie let him go."

"When was that?"

"Three and a half months ago. About two weeks after—"

"*Kylie* let him go? Are you sure?"

"It's right there in his record. To me it looked like Kylie was probably using him as an informant, so when Rydell got sober this morning I … let's just say I got it out of him that they did have a deal."

"What was it?"

"Don't know. I had to go to roll call, and by the time I could get back, he was out again."

"I don't believe this!"

"That kind of thing goes on all the time. It's how we get information about the big bad guys. We use the little bad guys."

"There is nothing little about Marcus Rydell. So this is little as in not as important."

"Little as in not gonna get Kylie a promotion to lieutenant. I'd bet my badge he's using him to get information on Sultan. Putting him away will get Kylie a lot of attention higher up."

I had never seen a sneer on Nicholas Kent's boy-mouth before, and it put five disillusioned years on his face. I was sure the one I was wearing added about twenty to mine.

"So all this time Marcus Rydell has been free and Kylie didn't bother to tell me so I could make sure Desmond was protected."

"Desmond *and* you." Nick slid the cup away from him with the back of his hand. "Look, I'll make sure Palm Row is heavily patrolled, and whatever else I can do."

"Thanks, Nick. I really appreciate this." I stared at his cup and looked back up at him. "Kylie promised me he'd keep me informed. *I* was the one who told him Sultan was still alive. Not only does he owe me, but you would just think that he would want to, I don't know, protect and serve."

"That's what he thinks he's doing." Nick looked at his watch.

"Go on if you need to," I said. "I just have to sit here for a minute."

He stood up and fished in his pocket. "I'm sorry we're not taking better care of you, Miss Allison." He dropped a dollar and change on the table.

"*You* are," I said.

But as I watched him make his way to the front of the diner, I wasn't sure of that at all. Nicholas Kent couldn't be everywhere, and evidently Marcus Rydell could. Even without closing my eyes I could see his massive black form in the alley behind Ms. Willa's and feel his hard shoe smashing into my side. And hear Desmond scream *Mama!* as he was flung from those monstrous hands.

There was no way I was ever going to hear that again.

I bolted from the booth and headed for the door. I don't know if I would have remembered Flannery if the Nudge hadn't hauled me back to some semblance of sanity. When I turned, Kade and Flannery were already on their way to me. Even in my current state I noticed that she was sneerless. And that she had fluffed up her helmet hair.

I forced myself to say, "How was the milkshake?"

"Not bad," she said. "Kade says they're not as good as the ones in Boston though."

I expected Kade to corroborate with some witty remark, but he was giving me a look so full of something unspoken I could almost hear it.

"So, listen, Allison," he said. "Call me later when you have a minute to talk in private ... about your financials."

What? Had he suddenly discovered an IRS problem over chocolate milkshakes?

He shifted his eyes to the top of Flannery's head and then back to me. She, meanwhile, was tucking her hair behind her ears and, quite frankly, looking coy.

Oh, for Pete's sake. Had she made a move on him, right there at the counter at Georgie's?

"Okay," I said. "I'll get back to you ASAP."

"Do," he said.

He glanced at his cell phone, muttered something about Chief expecting him, and took off. Flannery tracked his progress all the way out to the parking lot.

For the next two hours, all she could talk about was Kade. All I could think about was getting to Detective Kylie.

CHAPTER NINE

I couldn't go to Kylie right away. After I took a furious Flannery to Ms. Willa's for penmanship instruction, I had to pick up Desmond from school. He jettisoned himself out the front door almost before I pulled the Harley up to the curb. Four of his pubescent female friends cut a path for him, and he didn't give them a glance.

"I take it things didn't go well," I said as he jammed his helmet onto his head.

"You wanna know what I think about that Mosquito woman?" he said.

"We probably ought to wait until we're off the school grounds—"

"She need a man."

I nearly swallowed my tongue. "She what?"

"You tol' me I got to kill hate by showin' love, only I ain't got it in me, Big Al. Not with her."

"I didn't say you had to kiss her feet."

"That's good, 'cause that ain't happenin'. But somebody got to, 'cause she needs a lotta love if she gon' stop bein' hateful, now. And I know that thing."

I turned to adjust the mirror that didn't need adjusting so he wouldn't see my grin. "Do me a favor, Des. Don't try to find her a boyfriend."

"I was thinkin' Stan the Man."

"Absolutely not." Although the thought of the biggest player among the HOGs pursuing the Mosquito was the most amusing image I'd conjured up in a while.

I loved that kid so much.

It swelled in me so hard I had to force myself not to drive straight to the police station and crawl right across Detective Kylie's desk. As it was, I peered into every black car all the way back to Palm Row, looking for Marcus Rydell's dark face in the front, and a twisted man with an eye patch in the back. At the very least I didn't want to leave Desmond home alone while I went to pick up Flannery at Ms. Willa's, so I asked Owen to do it. That set me back approximately five light years in getting anything out of the girl.

"It wasn't bad enough I had to do freakin' calligraphy for ten hours?" she said when she stomped into the kitchen. "Then you had to make me ride with Mister I-have-to-give-you-sixteen-examples-for-everything?"

Owen may have been the master of metaphor, but Flannery was without peer as the queen of hyperbole.

She shut herself up in her room after supper, which gave me a chance to contact Kade. Since the September nights were finally cooling down to the low eighties, I sprayed myself with Off! and made the call from the side porch. The less Desmond was privy to info about Flannery the better.

"Thanks for getting back to me," Kade said.

"So what happened? Please don't tell me Flannery propositioned you. No, go ahead and tell me. Although what I'm supposed to do about it I have no idea—"

"She didn't proposition me. Geez, Allison, I didn't need that visual."

"Sorry," I said. "Occupational hazard. So …"

"We were talking. Well, *she* was talking, and she let it slip that she's from Hastings. I know she didn't even realize she said it."

"Hastings, Florida?"

"I asked her if she was enjoying St. Augustine and she said it was no big deal, that she used to come here for field trips when she was a kid. Then she went on about how this was a weird town but at least it was better than Hastings."

"That's just, like, fifteen miles south of here. Maybe less."

"I know. I looked it up. You want me to check—"

"No, I'll call Nick Kent. I don't want you mixed up in this any more than you already are. Could you get disbarred or defrocked or whatever it is they do to lawyers?"

"I'm good."

"You are. Seriously. I have to piece things together from things she almost says and then doesn't, and she won't even look at Chief. But you sit down with her for five minutes and we practically have coordinates."

"You're forgetting Desmond."

"I don't follow."

"He got her to tell him her name. She confided in him about the Hot Spot."

I moved further away from the door and lowered my voice. "I'm not using Desmond to get things out of Flannery. She uses him enough on her own. When she needs something, he's 'Desi,' her new best friend, and he gets all dewy eyed. The rest of the time she treats him like he's an annoying little creep, and I'm watching his heart break."

"Back away from the teenage romance," Kade said. "Mama can't fix this by teaching him to swim. You can't fix it at all. Besides, guys can handle getting their hearts broken a coupla times."

"Oh," I said.

"If Flannery lets anything else slip, I'll let you know. I'm not going to be too obvious, though." He laughed. "I don't really have to be. As much as she talks, sooner or later something's bound to squirt out."

When Kade and I hung up, I left a message with Nick Kent about Flannery. Then I checked Desmond's room. He was sprawled across the bed, fast asleep with his head on his sketchpad, a pencil still dangling from his fingers. He was going to be ticked off when he woke up the next morning to find out he'd drooled on his drawing. All I could see of it was a tangle of curls covering the top half of the page, and I hoped Kade was right about guys handling heartbreaks.

After I covered him up, I took the phone upstairs and curled up on my window seat to call Chief. When it came to things Desmond, I knew there would be no incomplete sentences.

As expected, he was thoroughly the Chief I knew as I filled him in on what Nick Kent had told me. There were engaged "uh-huh"s and calming, "Go on"s. By the time I finished telling him, I felt like Marcus Rydell was all but back in the slammer.

"I guess it's pointless for me to tell you not to go see Kylie," Chief said.

"I have to confront him about this."

"Is it also pointless for me to warn you not to inflict bodily harm?"

"I'll restrain myself." I sagged against the window. "I don't know how much good it's going to do. He'll do exactly what he wants to do."

"So why go?"

"Because–"

"You want me there?"

Okay, what was with the tears? I pressed my wrist against my mouth.

"I'll take that as a no."

"It's not that," I said. "If I go in there with legal counsel, won't he get all defensive?"

"Kylie's going to get defensive anyway, but you're right. I think the real question is how we're going to protect Desmond."

I took a second to savor the "we" before I said, "I'm not leaving him alone when I'm not here."

"I can help with that. How 'bout I take him this weekend? There's a ride Sunday, and he and I will figure out something to do Saturday."

How 'bout you take me, too?

I pressed my lips together to keep from saying it out loud.

"Desmond's not the only one who needs protection," Chief said. "Sultan is after Desmond to get to you." I could almost see him tilting his head. "We don't even know if Rydell is still working for Sultan, but—"

"Kylie wouldn't care about him if that wasn't the case."

"Which is why we need to assume that both you and Desmond are in danger."

"Nick's on it."

"I'll see what else I can do. Just watch your back, Classic. We don't want to lose you."

That "we" I didn't like. It made me sit straight up on the window seat, insides twisting.

"Chief, where are we? You and I—where are we?"

In the silence I could hear him shifting gears. "I love you."

"I got that part. But the other day at the beach you started to say that you can't be my 'something.' My what? My partner?"

"No—"

"The love of my life?"

"No—"

"Then what? Tell me what it is that you can't be, and I'll tell you if I need for you to be it."

"I can't be your Band-Aid," Chief said.

I shook my head. "My '*Band*-Aid?' You're gonna have to explain that one to me, pal."

"I can't be the one who covers up the wound so you think it's fixed."

"If you're talking about Troy Irwin, he is not a 'wound.' He's a 'scar.' We all have scars. Except maybe you, which is probably why you don't get this. At all."

"Let me guess what you're doing right now, Classic. You're pacing around the room, messing up your hair, picking up things and throwing them back down. Am I right?"

I stopped in the middle of the floor I hadn't realized I'd crossed and pulled my hand away from my scalp. A pillow from the window seat lay at my feet.

"Lucky guess," I said.

"That's what you do when the truth makes you mad."

I marched back to the window seat, holding the phone with *both* hands, but I couldn't deny the surging anger. Maybe that was what kept me from being too afraid to ask, "Where does that leave us?"

"Right where we are. I'm there for you. I'm there for Desmond. But until I know I'm not just a cover-up for unresolved feelings, I'm not going any further."

"How are you going to know that?" I said.

"When you know it," he said.

I didn't ask him how. I didn't have to. The words were already Nudging in my head.

I told you: You're going to have to go another mile.

"Are the doors locked?" Chief said.

Another gear change. For me, the temptation to shift into sarcasm was strong. *No, the doors aren't locked. I thought I'd just air out the house tonight and let Marcus Rydell breeze on in here and take us all.*

Only through sheer willpower did I say, "Yes. They're all dead-bolted."

"You want me to look into a security system?"

"No."

Long pause. Then, "Get some sleep, Classic."

Sleep? Was he serious? When we hung up, I curled up in the window seat, clutching a pillow and knowing I would never sleep again until Troy Irwin was completely out of my life.

I woke up several hours later, startled by a dream of the Road King purring into Palm Row. Still, I peeked through the slats in the plantation shutters. Chief's bike was parked in front of my garage. Once again with the tears as I crept downstairs and parted the curtains in the kitchen window. He sat with his back to me on the side porch, feet propped up on the railing. Waiting for something.

I spent the rest of the night in the red chair.

The next morning I walked Desmond into school, partly because I was convinced Rydell was hiding in the campus bushes and would grab my kid the minute he got off the bike, and partly because Desmond was so agitated about the slobber on his drawing and the Mosquito who waited for him on his last day of ISS, I was afraid he'd split before he got to the door.

Skeeter Iseley was right there waiting for him. She looked at me like she wanted to inject me with West Nile fever and pointed Desmond through the office door.

He was probably right. She did hate me. I prayed *GodloveherGod loveherGodloveher* all the way back out to the Harley and came to the conclusion that Desmond was wrong about her needing a man. I wasn't sure any guy could survive.

I picked up Flannery and took her with me to communion at Sacrament Two. It was Mercedes, Zelda, Ophelia, and Gigi's turn to host it, and Mercedes was at the front door taking the to-die-for homemade bread from Hank when we arrived.

Bonner was just pulling up behind us in the Jaguar that had been Sylvia's. He'd bought it from me so I could pay for the Harley, and he coddled the thing like it was a newborn infant.

"What does that guy do for a living?" Flannery murmured to me as we crossed the tidily mowed lawn to the front door. "Those things cost over a hundred thousand dollars."

"How do you know that?" I said.

"I was supposed to be paying for one," she said.

She looked quickly at me, aware, I was sure, that something had "squirted out." The self-loathing in her eyes stopped me from pursuing it.

All I said was, "They ought to declare open season on these men."

"What men?" she said.

"The men in our lives who've made us hate ourselves," I said.

"Who made you hate yourself?" Flannery said.

I let Bonner pass us into the house and looked at her squarely.

"Here's how this is going to work," I said. "For every question about my past that I answer for you, you'll answer one for me about yours."

"I don't really want to know," she said, and banged through the screen door.

Nice try.

When I followed her in, Bonner was helping Zelda set up the communion elements on the coffee table.

Mercedes emerged from the kitchen and exchanged glances with Jasmine, who took my hand and pulled me until the three of us were crammed in between the refrigerator and the butcher block island.

"I know you want to talk about Flannery," I said, "but we're about to start—"

"Just this one thing, Miss Angel," Mercedes said.

She pulled the pocket door closed and even at that brought her voice down to a gritty whisper. "Ophelia and Miss India are all *about* that child workin' at Second Chances, designin' outfits and helpin' with customers."

"India and I haven't discussed that," I said. "But Flannery isn't working age. We can't pay her."

"We don't care about that, now," Jasmine said. "It's just that it don't seem fair that she won't do the work on herself, but she gets to come in there and do the fancy job while Gigi and Rochelle, they startin' to really try and they stuck plantin' colly-flower with Mr. Owen."

I looked at Mercedes, expecting the folded arms and the flashing eyes. But she was watching Jasmine and nodding.

"You agree, Merc," I said.

"Yes, ma'am, only I think this got to be handled right so the child don't—doesn't—clam herself up any more than she already doin'."

She was so beautiful at that moment I just wanted to stare at her and take her in. She pulled her velvety brows together. "Somethin' wrong, Miss Angel?"

"No. But we need to get the whole group together and work this out. Flannery, too."

"Mm-mm."

"It's what we do," I said.

They both looked as if they would rather plant "colly-flower," but they followed me. The rest of the group was gathered in the tiny living room, and Hank raised her hands, ready to say "The Lord be with you."

"Wait," I said. "We need to talk first."

Bonner groaned. "I hate it when a woman says that."

Hank punched him on the shoulder.

"Go ahead, Mercedes," I said.

The Flannery issue rolled out like a skein of silk. The only person not nodding when she was through was Flannery herself.

"I didn't *ask* for the job," Flannery said. "I can't help it if I'm better at it than they are."

Mercedes drew herself up so far I was surprised her head didn't hit the ceiling fan. "Girl, that is ego talkin' now."

"Whose ego?" Hank said.

We all looked at her.

"This child's," Mercedes said.

Flannery drew herself up too, although on her it bordered on comical. "If Ms. Willa were here, she would say it's rude to talk about people like they're not here. And just so you know, I might only be fourteen, but I am not a child. I've seen as much as any of you—"

"I don't believe that, now," Zelda said. "Have you ever—"

I put up my hand. "This is not a contest to see who's suffered the most or done the worst. I think Hank was about to get us on track."

Arms folded and eyes narrowed, but the respect for Hank was palpable. I didn't look at Bonner. I knew he was probably edging toward the door.

"We're all responsible for our own egos," Hank said. "If we see a Sister acting out we call her on it, but then it's up to her and God to work it out."

"God and I aren't speaking," Flannery said.

Sherry sniffed. Jasmine said, "See?"

Hank just turned to Flannery. "Look at me, hon."

Flannery did. That happened when Hank D'Angelo used that tone.

"Your ego isn't the deepest truth of your being. What Allison has taught us each to do is find our deep self—our God-made self, so it can confront our shallow self—that ego we're talking about. As soon as you start doing that, you're talking to God." Hank swept her gaze over the Sacrament Sisters. "It's not the job of *your* selves to confront Flannery's self. It's your job to make this a safe place for her to do that."

Ophelia was the only one who nodded this time. Nobody else was ready to buy it. Until Gigi raised her hand.

"Yeah, Geege," I said.

She bugged her eyes at Hank. "So what you sayin' is, we got to stay at the table with people we don't like 'cause they been invited to supper too."

Hank's lips twitched into a rare full-blown smile. "That is exactly what I'm saying, only you said it better."

Gigi jerked a nod. Mercedes said "Mmm-hmm." Jasmine, naturally, cried softly. Even Rochelle grunted.

"Well then," Sherry said, "I guess we better do this thing."

"The Lord be with you," Hank said.

They all responded.

All except Flannery. But she did take communion. I tried not to think it was out of sheer you-*have*-to-include-me-whether-you-want -to-or-not. It wasn't up to me to decide what Jesus was going to do with his body.

Flannery wasn't so sure she wanted to be included, however, when I told her I was leaving her at Sacrament House to study with Owen.

"I'd rather go back to Ms. Willa's," she said. "That old geezer makes me crazy."

"That old geezer bought this house," I said. "He deserves respect."

Rochelle handed her a pair of gardening gloves that had seen their share of rake handles and trowels. When Flannery curled her now healing lip at them, Rochelle shoved the things into her hands and grunted her out to the back porch where Owen waited, dentures gleaming in the sun. I decided not to worry about him, not with

Rochelle there. Kind of made me wonder how she'd ever been forced into prostitution.

"All right, ladies," Owen said. "Let's get to those weeds before they choke out the roots of our seedlings." He looked up at me. "Where is Gigi?"

"I'll get her," I said.

But Gigi was in the dining room, eyes protruding from their sockets, deep in discussion with Hank, who looked at me and shook her head.

I loved that she and I could have whole conversations without saying a word.

That wasn't going to be the case with Detective Kylie. I used plenty of words getting past the female officer at the front desk of the police station who had an outdated perm and always seemed to like me for some reason. I think we shared a mutual dislike for Kylie.

He wasn't all that crazy about me either, as was evidenced by the *you again?* look on his face when I burst into his cubicle.

"You couldn't call first?" he said, tossing his reading glasses onto the desk. The bags under his eyes looked fuller than they had the last time I saw him.

"You couldn't tell me you let Marcus Rydell go?" I said.

He looked only momentarily startled before he got up from his chair and came around the desk.

"You might as well have a seat," he said, pointing to a plastic chair.

"I'll stand."

He stood too. No way he was going to look up at me. Speaking of egos.

"So you don't deny it," I said.

"No, I don't, although just for the record, Miss Chamberlain, I am under no obligation to tell you anything."

"Maybe not technically, but ethically, yes, you are. If you'll recall, you thought Jude Lowery was dead until I told you otherwise."

"I would have gotten it out of Rydell eventually."

"What else have you gotten out of him?" I put my hand up as his face headed toward that patronizing expression that made me want to spit. "We both know you don't give a flip about him except for what he can tell you about Sultan. Matter of fact, you don't seem to give a flip about anything *else*—including my son's safety."

Kylie glowered at me. "Let's start with you telling me how you know I've been talking to Rydell."

I'd spent a good deal of my time in the red chair the night before preparing to get through this minefield. I was ready for this.

"I make it my business to keep up with who's being arrested for what," I said. "Rydell got picked up on a DUI, but somehow he's no longer a guest in the jail. That's a matter of public record."

"Somehow I don't see you looking that up."

"All you see is how good it's going to look for you when you take down the pimp of all pimps. And all I can see is the danger this puts my boy in. If you aren't going to protect him, then the least you can do is give me enough information to do it myself."

"You've been hanging out with those lawyers too much," he said.

Actually I was being Nudged so hard I was surprised I wasn't holding the detective by the collar.

"All right," Kylie said. "I'll tell you what little I know, although it's not much." He pointed again to the chair. "But sit down, will you? I feel like I'm the one who needs police protection."

Good. Now we were getting somewhere.

I obliged him and sat with both feet on the floor, body tilted toward him. That posture I *had* learned from hanging out with lawyers.

Kylie obviously wasn't up on body language cues. He leaned against his desk and shielded himself with his folded arms. "First of all, Marcus Rydell is one of the dumbest sons of ... he's an idiot, which actually works because he says more than he thinks he's saying."

"Hooray for stupidity," I said drily. "So what's he saying?"

"All of Sultan's 'salons' have closed down, which left me without much of a trail. I needed Rydell to sniff out where he's landed."

"Is he still working for Sultan?"

"No."

"How do you know that?"

"Because Jude Lowery *isn't* stupid. Rydell's been picked up one too many times. Sultan's not going to keep counting on him to keep his mouth shut, no matter how much he's paid him."

"How much has he paid him?"

"Enough to keep Rydell in the cars he keeps driving drunk in. I'm sure Sultan's the one who originally bailed Rydell out four months ago, but I can't prove it because he used a go-between. Like I said, he's not stupid."

"Okay. Go on."

He gave me an exasperated look. "I'm trying. One of the reasons I haven't contacted you is that what Sultan appears to be up to is nothing to be concerned about safety-wise."

"I'd like the opportunity to decide that for myself."

"How in the world does Jack Ellington deal with you?"

I just looked at him. Chief had been right to warn me not to inflict bodily harm. I was sorely tempted. When I didn't answer, Kylie continued.

"Sultan's been trying to get some lesser pimps to work for him as part of a network because all his former people have gone off to do their own thing since he was shot and, as you reported, is now disabled and disfigured." Kylie shrugged. "He hasn't been too successful at it because according to Rydell everybody knows he's crazy."

"You did say he's a psychopath."

Kylie nodded. "Without his stable of hookers, his cash flow has suffered, which has also eroded his drug business."

I moved to the edge of the chair. "It seems to me that the more desperate he is, the more dangerous he is."

"That's why I'm using Rydell to keep me in the loop."

I felt my eyes narrow. "How about from now on you keep me in the loop."

He narrowed his eyes at me. "I don't think I have to. I think you already have somebody doing that. Who told you I had a deal with Rydell?"

"Like I said—"

"I'm a cop, Miss Chamberlain. You can't hold a candle to the people who have lied to me over the last twenty years."

"Ah. Then maybe you don't know honesty when you see it. I have another question."

He sighed through his nose. "What is it?"

"If you know the pimps Sultan has tried to hire, why haven't you arrested them?"

"Because most of them are out of our jurisdiction. He was the Man here in St. Augustine."

"Have you reported them to the authorities who could arrest them?"

His brows twisted. "Are you telling me how to do my job now?"

"I'm telling you you're not doing it at all. You think pimps are basically harmless, that prostitution is a victimless crime. You're concerned about what they do with that money. You're thinking about the drugs and the big crime rings. You're not even giving a thought to the women who are being victimized."

"Prostitutes aren't victims. They make their choices—"

"They don't choose to be beaten. They don't decide they'd like to be abused several times a night so they can turn whatever they make over to some jackal who has complete power over them." I was almost off the chair. "They don't walk into that trap with their eyes open. They're lured with the world promised to them, but what they get is a world no human being should have to live in no matter how she got there."

"Then it's a good thing you find them," he said. "Because we don't rehabilitate here. We just enforce the law, and the law says prostitution is a crime."

"And what about pimping? Is that a crime?"

"Why the—why do you think I'm after Jude Lowery?"

I bit my lip. If I said any more, I would be serving Nick Kent up on a platter. I wasn't sure I hadn't already.

"I hope it's because you want him in prison as much as I do," I said. "For the murder of Geneveve Sanborn, for openers, and for all the other lives he's ruined. And I hope you want that to happen before my son's life is one of them."

I stood up, and so did Kylie.

"Make no mistake," he said, voice tight. "We're close to catching Jude Lowery, very close, and as smart as he is I'm sure he knows it. He isn't going to make a mistake that will cost him his freedom just to get to your kid, or even you."

"That's the smart side," I said. "What about the psychopathic side?" I took a step forward. "Keep me informed, detective."

As near as I was to him now, I could see the glitter in his eyes, and I could feel the chill. I was as close to hate as I was the night I looked Jude Lowery in the face. With a shudder I backed away.

"Get him because it's the right thing to do," I said. "Not because you despise him. That's dangerous for all of us."

I didn't wait for the biting retort already forming on his lips. I left, and I rode for thirty minutes—until I felt like it was off me, until I didn't feel the insane passion to destroy that emanated from the detective. I didn't want that in my soul.

When I was sure I could speak without hawking out nails, I went to C.A.R.S. If Sherry did have a stake in this, she needed to know everything I knew.

It was almost ten o'clock by then, so I was surprised to see the lights off in the shop. When I tried the front door it was locked. I peered through the window and suddenly Sherry's face was there looking back at me, though her eyes were so glazed I wasn't sure she saw me at all.

She disappeared, and I was left staring into the darkness again until I made out the shapes of Zelda's hubcaps in a vicious heap on the floor. Maharry crouched near them, shoulders heaving.

I banged on the glass. "Sherry! It's Allison! Let me in!"

All I heard was the sound of water abruptly splashing and Sherry's raspy voice cussing like she hadn't done in months.

"Sherry!" I shouted again.

But it was Maharry who made his way to the door and jerked at the lock, even as Sherry cried, "Don't let her in yet, Daddy!"

Maharry opened the door just wide enough for me to slide through and jammed it shut behind me. At least, he must have. From the moment I stepped in, I was aware only of the mayhem around me. Before Sherry could crunch her way across splintered glass, I groped at the wall until I found the switch. The fluorescent lights stuttered on, revealing in their garish glare a museum of horrors.

I wasn't paralyzed by the tires crashed into the shelves of headlights and windshield wipers and slashed into jagged ribbons of rubber. Or even by the fingers of glass clawing out from the window frame that had once separated Maharry's workshop from the showroom—or the shards of pottery from the potted plant, now lying in soil that reeked of urine. Not even the remains of the window to the office, still sparkling from Zelda's last shining and now lying on the floor in shattered bits—not even that rooted me to the floor. It was the lower half of the walls that froze me there.

All the price lists and faded posters of outdated custom jobs had been stripped from them. Soapy water from the now overturned bucket had been thrown against the naked space, but I could still see parts of the misshapen faces that had been painted there. One mouth was twisted in pain. A pair of eyes were wild, beyond frightened. One cheek was pinched with the same terror that was strangling me.

The painter had done his work in blood.

There was no mistaking it. Its metallic taste seared my tongue, and the odor alone was a brutal assault, even above the smell of urine. Sherry had obviously been trying to scrub it off, but some of it oozed the few feet to the floor and brought with it the slow, ugly realization that I knew those faces.

I turned to Sherry. Her skin was gray, her eyes colorless. She was holding the half-empty bucket in one hand and the scrub brush in the other as she looked right through me and headed back to the wall.

"What are you doing?" I said.

"I'm getting rid of this—"

I snatched the pail from her and smashed her against me with my forearm so that she faced outward. She swore into the mess in a voice raucous with panic.

"Turn loose of me! I got to get rid of this!"

"It's evidence, Sherry. The police will need to see it."

She let go of another barrage of profanity in the midst of which I heard, "No cops!"

I pulled her closer. "There's nothing to be afraid of. You haven't done anything wrong. They can find out who did."

"It was just vandals. You think you know this neighborhood, Miss Angel, but you don't. We just wash away vandals around here and move on."

"This wasn't no vandals."

We both looked up to see Zelda standing behind the counter with her bag still over her shoulder. Sherry wrenched away from me, her expletives now pointed at Zelda.

"I told you on the phone not to come in today!"

"And I tol' *you* that you sounded like somebody done strangled you. I don't just leave my Sister soundin' like that."

"Go home," Sherry said.

It was too late for that. Zelda was already out from behind the counter, moving closer to the walls. I knew the moment she registered what she was seeing. Her knees gave way and she slithered onto the floor. I felt the pain shoot up my own arms as her hands came down hard on the broken glass. But the guttural scream that tore from her throat had nothing to do with the shrapnel she was crawling in toward what was left of the gruesome portraits.

"That's you, Sherry. And Mercedes—and Miss Angel. Oh, *Lord*! That's me! Somebody done drew me in *blood*!"

Zelda caved into the fetid potting soil and buried her forehead in the rubble.

"I'm sorry, Sherry," I said, "but we are *getting* the police. I'll call Nick Kent."

"Please, Miss Angel—"

"This is a threat—"

"They'll say it was just somebody on drugs."

I didn't say this wasn't merely someone having a bad trip. I didn't have to. She couldn't meet my eyes because she knew it too.

"Just don't wash any more of it off," I said. "Okay? Help Zelda."

Sherry shook her head at me, but she set the bucket down and went to Zelda who had covered her face with two bloody hands. I turned to Maharry. He had managed to get to his feet, but he was shocked into stillness where he stood.

"What do you want me to do, Maharry?" I said.

"I'm through," he said.

"No you're not." I touched his hand. His skin was dry and cold. "In the first place, you didn't have anybody else's car in here, so you're not liable. Your insurance will cover this. But they'll need a police report—"

"I don't have insurance, you silly woman!" The old voice split. "In this neighborhood, it would have eaten up all my profits. I was about to get some. Things were looking up and I was going to get some."

He was slipping. Police or no police, I at least had to get him medical attention. And probably Zelda, too.

"Sherry," I said, "bring your dad some water. Get his pills. Zelda? Can you hear me?"

Zelda nodded as Sherry left her rocking on the floor to go to the back.

"How badly are you bleeding?"

"That's blood on the walls," she said.

"I know, but let's talk about *your* blood. Let me see your wrists."

She held up both hands as if they belonged to someone else. The blood wasn't spurting. By some miracle she hadn't severed a vein, and yet I felt a wave of nausea that nearly knocked me down.

"Somebody that knows us did that, Miss Angel," Zelda said.

There was no point in arguing with her.

The eyes in the drawing belonged to Mercedes, though I had never seen them that terrified. Nor did I tear out handfuls of my own hair the way a sick somebody had portrayed the remaining portion of me. As for Zelda, that mouth was hers. She was out of her mind on that wall, too far out to ever come back.

But the strangest of all was unmistakably Sherry. Her thin hair had been painted away from her face in cruel slashes, but what shot through my soul was the patch drawn over her right eye.

These weren't distorted depictions of Zelda and Sherry and Mercedes and me as someone saw us. They were precise portrayals of the way someone wanted us to be.

A net of fear dropped over me.

"Here, Daddy."

Sherry was there, pressing pills into Maharry's shaking hand. I pulled Zelda up and walked her gingerly among the fragments of glass to the counter, as if that could keep this whole ghastly scene from breaking down any further.

Behind the counter the file cabinet lay against Sherry's desk chair like a startled assault victim, its lock still stubbornly intact. It occurred to me that the lock on the front door was also still in place. Had this person broken in the back door, then? He had to be hard-core, because that door had four different dead bolts on it, one for each time a crime had been committed on Maharry's property.

Zelda wiped her seeping hands on the seat of her jeans and opened a drawer in the other desk, just beyond the small, now-broken window between Sherry's area and Maharry's office.

"They didn't take the money," she said.

"There's money in there?" I said. "What was Maharry thinking?"

"A customer paid cash yesterday, and Maharry, he finished up too late to go the bank, so he put it in the desk. Sherry was gon' deposit it this morning." Zelda looked up at me, eyes almost as wild as they were in the painting. "There's a gun in here too, Miss Angel."

"Don't touch it," I said. "Just come back out here."

Zelda pushed the drawer closed and stumbled for me. I caught her against my chest and held on. Her fingers latched on to the back of my vest which was by now saturated in sweat.

"Did you come in the back just now?" I said.

"Yes, ma'am."

"Were the locks broken?"

Zelda shook her head. "The door wasn't locked at all. That's how I got in. You know that ol' man ain't gonna give me no keys."

"Okay. How are your hands? Is there any glass in them?"

She pulled back and looked at her palms as if she'd forgotten she had been crawling through debris. The odor of blood and urine from the potting soil was almost suffocating. Whoever did this couldn't just leave the bodily fluids at blood?

"Okay," I said. "We need to wash those. You want help?"

Zelda shook her head again, but she stayed there, close to me.

"What?" I said.

"I liked workin' here. That old man was in my business all the time, but I was makin' a difference here. Now that's all gone."

"Not necessarily," I said. Lied. "Come on, Zel, let's get you cleaned up so I can see if you need stitches."

I had to steer her into the bathroom, but she did let me run warm water over her hands. Dirt and blood washed down the drain, leaving several angry contusions in view on her creamy palms, but remarkably, none of them was deep.

"It's not bad," I said.

"Not this time." Her still-wild eyes met mine in the mirror. "Only one person I know hates me enough to do somethin' like this. And he hates you, too, Miss Angel."

I waited. I didn't want to put anything into her head that wasn't already there.

"This have Marcus Rydell all over it," she said. "You remember me and him was together."

"Oh, I remember," I said. "But I didn't know Marcus was an artist."

"He design his own tattoos. And mine."

I didn't ask her where it was on her anatomy.

Zelda shivered. "You know what really creepin' me out about this, Miss Angel?"

"All of it?" I said.

"No. Where did he get all that blood?"

That was a thought I'd been shoving aside ever since I realized that was this sicko's medium. As I knew it would, it chilled me to the marrow.

"It's probably not human, Zel."

"Miss Angel!"

It was Sherry, screaming from the showroom. I pushed past Zelda and flew through the door and around the counter, skidding as I went. Sherry was kneeling on the floor next to a half-bald push broom and a rusty metal dustpan and her father. Maharry was motionless and ashen.

"He's not breathing!" she said.

I virtually threw the phone behind me at Zelda. "Call 911," I said, and then flung myself at Maharry.

"What are you doing?" Sherry said.

"CPR."

"What can I do?"

"You pray," I said. "Pray hard."

CHAPTER TEN

Somewhere between the paramedics taking over and Maharry threading his way back to life, the police arrived. By then Sherry didn't seem to notice, or care, that within ten minutes C.A.R.S. was being sifted by two crime-scene investigators and a pair of officers. She sat by her father's head, rocking back and forth and whispering, "Please, God, don't take my daddy," until a female paramedic with soulful eyes led her to the front seat of the ambulance. Even then, Sherry leaned out the window and reached for me. Her hands were icy between mine.

"God won't take my daddy now, will he, Miss Angel? Not right when he started to trust me again?"

"If your daddy leaves us now, Sher," I said, "I'm not sure that's God's doing."

"Then it's mine."

Her face crumpled, but there was no chance to take that further. The paramedic slid into the driver's seat and patted Sherry's leg.

"Let's get your dad to the hospital," she said.

"This is not your fault, Sherry," I whispered.

But she couldn't have heard me over the sudden shriek of the ambulance, warning everyone in its path that this was a crisis worth getting out of the way for.

Nick Kent pulled up just as they were leaving. Without him there, I wasn't sure I could have gotten either Zelda or me through the questioning by the investigating team. Their biggest concern seemed to be why Sherry had tried to wash away evidence.

"Wouldn't you freak out if you saw your portrait in blood on the wall?" I said to a particularly scoffy boy-man who already had a minigut on him.

"What makes you so sure those are portraits?" he said.

I didn't answer.

"You got everything you need?" Nick said to him. "The paramedics said Miss Zelda needs a tetanus shot."

"I'd get about three of them," the other officer said. "Somebody took a leak in the plant."

My precious, freckle-faced Nick gave him a searing look.

"We're going to need to question"—Boy-Man glanced at his notebook—"Sherry Nelson."

"She's with her dying father," I said.

"It'll keep, Hickson," Nick said.

I didn't hang around for the rest of that discussion. Zelda was back to staring at the grisly gallery and melting toward the floor, and I needed to get her out of there. On the way to the bike I called Liz. She was the only person who could keep Zelda from tumbling over the precipice she was looking over.

Liz arrived at the hospital the same time we did, hair askew and eyes blinking, but able to soothe Zelda almost at the sight of her. Still, it took two of us to keep her from curling into a fetal position when the nurse produced the syringe. Most of the Sisters had used more needles than the average person saw in a lifetime, but break out the legal injections and they were like preschoolers facing their vaccinations. Maybe it simply stirred the memories from their graves.

When Liz left to take Zelda back to Sacrament House, I went to check on Maharry. They were still working on him in the ER, but I found Sherry in the same small, stark waiting room where I'd spent a tortured hour five months ago when Chief was hurt. She was spending hers with Officer Boy-Man.

"You couldn't give her a minute?" I said to him.

Hickson stood up from the faux leather couch, leaving a damp imprint behind him. "We don't like people's memories to get cold. We're through for now."

"For now?"

"She's a little foggy on a few of the details." He looked down at Sherry, who was staring at the knees she was knocking into each other, over and over, faster and faster. "Where can I reach you if I have any more questions?"

"Through me," I said.

I extracted a card from the back pocket of my jeans and handed it to him.

"Sacrament House." He looked at me in midscoff. "Oh. Yeah."

I could see him dumping the case in the Pointless Investigation file, the same way he shoved the card into his shirt pocket. I would have said, "*Oh, yeah* what?" if Sherry's thighs hadn't threatened to shake her right off the chair. I might have said it anyway if Hank hadn't come in just then, bringing her endless supply of calm with her.

She nodded at Hickson and we all watched him saunter out "like a bad dude," as Desmond would say.

"Liz told me what happened," Hank said. "You okay, Sherry?"

"He didn't believe anything I said."

I sat on the magazine table to face her. "What did you tell him?"

"That I was trying to wash that stuff off the wall so my daddy wouldn't have a heart attack when he figured out what it was." She jerked her head. "I guess I wasn't fast enough."

"Did he get on your case about destroying evidence?"

"He just said I made it harder for them to find out who did it." She glanced at me with eyes that still hadn't regained their color. "I told him it was probably taggers. Things have gotten worse since just about everybody left the block."

"Why did you tell him that, Sherry? This was clearly done by someone who knows us. Zelda thinks it was Marcus Rydell—"

"You're as bad as that cop!"

Sherry shot out of the chair and crossed to the wall under the television flickering soundlessly above her head. She stood with her rickety back to us, clutching at her sides.

"I can't talk about this while my daddy is in there dyin' and nobody will tell me anything."

"I'm sorry," I said. "You're right. Let's focus on Maharry."

"Ms. Nelson?"

A nurse in blue scrubs swung into the doorway. Sherry turned and froze.

"You can see your father now. But just for a few minutes."

Sherry went for the door and I started to follow, but she shook her head at me and said, "I can do this on my own."

When she hurried off with the nurse, I sank against the door jamb.

"Nicely done, Allison," I said.

Hank touched my shoulder. "Don't beat yourself up. She doesn't know what to do right now."

"Evidently neither do I."

"You want a sandwich or something while we wait?"

"Good grief, what time is it?" I looked at my watch. "It's after noon. Flannery's still over at Sacrament House."

"Why don't you go get her? I'll stay with Sherry."

"You sure?"

"This is family, Al. I'll keep you updated. Go on, get out of here." Hank waggled her fingers at my chest. "And, uh, I suggest you clean up a little before you show up at the house."

I looked down at myself. The front of my vest was like something out of a Hieronymus Bosch painting. And so, I knew, was my soul.

When I finally got to Sacrament Two, Gigi was serving a salad to Liz and Zelda that must have emptied out Owen's entire crop. Rochelle sat at the table with them, still wearing her gardening gloves. Flannery's were nowhere to be seen.

"This just torques my jaw," Owen said from the front window where he was peeking out between Ophelia's curtains as if the C.A.R.S. vandals might be heading up the driveway and he was going to be ready for them. "It gets my dander all the way up. I'm telling you, it jars my preserves."

"It does *what*?" Gigi said.

Flannery tugged at my sleeve and put her lips so close to my ear I was sure my lobes were being glossed. "Can we go? If I have to be around him one more minute, my head is going to explode."

I couldn't say I felt that much different. As much as I loved him, the day had frayed my nerves beyond Owen toleration.

Liz assured me she'd stay with the group for the rest of the afternoon until Mercedes got home. Flannery didn't register her usual complaints about having to ride on the Harley. She donned Desmond's helmet almost before I got to the curb. But I was more surprised when she said, "So does everybody always just, like, drop everything when something like this goes down?"

"We do," I said. "Nobody can get through this kind of thing alone."

Her chin came up, tilting the too-big helmet backward. "I've gotten through plenty of stuff by myself."

"I guess that depends on your definition of getting through. You can either stuff it and keep going and not let anybody know it's getting to you. Or you can deal with it, and that usually takes more than just you."

"What happens if you don't?"

I looked into the eyes that questioned me through the smoky visor. At least for that moment, she didn't appear to be throwing down the gauntlet, so I pieced the fragile words together.

"If you don't let somebody in to help you face it, a place in you is wounded. We're about healing wounds here."

Flannery looked away as if someone had tapped her on the shoulder and reminded her to stay buttoned up.

"I was just curious," she said. "So don't bother asking me if I've got any wounds."

"I don't have to," I said.

I left it at that and swung onto the bike. She stood there for another few seconds before she climbed on behind me. As we pulled away from Sacrament Two and eased around the corner toward West King, I wondered whether it was my wishful imagination, or if she really was holding onto me less like a terrified spider monkey than usual.

Until we got halfway down the block of West King where the Magic Moment Bar was losing the battle for survival. Without any provocation that I could see, Flannery suddenly grabbed my left arm and sent the bike wobbling. I gave it some gas and focused on straightening the wheel until I could steer it into the pockmarked parking lot in front of what was left of Titus Tattoo.

"You don't have to stop!" Flannery said.

"Yeah, I do. We almost lost it." I twisted to look at her. "Are you okay?"

"Yes," she said, though judging from the terror in her eyes she was anything but. "Let's just go."

"Not until you promise you're not going to grab my arm again."

"I'm sorry, okay? You don't have to lecture me."

It was perfectly obvious the possibility of a lecture wasn't the thing making Flannery dig her fingernails into my ribs and all but push the Harley forward with her feet. I could feel her heart beating against my back.

I added that to the stack of Things to Get Out of Flannery Later. I was a little freaked out myself sitting there a block from C.A.R.S. My own fear was overtaking the need to simply get things under control. Maybe one too many inhuman things had happened on old

Maharry's property. And if he couldn't make it, what hope was there, really, for the rest of the neighborhood?

For once I was grateful for Flannery's clinging. It kept the fragments of me from flying apart as we rode home to Palm Row.

Flannery spent the rest of the afternoon up in her room, and so, for that matter, did Desmond after I brought him home from school. I didn't know what Flannery was doing, but Desmond was sulking. I'd seen that lip-like-a-foldout-sofa thing before.

I didn't interrogate him because I needed a chance to call Chief from the side porch and bring him up to speed. He was with a client so Tia connected me with Kade, who said he would hit the high points with Chief.

"Mind if I come by tonight to go over a couple of financial things with you?" he said.

"That would be great." I slouched into an Adirondack and propped my feet on the rail. It was the first time I'd sat down that day without somebody's terrified face in front of me. I had a flash of normal. "Come for supper?" I said. "It's nice enough to eat outside, actually. I'll light some tiki torches for the bugs."

"You cooking?" I could hear the grin in his voice.

"A Hank casserole from my freezer."

"You're on. Who knows, maybe I can get some more info out of Flan."

"That would also be great," I said, because right now she could probably have poured out her entire life story to me and I'd miss it.

The minute Kade and I hung up and I had time to think, normal went out the way it came in and the faces on Maharry's walls were the only thing in my mind, like an assault on my sanity.

They were not the work of bored teenage taggers looking for action on West King. Nor could I believe some whacked-out druggie did the deed. Addicts always looked for cash, and Maharry hadn't even locked his up. Or his twenty-two.

Zelda might be right, especially if Marcus Rydell was capable of that kind of artwork. I wouldn't know. My only experience with that hideous hulk of a human being did not involve creative talent. Besides, there was something else about it that didn't ring true. I just couldn't get it to come into focus.

My phone rang and I jumped so hard it fell out of my hand and onto the deck. By the time I answered it, on hands and knees, Nick Kent was about to hang up.

"Hey, thanks for being there today," I said, "even though it wasn't your case."

I waited for him to say that he'd keep an eye on it and update me. He didn't. He ended the awkward pause with, "I looked into that Hastings thing."

"Oh. And?"

"There's a Brenda Donohue living there. Thirty-eight years old. I have an address."

I sat back on my knees. "Could she be Flannery's mom?"

"There's no way to tell. All she has is a driver's license. There are no properties or utilities in her name, and there's no Flannery Donohue registered in the public school system." I could hear him tapping computer keys. "She doesn't have any credit cards, not even a bank account."

"That's really strange. I mean, isn't it?"

"Yes, ma'am. I'm happy to give you her address."

There was something final in his voice.

"What's wrong, Nick?" I said. "You sound funky."

He paused again, long enough for the truth to dawn on me.

"Dad-*gum* it!" I got up and paced the porch, free hand in my hair. "Kylie, right?"

"Yes, ma'am. He called me in at the end of my shift and accused me of giving you information."

I flopped miserably onto the porch swing and knocked an innocent cushion over the edge. "Nick, I am so sorry. I tried really hard to make him think I checked out the arrest records myself. I definitely didn't mention your name."

"I knew when I told you I was taking a risk. It's not your fault."

I could almost see his eyes going Opie Taylor–sad.

"Are you in serious trouble?"

"No. He knows he can't prove anything."

"But."

"But he'll be watching to get me on some stupid little thing."

"Jackal." I pulled down at the sweat beads I could feel forming on my upper lip. "Okay, so, you need to stop giving me information. I don't want you going down for this."

"If I can do it without—"

"No. Absolutely not. Unless you're on duty and it's something you can report, I'm leaving you out of it."

In my mind, his eyes drooped even further.

"I'm sorry, Miss Allison."

"I'm the one who's sorry. Don't worry about it. Just watch your back."

He thanked me and hung up. I pushed the swing into motion with my foot and rocked until my heart sank to the pit of my stomach. I'd just lost a valuable ally.

When I was on the verge of nausea again, I looked at the clock on my phone and forced myself to get up. Time to thaw out the casserole and get ready for Kade. Then I'd call Hank and check on Maharry and Sherry.

"Desmond," I called out as I pushed through the back door and into the kitchen. "I need you to set the table. Cappuccino's coming over. "

Normally anything Kade-related brought him out of sulk mode, but there was no answer from his room. Probably had his headphones on, which was his MO when he was pouting. I pounded on his door, but he still didn't respond. When I realized I wasn't feeling the vibration of his subwoofer in the floor I opened the door. The room was empty.

Although I told myself it was ridiculous to panic, I was already praying *pleaseGodpleaseGodpleaseGod* as I searched the dining room, the living room, the foyer and the closet under the stairs. The shrill panic in my voice as I yelled, "Desmond! Desmond, answer me!" was enough to bring him all the way from St. George Street.

But he couldn't have gone out. From the screen porch I'd have seen him leave, even through the front door. His room was window-less, so nobody could have climbed in and snatched him.

That, however, was exactly what I was convinced had happened as I took the steps two at a time, still crying, "Des-*mond!* Where are you?"

It didn't dawn on me until I'd virtually ransacked the bathroom and checked the windows in my room that my hysterical shrieking hadn't brought Flannery out of *her* room either. I stopped in the middle of the upstairs hall and stared at her door. It was hard to hear anything over my own ragged breathing, but there it was: just-audible whispering from the other side.

It was a Sacrament House rule to knock before entering anyone's space, but I marched to her door and pushed it open. Desmond looked up from the bed where he leaned against the headboard with a sobbing Flannery in his arms. He didn't even have the good sense to look guilty.

Lucky for him I was more relieved than angry, at least for the moment.

"You need something, Big Al?" he said.

"Yeah, I need something. You."

He nodded as if he totally understood that and yet ... "Flannery needed me too."

Flannery sat up and pushed herself away from Desmond. The front of his T-shirt was soaked.

"I'm okay, Desi," she said.

Ah. We were back to you're-my-best-friend.

"Go ahead with your mom. I'm fine now."

Desmond got up and started past me but I planted a hand in the middle of his damp chest.

"Nobody goes anywhere until you two tell me what's going on. Desmond—dish."

He began to turn his head toward Flannery, but my eyes must have been steely enough to stop him. Yet he still sighed as if I just didn't get this at all.

"I was down in my room and I heard her up here cryin' and you was on the phone so I thought I oughta come up and make sure she wasn't in some kinda trouble."

"Even though you know this room is off limits."

"I was thinkin' this'd be one of those times when we got to be flexible."

"If I hadn't been here, sure. But I was right there on the side porch. All you had to do was stick your head out the door and tell me."

"She was cryin' real hard."

I looked at Flannery, who was doing absolutely nothing to get Desmond off the hook. Her tear-swollen eyes went from one of us to the other as if she were dumbstruck by the conversation.

"Were you being attacked by aliens when Desmond came to the door?" I said to her.

The chin came up. "What? No!"

"Were you getting ready to slit your wrists? Hang yourself from the ceiling?"

"Hello-o!"

"Suffering from severe abdominal pain? Bleeding? Vomiting? Experiencing a fever of over 102?"

She shook the curls, mouth hanging open. I turned back to Desmond.

"Since the answer to all of the above is no, son, you should have left the room and come down for me."

"I asked him to stay," Flannery said.

I shot Desmond another look but decided not to beat that already dead dog. This was a glimmer of a chance to get something from this child.

"All right." I pressed my shoulder against Desmond's. "And you, being the compassionate person you are, wanted to help."

Desmond stiffened.

"I'm being serious," I said. "I know you didn't hang out up here just for fun."

"That's what I told you," he said.

I sat on the edge of Flannery's bed. "And why did you need a friend?"

"I was upset."

"By whatever happened when we were driving down West King."

Her eyes startled just enough for me to know I was right before she hugged her knees and lifted her chin yet again. "It's whatever made you grab my arm," I said.

"Whoa," Desmond said to her. "You can't be doin' that now. I done that once and me and Mr. Chief ..." He cut himself off and nodded at me. "Go on ahead, Big Al."

"Whatever it was that scared you, Flannery," I said, "we can help you get beyond it—even if it was just something that reminded you of something else bad."

Her nod was too quick. "That's it. It just made me think of the night I ran away and got lost and ended up right there, where we were today, and that guy wanted ... you know."

Her eyes darted to Desmond, and I realized I was seeing the first sign of shame she had shown us.

"Des," I said. "Kade's coming for supper. Would you go down and set the table and get that casserole out of the freezer, the one that says 'mushroom ravioli'?"

"Kade's going to be here?" Flannery said. "When?"

"In about thirty minutes, so until then you and I can talk—"

"I have to take a shower," she said, and leapt from the bed, hands dancing through her hair. The switch in mood was dizzying.

I could feel Desmond's heart shrivel and Kade's voice echoed in my head: *Step away from the teenage romance.*

It was one hard, reluctant step.

By the time supper on the porch was over and the kids were cleaning up the kitchen while Kade and I sat in the living room with a stack of files, I was almost too brain dead to care if I went bankrupt. Hank had assured me on the phone that Maharry was stable and so was Sherry, and that Liz was seeing after Zelda. Maybe it would be okay to just shut down until tomorrow morning.

Kade flipped open a folder and grinned into it.

"I have never found anything even a little bit funny about my bank account," I said.

"It's not that. I was just thinking about Flannery. Does she ever take a breath? I don't think any of the rest of us said more than two words through the whole meal."

"Oh, she talks, all right. She just never tells us anything we want to know."

"Give me ten minutes with her."

"Unh-uh." I sat up straight in the red chair. "She's crushing on you so hard, you can't even look at her without her making wedding plans in her head."

"Get outta town."

"In her mind, she's Julia Roberts and you're Richard Gere."

"Huh?"

"You never saw *Pretty Woman*?"

"Is that a movie?"

"Omygosh you're so young." I leaned toward him. "Listen, I would appreciate whatever you can learn from her about her past, but don't do anything that would even remotely encourage her romantically. The child is smitten with you."

"Does Desmond see that?"

"Are you serious?"

"Aw, man. I feel like—"

"What was that?"

Kade followed my gaze to the kitchen. "What was what? Did you hear something?"

"I thought I heard the side door close."

He cocked his head and nodded at me. "What's weird to me is what I don't hear."

He was right. The kitchen was quiet. Too quiet for a pair of teenagers who five minutes before were arguing over who had to scrub the burnt cheese off the casserole dish.

"You think they're in *his* room this time?" Kade said.

"If they are, Desmond's never going to sit on a Harley again until he graduates from high school."

But even as I said it I dismissed it. I had clearly heard the latch on the back door click into place.

"Will you check his room?" I said. "I'm just going to look outside."

"What do you want me to do if they're in there?"

"Read them their rights."

I went to the foyer and eased the front door open. A soft darkness had fallen, and the streetlights had winked on so I could see clearly up and down Palm Row. A breeze ruffled from the bay, only slightly stirring the palm fronds. Other than that, all was still.

I slipped out, swatting at the night bugs swarming around the front porch light, and padded barefoot across the grass to the side of the house. Kade had flicked that light on too, so that my property, all the way to Miz Vernell's, was flooded in yellow. The porch was just as we'd left it after supper, complete with the fading scent of the tiki torches.

Forcing myself to look up, I scanned the edge of the roof, although what I thought I was going to find there I had no idea. Despite the shiver that went through me I told myself I was being as ridiculous now as I had been earlier, before I found Desmond playing Cyrano to Flannery's Roxanne in the upstairs bedroom.

Come on. It wasn't Sultan's style to simply have Desmond kidnapped from the kitchen. He could have done that a hundred times before. He was more about forcing people to join him at the edge of sanity and trying to shove them over it—

"Allison!"

I clawed at my chest and stared at Kade, who was tilting out the side door.

"I didn't mean to scare you," he said. "But I think you better come talk to Desmond."

Heart still slamming, I found my son at the bistro table. He was swinging his lanky legs and looking everywhere but at me.

"Where's Flannery?" I said.

He didn't answer until Kade poked him.

"Out," he said.

"Out? Out where?"

His Adam's apple went up and down so hard I could almost hear it scraping his throat.

"Look, bro," Kade said, "if you know, you gotta tell us. She could get into serious trouble out there."

Desmond catapulted himself out of the chair and paced to the sink and then to the refrigerator and back. Kade opened his mouth, but I put my finger to my lips. Finally Desmond stopped with his back to the pantry door. "I was puttin' the dishes in the dishwasher," he said. "And I thought she was cleanin' that nasty pan in the sink."

I nodded him on.

"But then I turned around and she was just about out the door. I axed her where was she goin' and she jus' said, 'Imma be back. I got to go do something. Cover for me.'"

I'd have bet my Harley she called him Desi somewhere in there.

"But I wasn't gon' cover for her, Big Al." Desmond's voice shot out of man-range, up into scared-boy territory. "I was just thinkin' for a minute how much she gon' hate me when she finds out I busted her."

"She'll get over it," Kade said. "Did she tell you where she went?"

"Desmond," I said, "where is the Hot Spot?"

He lost three inches against the pantry door.

"Remember what I said: If the time came when I really needed to know, you were going to have to tell me."

"Corner of Sevilla and Valencia."

"You won't regret this, bro," Kade said to him.

I was on my way to the door, phone in one hand, my boots in the other. "Desmond, stay here," I said.

"I think I'd better come with you," Kade said.

"Okay—" I pressed a hand to my temple. "Then, Des, I'm calling Mr. Schatzie to come over in case you need a grown-up. You can call Mr. Chief if you want."

He didn't argue.

"Lock the door. Don't let anybody in."

When I got a nod from him I bolted out with Kade on my heels.

"Let's take my car," he said. "If she's there she'll hear the Harley and maybe run."

Under any other circumstances I'd have called Kade a chicken heart. He had ridden with me one time and swore he'd never do it again. But at this point, there was no sign of my sense of humor. I called Owen and got in Kade's Mazda.

"I can't deal with this kid anymore," I told him as we wove our way from Palm Row toward Valencia. "Adults are one thing, but I'm not equipped to handle kids, not girls anyway. And definitely not this girl."

"You know if you actually catch her in the act of … soliciting … you're not going to have much choice but to turn her over to—"

"Are you speaking as my attorney?"

"It's what Chief would tell you."

"Wait, what's the address again?"

"Valencia and Sevilla. This is the way, isn't it?"

I stared through the windshield. "That's where the church is—where I used to go."

Kade swerved onto Valencia Street and into a now vacant Flagler College parking lot where he turned to look at me. His clear blue eyes were heading toward angry. "You think Desmond was feeding us a line to give Flannery time to—"

"No. He's never even been there. It just blows me away that this kind of thing could be going on right in front of the dad-gum *church*."

Mind still reeling, I scanned Valencia. The always-quiet avenue was lined with magnolias that even in mid-September were thick and shiny with leaves. I couldn't see Flagler Community Church, but it was there, ignoring the world from behind its Henry Flagler opulence. Just like it always had.

"Let's leave the car here and walk down," I said.

I went for the door handle, but Kade put his hand on my arm. His skin was clammy. "I'm thinking we should call Nick Kent."

"Can't."

"So we're going to do what if somebody pulls a knife?"

"I don't know, but I can't sit here any longer."

That was truer than he could know. The Nudge was so strong I was surprised I wasn't halfway down the street already.

"You coming?" I said. And then I got out of the car and took off toward the corner.

Kade caught up and took my elbow, for all the world as if he were escorting me to the opera. When we were almost to Sevilla, he squeezed my arm and pulled me out of the bright circle cast by the streetlight.

"I see some people down there," he whispered.

"How many?"

"Maybe four."

"*Big* people?"

Even in the shadows I could see him grinning. "Nah. They actually do look like kids."

I nodded. That was what Desmond had told me before: it was a place for kids to hook up.

"Do you see Flannery?" I said.

Kade shook his head. "There's a girl, but that's not Flan's hair."

I pulled away and hurried toward the corner, staying out of the lights, hugging the line of trees. A veil of Spanish moss hit me in the face and I brushed it behind me. Kade muffled an epithet.

By the time I reached the street sign I could see the figures Kade was talking about. A girl only slightly taller than Flannery, and two guys, both gangly and slope-shouldered like wannabe basketball players. They stood with their hands jammed in their pockets, the way men wait for women outside a ladies' room. Impatient, but not aggressive.

Their heads were turned toward the girl, but she faced away from them, hands working the air like she was hell-bent on convincing someone of something. I felt Kade's restraining hand on my shoulder, but I took another step forward, and there she was, in the shadows: Flannery, just as hell-bent from the other direction.

"He's after us, Tango!" she said. "You have to come with me!"

"They don't even know where we are," the other girl answered.

"New York accent," Kade whispered to me.

"Yes, they do. I told you—"

"Hey, are we gonna get any action or what? We got the cash."

That came from one of the boys, who moved just far enough out of the shadows to expose a pimpled face and a hard mouth.

"Just chill," Tango said. "I'll be right there."

Flannery grabbed her wrist. "No! Come back with me and you'll be safe. I swear."

"What do I look like? You'll just come back and take my clients."

Tango jerked her hand away and pulled it behind her head in a fist. Flannery cringed.

"Hey, all right—girl fight!" the other kid yelled.

"We have to stop this," I hissed to Kade. "Get Flannery."

Kade was on the two girls just as Tango set herself up for another try at Flannery's face. He put both arms around Flannery and turned her away. I attempted the same move with Tango and was rewarded with a bite on the wrist. When I jerked loose and lost my balance, she shoved herself against me and we both went down. She scrambled to her feet and stuck her foot in my chest, hurling obscenities through it all.

"Hey, who are you?" one of the boys called out, voice indignant.

From the ground I saw Kade hold up his open wallet with the hand that wasn't holding onto Flannery. With a string of expletives, both boys took off across the street and disappeared into the churchyard. Tango looked down at me, spit like a snake, and went screaming after them. But not before I got a full view of her perfectly round, exquisitely chiseled face.

"You okay, Allison?" Kade said.

It was no surprise to me that Flannery was limp in his arms. If his being here for this wasn't a God-thing, I didn't know what was.

I pulled myself up and examined the teeth marks in my arm. Beyond us a siren began to wail, and so did Flannery.

"Kade," I said, "take her to Sacrament House, okay? I'm going to stay here and tell the police what goes down here."

"How are you going to get back?"

"I'll figure it out. I'll call Chief."

Kade looked at me over the top of Flannery's head. "I don't like leaving you here."

"Oh, gee, Kade, what can happen?" I said. "I'm right in front of a church."

Sometimes sarcasm really did hold me together.

Kade half carried a strangely silent Flannery to the car. I was standing there listening to the sirens shriek toward me and figuring out just how I was going to explain why I knew about the Hot Spot, when I heard footsteps pounding toward me from the direction of the church.

Did those hormonal little morons have some coconuts or what? They were coming *back*?

But when I turned, ready to take them on, I saw that it wasn't one of Tango's clients but a man in perhaps his late thirties who jogged like he did it on a regular basis. His hair was cut close to the head that jutted forward, on alert.

"Hey," he said, "everything all right out here?" The accent hailed from someplace deeper South than north Florida. Alabama, maybe, or Mississippi.

I waited warily until he got closer and I could see concerned brown eyes and a plain wooden cross bouncing on his chest as he came to a halt a few feet in front of me.

"I heard some commotion," he said. "Those cops on their way here?"

"Sounds like it. And you are?"

"Yates Chattingham." He put out his hand. "I'm the pastor here."

I let my hand stay in his for no longer than three seconds. "The *new* pastor," I said.

"Been here just over eight weeks."

"Not long enough to know you have child prostitutes out here doing business with the local boys."

The brown eyes expanded. "Apparently not. I had no idea."

"Well, now ya know. What do you think you'll do about it?"

He shook his head.

I shook mine too. "Nothing is not the correct answer, reverend. The correct answer is: 'We have girls in our community who are desperate and neglected and unvalued enough to stoop to this? We'd better help them!'" I narrowed the space between us. "Just let me warn you, Mr.—Cunningham, was it?"

"Chattingham—"

"You're not going to get any support from your congregation on this. They're going to tell you this isn't the business of the church, which is why you won't find me sitting in one of your pews on Sunday mornings like I did for seven years. You want to know what drove me out?"

He nodded.

"It was the indifference. I hope it doesn't drive you out too."

I cocked my head. The sirens faded toward the bay.

"I guess they weren't headed here," Yates Chattingham said. "Would you like to come in for some coffee? Maybe talk about this some more?"

"No. I have to talk a wounded child out of the crazy tree."

"At least tell me your name," he said.

"Allison. Allison Chamberlain. But if you want to stay here very long, don't mention that to your flock."

I left him standing there and stomped off down Valencia Street.

CHAPTER ELEVEN

Although I was only wearing shorts, a sleeveless T, and a pair of flip-flops, I was marinating in my own sweat before I reached the traffic light at Cordova and King. The evening itself was cool; I was not. Even with a blister forming where the thong of my shoes cut between my toes, both my speed and my anger continued to ratchet up. Several notches for spoiled teenage boys with too much money and not enough supervision. Several more for the cops who never saw it going down and the members of Flagler Community Church who, bless their hearts, wouldn't know it was going down if they walked right into it. At that proximity some of them probably had.

But the rest of my rage I reserved for myself. The questions slapped me with every flop of my rubber soles on the brick sidewalk.

Why hadn't I pushed Desmond before to tell me where the Hot Spot was?

And how could I have let that little Tango girl get away? The fact that I'd have needed a black belt to hold onto her was beside the point. Why didn't I run after her and tackle her and drag her to Sacrament House before she caught up with those junior jackals?

I finally noticed the foot pain as I passed City Hall, and kicked off my flip-flops to carry them the remaining block to Palm Row. But the real ache, the one forming smack in the middle of my gut, didn't subside. That one was for Flannery.

I had seen the manipulative "bite me" blankets she stayed hidden under. She'd made sure I didn't miss those. And yeah, I'd lifted the corners of those covers and gotten a few glimpses of her fear and shame. But the capacity to care, and the courage to act on it—she'd kept those completely under wraps until I witnessed her begging Tango to come with her to my house. Even when Tango reared back to slug her, Flannery had done nothing more than cringe.

I stopped at the corner of Cordova and Palm Row, shoes still in hand. My eyes closed and I searched behind them for Tango's face. Round. Beautifully childlike. And without a mark.

Not a green and yellow bruise like Flannery's, not a single laceration or scratch such as the ones Flannery was still healing from. Not a sign that Tango had been in a fight with her just five days before.

Either Tango wasn't the one who'd tried to rearrange Flannery's facial features, or Flannery had simply stood there and let her do it. From what I'd just seen, I was inclined to believe the latter. But nobody could have convinced me of that an hour ago.

I ran barefoot the rest of the way, Flannery-pain still tearing at me. Just as I'd instructed Desmond, the side door was locked, and I'd barely started knocking when Chief was there opening it. His big safe shoulders brought my heart rate down a few beats per second.

"Where's Desmond?" I tossed my flip-flops under the table and grabbed my motorcycle boots.

"Taking a shower."

"Good. Okay—I need to put on some jeans. No, I'll just ride in my shorts—"

"What are you doing, Classic?"

"I'm going over to Sacrament House." I shoved my feet into the boots and flipped through the keys on the hook until I located the one for the Harley. "Kade took Flannery over there after we found her at the Hot Spot, trying to get Tango to come back here with her." I stuffed the key in my shorts pocket. "Tango chose two teenage johns over us and took off. Do you mind staying with Desmond until I get back?"

Chief put himself between me and the door. "I can't let you do this, Classic."

"I've got to get over there!"

"Then I'll take you. If you get on that bike in this state, you'll get yourself killed."

"I can't leave Desmond here by himself."

"Owen's still here." Chief's eyes crinkled for a second. "He said he'd guard the front door if I'd take the back."

I shoved my hair into a messy bun. "Okay, okay. I'll tell Owen and we'll go."

"I'll tell Owen. You go get long pants and a jacket."

I didn't tell him I'd given my jacket to Flannery, who was currently wearing it. I went to the laundry basket on top of the washing machine and pulled out some still-damp Levis and one of Desmond's Harley sweatshirts. Chief was waiting for me next to the Road King when I joined him. He put his hands on my shoulders.

"Breathe, Classic."

I started to deflate. "I think I've really messed this one up."

"Then breathe deep."

I sucked in air, but the look he gave me was all I needed.

I climbed onto the bike behind him and rubbed a new round of palm sweat on my thighs. Chief took my hands in mid-wipe and wrapped my arms around him.

"Hold on," he said.

This isn't fair, I wanted to say to him. But I needed to hold on far too much to go there now.

I did breathe, so that when we pulled up to the curb on San Luis Street and Mercedes waved to us from the window of Sacrament One, I could at least hope I would know what to say to Flannery. As for exact words, God wasn't providing any yet.

When Mercedes let us in, only Jasmine was in the living room with Kade and Flan. Someone had turned on the eclectic pair of lamps and lit a candle on the cable spool repurposed as an end table. An untouched mug of tea was next to it, and Flannery was wrapped in the blanket I recognized from Rochelle's bed, although Rochelle herself wasn't present. Another sensitive move on somebody's part.

"I told Ophelia and Gigi to stay over at Two with Zelda," Mercedes said. "She still goin' back and forth between havin' it together and fallin' apart."

I knew that dance.

"Sherry?" I said.

"At the hospital with her daddy. Miss Hank gave her cab money to get home." Jasmine's eyes bore all the signs of an afternoon of weeping. "Miss Angel, is it true what Zelda said, 'bout them pictures on the walls?"

"Jasmine, this ain't the time," Mercedes said.

I thanked her with my eyes and sat on the edge of the chair

Jasmine was leaning against on the floor so I could squeeze her shoulder. "We'll get to that later. How are you doing, Flannery?"

I didn't really have to ask. The child's face was so pale it bordered on blue and her tiny fists stroked the tops of her legs. Even with Kade beside her on the couch with his arm stretched across the back she still looked as if any passing person was likely to snatch her up and cart her off. Or perhaps punch her in the face.

But it was her eyes that looked the most wary as she pointed them straight at Chief. He was perched on the arm of Mercedes's chair, face at ease. Mr. Rogers couldn't have been less threatening, but Flannery shrank under Kade's arm.

"You ready to talk now?" Kade said to her.

"I was, but …"

Chief nodded and stood up. "I need to get back to Desmond. Kade, can you make sure Allison and Flannery get home?"

"On it, Chief," Kade said.

Flannery visibly relaxed when she heard the Road King rumble down San Luis. I still had no idea what that was about, but it was so heartbreakingly like Chief to know what to do with it.

Kade looked at Flannery. "Okay?"

She gave the front door one more scan and tucked back the curls that seemed to have doubled in the night air. "I haven't been totally telling the truth," she said.

I looked at Mercedes, but she didn't respond with an *mm-mmm*. We all waited.

"I did have a pimp. The same one as Tango. In Jacksonville." Flannery shook her head. "I didn't pick him. He picked me. I didn't even want to be a prostitute."

"Don't nobody make that they career choice."

Flannery glanced at Mercedes and then turned her gaze to the fists that had to be rubbing her skin raw by now. "That first day I was here, you told me I had choices, but I didn't. He had total control over my life. I don't care what anybody says, I couldn't just walk away, because I didn't have anywhere to go."

"Ain't nobody judgin' you here, baby girl," Jasmine said, voice thick.

Mercedes came forward in her chair until her knees touched Flannery's. She stopped both of the pink fists with one hand.

"You think I don't know what it's like? I was in a trap, same as you, only worse because I got in it for drugs. That man forced you, didn't he?"

"Yes." I was surprised Flannery left her hands where they were, smothered by Mercedes's. "So I *didn't* have a choice."

"Then how did you get here?" I said.

"Sherry and Zelda. They didn't give me a choice either."

"No, I mean how did you get to St. Augustine from Jacksonville?"

I watched her press back into the sofa, but Mercedes pulled her forward. She was on the coffee table now, and her eyes were as latched onto Flannery as her hands.

"You start holdin' back and you lost, honey," she said. "We not gon' force you, but don't pass up the chance for us to come alongside, now."

My worry about knowing what to say had been completely pointless. Even Kade couldn't make this kind of progress with Flannery. I obviously wasn't the only one God gave words to.

Flannery talked straight to Mercedes, as if the rest of us had left the room. "He put us, Tango and me, on a private plane with two clients. He called them clients like it was a real business."

"Mmm-hmm."

"We were supposed to spend the week here with them, but they got totally wasted the first night in the hotel so while they were passed out, we got away."

"You see?" Jasmine said. "You stronger than you think."

Mercedes jiggled Flannery's hands. "Where did you go?"

"Tango knew that there was a Hot Spot. She found out about it on Facebook or something, I don't know. We were going to try to find out where it was so we could … make enough money to get a bus ticket." Flannery let her head fall back, and I could see how hard she swallowed before she went on, eyes closed to the misery. "I have a great-uncle in Fort Myers. I thought we could go there, but we needed money."

"So you tried to find out where the Hot Spot was," Kade said.

"She thought she could find it from what she picked up on Facebook and we were, like, basically just wandering around, when, this police car went by and I flipped out and ran. I thought Tango was behind me but she wasn't. I got so lost, and when I tried to call her, my cell phone was dead."

So far the pieces fit together, but I could see spaces where several more were missing.

"You're doing great, Flan," I said. "Keep going."

She shrugged the shoulders that had surely grown smaller since she'd last told me to butt out of her business. "That's mostly it."

"Mmm-hmm," Mercedes said, "'cept for the part where you got picked up by that pimp in the first place. He come to your house?"

We didn't get the expected, "Hello! No!"

"I don't remember how it all happened exactly," Flannery said to her lap. "I was messed up, and he said he'd take care of me and make sure I had everything I needed. More than I needed."

"And he done that at first, right?" Jasmine said. An unusual anger tinged her voice.

"I was like his little princess. Pedicures and clothes and the cell phone. Any lessons I wanted. Other stuff." I saw her neck tighten. "I don't even want to talk about that. It just grosses me out."

"And then?" Mercedes said.

Flannery closed her eyes again. "And then he just turned into somebody else. I wouldn't even be doing anything wrong and he'd just slap me or do whatever, and I'd try to figure out what I did so he'd change back into the way he was before."

"That's a big dog barkin' there," Mercedes said.

Flannery looked at her, eyes puzzled.

"Ain't never gon' happen, baby girl. All that slappin' around and takin' over your life, that's the real pimp. The treatin' you like a queen, that ain't nothin' but a act."

"Did that happen to you?"

"For 'bout ten minutes 'fore he threw me out on the street and tol' me I wasn't gon' get a fix till I brought him back some john money."

"I didn't get no princess treatment at all," Jasmine said, "but now Geneveve, she did."

"Who's Geneveve?" Flannery said.

"Desmond's mama before Miss Angel. Sultan had her believin' he was gon' marry her and take care all her problems and then next thing you know, she on his leash like the rest of us, only worse."

"What happened to her?"

Before I could stop Jasmine she said, "He killed her."

Flannery's face went dead. I wanted to grab her by the shoulders and make her believe that couldn't possibly happen to her. Kade was already going in that direction as he let his arm slide to her shoulder. But it was Mercedes who said what needed to be said.

"Maybe that pimp you had, maybe he's not as evil as Sultan. But once they get thinkin' they own you, you can't never trust they gon' just let you go. Miss Angel and all of us, we'll try to protect you, but the best thing you can do is know God loves you." Flannery's gaze headed for her lap again, but Mercedes tilted her fragile chin with her brown fingers. "And you got to let us see the real human being God put inside you."

Flannery collapsed against Kade. We couldn't push her any further tonight. I believed everything she told us, but I also knew she'd left some large chasms in her story. I just hoped she wouldn't fall into them before we could close them up.

After Kade dropped us off at Palm Row and he and Chief went out to the side porch, I did sit Flannery down at the bistro table and explain that if we *were* going to protect her, we had to have her mother's signature so she could stay with me until we got things straightened out.

I watched her closely as I said, "If Brenda will give me temporary legal custody of you—"

"How did you know her name is Brenda?" Flannery's knuckles

whitened on the edge of the table. "You don't even know where she lives."

"Hastings," I said.

"Did you already talk to her?"

"No. I thought we should do that together."

Actually, I still didn't think Liz's idea was the best one and neither, apparently, did Flannery. I waited while she did everything but split the wood on the bistro table.

"I'll go on two conditions," she said finally.

"One," I said.

"She has to promise me she's alone. Totally alone."

My stomach seized. Was she expecting her pimp to be there, at her house, with her mother? I had to push that aside to get out, "And two?"

"I want Kade to come too."

I forced myself not to sigh.

"Is he still out there?" she said, one foot already feeling for the floor.

"*I* will ask him," I said.

"Then can I go to bed?"

"Absolutely," I said.

The poor kid had been through as much as I had that day, and I could barely put two thoughts together at that point. But there was still one more thing to deal with.

After I saw Flannery to her room and smoothed the covers over her and stood outside her door to breathe a prayer, I went back downstairs where Chief was pouring me a cup of Earl Gray. I wrapped my fingers around the mug handle and held the cup against my temple.

"You've had quite the day, Classic."

"It's not over yet. I need to talk to Desmond."

"He's asleep. I talked to him."

I nodded Chief to the living room where he tucked the Harley throw around my feet in the red chair and put the cup back in my hand. Strange behavior for somebody who couldn't commit.

There was still so much steam rising from the cup I set it on the table. "What did Desmond say?"

"He didn't have to say much." Chief stretched back on the couch. "It's obvious he really cares about this girl."

"He has a crush on her."

"It's more than that. He relates to her, which makes sense. Both from messed-up backgrounds, both having to trust that somebody gives a rip about them when they never had a reason to before." Chief shrugged. "I think he puts up with her using him because he understands why she does. There's your trouble."

"Meaning ..."

"Desmond isn't what Flannery needs."

"She isn't what Desmond needs either."

"Right. Plus, she's transferred all her affections to Kade."

"*Oh* yeah. And I can tell you where they were before."

"Pimp?"

"Uh-huh. Only, you know what's really heinous?"

"I'm afraid to ask."

"I get the impression she didn't run away from her mother and *then* get hooked up with this piece of slime. I think he was part of her life at home."

Chief winced.

"I know."

"You didn't get the whole story though."

"Not yet. But she did say she'd go with me to get a signature from her mother. She wants Kade to come along."

"Big surprise."

I shook my head and felt the messy bun come loose. "What I still don't get is why she's so afraid of you."

"No idea." Chief surveyed the ceiling. "There's something else we need to discuss."

I picked up the cup and blew into it. "Good or bad?"

"Strange."

"What hasn't been today?"

"Desmond told me he saw the Mosquito talking to somebody at school this afternoon who knew you."

"Who?"

"He wasn't sure about the guy's name. Roy, maybe. He said this dude stepped out in front of you on the bike down on Aviles Street one morning when you two were out riding."

The mug went back to the table. Could I not catch a break?

Chief's eyes took on their eagle quality. "Desmond said you didn't like this guy, and he didn't much like him either. This ringing any bells, Classic?"

"It was Troy Irwin. But I think you already figured that out."

"Knew it the minute Desmond described him as 'some dude in a pimp suit.'"

I guffawed in spite of myself. Chief didn't join me. He just leaned forward.

"Come *on*, Chief. It was a chance meeting. He just showed up out of the blue."

Chief looked as if I'd just smacked him in the face.

"*What?*" I said.

"You weren't going to tell me about it?"

"There was nothing to it."

"Desmond said you were so freaked out when you drove away, you almost hit two cars and a pickup truck." Chief's eyebrows lifted. "That sounds like something to me."

I kicked off the blanket and got myself out of the chair to pace to the bookcase. "We keep having the same conversation," I said to the spine of a Robert Frost collection. "When have I had a chance to do anything about this Troy thing? I guess I could have gone to his office, somewhere between taking Zelda to the hospital and keeping Flannery from getting her nose broken and—"

I turned from the shelves, and my breath caught. Chief was examining his left palm as if a gash had appeared there, but the wrench in my chest said the hurt was someplace else. His hand closed as he looked up, in time for me to watch a memory escape from his eyes.

"This isn't just about *my* stuff, is it?" I said.

He stood and reached for my cup. This time I blocked his path. "I'm thinking I'm not the only one in this relationship who has issues with the past."

For the first time since the day I met him, Chief couldn't meet my eyes. It was hard to tell whether the pain that cut to my core was his or mine.

"You always tell me whatever goes on inside needs to come out where we can deal with it." I pressed my hands against his chest. "But that goes for both of us."

"Always has."

"Really? Because that's not what I'm feeling here."

Chief rested his forehead against mine. "Your tea's getting cold."

Maybe it was the fatigue that made my brain suddenly heavy. Or maybe the press of his Chief-ness into my skin. Whatever the reason, I let it go.

"We're not done with this," I said. "But right now—"

"Right now you're the walking dead. Get some sleep, Classic."

He started to pull away, but I put my arms around his neck. "Just tell me we're not over."

I watched his face struggle. "I don't want us to be over."

"That's good, because you're the best thing that has ever—"

Chief pressed his finger against my lips. "'Night, Classic," he said.

With a kiss on each of my wrists he was gone. Even as I listened to the Road King growl away I crawled into the red chair, pulled the Harley blanket over my head and whispered, "You infuriating man."

But I couldn't escape the pain that clenched my chest. Again, and then again, until I had to gasp for breath.

I sat up and let it throb. This time I knew it wasn't just mine or Chief's. It was God's.

And I wasn't going to be able to let it go forever, because the aching, breath-stealing pressure to hang on—that was God's too.

Desmond was distant the next morning, and between the stiffness from sleeping like a pretzel all night in the red chair and the dread of making the phone call with Flannery, I wasn't in the right frame of mind to question him. All I said when I dropped him off was, "I understand why you want to help Flannery."

And all he said was, "She rather get her help from Cappuccino."

As I pulled the Harley from the curb I hoped Kade was right about boys surviving those heartbreaks, because Desmond Chamberlain wasn't just any boy.

When I got back to Palm Row I hauled Flannery out of bed and down to the kitchen and set an English muffin in front of her. While she pulled it apart into tidbits, I slipped out to the porch and called Liz.

She was ecstatic to hear that we had a name and address for Flannery's mother, but her voice quickly hushed to a husky whisper.

"Let the mother do most of the talking," she said. "Questions about how long the girl has been with you and the circumstances of her winding up with you are better left unanswered. You have to protect yourself."

"I'm more interested in protecting Flannery."

"And you can't do that if Judge Atwell takes her away from you. All you're doing in this phone call is setting up a meeting."

"Got it. And Liz?"

"Yeah?"

"Any time you want to step out of this, I'll understand. I've already put one person in a bad position."

"You know what, Allison? You aren't the only one who gets Nudges." I heard a door squeak on her end, and her voice changed to something between professional and are-you-getting-this-Allison? "Gotta go. Get back to me on that, would you?"

As I hung up, I could imagine her nodding too cheerfully at whoever had walked in on her breaking the law.

Flannery was waiting for me in the living room where I had told her
we'd make the call on her phone, thanks to Kade's provision of a charger.
She looked tiny and pale and still-bruised in the red chair, and I won
dered if she was feeling any of the same pain I'd spent the night with.

"I'm going to put us on speaker phone," I said. "Not because I don't
trust you—"

"Nobody trusts me," Flannery said. "Why should they?"

"Because." I sat facing her. "You're starting to tell the truth."

She toyed with a curl, eyes away from me. "You believe what I said
last night?"

"I do. I also believe there's more."

I gave that about ten seconds until she said, "Can we just get this
over with?"

I nodded and handed her the phone. As she deftly punched in a
number with her thumbs, I tried to read her face. It was pretty much
as guarded as it had been when I first saw her at Sacrament House, but
the place between us was thinner now. I just hoped the woman we were
about to talk to didn't thicken it up again.

The ringing was cut off abruptly with a "Hello?"

The voice was crisper than I expected, and more confident. Until
Flannery said, "Hi, Mom." Then the air crackled with silence, followed
by an almost timid, "Flannery?"

"Yeah, it's me."

"Darlin'—they let you call? Are you supposed to be calling?"

That was not among the possible maternal responses I'd imagined in the wee hours of the morning. I had to grip the sides of the

ottoman to keep from grabbing the phone and screaming, *You were in on this?*

"The school is allowing you to call?" the woman said.

"What school?" Flannery said. "I'm not at any school, Mom. I never was. Is that what Elgin told you?"

"Where *are* you, Flannery?" Brenda Donohue's voice now climbed to the place I'd expected it to be. I'd heard that same mother-fear in my own voice more than once.

Flannery looked at me, shoulders to her earlobes, as if she'd just realized I might actually be able to help her.

"Ms. Donohue?" I said. "I'm with a nonprofit that helps young women in trouble."

There was a pause as she apparently put it together that someone else was on the line. "What kind of trouble?" she said. "Flannery, who is this woman?"

"Ma'am—"

"Mom, she's been taking care of me, okay? I'm fine."

"I don't understand any of this. You're not at New Beginnings? I signed the papers. Elgin said it would—"

"Straighten me out?" Flannery's practiced insolence kicked in. "He's the one who screwed me up in the first place."

Brenda didn't answer, which gave me a minute to sort through what I'd just heard. This mother thought her daughter was away at a residential facility all this time? She let this Elgin person put her there, with no way of being in touch with her? I had been a mother for less than a year, and on my worst I-want-to-quit Monday I could not imagine myself doing that. Either this woman was a complete mess, or Elgin, whoever he was, had a hold over both of them that made my insides tie themselves into a whole series of knots.

"Flannery, I don't understand," she said.

"Did he come looking for me?"

"No! I told you, I thought you were in Huntsville, Alabama. What about the emails you sent me?"

"I never sent you any emails." Flannery put her hands up like she was trying to stop a train. "You haven't seen him?"

"No. He's working in Jacksonville. Flannery—what happened?"

"You really don't know?" Flannery's voice trembled on the near side of vulnerability.

"If I had known you were someplace besides that school, I would have come and found you and brought you home. What is going *on*?"

By then Brenda was clearly close to tears, and she wasn't the only Donohue in that place. "Do you swear to me that you will get him out of our life?" Flannery said. "Because if you do, if you *swear* to me, I'll come home. Only we have to go someplace where he'll never find us."

Whoa.

"I swear, Flannery."

"Do you? Because if I come home and he's still there, you'll never see me again."

"Okay," I said. "Let's take this one step at a time. Ms. Donohue, I need some assurance that Flannery is going to be safe at home."

"Are you with the county?"

"No, like I said, I'm with a nonprofit, but I do have a responsibility to Flannery."

"You can't keep her away from me."

I didn't point out that she had apparently let somebody else do that. Flannery snatched up the phone and brought it close to her face, as if she were trying to see her mother on the screen.

"She won't keep me from you. But if he ever comes back, you will *never* see me again. You have to make it so he can't ever hurt me anymore."

"What did he *do* to you?"

Brenda was near hysteria. Flannery, though her eyes still streamed, was almost unnaturally calm.

"It doesn't matter now," she said. "Miss An—these people are helping me get healed. I just want to go forward, but I can't do it with Elgin there. You have to promise me."

"I promise."

I watched Flannery. This obviously wasn't a new way of relating for these two. Flannery was more the mother than the child. I could almost feel Brenda Donohue drawing strength, no matter how misguided, from her daughter.

"Give me until Sunday," Brenda said. "I can make this happen by Sunday. Can you come at two thirty? Maybe three? I'll be off work."

Flannery's eyes rolled. "Mom, you don't get it. You have to quit your job so we can leave. For good."

I eased the phone from Flannery's hand. "Actually, Ms. Donohue, I wouldn't give notice. You don't want to arouse any suspicion."

"All right. That's right. I'll work that last shift and then I'll meet you at the house. All right? Is that all right?"

"Three o'clock Sunday," Flannery said. "You have to be ready, Mom."

This poor woman was unraveling. How was she going to make arrangements for them to go into permanent hiding from a man Flannery was obviously terrified of? And how was I going to let her?

"I love you, darlin'," Brenda said.

"I love you, too, Mom. I'm coming home."

Squeezing the phone in my palm until I felt the ooze of sweat, I watched Flannery visibly shed the bravado that had kept her in charge of the call. Only the bare, vulnerable shell of a frightened child was left in view.

"Flan," I said, "that didn't go the way I thought it was going to go."

"Me neither."

"Really?"

She nodded. "When I heard her voice, I just wanted to go be with her."

I tried to tread carefully. "Even though she didn't protect you from Elgin?"

She looked up. "You obviously haven't experienced somebody like this. He is—was—her boyfriend, but he didn't love her. He just *controlled* her, and I didn't ever think that could happen to my mom."

"And that's how he was able to be your pimp?"

"It doesn't *matter!* "

I put out a hand to stop her as she tried to wriggle from the chair. "It does matter. He should go to prison for what he did to you."

"No, Allison! Just leave it alone, okay? You don't know him. He'll get out of it and come after us."

Everything on her shook. I put my hands on the curls and pulled her head into my chest. A protective wave pushed me to hold her in spite of her stiffening in my arms.

"We'll make sure you and your mom are safe. God'll show us what to do next."

Flannery pulled back far enough to scour my face with her eyes. "How do you know that?"

"Because I *have* experienced somebody like God, Flan. And I just know."

CHAPTER TWELVE

Everyone got on board for me to take Flannery to her mother on Sunday. Gigi and Rochelle were going on a weekend NA retreat with Leighanne and Nita where we hoped they would be able to pair up with potential sponsors, and I wasn't concerned about other Sisters being on their own for the day. Kade agreed to go with us, as Flannery requested, but he said he'd stay away until then so he wouldn't "exacerbate Flannery's romantic inclinations" toward him. He could definitely sound like a lawyer when he put his mind to it.

Desmond was the only one who balked. After I told him Thursday night that Flannery might be going home to stay, he shut himself up in his room to continue the pouting he'd already been doing for days, and he wouldn't say a word on the way to school Friday morning. I could feel the resentment seething through my back as we rode, even though he was going to great lengths to keep from touching me all the way there. When I pulled the Classic up to the front of the school, I could almost hear Kade telling me to just let him be, but the mother voice in my head was louder.

"Jacket," I said like I always did when I dropped him off.

"I ain't even wearin' it."

I had to take off my helmet and do a double take to realize what I hadn't before. It was the first time he hadn't put it on, or tried to get into the building with it *still* on, since Chief gave it to him.

"How come?"

He shrugged.

"You want to try that again?" I said.

"'Cause I guess it don't matter what your last name is on the paper or anyplace else. If you ain't born into it, then you ain't really family."

I kicked the stand into place and swung my leg over the bike, just in time to curl my fingers around the retreating back of the denim jacket he *was* wearing.

"Imma be late," he said, still facing away from me.

"I'll go in with you and tell them you woke up sick this morning," I said, "because you *are* sick, in the *head*, to say something like that about me."

He didn't try to pull away. That was my only clue that he actually did want me to argue with him.

"This is about Flannery, isn't it?"

I took his silence as a yes.

"I can't make her stay here, Des."

"You made *me*."

"You want to rethink that statement?"

Desmond wheeled on me.

"If you let her stay home with her mama like she was, it's gonna go right back to what she was runnin' from—now I *know* that thing."

I couldn't deny it. If I didn't already feel that in my very soul, the wisdom in my son's eyes would have convinced me.

Resisting the urge to fold him against me, I said, "I promise you, Des, if I get even the smallest Nudge that it's dangerous to leave her with her mother, I will find a way to bring her back. I promise you."

He swallowed hard. "I know Flannery don't feel the same way 'bout me as she do 'bout Cappuccino, and I been doin' a lot of thinkin' and prayin' on that."

That would account for the pouting. I felt a twinge of guilt for giving him less credit than that.

"Did you come to any conclusions?" I said.

"I don't know 'bout no conclusions, now." The Desmond light flickered faintly in his eyes. "But I'm feelin' like she don't need no more boyfriends. She had plenty that didn't love her." He put up a hand, lest I should misunderstand. "I ain't talkin' 'bout Cappuccino. He love her in a different way, but he way outta her age group."

"Uh-huh," I said.

"What she need is a brother, and that's what I am." To my surprise I saw a thin sheen of tears. "But if she go back to a mama that ain't gonna protect her—"

I blinked against my own sheen. "I have to take her back to her mom, Des. That's the law. But the same law says that if I see any signs that she isn't safe, I don't have to leave her there."

"What if her mama won't let you bring her back?" he said.

I was going to have to work on my poker face.

Or not. Because a soft Nudge made me open my mouth and let out the words I didn't think of.

"Then Kade and I will try to convince her mom to come back with us so we can protect both of them until Flannery's pimp goes to jail."

Desmond didn't look at all surprised. He just nodded his won-derful fuzzy head sagely. And then he knocked at the side of it with the heel of his hand.

"What was that for?" I said.

"For not knowin' you and God woulda had this all figured out."

"Yeah, well, before you really start beating yourself up, I didn't know God and I had it all figured out until I said it."

He nodded again. "That happen to me sometime too."

"Yeah?"

"Like yesterday when I seen that Roy dude with the Mosquito in the office. He was flashin' them teeth at her and she was all turnin' pink, and when he left I told her she better not be gettin' mixed up with him 'cause he bad news."

"Desmond, you can't be telling adults who to hang out with, especially not *that* adult."

His voice went up into dogs-only range. "I was jus' tryin' to show her I don't hate her like she hates me."

"Do I dare ask what she said?"

He shrugged. "She tol' me I better mind my own business."

For once I agreed with her, but to Desmond I said, "I think the best way to show the … Coach Iseley you don't hate her is to avoid her. I think she'll really appreciate that."

The first bell saved me from the argument already forming on his lips.

"Go," I said. "Oh, and Des."

"Yeah, Big Al?"

"Flannery couldn't ask for a better brother."

"That's what I'm thinkin'," he said, and loped on up the steps, once again like the outrageous boy I loved more than life itself.

With our meeting with Brenda not being until Sunday, I had two more days to keep Flannery off the radar. I was trying to figure that out during my quiet time on the side porch later that morning when I got a call from Jasmine.

"Miss Angel," she said. I could practically hear her chin quivering. "I thought you oughta know that Sherry, she didn't come home last night."

"She might've stayed with her dad. Did you call the hospital?"

Jasmine sniffed. "They don't tell nobody nothin'."

I didn't know whether that was a yes or a What's the point in even trying? so I told her I would look into it.

That, of course, meant finding a place for Flannery in the meantime. I was more comfortable taking her to Second Chances now that Mercedes had stopped referring to her as "that child." Flannery was good with that too, once I got her up and vertical. She was truly a teenager, nocturnal and all but chemically allergic to morning. I bought her a hot chocolate at Sacred Grounds, deposited her upstairs with the Sisters and the potentially cool clothes, and took off for the hospital.

I hadn't had much chance to even think about Sherry since the day of the break-in at C.A.R.S. Hank was spending time with her when she could, and so were Bonner and India. I had to wonder now as I parked the bike and found my way to Maharry's floor

whether she would be all that happy to see me if she *was* there. Our
last conversation hadn't ended well.

I found her in the room Maharry had been moved to from
ICU. She was asleep in a stiff-looking reclining chair, and he was
sitting in front of a gelatinous breakfast I didn't blame him for not
eating. He nearly knocked the oxygen tube from his nose as he put
his finger to his lips.

"This is the first time she's slept since it happened," he said.

His attempt at a whisper was loud enough to wake her with
the nightmares still in her eyes. It seemed to take her a full five
seconds to realize who I was. I was relieved that she didn't bolt out
of the room, but, then, she looked too exhausted to even sit up in
the chair.

"Just stay there, Sher," I said. "What can I get you?"

She shook her head, but her hair didn't move. It was stuck to
her scalp in greasy strips. Sleep wasn't the only thing she hadn't done
since Wednesday. I could only imagine what the breath situation
must be, so I poured her a glass of water and put it in her hand.

"Glad you came by," Maharry said.

"Me, too. You don't look like a man who had a heart attack
two days ago."

He dismissed that with a hand still attached to a tube that
snaked its way out of a bottle hanging above. "It was just the shock.
I'm over it now."

"No you're not, Daddy," Sherry said.

"Am too. Tell her the good news."

I looked at Sherry, who was digging crust from her eyes with
her fingers. "You tell her."

"Somebody tell me," I said. "I want to know who's responsible for you looking like you just won the lottery."

It was true. Maharry's color was better than I'd seen it since, well, since I'd known him, and although his hands still shook the way they always did, less anxiety seemed to be running under his skin.

"Your HOGs are buying C.A.R.S.," he said.

My hand stopped halfway to the Kleenex box I was going to toss to Sherry. "I'm sorry ... what?"

"Three of 'em come in here last night," Maharry said. "What were their names, Sherry Lynn?"

She licked at lips that had to be pretty much the consistency of sand. "Stan the Man, or whatever it is Desmond calls him. Ulysses. And that guy with the weird accent."

"Rex. He's French."

"I don't care what he is as long as he's telling me the truth," Maharry said. "They want to buy me out and open a used motor-cycle shop."

Knowing those guys as I did, I didn't even have to wonder if this was the real deal. I felt my hanging-open mouth move into a smile. "Are you serious? Really?"

"That's what they said." In spite of her obvious fatigue, Sherry did seem a thin layer lighter in spirit.

"You have to feel like the weight of the world has been taken off your shoulders, Maharry," I said.

"Almost." He squinted his eyes down further than I thought possible behind the thick glasses, which were, for once, sparkling clean. That alone had to make him feel better. "Only thing that'll set everything right is if that Zelda woman will admit she let somebody take those keys and make copies." He jabbed the tube-laden hand at me. "I told you she was smart."

I closed my eyes but it didn't help. My hackles still stood up.

"Why would she do that?" I said. "The cash was still there, and so was the gun, so it wasn't a robbery."

"She just did it to get back at me for fussin' at her so much."

"That makes no sense. Zelda has been fussed at all her life. I don't think—"

"She knew that I knew she was tryin' to take over. I told you that, too."

I looked at Sherry, but she avoided my eyes and stomped into the bathroom and shut the door.

"When I went to lock up Tuesday night"—Maharry's voice cracked like the dried-out lines on his face—"the keys were *not* exactly where they were when I put them there last. I am *always* careful about that."

"That doesn't mean Zelda took them out and had copies made and brought them back. How could she do that, Maharry? You said yourself you watched her like a hawk."

"I know what I know!" he said, and then collapsed into a fit of convulsive coughing that brought Sherry out of the bathroom and a nurse in from the hallway. She gave Sherry a deep, *V*-between-the-eyebrows frown as she pushed me out of the way and went to her patient.

"I told you not to let him get upset," she said to Sherry. "You two need to leave until I get him settled down."

I had to agree. Even in the midst of choking on his own mucous, Maharry was still stabbing his hand at me.

"Come on, Sher," I said. "I'll buy you breakfast."

She let me usher her down to the cafeteria and nodded at my attempt to apologize for setting her dad off. But by the time I sat her down to a less-than-appetizing plate of scrambled eggs and turkey sausage, she was awake enough to drive the wedge between us again.

"If you came here to talk about you know-what again, Miss Angel, I'm not interested."

"Okay," I lied. "You want to hear what we learned about Flannery last night?"

Her nod was halfhearted, but I filled her in anyway. Gradually she stopped poking the fork into the sausage as if it threatened to attack her first. I felt only a little guilty about lulling her into a false sense of we're-only-going-to-talk-about-safe-topics.

"So basically," I said, "we know she was forced to work in Jacksonville for a pimp named Elgin." Something occurred to me that hadn't before. "You ever hear of him when you were in the life?"

For the first time since the one-sided conversation started, her eyes tracked as if she were actually seeing me.

"No," she said. "But I've heard that name recently, only not in connection with that." She seemed genuinely puzzled. And as long as we were being honest …

"Let's talk for just a minute about you not letting the Sisters know you were going to spend the night here again."

At once the fork poked at the rubbery eggs, and the eyes all but glazed over. "I just assumed they'd know."

"Better not to assume," I said. "I'll call Jasmine for you. I think she'll understand."

Sherry nodded, but I wasn't sure she cared whether Jasmine understood or not. I tried to keep my voice out of what-the-devil-is-the-matter-with-you range.

"Your dad seems to be doing so well. Do you really need to stay with him 24-7? You look like you could use some real sleep."

"I just don't want to bring anything else down on my Sisters," she said, egg in her cheek. "You saw those drawings on the wall. Whoever did that is after *me*."

"We were all up there," I said. "Why would you think it was specifically an attack on you?"

"They could have done it anywhere. But they did it at C.A.R.S."

She pushed the plate away and covered her mouth with the napkin. I suspected most of the eggs were coming back out. She couldn't sleep. Couldn't take care of her basic hygiene. Couldn't eat. She was suffering from a classic case of fear I could feel in my own marrow.

"Sherry," I said, "what did you wash off of the drawing of you before I made you stop?"

"I don't remember."

"I saw the eye patch."

"Yeah."

"Sultan has an eye patch now."

The look she gave me was brutal. "I told you I'm not interested in talking about him."

"Neither am I. So let's consider who else might be behind it. Who besides you and Zelda had access to those keys?"

Sherry set her jaw. "No one."

"No customers could have gotten to them?"

She started to shake her head, but she stopped and looked at me, eyes following again. "They might have. Some people do kind of hang out when Daddy's working on their car. OSHA would fine us for that if they knew, but he likes the company. He says it's like the good old days."

"Anybody recently?"

"I'll have to think about it. I'll go through the files …"

"What?" I said.

She put both hands behind her and leaned back into the chair. Something had stirred her to go back into hiding. "For a minute I forgot," she said.

"Forgot what?"

"That maybe I won't be around that much longer."

"I'm sorry?"

"As soon as the sale of the shop goes through, I'm going to get Daddy settled someplace comfortable and then I'm going to go … somewhere else." She set her jaw again. "Don't you think I'm ready to go out on my own soon?"

"That would be your choice." I ran a finger around the top of my coffee cup to disguise the fact that I had no idea what to do with this, and I was getting no God-help. "Any thoughts on where you'd go?"

"Far away."

"Are you sure you want to go far away right out of the gate, Sher?"

"I can't do this anymore, Miss Angel!"

The blurt and the tears and the sheer panic in her eyes came so out of nowhere I didn't have a chance to put a thought together before she jerked forward in the chair and pulled my wrists so that I had to come across the table.

"You've been trying to get this out of me for a long time," she said, "so before I go I'm going to tell you."

"Sherry—"

"I saw them taking his body away."

"Sultan's," I whispered.

"After he got shot and you got away, they came out of nowhere and—"

"They?"

"I couldn't see. Just his people. I heard somebody say he was still alive."

"Did they know you were there?"

"I don't think so. I was hiding."

Memories flipped through my head like old Rolodex cards. Sherry telling me to leave it alone. Sherry fighting the proof that Sultan wasn't dead. Sherry now believing that the attack on C.A.R.S. was about her.

This revelation wasn't a surprise. The secrecy of it was.

"What kept you from telling me about this when it happened?" I said.

"Because I didn't think he'd live. I never thought he'd come back."

"But when he did—"

"What difference did it make then?"

We were hissing back and forth across the table, but whatever the passersby couldn't hear they could certainly see. A maintenance guy mopped in slo-mo under the next table, and a bag-eyed new father looked up more than just curiously from his text message.

"Let's go someplace a little more private," I whispered.

"No," Sherry said, "I'm done."

She scraped the chair back so hard it fell against the one behind it, startling two women in scrubs to their feet. But I didn't go after Sherry as she stumbled across the cafeteria and disappeared into the elevator. I just stitched my way among the people trying not to stare at me, bussed Sherry's tray, and headed for the exit. Pain clutched at my throat.

"Ms. Chamberlain?" a voice behind me said.

I didn't recognize it, and I would have pretended not to hear it, but it was persistent. Again, "Ms. Chamberlain, right?"

I found myself looking into a face that was unfamiliar only for that moment it takes to recognize someone you've met once, in the dark.

"Yates Chattingham," he said, offering his hand.

"Right. The new pastor."

I shook his hand only because I didn't have the energy not to. I also didn't have the energy to make small talk, so I just stood there. He seemed unruffled by that.

"I'd like you to meet my wife. Christine, *this* is Allison Chamberlain."

The woman who took my hand looked as if she already knew me. I was sure I'd never seen her before, and I was struck now by the fact that she would be fairly homely if she didn't know how to make the best of what she had. She obviously refused to be plain.

She let go of my hand just at the moment I was about to withdraw it. "Yates told me he met you the other night. You made quite the impression."

I didn't have to recall my exact words to know I'd pretty much let him have it between the eyes.

"I'm glad we saw you here," he said.

I waited for a toothy smile, maybe a pastoral invitation to join them for coffee, but he said instead, "We won't keep you, but I do want to talk to you, soon, about what's going on on that corner."

"We can do that, but only if you're ready to get some of it on you."

He moved his fingers as if he were beckoning me forward. "Talk to me about that."

"I'm not interested in chatting about the problem unless you really intend to get in there. You can't do this from a distance."

"That would be hard since it's right in my yard."

There was nothing condescending about the statement, but I was already fired up from—everything.

"You have to get to know those kids and let them get to you." I flattened my hand to my chest. "In here."

"Well," his pretty-homely wife said. "Yates told me you were passionate."

He nodded toward the exit I'd been going toward. "I know you need to get out of here, so if you want, you could come out tonight and join us for drinks and pizza—"

"I don't think so—"

"At the Hot Spot," Christine said. "I did it last night and the boys all took off and the girls weren't that happy with me, but they ate, and I told them I'd be back tonight."

"We have a lot in common with you. More than we have with the congregation, unfortunately." Yates gave the exit another nod. "If we don't see you tonight we'll connect another time."

I almost had no choice but to turn around and go. I did so feeling like the schoolyard bully whose target just brought her a batch of cookies.

I put that encounter in my Things To Sort Out Later pile and picked up Flannery at Second Chances, where a new batch of one-of-a-kind skirts and dresses hung over the balcony, tempting the shoppers below. She didn't seem that unwilling to go to Ms. Willa's for tutoring while I took care of some things. She was, in fact, out the door ahead of me, but Ophelia caught me by the arm before I could follow.

"Miss Angel," she said in that soft velvet voice that could charm a snake and probably had a time or two. "We're worried about Zelda."

"I'm sure she's still pretty shaken up." I probably would be too if fifteen other things hadn't happened since I'd had my portrait done in blood on a wall.

"She just can't get past Sherry's father thinking she gave somebody those keys," Ophelia said.

"Zelda told you about that?"

"She can hardly talk about anything else. We said she needed to put that behind her, but she's just having a hard time. Could you …?"

"I'll talk to her. Y'all just keep praying with her and supporting her, okay?"

Ophelia nodded but her warm hand stayed on my arm. "She needs more than us, Miss Angel."

She wasn't talking about God. She was talking about me. I pushed aside the guilt that was going to get me nowhere and

hugged her neck and promised to see that Zelda got all the attention she needed. Before I reached Flannery at the bottom of the
steps, I texted Liz and asked her if she'd see to Zelda until I could
talk to her.

I still expected Flannery to give me just a little bit of grief about
Ms. Willa and penmanship, but as we threaded our way through
the shoppers in the Heritage Walk Mall, the shortcut to where I'd
parked, her face was pensive. When we reached the Harley, she
hugged the helmet to her chest instead of putting it on.

"Something you want to say?" I said.

"Something I want to ask."

If it was Kade's phone number she wanted, I was ready.

"Do you think you could find out what's happening with
Tango?"

How many times in one day did I have to be called on selling
people short?

"I can try," I said. "It might be hard, not knowing her real name."

She lifted that chin. "I was telling the truth when I said I didn't
know."

"I believe you. I'll see what I can do."

"Then I believe you, too."

I tried not to stare as she strapped on the helmet and climbed
onto the bike.

I didn't go to the Hot Spot that night because I wanted to stay near
Flannery and give Desmond some much-needed attention. Chief

and I took them to the Santa Maria so they could feed pita bread to the catfish, where we all pretended we were a normal family until it wore us out.

Chief didn't stay when we got back because he was taking Desmond home with him. We made arrangements to meet up at the F. A. Café Sunday afternoon after the HOG ride.

That was fine because I needed to get my head straight for the next day. I did call Liz to thank her for faxing the signature form to Kade's office, just in case Brenda did decide to turn Flannery over to me.

"I got your text message," Liz said. "I've been spending as much time with Zelda as I can, but it's not as much as she needs."

"I hear that," I said.

"But I did ask Bonner to fill in some and he said he would. Is he the best *man*, or what?"

"He's pretty good."

There was a tiny silence. "I want that for you, Allison."

"Hey listen." I switched the phone to the other ear. "Would you mind keeping your eyes open for another exploited teenager? She goes by the name Tango. Flannery knows her and she's worried about her."

"Do you have anything more than that?"

"No. But she's here in town, at least she was Wednesday night, down at the ..."

"At the what?"

"Just hanging out with some kids. Let me know if you see her come through the system, will you?"

"Oh, Allison, you have the biggest heart."

"Right back at ya, babe," I said before I hung up. I wasn't feeling so big-hearted. Mine didn't seem nearly large enough to hold all God was asking it to hold.

I couldn't dwell on that at the moment, so it went into some pile while I took a chamomile tea to the red chair and considered the two things that had come to me during my conversation with Liz.

One, if Tango went back to the Hot Spot, she might meet up with Christine Chattingham. I hesitated to call the pastor's wife, though. It sounded like they were on the same page I was, or at least somewhere in the same chapter, but I needed to be sure. What were they planning to do if they gained the kids' trust? Turn them over to the system with all good intentions? Maybe I should call the Reverend Yates C. for a talk.

In my spare time.

The other was more a longing than a thought. I was missing Nick Kent. Before Detective Kylie called him on the carpet, I could have asked Nick to keep an eye out for Tango too, and bring her to me instead of taking her in. But I refused to pull him in any deeper. I was trusting Kylie less by the minute.

It wasn't a good thought to fall asleep on.

I tried again early Saturday to pray and shape some thoughts for our meeting with Brenda Donohue, but I no sooner got settled at the bistro table with a cup of coffee and an almost-centered soul when my phone dinged with a text from Kade. MEET ME AT GEORGIE'S AT TEN?

I texted back YES. Kade must be thinking about tomorrow too. It would be good to process it with him.

Flannery was up early, nine being early for her, and she seemed on edge. Not that I could blame her.

"I have to go to a quick meeting," I said. I left out the Kade part. "You want to stay here or—"

"No," she said.

"Then where—"

"I'll go to Ms. Willa's."

She could have given me a bigger surprise, but I wasn't sure how. Unless it was her saying as we were about to pull into the alley behind Ms. Willa's place, "Just drop me off in front of her house."

"I'll wait for Maria to let you in," I said.

"You don't have to. Ms. Willa gave me a key."

I turned onto Cuna and let the engine idle at the curb. "How do you rate? Ms. Willa never gave me a key."

"She says I need options. A woman should always have options."

"Oh," I said, and watched the little redhead bounce up to Ms. Willa's porch and let herself in. She looked so tiny, like a small child going to see grandma.

It grabbed at me.

Kade was already at Georgie's when I arrived. Nobody else was there for breakfast, which made Neil Sedaka seem even louder than usual as he informed us that breaking up was hard to do.

"What is with you and this place?" I said as I slipped into a booth across from him.

"Kind of reminds me of back home," he said. "It's too new to be authentic though."

The red-and-white checked floors and the metal edged tables and the neon tube lighting did seem to be trying a little too hard. The only thing missing in the booth itself was tuck-and-roll and a miniature jukebox.

Kade, however, was clearly not there to talk about the decor. He hadn't touched the coffee in front of him, and his face was ruddy with obvious excitement. It made his eyes seem even bluer. I forced myself not to compare them to Troy's.

"You need to know something," he said.

"I feel like I know more than I can handle already."

"No, this'll make your day."

I nodded at the college kid who put a cup of coffee in front of me and left. Kade produced a sheet of paper from a folder on his seat and turned it face down between us.

"Before I show it to you, you have to promise not to breathe a word of this to anybody. You won't have to keep it to yourself for long, because I'm sure it'll be announced publicly soon, but until then—"

"What on earth are you talking about?"

"I got an email this morning." He turned the sheet over. "You can read it, but the upshot is: Troy Irwin is being removed as CEO of Chamberlain Enterprises."

I must have blinked five times before I got anything out. And even at that, I could only say, "Are you sure?"

Kade tapped the email I still hadn't looked at. "I've been working pro bono as a legal consultant for a group of minority stock holders who are watching their investments dwindle because of the bad press Troy got when he was being questioned by the cops last spring."

"What bad press?" I said. "It barely made the news."

"It was enough to make some people nervous."

"I don't get it. If the value of the stocks was going down, wasn't Troy losing money too?"

"He has so many shares it doesn't hurt him that much. Besides, that's not the only way Troy Irwin was making money, or the only reason these people want him out of there." Kade was all but rubbing his hands together. "I've suspected there was more going on than that, and I finally found somebody on the inside at CE who would work with me."

By now my body was starting to go cold, one extremity at a time. "Work with you how?"

He flattened his hands on the table. "It was all perfectly legal."

"I didn't say—"

"And ethical. Once we were able to prove he wasn't carrying out his fiduciary responsibilities—"

"In English, Kade."

"We're talking mismanagement of funds. Embezzling, basically."

"Embezzling? Troy?" All I could seem to do for body language was shake my head, over and over. "Why did he need to make money illegally? He's a multimillionaire already."

"You know as well as I do it wasn't about money. It was about proving he could do whatever he wanted to whomever he wanted to do it—including his own stockholders. And they're done with it."

"So you've helped them and now Troy's getting fired."

"Essentially, yes. Like I said, the official announcement hasn't been made yet." Kade folded his arms. "He's so arrogant he probably doesn't even see it coming."

"I think he does."

Kade unfolded. "Why do you say that?"

"Chief and I were at Columbia one night and I saw Troy come out of a private dinner meeting raging like a bull. He was yelling something like, 'They can't do it.' Or 'They can't prove it.' I think he saw it coming, Kade, but he was sure he could stop it."

"You could tell all that just from watching him?"

"I wish. No, we had a bit of a confrontation."

He watched me for a moment, until something dawned in his eyes. "That started the rift with Chief."

"Yeah, you could say that."

"Then this is double good news for you."

"I'm not so sure about that. You've seen how ruthless he is. He already blames us for his trouble with the police. He puts total responsibility for his failure with the West King project on me. It doesn't matter that he's the cause of every one of his own issues. He has always and will always punish other people for his unconscionable ... stuff."

"Then we'll take precautions."

"How can we take precautions when there is no telling what he'll stoop to? Especially now that he's losing power. That means he won't be able to control the mayor or his attorneys or the DA or whoever else's strings he's been pulling for the last ten years."

For the first time, the victory gleam dimmed a few watts in Kade's eyes. "You're scared, aren't you?"

"I am terrified, and you should be too." I drew in my shoulders. "I'm glad you told me, and I'm sorry to take the wind out of your sails. I really am proud of you for doing this the right way. I'm sure Chief is too."

Kade looked down at the table. "Chief doesn't know about it. And ... I'm asking you not to tell him until the official announcement is made."

"Why?"

"I've done this totally without involving Chief. That's why I'm not going to represent these people in court if it comes to that. I've been really careful not to use the office to pursue this, just to keep Chief completely in the clear. Just in case Troy does find out it was me."

"I don't know if I can do that," I said. "If I keep something from Chief that involves Troy, and he finds out about it, which he will because he always does, that could be the final death blow to our relationship."

"Worse than having his name dragged through the mud Irwin's going to sling over this?"

I closed my eyes for a few seconds. Nothing came. At least nothing more than I already knew, which was that not telling Chief was a huge mistake.

"Hey," Kade said.

I opened my eyes.

"It will probably hit the papers Monday morning. You aren't even going to see Chief until late Sunday. Later, if he finds out you already knew, I'll go to bat for you and explain to him that we were trying to protect him, which is the absolute truth."

He reached over and teased at my arm until I pulled out a hand. He squeezed it, hard, and looked straight into me. "I've got your back."

This time all I could do was nod.

But that didn't mean I wasn't disturbed down to the very core of myself as I drove the Classic around the perimeter of the historic district and over the newly renovated Bridge of Lions out to Anastasia Island. The Harley grumbled, tough and reassuring under me. The St. Augustine lighthouse stood tall and straight and sure the way it had for so many years and so many wars and more storms than both put together. When I let the bridge lift me back into the noonday traffic and the fall tourists and the tour carriages waiting hopefully at the bayfront, I could see the great fort, the Castillo de San Marcos, keeping watch as it had done since the seventeenth century. I needed to see things that weren't going to be something else the next time I blinked.

God was still there too. Murmuring right along with the engine's constant, protective growl. Telling me the same thing, again and again. *Go another mile.*

I did. Until Hank's voice seemed to join God's. *It's your enemies Jesus is referring to when he says to go another mile.*

I pulled the bike off the road in front of the entrance to the Fountain of Youth.

"You want me to go there, I'll go there," I said out loud. The engine idled over my voice, keeping me from looking too crazy as I talked to myself. "Troy's place is more than a mile from here, but I'll go—"

My phone vibrated in my pocket, and for a second I thought maybe I *was* nuts. But it wasn't God. It was Flannery, and I knew from her shallow, frightened breathing that she was near panic.

"It's Ms. Willa," she said. "She's really, really sick."

I turned off the engine. "What does that mean, Flannery?"

"She keeps passing out and coming back. She's almost blue, too. This is serious."

"Okay, I want you to call 911. I'll be right there."

"911," she said.

"No hospital," I heard a thready voice cry in the background.

"As long as she can still give orders, she's not dying," I said. "Call no matter what she says. I'm on my way."

"I'm calling, Ms. Willa," I heard Flannery say.

By the time I got there exactly seven minutes later, the paramedics were already knocking on the front door. By the time I got up the steps they were letting themselves in as Flannery called out, "It's unlocked."

She and Ms. Willa were both on the couch and for the life of me I couldn't see how Flannery had managed it. Ms. Willa was propped against her, face the exact shade of blue as her hair, breathing raggedly as Flannery stroked her arms.

"I don't need these people," the old lady said.

"You promised me, Ms. Willa."

To my amazement Ms. Willa closed her mouth, and her eyes, and sank further into Flannery. The longing in the air was palpable. I didn't even try to sort out whose was whose as I watched the paramedics go to work.

CHAPTER THIRTEEN

For the second time in four days I helped check an elderly friend into the hospital. It made me want to order Owen to go immediately to the clinic and have a complete physical. That wouldn't have done a whole lot of good; he refused to leave Ms. Willa's side, even when more than one nurse made it abundantly clear that he was in the way.

"We should have made her go to the hospital days ago," he said to me when one particularly militant nurse forced him to wait in the hall.

"Owen, you know Ms. Willa," I said. "There is no making her do anything."

"That little redhaired girl did."

I looked over at Flannery, who was sitting on a bench against the wall repeatedly pulling her hair onto the top of her head and letting it fall back to her shoulders. All I'd been able to get out of her was that she just talked to Ms. Willa the way she did the people at the nursing home. I wondered if her attachment to the old lady had something to do with a grandparent she'd visited there, but I didn't push it. With what she had staring her down tomorrow, and now this, there were probably enough memories to tangle with right now.

Finally a doctor emerged and gave us the news: Ms. Willa had had an attack of angina and was resting comfortably. They would be discussing her treatment plan, but in the meantime her visitors were to be limited. I was able to talk Flannery into going home, but Owen almost literally dug his heels into the linoleum. He promised to keep us posted.

"Who are they?" Flannery said as we walked toward the elevator.

"I'm sorry?" I said.

"Who are the they that doctor is going to discuss her treatment plan with? Does Ms. Willa have any family?"

"Good question," I said.

I gazed at Flannery's back as she preceded me into the elevator. That sealed it: there was way more to this little woman than any of us thought. Except maybe Ms. Willa herself.

"Does she have any kids?" she said.

"No. And she's a widow."

Flannery pushed the button for the lobby. "Then who's going to help her make decisions about her health care?"

It was hard for me not to demand to know where she learned to talk like a patient advocate.

"I doubt she's given anybody medical power of attorney," I said.

"What about a living will?"

"It does sound like something Ms. Willa would have, doesn't it?" I said. "So she can stay in charge."

"Let's just hope so," Flannery said.

Okay, someday I was going to get to the bottom of that.

All the way home I thought about a hot bath and a steaming cup of chamomile, but Bonner was there on the side porch when we arrived. Zelda was with him. Judging from the size of her eyes as she rocked the swing with a vengeance, they hadn't just dropped by for a chat.

I sent Flannery inside and managed to catch the swing and hop on to join Zelda. Bonner sat across from us in one of the Adirondacks, hands pressed between his knees. He had so many great skills, but dealing with hysterical women wasn't one of them.

"What's up?" I said to Zelda.

"You tell her, Mr. B. I'm too upset. It'll all come out wrong."

I looked at Bonner.

"Zelda and I talked last night, and we decided that the best thing for her to do was go to the hospital and discuss the key situation with Maharry, face-to-face." I opened my mouth, but he stilled me with his hand. "I said I'd take her and stay there with her."

"So what happened?" I addressed that to Zelda, but she still pointed at Bonner.

"We never had a chance to talk about him accusing Zelda because he was too worked up about Sherry."

"He wasn't just worked up! He was fixin' to lose it right there in that bed. Two nurses had to come in and get him calmed down, and they told us we had to leave."

For someone who was too upset to talk, Zelda was doing rather well.

"That one nurse, she kep' sayin' everybody that come in there got him all coughin' and not bein' able to breathe."

"Maharry's blood pressure isn't their only concern," Bonner said. "From what I gathered, he has some lung damage, which is why they're keeping him."

Zelda planted her feet so that the swing came to a jerky halt. "That ain't what I'm upset about, Miss Angel. It's Sherry."

"Wasn't she there?"

"Maharry said she ain't been there since the day *you* was there. She come up from talkin' to you and said she need to go home and sleep, and she ain't been to see him again."

I squinted back to the day before. "When I tried to call her yesterday at Sacrament One, Jasmine told me Sherry was still staying at the hospital."

"That's what she *told* Jasmine, but that ain't what she did." Zelda grabbed my forearm with both hands, so hard I was sure she was leaving her fingerprints in my skin. "You think somethin' bad happen to her, Miss Angel? She wouldn't just run off and leave her daddy. Or us. Now, I know that."

Her head bobbed in an attempt to get me to nod too, but I couldn't. Yet I couldn't tell her what Sherry had said to me either, not yet.

"So it's been, what, twenty-four hours?" I said to Bonner.

"Yes. You think we should file a missing-persons report? I'm not sure what the time is on that for an adult."

"Why don't we check?" I said. "Zelda, you need to stay hydrated. There are drinks in the fridge."

She went dutifully into the kitchen, as if she were glad someone was telling her how to be in this situation. I waited until she shut the door behind her to cross to Bonner and sit in the other chair.

"I'm not sure she's so much missing as AWOL," I said, and told him about part of my conversation with Sherry. I left out her confession about Sultan.

"She picked a strange time to decide to go off on her own with her dad sick like this," Bonner said.

"True. She told me she was going to wait until the sale of the shop was final and she got Maharry settled."

"So we're back to she's missing."

"I think I upset her."

"Enough to make her leave town?" Bonner pulled his glasses down his nose and looked at me over the top of them. "I'm not buying that."

I was tempted to tell him the whole story, but I wasn't sure that what she told me about Sultan was the reason for her disappearance. She certainly didn't think I would tell Detective Kylie that she had seen Sultan's body being carried off. Why would I? We'd all established the fact that he was still alive.

A deep sigh welled up without my permission. Whatever she was thinking, I might have stopped this if I had gone after her.

"I brought y'all some sweet tea," Zelda said from the doorway.

She was visibly calmer; at least she was able to carry three glasses without jittering the ice cubes out of them. But once the drinks were served, her eyes went right back to begging me for reassurance.

"We're going to try to find Sherry," I said. "But just so you don't worry about this too much, she did tell me that she was thinking about going on her own. She probably didn't know they found lung issues in Maharry, or she wouldn't have left. He's coming into some money, and she most likely thought he'd be okay."

It was the truth. It just wasn't the whole truth. And judging from Zelda's "Mmmm-mm," I knew she knew it.

If I hadn't been looking right at her, I would have thought that came from Mercedes herself.

I felt like Gumby Sunday morning, stretched between Ms. Willa and Sherry and Zelda and Maharry as I got ready for the drive to Hastings with Flannery and Kade. As usual, the family snapped me back into shape.

Hank said she'd go to Sacrament One and talk to all the Sisters about Sherry. Bonner and Liz promised to keep Zelda with them for the day. I couldn't have torn Owen away from Ms. Willa, and India said she'd go by the hospital too, and take Ophelia with her. Their love surged through me, their love and their willingness to go the extra mile.

Especially when God kept asking us to keep going.

The drive to Hastings was mercifully short. We had only twenty minutes with Flannery in the backseat of Kade's tiny Mazda, chattering nonstop all the way down route 207 about everything from how weird it was that cranes hung out with cows to why anybody would name a place in Florida Vermont Heights. As soon as we passed the wide space in the road called Spuds—now *there* was a name she thought was cool—I got her to talk about just exactly where it was we were going once we got to Hastings.

"Turn left after you pass the Potato Building," she said.

Kade snickered. "They have a building for potatoes?"

Flannery automatically went into flirt mode. "What's wrong with you, Kade? You didn't know Hastings is the Potato Capital of Florida?"

"I'm a loser," he said.

Quite the contrary. He was a complete winner for keeping the poor kid from chattering herself right out of her skin. We got the rest of the directions without having to chase her down any more verbal trails.

We probably could have found Brenda Donohue's house simply by knocking on every door in the town. There were only about
two hundred homes in the whole place, though the one Flannery
had us stop at was a step up from the rundown dwellings surround-
ing it.

It was a simple rancher with a carport. The white siding was
clean, and the black shutters and trim were freshly painted. Brenda's
azalea bushes would have met Owen's approval, and the wreath of
autumn leaves on the door would have met India's. Even the garbage
cans and recycle bins looked as if they were hosed off on a regular
basis. I was actually a little surprised by the neat, middle-class look
of the place. Between her understanding of fashion and the gymnastic lessons, I'd expected more from Flannery's background.

What didn't strike me until the three of us were walking up the
driveway was that this didn't look like a house someone was about
to abandon. Before I could warn Flannery that maybe Mama wasn't
totally going for the let's-run-away-together plan, the front door flew
open and a small woman with fading red hair skittered squirrel-like
down the steps and ran toward us. She was the spitting image of
Flannery. Right down to the bruised, swollen eye.

Until then, Flannery was running ahead of Kade and me, arms
spread. At about the same moment that black eye registered with me,
Flannery stopped and screamed, "You lied to me! He's here!"

She turned so hard she left a divot in the lawn. Only because
I was right behind her by then was I able to grab her and flatten
her against me. Otherwise, I knew she'd have run all the way to St.
Augustine. Or further.

She continued to scream, "I'm not staying here! I'm *not!*"

I didn't bother to introduce myself to the woman who stood there with what was left of her face twisted in anguish.

"Ms. Donohue," I said, "there has obviously been abuse here. This child is terrified—"

Terrified and, apparently, enraged. Flannery got one elbow loose and jabbed me soundly in the gut, which gave her a chance to wriggle free and bolt. She had already put two other front yards behind her by the time Kade got to the Mazda and took off after her.

Brenda Donohue, on the other hand, had her remaining eye fixed on another vehicle, a red Mustang that squealed around the corner from the opposite direction and careened into the driveway. It spit out a large man with shoulders as big as Chief's. His whole physique could, in fact, have been Chief's if not for the paunch that spilled over his belt buckle as he stormed toward us.

Beside me, Brenda crossed her forearms over her chest and tucked her head. I knew in that moment that I had never seen true cowering before. Just as he got within grabbing distance I stepped in front of Brenda and pushed her two steps backward. I barely avoided a head-on with the man I knew was Elgin.

My mind raced straight to God. *Pleasepleasepleaseplease—*

He yelled, "Who are you?" Basically. I was amazed he could get as many expletives as he did into that three-word question.

"I'm here for Brenda," I said. "I took one look at her and called the police." It was a lie I knew I was already forgiven for. And for the next one. "They're on their way. If you did this to her, you might want to consider getting out of here in your Mustang."

The steady sarcasm was not in line with the shaking terror going on inside me. This man was far more menacing than the typical redneck wife-beater. His iron-gray eyes were as hard as fists, and his lower lip flattened over the upper one and held it like a vice. I'd seen a lot of hate in the last year and he personified it.

PleaseGodpleaseGodpleaseGod—

You've stood up to more professionally vicious men than this, Allison. Go ...

"Are you thinking of adding me to the list of assault charges, Elgin?" I said.

His arm lashed out and slammed me aside. From the ground I could see both of his hands already shaped to fit Brenda's neck.

"What did you tell her?" he screamed into her face.

"Nothing!"

"How else does she know my name, you—"

The profanity spewed upward as Elgin went down, buckling from the kick I delivered right behind his knees. I didn't have another move planned as I scrambled up, but Kade was suddenly there with his foot planted in the middle of Elgin's chest and his hand reaching under his jacket. I forced myself not to look around for Flannery and kept my eyes, and my prayers, on Kade. This wasn't going to be a fair fight. Kade might be scrappy, but he was no match for this behemoth, in either size or rage.

"I told him I called the police," I said.

"Great minds think alike," Kade said. "I did too. Looks like you got double trouble coming up, buddy."

Elgin shoved Kade's leg out of the way and got to his feet. Kade, hand still inside his jacket, didn't back down. If he was trying to make Elgin think he was carrying a gun, it seemed to be working.

"You better be off my property before I get back," Elgin said, though how I had no idea, because his lower lip was almost to his nostrils.

With that he stormed back to the Mustang and came just short of breaking all the windows as he slammed the door and peeled out of the driveway. All I could think as he burned rubber in the opposite direction from the way Flannery had run was *ThankyouGodthankyouGodthankyouGod.*

"Where is she?" I said to Kade.

"In the car. I parked it around the corner and a couple of blocks down. She promised she'd stay there."

I nodded and turned to Brenda. She was no longer in a fetal position, but she was clearly shutting down. Although she shook head to toe, her eye was guarded and her chin tilted upward in a way that was all too familiar to me.

"You shouldn't stay here, you and Flannery," I said. "You can both come back with us to St. Augustine, and we'll protect you until he's locked up."

"He'll find us."

"You don't understand, Brenda. We can—"

"No, you can't! No one can!"

This was just like my conversation with Flannery, and yet this woman was doing something her daughter hadn't. She was backing toward her front door with a determination in her eyes she must have had to scrape the bottom to find.

"You take her with you," Brenda said. "And don't bring her back here until I call you."

"Please," I said.

"That's the only way. Take her!"

"Okay." I took a step closer but she put up her hands. "I'll take her, but I'm going to need for you to sign the paperwork saying you give your permission for me to keep her with me."

I stopped, because her gaze had left me and gone to Kade, who was just closing his phone.

"Who did you call?" Her voice rose to a shriek. "Did you call the police? Really?"

She didn't give Kade a chance to answer. Stiff-arming us both, she backed to the steps and half-ran, half-crawled up them and into her house. I heard three deadbolts click into place, locking her away.

Kade smacked himself in the forehead. "I totally blew that."

"She wasn't going to sign anyway." I nodded at his phone. "Did you call the police?"

"No. I took her picture. Maybe the broken nose will get us probable cause for an arrest warrant for her old man if she does decide to press charges."

"Like that's going to happen," I said.

"Come on," he said. "We better get back to Flannery."

When we were almost to the corner I sneaked a glance at him. Despite the heat and the scene from *SmackDown*, he was impressively calm.

"You sure know how to bluff," I said. "Flashing your wallet like a cop the other night. Acting like you were packing heat today."

His eyes shifted away. "I *am* packing heat."

I skidded at the end of someone's driveway. "Are you *serious*?"

"I wasn't going to use it. I just thought it might make a good visual aid in case we got into trouble."

"I don't even know where to put this. You have a permit, right?"

"Yes, I have a permit. And Nick Kent helped me pick it out and spent some time with me at the range. It's a Glock, same as the kind he carries."

I shuddered. "I don't care what kind it is. I hate guns."

"So do I," he said. "The car's about two blocks down."

That gave me approximately two minutes to get back into Flannery mode and figure out what I could say to her. The few words I did come up with fled when Kade's Mazda came into view, and there was no silhouette of Flannery in the backseat.

"Kade, she's gone," I said.

"Nah. She's just doing what I told her to do."

"Which was?"

"Lay low."

Indeed, she was about as low as she could get behind the front seat with a beach towel over her head. The mixture of anger and disappointment and fear I could almost smell in the car was like a simmering bad stew.

Kade opened the rear door. "You okay?"

She gave him a deadpan look from the floor. "How could I possibly be okay?"

"All right—stupid question."

"I don't want to talk about this right now. Except to say one thing."

I stuck in a hand to help her get herself untangled and onto the seat. "Go ahead," I said.

"I knew I couldn't trust her," she said. "I can't trust anybody."

"Really? We're taking you home with us, Flan. We're not leaving you there."

"But what's going to happen now? Don't you have to turn me over to DCF?"

"Have you seen me do that so far?" I said.

Then I held my breath. It was the best I could do without totally lying to her. If she pushed this any further, she'd have me against the wall.

"Whatever," she said.

We rode all the way to the F. A. Café in silence, except for the occasional squeak of Kade's hands gripping the steering wheel. Fortunately they couldn't hear the tortured groans in my soul.

No one really knew why the funky little joint on Anastasia Island was called the F. A. Café. I was told it stood for First Attempt, since so many surfers made their initial try at the sport on the tame waves of St. Augustine Beach. The name didn't quite fit my situation when we joined the HOGs there. I was way beyond my first attempt to deal with Flannery. More like the fifteenth, and at that point I had no idea what my next one was going to be.

Still, if a person was feeling bummed, this was the place to come to. It was no bigger than my side porch and was dotted with brightly colored fish-shaped tables. There was just plain stuff attached to every vertical surface: old license plates, almost-funny signs, bumper stickers supporting a myriad of causes, some of them contradicting all the others. It was like the proprietors hung up anything anyone wanted them to, even in the restrooms. It was possible to learn The Redneck Ten Commandments while sitting on the john.

The HOGs were there, Rex, Ulysses, and Stan among them, and of course Chief, who was in the farthest corner from the door. Leighanne and Nita had obviously just arrived, fresh from the NA retreat and ready to be brought up to speed on the ride they'd missed. Desmond sent them all rocking as he plowed through to get to Flannery. He gave her no choice but to hug him back when he threw his lanky arms around her. I couldn't hear it, but I could see her shoulders shake as she started to cry.

"Should we do something?" Kade said close to my ear.

I shook my head. "Whatever it is, I think Desmond can do it better at this point."

Desmond took Flannery to the far end of the counter that ran along the front window and Kade started the trek to the back counter to get us drinks. I tried to make a beeline for Chief, but Leighanne and Nita got to me before I could get past the first table.

"This can't be good," I said to them.

I tried as I always did not to stare directly into the cleavage that habitually peeked from Leighanne's T-shirts. Nita grabbed my hand and cradled it. She was wonderfully Hispanic and touchy and warm.

"It *is* good," she said.

"Don't tell me Rochelle actually spoke during the retreat."

"She did." Leighanne tucked a curve of her silvery bob behind her ear. "I gotta tell you, she and Gigi both are way further down the recovery road than any of the other newbies that were there."

"Really."

Nita squeezed my hand. "And someone has said she'll be their sponsor."

"Seriously?"

"They both liked her and she said yes."

"And she knows their history?"

"Oh, yeah," Leighanne said. "I think Gigi told her more than she really wanted to know. Rochelle, not so much, but the sponsor gets it."

"The woman's an angel from heaven," I said.

Nita stopped massaging. "We can't give you a name or anything, but you would like her."

"Really, thanks," I said to them. I was oddly close to tears. "We need this right now."

Nita's eyes immediately drooped. "We heard about Sherry. Any word from her?"

"Not that I know of. In fact, I need to call the house."

I pulled out my phone and they took the cue. Once they'd melted into a conversation with Rex and Ulysses, I tried again to head for Chief.

"Hey, Allison!"

Oh, for Pete's sake.

I turned to look at Stan—Stan the Man—who was standing in the middle of the room, pointing his finger at me.

"*What?*" I said.

"What's with you ditching us and going off doing your own thing?"

"When did I ditch you?" I said, still trying to inch my way between two stools to get to the back.

"Today. We had one he—wait, sorry—one heck of a ride. Do I hear an amen to that?"

Several renditions of "amen" went up with the glasses being raised. Kade got there in time to stick a 7-Up in my hand.

"Did we go far?" Stan shouted.

"Yes!"

"Did we go far enough?"

"No!"

"And why is that?" Stan cupped his hand around his ear and squinted.

"Because we've come too far to say far enough!"

They went back to toasting each other over the pound of Grand Funk Railroad somebody turned up. I just stood there, stunned. All I could hear was—

Isn't that what I've been trying to tell you?

"Hey, Allison."

I jumped at Leighanne's touch.

"Who's the new girl?"

I followed her gaze to Flannery, who had stopped crying and was listening with her eyes as Desmond talked with his hands. It hadn't even dawned on me that someone might ask questions about her here.

"She looks young," Leighanne said.

"Mmm. She's younger than most."

"She doesn't look like an addict."

"She's not."

Someone jostled my elbow. "We have not clinked our glass."

I smiled at Rex, our HOG chapter president. He was the diametrical opposite of the stereotypical motorcycle dude, and that included his impeccable manners. I lightly touched my glass to his.

"What are we talking about?" Stan said.

His manners on the other hand were right up there with the Hell's Angels. Right now his grinning blue eyes were several inches into my personal space.

"The new Sister," Leighanne said, gesturing toward Flannery.

"Yeah, what is she, about eighteen?"

"She's working on her high school diploma," I said. Okay, blurted. That was an Allison cover-up. The rest came from Somewhere Else. "We need some tutors. Anybody want to volunteer to share his expertise?"

At that precise moment the song ended, all conversations halted, and Chief looked directly at me from his corner of the café. It was a perfect storm.

"I would love to help," Nita said. "English is not my first language, but I have studied the grammar until, ugh, I am cross-eyed." She proved that and laughed.

"You're on," I said.

There were two more takers before Chief started toward me. If I'd known that was all it took I'd have done it sooner, although, in truth, that idea hadn't come from me. Only because I believed it came from God did I not declare myself insane. Still, it could mean more protection for Flannery, even if people didn't know that's what they were doing.

My phone vibrated in my hand. It was Liz, and I had to answer it. Finger in my ear, I said hello and slipped out the door.

"How did it go?" she said.

"Uh, down the tubes," I said.

I told her the story as I leaned on the splintered porch railing and looked out over the sea of Harleys still shiny in the fading sun.

"Are y'all *okay*?" she said. "I mean, you're not hurt, right?"

"I guess not. I sure hope you have a plan for me because I am clueless right now."

I imagined her blinking. "All right, two things. One, we know Flannery has been abused by this man. You are going to have to get a statement from her, and then you need to go to the police so that this will become a civil case, rather than a criminal case for Flannery. We've always known we would have to do that eventually if the mom didn't sign her over."

"I think Flannery'll do that now," I said. "She's pretty much given up on her mom."

"For the moment she has, but don't underestimate that bond. You need to get her to talk right away while she's still angry."

"Okay. What's the other thing?"

"You just have to get that signature."

"I think we blew our chance, Liz."

"I can give you some suggestions for ways to set that up. We can talk tomorrow. Right now I'm on my way to Sacrament House with Zelda to get her things."

"Oh?"

"She's going to stay with me for a few days if that's all right with you. There's still been no word from Sherry, and I think Zelda needs a lot of one-on-one. I'm taking tomorrow off work."

"Do you think she's thinking of using?"

"No, but I just don't want her to get there."

I sank onto the railing and let out all my air. "Talk about a big heart, Liz."

"There's one other thing, and I wouldn't suggest this if I didn't think you need to see how serious this is with Flannery."

"What is it?"

"I'm going to send you a link to a website. You'll see what I mean when you look at it." She paused. "Just don't throw your computer monitor."

I was afraid to ask what that meant. After I hung up I looked past the Harleys to the last of the clouds that hovered on the horizon like pink-tinged battleships. If I could just escape back to the times when all we had to do was lie on our backs in the sand and make up stories about the clouds.

"Classic."

I grabbed at the rail to keep from tumbling off into somebody's gold Sportster. Chief steadied me with a hand around my arm.

"Off someplace?"

"Anyplace," I said.

He perched on the railing next to me, for all the world like an eagle merely coming to rest for a moment. I wanted to lean my head against his shoulder.

"I'm not going to keep you out here," he said. "I know you need to get back to the kids."

"How was Desmond this weekend?"

"Not as happy as he is now. He was setting himself up for you not bringing Flannery back."

I prayed my hands together in front of my face and blew into them. "Did Kade tell you what happened?"

"He did. Classic."

I looked up at him.

"Please, please be careful."

"I am."

"Are you? Announcing to the entire chapter of HOGs that they can volunteer to be this kid's tutors?"

"That wasn't my idea."

"Nudge."

"Yep."

He gave a slow nod. "Then I guess we have to assume that God'll provide protection."

It still surprised me when he said things like that. Suddenly emotion clogged my throat again. For so long I'd thought it would be God who would come between us. Not Troy.

"I missed you this weekend," he said.

"Enough to tell me what this whole thing is really about?"

"I'm working on it, Classic."

He looked at my lips. The longing was more palpable than the railing under us. We hung there, wanting this thing to get out of our way. We were still hanging when Stan opened the café door and said, "Kiss her already."

I closed my eyes. When I opened them, Chief was halfway to the door.

"Hey, sorry, dude," Stan said. "I didn't mean to break that up."

Chief squeezed his shoulder and disappeared inside. Stan looked sheepishly at me.

"It's okay," I said. "That wasn't going anywhere anyway."

"Huh."

Stan strolled toward me, bottle of something in hand, and put his foot on a picnic table bench. Above his shaggy blond head the night bugs swarmed around the porch light that had just snapped on. With any luck they would drive him back inside before he asked too many questions.

"What's up with you two?" he said. "I thought you were on your way to the altar."

I shrugged. "Just stuff."

"Yeah, well, don't let stuff get in the way of a good thing."

I felt my eyebrows rise. If I wasn't mistaken, Stan was actually serious, which was not something I often saw.

"You can't give up on him, Allison. He got hurt bad by his ex, but if anybody can heal that, it's you."

"You know her?" I said.

"Knew. Past tense, and it'll stay that way if I have anything to say about it."

"I had no idea."

I nodded for him to join me on the railing. He looked warily at the door but he sat down.

"I'm not trying to pump you for information," I said. "If you don't feel comfortable telling me—"

"It's okay. I don't know that much." He took a long haul out of the bottle and wiped his mouth with the back of his hand. "All three of us were in the same HOG chapter down in Orlando. Joy was her name. Name didn't fit her, but she was a looker. And you think Leighanne has it going on—"

"Too much information, Stan."

"Anyway, it seemed like they had it all. Both lawyers. Nice house. Very nice house. Two Harleys." He gave me a grin. "He and I, we didn't talk that much about our feelings."

"I'm shocked," I said.

"But I knew he was happy. And then one day it all went down." He stabbed his thumb toward the ground. "Just like that."

I looked down at my sandals, dangling below.

"Y'know what, Stan," I said. "Thanks for telling me this. But I don't think you should say any more. I think I need to hear the rest from Chief."

"Good call. Besides, I don't know all the details. Don't want to. All I know is that I'm glad I got him to come up here with me when I moved to St. A. This gave him a new start. And then when you came along, I thought, now he's gonna make it." Stan leaned his shoulder against mine before he slid off the railing. "I still think that. Like they say, you've come too far—"

It was a blessing he was cut off by Kade poking his head out the door. Tears were once again imminent.

"Allison," Kade said. "You need to come in here."

I brushed past Stan and followed Kade inside, ready for the next disaster of the day. But when he led the way back to Flannery and Desmond, neither of them appeared to be standing on a ledge.

"Tell her," Desmond said to Flannery, jerking his head at me.

I sat on the stool next to her, although my behind barely hit the seat before she said, "I want to talk to that cop. I want to tell him everything."

"That's … a good thing, Flannery," I said.

"But it has to be that friend of yours," she said. "The one that picked me up that day."

"Officer Kent."

"Yes. I won't talk to anybody else."

"I told her Opie was cool," Desmond said.

I nodded, even as I made my mental way through that mud. Would this put Nick in jeopardy? He said Kylie was going to be watching him, ready to pounce any time Nick colored outside the lines.

"I know I can't go back to my mom," Flannery was saying. "She can't protect me. She can't even protect herself. She doesn't want your help, but I do, and I'll do whatever it takes."

I took both of her hands. "It's going to mean two things. Telling the police, yes, and helping me talk your mom into giving me her signature."

Her small shoulders dropped. "I know she won't let you back in the house."

"What about where she works?" Kade said.

"I don't know where that is. I don't think she works at the same nursing home now."

I heard another piece of the puzzle drop into place in my head.

"We'll figure it out," I said. "The good news is that you don't have to worry about being punished for anything you've been forced to do. Your statement to the police is going to ensure that."

"Then let's do it right now."

Kade squatted beside her. "We're going to have to wait until tomorrow. And so that we don't put Officer Kent in a bad position, we'll probably need to do it at the police station."

She started to shake her head, but Desmond put his hand on the top of it, fingers lost in the curls. "You don't got to do it alone, sis. Everybody you need gonna be right there with you."

"It's true." I smiled at Kade. "Even your attorney."

"I wouldn't let you talk to anybody without me there," Kade said.

Then we all went still and watched Flannery. She, too, was still, except for the wheel I could almost hear, turning in her head as the frightened hamsters whirled it round and round. But in that silence, surrounded by HOGs and Grand Funk Railroad and somebody's Harley growling to life outside, I felt a longing as deep as the longing that had pulled Chief and me together on the railing. I wanted this girl to have a life. I wanted her to know the love that Desmond knew. I longed for it.

And in the longing I felt more longing, pulling and hugging and holding.

It was God's longing for his little redhaired girl.

It was almost completely dark when Kade, Flannery, Desmond, and I pulled up to the Palm Row house in Kade's car. I was still a little preoccupied with the fact that the Harley I'd heard leaving the café was Chief's Road King, when Desmond said, "What's Mr. Schatzie doin'?"

I peered through the window on the passenger side to see Owen standing on my lawn between the lane and the side porch. He was bent at the waist, arms sprung out to either side of him like wire coat hangers, yelling something into the pyracantha bushes. They were past their due date for a trim, but that couldn't account for his screaming something unintelligible into the foliage.

I heard Desmond's window go down. "Hey, Mr. Schat-*zee*!" he called.

Owen turned, teetering on one foot on the uneven ground. The hulking figure who burst from behind the bush knocked him the rest of the way off balance and took off like a buffalo around the side of the house and behind Miz Vernell's. The motion sensor bulb affixed to her eave flashed on, drenching his thick back and bush of hair in light before he was swallowed up in the shadows.

Kade was already out of the car, sprinting after him. I told the kids to stay put and ran to Owen. He sat trembling in the grass, clutching his cell phone in his hand.

"I called the cops," he said.

"Are you all right?"

"I'm just madder than a wet hen that I couldn't stop him."

I waited for the rest of the similes but he just shook his balding head. "I'm just no good to anybody these days."

My arms were about to go around him when blue lights jarred the night and a siren whooped to a stop. I almost dissolved right alongside Owen when I saw that the driver was Nicholas Kent. In uniform. *Thankyouthankyouthankyouthankyou.*

"He got away, " Owen called to him.

His voice was creaky. Were we going to have to call yet another ambulance?

Nick said something into the radio on his shoulder and crouched beside Owen.

"Are you hurt?"

"No, I'm not hurt!" Owen barked at him. "Just go catch the son of a gun."

"I called in backup to do that. Let me help you up and you can tell me what happened—"

Owen swatted at the freckled hand Nick offered. "I don't need any help. I'm not that useless."

Nick nodded patiently. I turned my attention to the car where wails were coming from the backseat. I started toward it, but the door came open and Flannery flung herself out, followed by a grasping Desmond. I caught her before she could get up any momentum. She scratched at me without really trying to get away and I managed to pull her to the front steps and make her sit between Desmond and me.

"It was him!" she said.

"Who?"

"Elgin! That was Elgin!"

"That's her old pimp," Desmond informed me.

"Flannery, there is no way that was Elgin. He couldn't possibly know this is where you're staying."

"He has ways! He always gets what he wants! He knows!"

Everything was coming out with an exclamation point attached to it. I pulled both her frenzied hands into mine and shook them until she finally let her eyes land on my face.

"Listen to me," I said. "I had a very close encounter with Elgin today, and that guy was not him."

"He was big. Elgin is that big."

"Elgin is taller." This I knew because Elgin was Chief's height ...

Another piece snapped into place. Chief had Elgin's build. It was no surprise, then, that Flannery could barely look at Chief.

"I saw the back of his head, Flannery," I said. "That guy was—"

She yanked her hands from mine and pulled back until she was nearly in Desmond's lap. He folded his arms around her.

"He knows," she said. "Elgin knows I'm here. I can't talk to the police now."

"All the more reason *to* talk to them. If you think Elgin's around here, they need to know so they can be on the lookout for him."

"You don't get it."

"What don't I get?"

"Miss Allison?"

Flannery took one look at Nick Kent standing a few feet from the bottom of the steps and she closed down everywhere at once.

"Why don't you take Flannery inside, Des?" I said. "Make her some tea."

I didn't protest when Desmond scooped her into his arms and carried her past the cop randomly shining a flashlight into the bushes. I turned to Nick, who by then had been joined by a breathless Kade.

"Lost him," Kade said. He bent over at the waist, hands on his knees.

"Backup will catch up to him." Nick tapped Kade on the back. "Sheesh, dude, how far did you go?"

"Till I got to a freakin' hedge of palmettos. Who uses those for landscaping?" Kade straightened. "Did you get the picture I texted you?"

"Of the girl's mother? Yeah." Nick looked down at me. "She has to press charges for that before the county cops can do anything about it."

"I know. We had Flannery all ready to report *her* abuse to you and then this happened and freaked her out. She thinks the guy in the bushes was her pimp, which it wasn't. The guy ramming around in my shrubs was African American."

Another cruiser pulled in front of the house, and the driver leaned out the window. "He got away from me," he said. With a shrug.

"That's it? 'He got away'?"

We turned as one to look at Owen, who was walking unsteadily from the side porch where Nick had taken his statement.

"Why aren't you out there trying to find him? Somebody hides in the bushes at Ms. Chamberlain's house and you act like it's no big thing." Owen waved vaguely in my direction. "After all she's been through you're gonna shrug it off like a sweater? Swat it away like it's an annoying mosquito. Chalk it up to—"

"Sir, there's nothing more I can do," the cop said. He was either blind, deaf, heartless, or all three.

Owen stomped across the lane and leaned into the passenger window of the police car. Nick stirred and started toward him. Officer Whoever probably had his hand on his service weapon. The one who'd been aimlessly pointing his flashlight into the bushes definitely did.

"I want Palm Row protected!" Owen shouted. "You work for me, the taxpayer, and I want this resolved. Do I make myself clear?"

"Perfectly, Mr. Schatz," Nick said, hand on Owen's shoulder. "Don't you worry. I'll see to it."

Owen paused a moment longer in the cruiser window. I could see only the back of his head, but I knew he was delivering a long, searing look at Officer Shrug. When he finally stood straight, the other cop got in and the car turned up gravel as they drove to the end of Palm Row to turn around.

Nick reassured Owen again, and after promising me that we would talk tomorrow, he left. Kade went inside to check on the kids, while I put an arm around Owen and coaxed him into sitting with me for a minute on the side porch.

"You need something to drink?" I said.

He shook his head and rubbed at his knees with age-spotted hands. He seemed so much older than he had just a few days ago.

"Maybe I shouldn't have gone off on that policeman that way," he said.

"Oh, I don't know. He probably deserved it. I thought he was a pretty lackadaisical about the whole thing too."

"It's not just that. I'm mad at myself because I can't take care of everything the way I used to."

"Yikes, Owen, if I got mad at myself every time I couldn't take care of everything, I'd be ticked off all the time."

He looked at me, his eyes red-rimmed. "I'm worried about Ms. Willa."

"I know."

"She kicked me out this evening. Said I was no good to her if I didn't get some sleep."

"She's right."

"And tomorrow I've got to go work with Rochelle at the house."

"I'll look in on Ms. Willa, Owen," I said. "It's not all on you. We're in this together, the whole bunch of us."

"You think?"

"I know."

He nodded, so sadly.

When he'd gone home I stayed on the porch, feet stretched out on the swing, looking toward Miz Vernell's backyard. I hadn't been lying to Flannery. There was absolutely no way the figure I'd seen hurtling himself into the dark was Elgin. He wasn't the right size. He wasn't the right race.

And he didn't have the kind of controlling power I'd seen in Elgin. Flannery's pimp would never lower himself to lurking in the bushes; he'd have somebody else do it. And even if he had done his own dirty work, I could say with certainty that he wouldn't have just knocked an already unsteady Owen to the ground and run off. He would have taken us all on, at least until he heard Nick Kent's siren. He and Flannery both seemed committed to avoiding law enforcement officers, though now I knew it was for different reasons.

I shivered and shoved that thought into the pile of Things That Make Me Ill. Things I was going to have to look at if I was ever going to help Flannery dig out of the pit that went even deeper than I'd thought.

Right now, I had to wrestle with this thing, this new intrusion. It wasn't Elgin, so who was it?

Black. Hulking. Not personally attached to whatever it was he was doing.

Or had been sent there to do.

The thing smacked so hard of Sultan's lackey I could feel it stinging my face. My hands were uncannily steady as I pulled out my cell and scrolled for Detective Kylie's number. When his voice mail finished its drone, I spoke distinctly into the phone.

"This is Allison Chamberlain. Please call me. We've had a sighting."

CHAPTER FOURTEEN

I had only been asleep for an hour, after tossing for two, when I was awakened by someone crawling into bed with me. I rolled over to find a mass of hair in my face.

"Flannery?" I said. I wasn't always coherent in the middle of the night.

"Yeah."

Her voice was so small and quiet I peered closer to make sure it was actually her. For good measure, I snapped on the light over the bed. She was curled into a tiny ball with her back to me, like a kitten disconnected from the litter. Complete with trembling.

"You cold?" I said.

"No," she said.

"Scared?"

"Uh-huh. I keep thinking he's out there."

I started to tell her again that he had never been out there in the first place, but I had a flash of Sylvia, coming to me in the wee hours when I cried out that the alligators were under my bed again. She never once said, "Oh, for the love of Pete, Allison, there are no alligators under your bed." Every time, she said, "I better look, then." And while I waited with the covers pulled up to my nose, ready to scream when she was eaten alive, she squatted down, pulled up the bed ruffle, and stuck her head right under the box spring to inspect. I never ceased to be awed by her courage. "No gators," she would say. "We're safe for now." Then she snuggled in beside me and stroked my hair until the specter of reptiles stopped taunting me and I fell asleep against her saggy chest.

"I better look, then," I said to Flannery.

She sat up and waved her hands at her hair until her eyes could peek out.

"What if he sees you?"

"I'll be stealthy," I said and squeezed her knee. "I've always wanted to use that word."

She didn't seem to find that funny, and quite frankly neither did I. Every thought while I'd lain awake earlier had been some version of, *What if that* was *Marcus Rydell?* If I expected to see anybody outside, it was him, not Elgin the Pimp. And that thought was beyond horrifying.

But I tried to keep a cool exterior as I made a slight adjustment to the plantation shutter and peeked out. Only the light from my front porch shafted through the velvet blackness, just enough for me to see the vehicle parked in front of my garage.

I must have changed my breathing or flicked an eyelash or something because Flannery whispered, "What? Did you see somebody?"

"Yes," I said. "Come look."

I held out my arm to her and she crept from the bed to the window seat, dragging what I now saw was Desmond's Harley blanket with her.

I opened the shutter a little further and pulled her closer to it. "See?"

"Is that a police car? Really?"

"Not just any police car. That's Officer Kent."

She relaxed against me, but only momentarily. "I can't talk to him now," she said.

"Well, no. We aren't dressed for it."

"No, I mean ever. Elgin will know."

"What is he, clairvoyant?"

Her nose wrinkled. "What does that mean?"

"It means you can see things other people can't."

"Oh. Desmond says that's what *you* do."

My breathing definitely changed then, because she took it away.

Flannery pulled the blanket around her and hugged her knees. "Are you really a prophet?"

It wasn't a challenge, or even a prelude to *You have got to be kidding me, lady.* There was actually something hopeful in her voice. Something I had to be careful with.

I leaned against the short wall that formed the window seat so I could face her. "I seem to have a prophetic gift," I said.

"So ... does that mean you could tell someone what was going to happen next?"

Ah.

"I can look at a situation and tell someone what's *probably* going to happen because I see some things as they are, rather than just the way I want to see them."

"Some things. Not everything."

"The things God shows me."

"Does God, like, show up and talk to you?"

"I've never seen God, if that's what you mean—at least not in person. I see God in people's faces, in the things they do that couldn't be anything else but God working in them."

Flannery studied her knees, frowning.

"That wasn't the answer you wanted to hear," I said.

"When Desmond told me you got pokes from God—no, that's not right …"

"Nudges."

"Yeah, that was it. When he told me that, I thought maybe God had nudged you about me."

"How about until I'm black and blue?"

Her face came up. "Are you serious?"

"You wouldn't still be here if that wasn't the case." I put up a palm. "Not that I'm not delighted to have you."

"Uh-huh. So are you getting what I'm supposed to do? Because all I want to do is run." Her face was on the verge of crumpling, and I could see her fighting it. "That's the only thing I know how to do. Everything else I tried didn't work."

"What else did you try?"

She looked at me sideways. "Off the record?"

"I'm sorry?"

"That's what Kade always says when I won't talk. 'This will be strictly off the record.'"

She sounded so like him I snorted.

"Okay," I said, "off the record. What else did you try besides running away?"

It took her a minute to get started. I waited.

"This one night Elgin took me down to the lobby of the hotel to meet a client. He told me to wait while he went into the bar to look for him, and this cop came in. He didn't have a uniform on, but I'd seen him before when he did so I knew. I went up to him and I told him that I needed help and to please take me to the police station."

I didn't want her to tell me the rest, but I nodded.

"He was the client," she said.

Just when I thought I couldn't be stupefied by anything worse than I'd already heard, something like this came out and clawed me in the face.

"And after that, there were other cops. They liked to take me out on motorcycles and scare the pee out of me and then they'd strip me down except for chaps and a leather jacket and pretend they were arresting me." Flannery dug her fingers into the blanket. "That's what you don't get, Allison. They're in on it."

I didn't know what else to do but put my arms around her and hold her, even though her tiny body was stiff and unbelieving.

"It's hard for me to even think about God," she said, "when God's the one who created this whole messed-up world and isn't doing anything to change it. But I thought if you knew something, since you see ... I don't know."

She pushed me away and I let her, so I could look into the face she could no longer control. Anguish was taking it over, just as I'd watched it do to her mother. And I couldn't let that happen.

PleaseGodpleaseGodpleaseGod.

"Here's what I know," I said. "I know God loves you." I let a corner of my mouth go up. "If *I* can love you, I *know* God does."

"Then why—"

"I'm getting to that. I also know that God didn't create the messed-up parts of this world, but God does help *us* change them. That's what Sacrament House is about. One woman at a time. Before

Zelda started healing, I watched her flip her stuff all the way out in front of three policemen down on West King Street. I pulled Desmond's mother out of a garbage can in a back alley. Ophelia used to turn tricks where you're selling artwear to customers." I scooted closer to her, shaped the words with my hands. "The first thing they did was accept that we loved them—me and Hank and India and Chief, all of us. Then they started to wonder if God cared about them, too, so they bought into that because we did." I smiled at her. "And then things started to change. They didn't just get clean and sober and stop hooking. They turned into the beautiful people they were meant to be, before *their* Elgins or the drugs or whatever else got hold of them. Then … they started taking it outward. Who made it safe for you to tell us about Elgin the other night at the house?"

"Mercedes."

"Who told you that you had a way with the customers up at Second Chances?"

"Ophelia."

"Who saved you from that john who was slapping you around behind C.A.R.S.?"

"Sherry and Jasmine."

"They didn't trust anybody either until they started trusting God. And then people started trusting *them*."

"Did they have people after them?"

"Oh, yeah," I said. "But they didn't let those people win."

She lost the battle with her face and choked out a sob.

"I hate Elgin so much," she said.

"I hear that."

"I bet you never hated anybody enough to want them dead."

She watched me as she sobbed. *PleaseGodpleaseGodpleaseGod don't let me mess this up.*

"I could hate somebody that much," I said. "But that makes *me* hateful, so I fight it every day."

"Are you winning?"

I hadn't lied to her yet, and I couldn't start now.

"I'm still working on it," I said. "That's why I know I can help you."

She closed her eyes and she cried. I pulled her into my lap and rocked her and she cried some more until she went limp and breathed sleeping sobs.

I had told her the truth. Now I had to make sure it remained the truth.

I never did go back to sleep. After I tucked Flannery into my bed, I went downstairs and drank tea in the kitchen, between the door and Desmond's bedroom. At dawn, I greeted God and Monday and smacked aside the weekly urge to quit. There would be none of that now.

That done, I called Chief. He never sounded groggy when I called him at weird hours. It made me wonder if he was always expecting the next crisis. I filled him in on this one, and he was there before I got the coffee made.

"I have a plan," he said as he tossed the newspaper on the table. He took the coffee canister away from me and nodded me toward one of the high chairs.

"Bring it," I said.

But before he could launch into it, my phone rang.

"It's Kylie," I said. "Hello?"

"Got your message." Kylie's voice was gruff. I couldn't tell if he was annoyed or just hadn't had his caffeine either. Kylie *after* morning coffee was bad enough.

"What's this sighting you're talking about?" he said. Oh, yeah. He was annoyed.

"I'd rather tell you in person," I said. "How is nine for you?"

"Fine. Just tell me—"

"I'll see you then."

I hung up and looked at Chief.

"Y'know," he said, eyes crinkling, "one of these days I'm going to have to teach you how to talk to law enforcement."

"Maybe when he starts actually enforcing the law." I twisted in the chair as Desmond stumbled out of the bedroom. "Mornin', Des."

He grunted at me and slapped hands with Chief.

"I'll be taking you to school this morning, buddy," Chief said. "Why don't you go up and hose yourself down and I'll wait for you."

Desmond nodded and continued his stumble out of the kitchen.

"Is that part of the plan?" I was still watching the door swing. "I hope it includes a full-time bodyguard because I can hardly stand to let him leave the room."

"You stayed up all night, didn't you?"

"Uh-huh."

"Here. Drink this first and then we'll talk."

I obeyed, happy to have somebody else making a decision. Chief sat opposite me and opened the paper. The longing stirred in me again. Him in the kitchen with me, first thing in the morning, making me coffee, getting our son off to school. It was so normal I wanted to freeze the moment.

Chief let out a long, slow whistle.

"What?" I said.

He tapped the front page. "Troy Irwin has been ousted as CEO of Chamberlain Enterprises."

The moment did freeze, except for my heart, which slammed against my chest wall. Chief handed me the paper and I stared at it, seeing nothing. I couldn't even think *pleaseGodpleaseGod* because God was probably looking at me the same way Chief was. I could feel it right through the newsprint.

"Don't you do it, Classic," he said.

"Do what?" I said.

"Act like you didn't already know this."

I lowered the paper slowly. "I found out Saturday."

"How?"

"I can't tell you."

"Why not?"

Because Kade said he'd have my back, and I had to have his, too. Just how I was supposed to do that with Chief's eyes boring into me, I had no idea.

"He told you, didn't he?"

"Who?"

"Irwin."

"No!"

Chief hung his hand on the back of his neck. If I'd touched my own neck, I knew I would have found my hackles standing straight up like a razorback hog's.

"You don't believe me?" I said. "You really think I would lie to you about something like this?"

"'S goin' on, Mr. Chief?"

Desmond was in the doorway. Of course. He was only half dry, but all the way concerned.

"Don't worry about it, buddy," Chief said.

"Y'all sittin' here fightin and I'm not s'posed to worry about it?"

Chief shook his head. "We're not fighting. We're having a disagreement. People do that."

"Well I hope you be fixin' it," Desmond said. "'Cause it's stressin' me out, now."

Any other time I would have had to stifle a grin at the thought of Desmond being stressed out. This wasn't any other time.

"Get dressed," Chief said. "We'll grab some breakfast on the way to school."

Before Desmond even closed his door behind him I was out on the screen porch. It was the first morning since May that the heat didn't hit me in the face like a pillow when I walked outside. I could have even used a light hoodie. But I just hugged my arms around me and went to the railing and fumed. Chief fumed right behind me.

"Well, are we going to give the boy what he wants?" I said.

"Which is?"

"Are we going to fix it?" I whirled to face Chief, who had his own arms folded so tight his hands were lost in his armpits. "This can't go on any longer. Something besides my issues is keeping you from trusting me when it comes to Troy Irwin. Put it out there, Chief, because now it's not only affecting you and me, it's affecting Desmond."

"I told you I'm working on it."

"Not hard enough, evidently."

"And how about you? This is going to blow up. Are you ready for that?"

The door creaked. Before Desmond could get the screen door open, Chief had turned away from me.

"I'll get the bike started," he said to Desmond, and strode off the porch.

Desmond looked at me. "You was just fixin' it out here, right?"

"Yeah, Des," I said.

He let his look linger and then loped off to meet Chief.

As I watched him go, and then watched them both go, on the Road King, riding off like one bonded-together hunk of love, the longing went so deep and so hard, I had to sink into the swing.

"It's your longing for us, isn't it?" I whispered.

Love another mile. Go. Go now.

I rocked the swing and waited for more and there was no more. Maybe I didn't need any more. Maybe that was all I needed to know to go fix it.

As for love … it suddenly seemed harder than hate. But I had no choice.

I got Hank to come and stay with Flannery until it was late enough for her to go to Second Chances, where, according to Ophelia, they were waiting for more of her creativity. I went straight to the police station and was there a few minutes before nine. Detective Kylie looked up from his piles of envelopes and folders and sighed when Officer Bad Perm showed me into his cubicle. I bit back what I wanted to say, which was *You picked the wrong time to pull attitude with me,* and sat in the chair he neglected to offer me. I couldn't get snarky if I was going to find out what I came for. If that was what was meant by *Love another mile,* I had to make sure I could do it.

"I think I can help," I said.

"Well now, isn't that nice?"

Really, God? Really?

"I don't know about nice. Just honest. My neighbor flushed somebody out of my bushes last night just as I was getting home. You can check it out on the police report. He got away, but it sure looked like Marcus Rydell to me."

Kylie straightened slightly in the chair, but his eyes remained mildly incredulous. "You saw his face?"

"Didn't have to. If you'll recall, my view of Mr. Rydell is usually his back as he runs away like the complete coward he is. I'm not thinking you sent him."

"What the ... why would I send him?"

"He's working for you. I just thought if you didn't send him, you'd want to know that he's obviously got something else going on the side." I leaned forward. "Like maybe working for Sultan again."

Kylie grunted. "I think your imagination is getting the better of you, Miss Chamberlain."

"No, if anything, it's my fear. I don't like the fact that Rydell is walking around free as it is, but if he *is* working for Sultan—"

"Look, even if he were, Sultan's done."

"What do you mean he's done?"

The detective pinched the bridge of his nose like a father whose aggravation with his teenage daughter was giving him a migraine. "All right. Rydell told me that the only action Sultan has been able to get going recently is one small-time pimp who's joined his new line."

"So that's it?" I said. "Because he's only responsible for a *handful* of exploited women you don't give a flip if you catch him now?" I took a breath. So far the love thing wasn't working well. "I'm sorry. There's no need for sarcasm."

He looked a little stunned.

"Sultan may not have the influence he once did," I said, "but we know from what he's done in the past that he has absolutely no conscience and that he is a threat to Desmond and me."

"Which is why I have Marcus Rydell working for me. Your words, not mine."

"Then let me just tell you what I want."

"There's no stopping you. What?"

"I want protection for my son. I want police cruising Palm Row on a regular basis. I want to be able to call you and report anything that seems suspicious to me and have you take it seriously." I spread my hands out on the desk, where I could find a place amid the piles that mimicked my own mental ones. "I'm on your side, detective. We both want the same thing. We want it for different reasons, and we seem to be going at it in entirely different ways, but really, we want the same thing."

I sat back. Kylie waggled his head side to side. Grimaced. And finally said, "What is it that we want?"

"Justice," I said. "Right?"

"Right," he said.

But I'd already seen the cynical glint. That was what I'd gone there to find out, and it surged up in me until I had to grip the arms of the chair to keep from flying across his pile-filled desk. What I was feeling was definitely not love. I had to pull in air to keep my voice calm, no matter what I felt.

"No," I said. "You aren't about justice, sir. If you were, you would never have let Troy Irwin go. He's going to be arrested today for embezzlement, and he'll probably go to prison for that, but not for what he did to one of my Sisters. That's not justice." I prayed my hands together. "But you have a chance now with Jude Lowery. And I'm praying that you'll take that chance—*not* just to get you out of this cubicle, but to protect my son and everyone else Sultan is threatening."

Kylie's face grew grave. "Who else is he threatening?"

"Have you read the police report on the vandalism at Choice Auto Repair last Wednesday, the twelfth?"

"What van—"

"Grisly portraits of me and three of my Sisters were drawn on the walls ... in blood. One of them was portrayed with an eye patch. Did anybody bring that to your attention?"

"These were actual drawings?"

"Caricatures," I said.

As soon as the word crossed my lips the vision was clear. Caricatures, good ones. Drawn with the same talent Desmond had.

"They were done by Sultan," I said.

His eyes narrowed. "You can prove that?"

"That's not my job. It's yours." I slid to the front edge of the chair. "Look at the crime-scene photos. Compare them to the copy of the drawing I showed you last spring that my son did. Sultan is Desmond's biological father. The only decent thing he passed down to him was his artistic talent. And while you're looking at those photos, notice that the drawings were all done low on the wall, where someone in a wheelchair could reach. You're a smart guy, Detective Kylie. You'll see it." I stood up. "I'd like regular police presence on San Luis Street, too, and a foot patrolman keeping an eye on our building on St. George. Second Chances. Used to be the Monk's Vineyard."

The scoff was gone from Kylie's mouth, though he did say, "Is there anything else you want?"

"I want you to care," I said.

And then I left, before the tears in my throat could catch up to my eyes.

As I made my way, half-blind, down the hall, I tried to assure myself that not grabbing Detective Kylie by the throat and shaking him was about as much of a demonstration of love as God could expect me to show. I wanted to. I also wanted to pick up the next trash can I saw and smash it—

I cut off that thought and fell against a doorway. Or maybe I was pushed. I felt pushed—back from the undeniable urge to hurt someone, the way the people I loved had been hurt and still could be. When there was no justice, it was hard not to seek revenge. As the urge pulled me and God pushed back, I could see Kade caught in that same riptide.

When I could stop dragging my hands through my hair, I started to step out of the doorway, but a voice in the hall stopped me.

"I have a right to an attorney. I'm not saying anything until my lawyer gets here. Don't try any of your big bad cop—"

The rest was profanity. I had never heard Troy Irwin swear like that before. I flattened myself against the recessed door.

"You have the right to remain silent too," Nick Kent said. "I wish you'd take it."

I expected a flock of attorneys to be scurrying around Troy already, but when they passed me, he was alone with Nick and a plainclothes guy whose open jacket unconcealed his concealed weapon. It was a far different scene from the one I'd witnessed last spring in this same hallway: Troy strolling confidently with his bevvy of advisors, arms swinging as if he were on his way to a three-martini lunch.

This time he was in handcuffs, and I was more frightened of him now than when he was walking free.

I waited until the double doors swung shut behind them before I emerged from the place God had pushed me to and hurried out of the building. So much for step two of my plan for fixing it. And I'd been so sure that *Love another mile* included *Go see Troy*. As opposed to my natural inclination as that was, I thought it *had* to come from God.

I was going to have to wait on that one. I paused when I got to my bike and sorted through one of the piles. Zelda was with Liz. Sherry ... I couldn't go there. Flannery was occupied for the moment.

I put on my helmet and headed for the hospital.

Owen, who surprisingly wasn't there yet, would have had more than the usual three metaphors for Ms. Willa's state when I got there, starting with "ready to blow a gasket."

I didn't even have to ask her what was wrong because she started in on me the minute she saw me walk in.

"You got me in here, Allison Chamberlain, and you'd better get me out!"

"Nice to see you, too, Ms. Willa."

"Don't you be smart with me. I told you people I was just having one of my spells. I would have been fine if you'd just left me alone."

I pulled a chair close to the bed where she was hooked up to a heart monitor and several other machines I couldn't identify. "Tell that to Flannery," I said. "She's the one who convinced you to come."

The inevitable blue-veined finger came out from under the sheet. "Don't you blame that girl. She was just doing what you told her to."

I laughed. "And since when does Flannery do *anything* I tell her to? Or you either, which I think is why you like her so much."

"She wouldn't let them treat me the way they're treating me in here."

My smile faded. "You're not getting good care?"

"Look at me. I'm a fright, and don't tell me I'm not because I looked." She flailed her hand at a small mirror on the rolling tray and then pulled fretfully at the defeated curls flattened to her head. There were tears in her eyes as she tried to push her dignity back into place.

"Do you want Flannery?" I said.

"Well, of course I want Flannery! Why didn't you bring her with you?"

"I'll get her here," I said.

I took my cell phone to the waiting room down the hall and called Hank. She said she and Flannery were just leaving my house so she'd drop her off at the hospital instead of Second Chances. I was on my way back to Ms. Willa's room when a graying nurse with still-bright eyes the color of blueberries stopped me.

"You're Ms. Livengood's visitor?" Her voice was the kind I'd want to wake me up in the morning, especially if I was in a hospital bed.

"I am," I said.

"Family?"

I shook my head. "I'm not sure she has any."

"No, there's no one listed." She bit her lip like she was trying to decide something. "I just think someone should be aware. I hate to see this all come down to a social worker."

I felt my eyes widen. "She needs a social worker?"

The nurse motioned for me to walk with her down the hall. She kept her head tilted toward me and her voice low.

"She has a number of different things going on with her. I can't—"

"I know."

"She's stable for now, but her doctor isn't going to release her until arrangements have been made for full-time care for her."

"You're talking about a nursing home," I said.

"I think so, unless she can afford round-the-clock nursing."

"She can probably afford it. I'm just not sure she'd stand for it. Or that anybody would last longer than about a day."

Her blue eyes twinkled. "I gathered that. When I asked her if she had a living will, she told me she wasn't planning on dying any time soon, unless I knew something she didn't, and in that case I'd better be telling her right now."

"I'm surprised she didn't order you out of the room."

"She did."

It felt good to laugh, even for a moment. I wanted to take this woman home with me.

"Anyway," she said, "I'll have HIPAA all over me if anyone finds out we had this conversation—"

"What conversation?"

"I just felt like somebody should know."

"I appreciate it," I said.

She went back to the nurses' station, and I turned to greet Flannery, who was hurrying toward me from the elevator. Hank wasn't even trying to keep up.

"She's waiting for you," I said.

Flannery all but danced into the room, to the tune of Ms. Willa's "Now where have you been?"

"Sounds like she's glad to see her," Hank said, mouth twitching.

"And I'm glad to see you," I said. "Can we talk for a minute? There's a room right down there."

Hank nodded and looped her arm through mine as we walked. "How you holding up, Al?"

"Better, now that I'm getting clear on the extra mile."

"Good."

She pulled off her bandanna and sank into a chair facing the couch. I sat on its edge.

"Now it's not just *go* another mile, it's *love* another mile."

"Shouldn't be too hard for you. That's all you do is love."

"Troy Irwin?"

Hank breathed in through her nose. "Well, we did determine that Jesus is talking about your enemies. Troy qualifies."

"Then I need you to pray for me."

"Because …"

"I'm going to go see him."

Hank folded her hands, neatly piling the fingers.

"You don't think I should," I said.

"I don't think you should do it alone. Not in a private place."

"Not a problem. It's going to be at the courthouse."

"When?"

"The minute he posts bail."

Her eyes popped. "Bail?

I told her about Troy's arrest. To protect Kade, I didn't include my issue with Chief. If she knew there was more to it, which she probably did, she didn't ask.

"When is this going to happen?" she said.

"I don't know. I have to find out. Today sometime I guess."

She rearranged her fingers. "And what will you say?"

"I don't know that either. I'm going to do the only thing that ever really works for me and what I should have been doing a whole lot more of lately."

Hank's lips did a double twitch. "Yeah, you pretty much insert a whole shoe store in your mouth when you don't wait for God."

"Thanks for that. You'll pray?"

She held out her hands and I took them.

Hank offered to stay with Flannery at the hospital until she herself had to get to work, and she'd drop Flan at Second Chances on her way. I went out to the parking lot and sat on Classic's welcoming seat and tried to figure out how I was going to find out when Troy would probably be released. It had to be somebody who wouldn't (a) try to talk me out of it, or (b) leave me for good without giving me a chance to explain. Somebody who was the very soul of discretion.

Of course.

Tia Davies picked up on the first ring with, "Ellington and Capelli. How may I help you?"

"Hi, Tia." I said "It's Allison Chamberlain."

"Good morning. I'll get Mr. Ellington for you."

"No, Tia, I don't want to bother him. I thought maybe you could help me. I just have a quick question."

"I hope I have a quick answer."

I decided she must practice these smooth responses in her spare time. I was grateful for that.

"If someone were arrested on a criminal charge—a white-collar crime—and he or she had the means to make bail, how long would it take for the person to be released?"

"From the time of the arrest?" she said.

"Right."

"Here in St. Augustine?"

"Yes." My nerves started to jangle. The more questions she asked, the more information she could give Chief if she mentioned it to him. Then he was going to have *plenty* of questions. Hopefully, this would be over by that time.

She was already answering, and I missed the first part of it. When I tuned in she was saying, "That would probably be between three and five hours."

I did a mental calculation. Not before noon and not after two. It was ten thirty.

"Is there anything else I can do for you?" Tia said.

"No. You have been wonderful as always."

"You sure you don't want to speak with Mr. Ellington? He just got off the phone."

"I'm good. In fact ..." I hesitated. If I asked her not to say anything to him, that would arouse suspicion. And make me feel like a sneak. If this was right it was right.

"I'm sorry?" she said.

"In fact, let's just let him keep his mind on what he's doing, okay?"

Her okay revealed none of the bewilderment she must be experiencing by that time. I was going to have to get me some of that decorum someday.

The wait was brutal. At eleven thirty I finally left the Harley in the parking lot at the courthouse and stationed myself on the shallow steps to wait in the sun that beat down on the cream-white walls. That morning's September cool had surrendered to a muggy midday, and even without my vest, and with my T-shirt sleeves rolled attractively up over my shoulders, the sweat pooled wherever it could find a place and ran in veritable bubbling brooks where it couldn't.

I was only intermittently aware of it. The real brutality was in my soul, where I was doing battle and being sorely beaten.

I didn't want to do this. Face Troy. Try to love him more than I could. Give him more than he asked for. Because that was the thing. I didn't need another message from God to know that was what this was about. That day on Aviles Street, I'd turned the other cheek. Not my idea, but I'd done it, instead of leaving fingernail marks in his. And that night at Columbia I'd refrained from kicking him in the groin and had given him my cloak, almost literally. He was probably hanging onto that scarf like a trophy.

And somehow that still wasn't far enough? *Really, God? Really?*

I knew the answer. I just didn't like it. It made me want to vomit; as it was I had to go behind a palm tree twice with the dry heaves. But if I didn't do this, if I didn't let God push me away from the hate that was pulling at me, then I was no better than Detective Kylie. And if I didn't love Troy Irwin one more mile, whatever that meant, I would lose Chief, and I would deserve it.

But Desmond didn't deserve it, and that kept me there, sweltering on the steps, until one thirty, when Troy came through one of the glass doors.

The ingratiating entourage was still missing. Troy made his exit with one smarmy-looking man with a greasy comb-over and sweat rings under the sleeves of what at one time had been a white shirt.

They didn't speak to each other when they stopped a few yards from me. The man just handed Troy a sheet of paper and heaved his bulging body laboriously toward the brick walkway. I watched him cross the parking lot to a van with the words *Goddard Bail Bonds* on the side.

"Did you come to gloat?"

I looked up at Troy, standing a few steps above me. His eyes were cruel blue in an inflamed web of red, and the sagging skin around them was refusing to support their struggle to stay in control. As I stood up to face him, I knew I was watching his power drain from his body.

"No gloating," I said.

"Good, because this isn't over—"

"Troy, stop. Just ... stop."

He put his hands on his hips and moved his mouth as if he was trying to get rid of something sour. I was sure that was a combination of a sleepless night with a bottle of Southern Comfort and his current nearness to me. I was supposed to love someone who saw me as a bad taste in his mouth?

Go another—

I know. PleaseGodpleaseGodpleaseGod give me the words before I spit.

"So what do you want?" Troy said. There was no sign of his well-oiled charm.

"That's what I came to ask you. What do you want from *me*, Troy?"

He looked to one side, as if he were used to someone being there to validate his disdain. "It's a little late for that, don't you think? This isn't what you said when I was offering you the moon for your whores."

I swallowed that one. "I'm not talking about money. I'm talking about you. Troy the person, not Troy the ..."

Please let me say jackal. *Please?*

Not happening. That got shoved back down my throat, so I started again, while Troy continued to deal with the moss on his tongue.

"Do you want me to say I'm sorry I kept you from knowing you had a son? Or that I ran and—"

"You're not sorry."

"I think Kade had a better upbringing than he would have with either of us. But you had the right to make that choice. Even though you wanted me to have an abortion, I should have told you I didn't."

"Where is this even coming from?"

Certainly not me. But now that I'd said it, I knew it was right. I took in a breath. "It just needs to be said."

"Look, forget it. I don't have time for this."

Troy tried to step around me but I put myself in front of him. His usual tennis-court sureness of foot failed him and he almost tripped. When I put out a hand to steady him, he smacked it away.

"I said I don't have time—"

"We both know you have no place to go," I said, not unkindly. "What do you need from me?"

"Not a thing." He inserted a sample of the profanity I'd heard at the police station. "I'm not one of your addicts who needs a rescue."

"I'm not offering one." I kept my eyes latched onto his. The fragment of pain I found there kept me going. "This is just us. Ally and Troy. No power play. No guilt trip. No revenge ... from either of us. So let's get down to it."

"Why?"

"Because you just lost everything, and that means there's nothing keeping you from starting over."

Troy put his face close enough that I could smell his hatred of me. "You should be careful what you ask for, Ally."

"There's nothing careful about it. We're talking reckless abandon here."

"You really are nuts. All right, first of all—" He thrust his index finger under my nose. "I haven't lost anything but your father's albatross. I'm independently wealthy. I'm going to rebuild Vilano Beach—"

"From prison?"

I had never heard my own voice sound that kind. For only an instant Troy leaned into it, before his eyes hardened again.

"You know what I want, *Ally*?" he said. "I want *you* to lose everything."

I felt like I'd been stabbed in the stomach, but I shook my head. "I can't lose what matters to me. And you want to know how crazy I really am?" I didn't wait for him to answer. "I want that same state of soul for you. Not because you deserve it. Definitely not because I *like* you."

"You hate me."

"No."

I sucked in air again. *Isn't that enough? Just not hating him—isn't that far enough?*

The answer came in my own words as I said, "I love you."

The fragment of pain in Troy's eyes tried to hide itself and couldn't. Still, he forced a laugh. "I'm not feelin' it, Ally."

"Neither am I," I said. "But I'm choosing it."

"You don't just stick the knife in, do you?" He stabbed his fingers just above my left breast. "You have to twist it. And then you twist it, and twist it, and twist it some more."

With each *twist* he turned his fingers until I let out a cry. He pulled them away, but he kept his tightened lips close to mine.

"That's what I want, Ally. I want you to hurt."

He left me standing there on the steps with my hand pressed against my chest. I could barely breathe. I could only whisper, "I already do."

Me, too, was the whisper. *That's the cost of loving as I do.*

"Classic."

I turned and looked at Chief, standing between me and the parking lot I wanted to run to.

"What were you *doing?*" he said.

"I was fixing it, Chief," I said.

And then I covered my face and wept.

CHAPTER FIFTEEN

Chief walked me across the drive and onto a mound of grass that displayed one of the palms. By then I had stopped crying and was blowing my nose on my do-rag.

"Tia told you," I said.

"Did you think she wouldn't?"

"I think I wanted her to tell you." I leaned against the trunk of the palm. "I think I wanted you to show up here and see that."

"I guess I missed it." Chief's voice was taut.

"Then see it now." I put my hands on either side of his face so he would have to look right into mine. "Are you looking at hate?"

"Classic—"

"I mean it. Do you see hate?"

Like the man he always was, threatened or not, he searched with those eagle eyes.

"No," he said.

"Do you see anger?"

"No."

"What *do* you see?"

"You're in pain," he said.

He closed his eyes. I waited until he opened them again before I said, "That's what I see in yours, too, Chief. You say you're working on it, and I believe you, but I'm not sure it's work you need to be doing."

His gaze went to the fronds swaying above us. "What do I need to be doing then?"

"Loving."

"Classic, you know I love you."

He tried to pull me into him, but I pressed my hands to his chest. "I'm not talking about loving me. I'm talking about loving Joy Ellington.

Chief's arms dropped to his sides. "Who told you her name?"

"Somebody who cares about both of us."

"That whole thing is behind me."

"That whole thing of unresolved issues?"

He looked away, but I took his chin in my hand and pulled it back to me. "I can't tell you what to do, Chief, but I know, I *know* now that nothing stays behind you until you leave it there in love." I kissed his mouth. "But not that kind of love."

"What kind?"

"The kind that doesn't expect her to give back whatever she took from you. The kind that gives her what she needs."

"She doesn't need anything from me," Chief said.

"Oh, yeah she does."

"*What?*"

"She's the only one who can tell you that."

He started to move, but I stopped him with a hard hug. And then because there was nothing else I could do, I pulled away from the tree.

"I love you," I said.

And then I crossed the wide drive to where Classic waited for me.

As right as I knew I was, I still had to bring myself back to center before I called Hank to find out where Flannery was. To my surprise, they were both still at the hospital.

"I thought you had a student today," I said.

"I got a sub. I think you need to get over here and see this."

I didn't ask which pile whatever it was belonged in.

Hank was leaning against the wall outside Ms. Willa's room when I arrived.

"Is Flannery in there?" I said.

"Oh, but definitely."

That was an understatement. Flannery was *in* the bed with Ms. Willa who, now combed and coiffed, was wiping Flannery's tear-smeared cheek with a Kleenex. When she saw me, Flannery stopped Ms. Willa's hand and gave me a watery smile.

"I want to call my mother, and I want to make her give you that signature. And then I want to tell the police everything."

"O-kay," I said.

I raised both eyebrows at Ms. Willa.

"You people don't know how to handle this child," she said.

"Apparently. You want to tell me your secret?"

She exchanged an eye roll with Flannery. An actual eye roll.

"It's no secret," Ms. Willa said. "You just have to stop doing all the work for her."

I couldn't even begin to sort that out, and for the moment I didn't need to. Ms. Willa's influence notwithstanding, I had to get

Flannery on the phone with Brenda ASAP. If she'd even answer now.

"All right, then," I said. "Let's do it."

Hank went to pick up Desmond from school, after assuring me at least five times that she would not let him out of her sight for an instant. There was some comfort in the fact that Marcus Rydell would have a harder time wrestling Desmond away from Hank than from me.

Flannery and I went straight to my house and used Flannery's phone to call Brenda. I almost cried—again—when she picked up on the first ring.

I still wasn't expecting much from her, now that the image of her cowering in front of Elgin was branded into my brain. But Flannery herself was strong enough for both of them. Whatever it was Ms. Willa told her she could do for herself, she was doing it as she put it on the line with her mother.

"I'll sign," Brenda said. "Ms. Chamberlain, was it?"

"Yes, ma'am," I said.

"I can meet you Thursday at noon."

My heart sank. I really didn't want to take the chance of waiting that long, but there was enough hope in the woman's voice for me to agree.

"Your place?" I said. "Or the nursing home?"

As subtle as I'd tried to be, she didn't bite.

"No. J. T.'s Seafood Shack, south of Marineland."

"I know where it is," Flannery said.

"I don't want you coming this time, darlin'," Brenda said.

"Mom, why not?"

"Just in case."

Neither of us asked her to fill in that blank.

"I love you, Flannery," her mom said before we hung up.

"I love you more," Flannery said.

I couldn't help thinking that might be true. Flannery was more the mother than Brenda, just as I'd seen before. Ms. Willa must have sensed something like that too.

I didn't hear from Chief that evening, which was only one of the many things that kept me awake half the night with Flannery sleeping close beside me. The next morning pure adrenaline got me on the Harley to take Desmond to school, early, so I could talk to Erin O'Hare. After sending Desmond off to class, I located her in the office.

"Allison!" she said, hugging me with arms so full of bracelets they looked like Slinkies. "I've barely seen you." She drew back and scanned my face. "What's wrong?"

"Can we talk?" I said.

I glanced at the crowd of tardy kids rushing the counter. Erin nodded and pulled me into an empty glass-walled conference room.

"I need you to keep a really close eye on Desmond," I said.

"He seems fine."

"He is. But if he starts acting like he did last spring ..."

She nodded, brow puckered, and then her gaze drifted past my shoulder.

"Don't turn around," she said, barely moving her lips.

"Who is it?"

"Coach Iseley. She's lurking."

"Do you think she heard us?"

"Hard to tell." I could see Erin watching her leave the window. "She's been in a really good mood for almost a week now."

"As in, she's seeing somebody."

"As in she's being wined and dined. That's all she can talk about in the teacher's lounge. I leave now when she comes in so I won't barf."

So Desmond had been right. For a moment I almost felt sorry for the Mosquito. "Roy" wasn't going to be in the mood to wine her and dine her that night.

But I shook that off. So none of my business.

"I'll call you if Desmond starts to slide," Erin said.

I left it at that.

My next stop was Kade's office. I wanted to tell him about my conversation with Troy, at least some of it. I could have just called him, but the nervous part of me wanted to get a glimpse of Chief, too.

When I walked into the reception area at Ellington and Capelli, Tia was a little more buttoned-up than usual. I felt bad for putting her in an awkward place with Chief and was about to tell her that, but she got the first word.

"Mr. Ellington isn't in today," she said.

"Oh?"

"And I'm not at liberty to say—"

"Of course not. Listen, Tia, I'm—"

"Hey. Just the person I was about to call."

I looked up gratefully at Kade, who already had his arm out to usher me into his office.

"She's mad at me," I said when the door closed behind us.

He grinned as he nodded me to a chair. "You can tell? I think she looks just like she always does."

"Bless her heart."

"Bless her heart. You Southerners. Anyway, you don't know where your old man is either, huh?"

"My old man? You Yankees."

Kade was still grinning, and again, I was grateful. There had been a real lack of mirth in our little community lately. I hated to let go of it now, but I had to tell him about Troy.

By the time I finished, he was frowning from his perch on the front edge of his desk. "He thinks he's going to take over Vilano Beach? What is he, delusional?"

"He can't let go of the power. If he does, who is he? I mean, in his mind."

"Just in *his* mind?" Kade said. "Actually you're right. I don't think there's anything else to him."

"There used to be."

"Huh. Like what?"

I sank back in the chair. "He was a much sweeter kid than I was. He'd play with me for hours when we were little, totally content. But when I got tired of him, I'd just bite him so he'd go home."

Kade let out a guffaw.

"Then Sylvia would make me go tell him I was sorry."

"And what did he do?"

I let my mind drift backward, to the clear blue eyes filled with big tears and the sandy hair sticking straight up because he'd pulled at it while he was crying.

"He always said it was okay. He always came back to play some more."

Kade cocked his head at me. "Really."

"Really."

"So what happened to that person?"

"Kade," I said, "you don't have that kind of time. I need to let you get back to work."

I started to get up, but he held up a hand and leaned back to look at his computer screen. "I was about to call you. I got an email this morning from an attorney at Chamberlain Enterprises."

"Do they want to give you a job?" I said.

"No, but she—a woman named Pix Penwell—wants to meet with us."

"Us?"

"You and your financial advisor."

"Did you answer yet?"

"I was waiting to talk to my client."

"Well, your client says no. And who names their poor kid Pix?"

"End of discussion?"

"End of discussion."

He was getting to know me well. I tucked that away in the pile of Things To Thank God For.

Between then and Thursday, when I would go to meet Brenda Donohue, I was on pins and needles. Or maybe it was thumbscrews and carpet tacks. Flannery showed no signs of backing away from her decision to tell all once we had her mom's signature, but the nearer the meeting time came, the more I wanted to know if she'd told Ms. Willa anything we didn't already know. It just seemed like the more information I had the better, in case it was Brenda who changed her mind.

Besides, it kept my mind off of not hearing from Chief, or from Sherry, or from Detective Kylie. Police cars made regular appearances on Palm Row and San Luis Street, and India told me there always seemed to be an officer in the vicinity of Second Chances. That only eased my mind a little bit.

I knew Desmond was feeling my anxiety. Thursday morning when I dropped him at school, he said, "You not gon' walk me in again, are ya, Big Al? You fixin' to ruin my reputation."

"No," I said. But I did watch until he was inside the building.

I went back to Palm Row and picked up Flannery to take her to Sacrament House so I could go see Ms. Willa without her.

"Why can't I go to the boutique?" she said when we pulled up in front of Sacrament Two. She sounded so much like a normal, whining, fourteen-year-old girl I didn't know whether to cry or ground her.

"It's not even open yet. Why don't you want to hang out with the Sisters at the House?"

She pointed to the shiny Lincoln in the driveway, parked in front of Hank's Sportster. "Because the Gardener Guy is here?"

"Who?" I said.

"Don't you ever watch HGTV? Oh, wait, you don't even have a TV."

"Why do I need one? I get all the entertainment I want from you and Clarence."

I climbed off the bike and hung my helmet from the handlebar. When I reached for hers, she said, "When am I going to get a nickname?"

"I'm sorry?"

"You call Desmond Clarence when he's being a pain. Why am I just Flannery?"

"It's not because you're never a pain," I said. And then I reached out and touched a curl. "You had to go through a lot to get your name back. I thought you might just want to keep it."

She just nodded, but I felt her deep longing as I followed her into the house. Hank was in the kitchen with Gigi.

"You want some breakfast, Miss Angel?" Gigi said. "I got French toast."

"You want to turn that before it gets too brown," Hank said to her.

Gigi flipped a piece and beamed. "Imma be Miss Julia Chiles 'fore Miss Hank gets done with me."

I looked at Hank. "Cooking lessons?"

"She's a natural."

The back door banged, and from down the short hall I heard Mercedes yell, "Don't you be slammin' that screen door now."

Owen scowled as he held it open for Rochelle, who had apparently been in the backyard with him. It was barely eight a.m. and the place was humming.

"Nobody's slamming anything," Owen said. "That wind's kicking up like a country hoe-down—"

"Do we have a storm coming in?" I cut in.

Hank poked me in the rib. If her mouth twitched any more it was going to leave her face.

"You haven't been watching the weather report?" Owen said to me.

"No." Flannery looked up from the half bottle of Aunt Jemima she was using to drown her French toast. "She watches *us*."

"They just upped it to hurricane status. It's due to make landfall here Saturday if it keeps up."

"Will you be in charge of battening down the hatches here?" I said.

"Already happening," he said. "Between that and Ms. Willa I'm busier than a one-armed paper hanger."

"Or a hill full of ants or a hive full of worker bees."

We all looked at Flannery.

"What?" she said.

I was really starting to like that kid.

Visiting hours hadn't officially started when I got to Ms. Willa's hall, but my favorite blue-eyed nurse seemed relieved to see me. She beckoned me away from the nurse's station.

"I am so glad you're here."

"Why? Is she okay?"

"The social worker's in there."

I groaned. I'd been so caught up in everything else, I hadn't had a chance to even think about this.

"Ms. Livengood's holding her own at the moment," the nurse said. "But this one's old school. She's not leaving without a signed consent."

There was a lot of that going on today. I thanked Blue Eyes, took a long breath, and opened the door—just in time to get a blast of Ms. Willa's Jack Russell voice.

"I'm going to say this one more time, and then I'm going to call security!"

The broad-faced woman on the other side of the bed merely tapped her clipboard with a pen. "There is no need for that, Ms. Livengood. I'm here to help you."

"Help me into an early grave! I know what happens to people when they go into a nursing home. They never come out!" Her eyes finally found me. "Tell her she's wasting her time with me, Allison."

"Could you give us a few minutes alone?" I said to the woman.

"Are you a family member?"

"Yes," Ms. Willa said.

The woman flipped through the pages on her clipboard. "I don't remember seeing—"

"We just need a few minutes," I said. "Please."

She stood up and glared at her watch. "I'll be back in twenty minutes, Ms. Livengood, and then we need to get serious about this. Okay?"

When she left Ms. Willa bounced her fist on the rolling tray. "No, it's not okay! Why do they have to talk to me like I'm five years old and deaf?"

I ignored that, though I'd wondered the same thing myself, and pulled the chair up to the bed.

"You don't have to go to a nursing home," I said.

"I know that!"

"But you can afford some pretty luxury assisted living. Some of them are like five-star hotels. You could be running the place in no time."

"They're telling me I've got failing kidneys and a dying liver, and I don't believe a word of it. I don't need any assistance to live."

"Yeah, Ms. Willa, you do."

She plucked at the sheet. "Where's Flannery?"

"It's not Flannery's job to make this better. It's yours."

Ms. Willa scowled, but I went on.

"What are the other options?"

"Private nurses. But I don't want to spend all my money on somebody's salary. And I don't trust strangers in my home."

"You gave a fourteen-year-old runaway a key to your house. You trust who you decide to trust." I put my hand over the fist she was balling up again. "Do you really think we're all just going to leave you with nobody to keep tabs? Owen would probably install a metal detector at the door so the nurses wouldn't get out with your silverware."

Ms. Willa studied the edge of the tray with her thumbnail. "I'd want complete background checks. You can't be too careful."

"Absolutely."

"I wouldn't care what race they were, as long as they were competent and didn't treat me like I'm in kindergarten. You know I'm open-minded that way."

"No doubt."

She raised a bony warning finger. "I will do all the interviews myself."

"That goes without saying."

There was a little more fist-bouncing, a few terrier growls from deep in her throat. Finally she said, "You can get that woman back in here. But just so she knows, I'm not signing anything until I've read every word. I want that lawyer of yours to double-check the documents too. Not the young one. The one you're in love with. I don't like the ponytail, but other than that he seems trustworthy."

The social worker was just coming down the hall when I came out.

"She's going to go home and have round-the-clock-nursing," I said.

"How did you get her to agree to that?"

"I just stopped doing it all for her," I said.

I left to the sound of Ms. Willa yipping at her as she opened the door.

Blue Eyes was on the phone so I just gave her a thumbs-up before I rounded the corner and went down the hall that ran perpendicular to Ms. Willa's. I'd meant to check in on Maharry the last two times I was there, but something had always come up. Guilt lapped at me as I approached his room. Without Sherry, he really was alone, and he had to be going crazy with worry.

But when I poked my head in, the room was empty. I hailed a nurse coming out of another room with a tray full of pill cups.

"Has Mr. Nelson been moved?" I said.

She shook her head. "No, ma'am. He's been released."

"He went home?"

"No. He was transferred to a nursing home." She began to edge away with the tray. "Beyond that I can't really tell you."

"I totally understand," I said.

As I retraced my steps down the hall to the elevator, a wave that could only be loneliness washed over me. Maharry, all by himself in some strange place with no idea where his only child was. Unless she had come back and gotten him settled, the way she'd originally planned to. But then why hadn't she at least told the Sisters?

I stepped into the elevator and jiggled my leg impatiently as I watched the floor numbers descend. I needed to get outside and make a phone call, because as soon as I got through this meeting with Brenda, I was going to go see Maharry. I knew the person who would help me find out where he was, the one person who wasn't already up to his eyeballs in all this.

I turned my phone on en route to the parking garage, and saw that I had a voice message. The number was vaguely familiar so I took a moment to listen.

"Ms. Chamberlain," said a crisp, I'm-in-charge-of-a-lot-of-people voice. "This is Pix Penwell. I'm an attorney for Chamberlain Enterprises, and I would like to make an appointment with you—"

"And I would not," I said out loud and hit Delete.

I dialed Bonner's number then and closed my eyes when I heard his voice. It was like putting on lotion. Quickly I gave him the nutshell about Maharry.

"Would you mind doing some calling around to see if you can find out what nursing home he's in?" I said.

"I will. And I'll go see him when I find out. I need to take Zelda anyway."

"You still have the Zelda watch?"

"Liz does. I'm just backup. I'm happy to do this, but … I'm surprised that all happened so fast. The sale of C.A.R.S. isn't even final yet."

"Are you handling that?" I said.

"Yeah. I usually only do residential, but Rex asked me to."

"It's in good hands, then. Listen, Bonner, I know I don't tell you this often enough—"

"I know you love me. You tell me all the time." He laughed his soft laugh. "You just don't usually use words."

CHAPTER SIXTEEN

The twenty-five minute drive to J. T.'s Seafood Shack made me feel like I was going a hundred "extra miles," especially with the gusts trying to push Classic and me around like mean girls on the playground. I felt like I'd been soundly beaten by the time I pulled into the gravel parking lot and nearly laid the bike down in the process. Chief would have told me not to even think about riding in that weather, if I could have found him to even tell him I was going. I put that in its own pile and went on into J. T.'s.

Although the entire front of the narrow restaurant was windows, the brooding cloud cover made it dim. The only other light came from the upside-down bait pots serving as fixtures over the tables, part of the overall fishing motif. Once I saw that Brenda wasn't there yet, I let an hourglass-shaped waitress with just about as much makeup as Flannery used to wear show me to a table.

"Honey, you want to go ahead and order?" she said.

"No, I'll wait. She should be here any minute." I hoped. This didn't look promising so far.

"How 'bout I just bring you some sweet tea then?"

I was sure I'd gag on it, the way my stomach was churning, but I told her that would be great. Then I opened the menu and pretended to read it, though I really didn't have to. The smells belting out of the kitchen told me every kind of seafood was served deep-fried with hush puppies and coleslaw. I toyed with a package of crackers and wondered what ever made me think Brenda Donohue was going to show up.

And then she was suddenly there, sliding into the booth across from me.

"Sorry I'm late," she said. "I can't stay long. I only have half an hour for lunch."

"We could have met someplace closer to your work," I said.

"I always come here."

Why did that kind of question always get characters in detective novels to spill information? That was the second time it got me nada.

"Do you have the papers you need me to sign?" Brenda said.

"Here she is!"

Brenda startled as if she'd just been shot. Her relief that it was just the waitress was visible.

"Y'all ready to order?"

I looked at Brenda, who was staring a hole in the tabletop. Although she'd obviously attempted to disguise her bruises, our server had given her a double take.

"Just a sweet tea for my friend," I said. "We won't be having lunch."

She opened her mouth, but I gave her bug-eyed head a shake. She winked as if we two were kindred spirits and hurried off.

When I turned back to Brenda she was digging in her purse. "I know I have a pen in here ... "

I had one, but I let her continue the search. Suddenly I had the need to get a better sense of this woman who had raised Flannery, and my five-minute encounter with her in her front yard had told me nothing more than that she had sunk to the bottom of her life. If I'd learned anything in the last year, it was that a desperate woman never willingly showed you who she was. Most of the time she didn't know.

Brenda really was a pretty woman, even with the upper quarter of her face looking like the hind end of a baboon. There was more tidiness about her today: thick curly hair tied neatly into a ponytail, flowered scrub top crisply ironed, nails trimmed and buffed. She did look like Flannery, except for the fragility in everything from her small, shaky fingers, to the nervous nibbling on those full lips. I had so many questions, but she looked as if even one query might crush her where she sat.

"I knew I had one," she said, producing a ballpoint with advertising on it.

It might show the name of her workplace, but I gave up hope of seeing it. She rolled it between her palms as she watched me.

"Do you have the papers?"

"I do. But can we just talk for a minute first?"

"I told you, I don't have much time."

"Ms. Donohue, I really need to know a few things about Flannery's past so I can help her." I took a cautious breath. "Maybe just some things in the last year or so."

She stopped rolling the pen. "You mean since Elgin came to live with us, don't you?"

"Is that when things changed? Because Flannery is so well-adjusted in so many ways, and I'm sure that has to do with your parenting."

"I raised her alone," she said, chin up.

"So I can only assume that what she's suffered has been at the hands of Mr. ..."

"Wedgewood." Brenda's brow furrowed. "I'm not even sure what all she *has* suffered, Ms. Chamberlain."

I gave her a listening nod.

"When I first met him, when she was twelve, he treated her like a princess. I scrimped and saved to make sure she got to go to gymnastics and things like that, but he bought her the best clothes and did homework with her when I was working. He was nice to everybody, actually. I thought he was wonderful the way he spent time with his grandfather every day in the nursing home before he died." She tilted her chin again. "I never let Elgin move in with us. I don't believe in that, especially with Flannery in the house."

"Of course," I said.

"And especially because she was turning boy crazy on me." A tiny smile peeked through. "She's such a cutie she could have any boy she wanted, and after she had gone steady with every boy in the seventh grade, she graduated to older boys." Brenda's eyes filled. "That was the thing. Elgin was so good with her about that. He'd stay with her when I had to work a night shift and he'd tell me how he talked to her about boys and what they think."

"How was Flannery with that?"

"For about a year she really took to Elgin and I just didn't hear her talk about boys at all. And then everything changed."

I only nodded. Any minute she was going to look at her watch again, and I didn't want to slow her down when we were just getting to what I needed to hear. "Elgin's grandfather died ... very suddenly." She seemed to back off from that, as if it were a turn she'd avoided before. "Anyway, he didn't leave him the money Elgin expected him to. That just seemed to twist his whole personality. He was like Dr.

Jekyll and Mr. Hyde. He would be his usual sweet self one minute, and then he'd just turn on me." She shook her head firmly. "He didn't hit me. Last Sunday was the first time he ever did that. But he always told me if I broke it off with him he would say …"

She stumbled on that, but I didn't push her, much as I wanted to. It was Flannery I needed to know about in the window of time that was closing fast.

"I didn't see him treating Flannery like that. If I had, I would have taken the consequences, but that would have hurt her even worse in the long run. She also got really distant with me, like she didn't want to be alone in the same room with me. I thought Elgin was telling her lies about me, but when I asked her about it, she said she didn't like the way he was treating me." Brenda tried to smile again. "She's always been kind of motherly with me."

So I hadn't been wrong there. For that matter, most of this was what I'd expected.

"He said he had to go to Jacksonville on business."

"What business was he in?"

"Investments. He was counting on an inheritance for that and it threw him when his grandfather left everything to charity. Elgin was gone for a while, several weeks, and Flannery kept saying, 'Are you going to break up with him?' and when I'd say, 'I think I should,' she'd say, 'You can't.' That didn't make any sense to me, but every time I tried to talk to her about it, she would shut down even more. Her grades went down. She was cutting school and back-talking her teachers, and I just didn't know what to do."

Brenda put her small hands to her mouth. The pen rolled across the table, but I didn't look at it. Her pain kept my gaze on her.

"He called me one Friday, at work, and he was crying on the phone and saying how sorry he was for how he had treated me and would I please take him back. I said I didn't know, but then when he asked how Flannery was, I told him how she'd been acting out. He was so concerned, like he always was before, and he said he would look into some programs that might help her."

My stomach lurched.

"I thought he meant group therapy or something. I didn't know he was talking about a residential program. Her behavior wasn't *that* bad, I didn't think."

The bubbly server arrived with a sweet tea for Brenda and a refill for me. I watched Brenda put on a smile for her, which faded the instant she was gone.

"So he came back," I said.

Brenda nodded. "The next day, while I was at work. It was Saturday and Flannery was home. When I got there, the entire house was torn apart like somebody had come in and ransacked it and Elgin was in a panic. He said they had a huge fight and she ran off."

"Did he say she tore up the place?" I said.

"Yes. He went looking for her while I stayed at the house in case she came back. He called me and said he found her in Palatka. Two policemen were asking her questions in a McDonald's. That's when he said if we didn't want her to have a record, we should put her in a residential facility where she could get turned around. He said he'd pay for it."

"Did you see her before he took her to—where was it, Huntsville?"

"She was home for two days, and she would hardly speak a word to me. I kept saying, 'You don't have to do this, darlin',' and she'd just say, 'Yes, I do.' That was all. So I signed the papers and Elgin took her. I wanted to go with them, but she said she didn't want me to." Her hands went back to her mouth where they trembled so hard I could barely stand not taking them into mine. "And now I find out she was never there at all. That she ran away from wherever he had her." She leaned into the table. "I looked you up, Ms. Chamberlain. I know the kind of women you help. Was she …"

The words caught in her throat, and I did grab her hands. "Don't you want to come with me and ask her that yourself?"

Her answer came without hesitation. "That isn't safe for Flannery."

"Because …"

"Because Elgin will follow me straight to her."

"He's still here?"

"I haven't seen him, but I know he is. I can feel him."

"Have you tried to get a restraining order? We can help you."

"Please don't push this. He'll …"

"We can protect you."

"Not from what he can do to me." I could see her shutting down again. "I know Flannery is safe with you until I can get myself straight. I'm no good to her like this."

"You seem pretty strong to me," I said.

The last of her doors slammed shut. "You don't know," she said.

"You sure y'all don't want anything?" I looked up at the server. "Just a basket of fries maybe?"

"Oh my gosh, what time is it?" Brenda said.

"Twelve forty-five. We serve lunch all day—"

Brenda snatched up the pen. "I need to sign right now. I have to go."

I shook my head at the waitress and pulled the form Liz had given me out of my bag. Brenda snatched it from my hand.

"Tell me what I'm signing," she said.

"You're giving me temporary legal guardianship of Flannery for thirty days. I can enroll her in school, obtain medical care—"

"Fine. I know she trusts you. Just take care of her."

She scribbled a signature where I showed her and pushed the form back at me. Before I could say another word she had stuffed the pen in her purse and slid out of the booth.

"Brenda," I said. "How do you know Flannery trusts me?"

"Because she asked me to sign that paper," she said, "when the last time I signed a paper, it led to something very bad." She shook her head. "Flannery is not like me. She won't let that happen again."

I didn't try to stop her as she rushed for the door. The server sidled back to the table.

"This is none of my business," she said, "but I hope she's not running back to the jerk who did that to her face."

"Me, too," I said. "Me, too."

I got Nick Kent on the phone from Palm Row before I picked up either of the kids and asked him to set up an interview for Flannery.

"I gotta tell ya, Miss Allison, this is, like, a huge relief. I wasn't liking the thought of taking you in for … whatever. Anyway, yeah. We can do that tomorrow." He paused. "You know it's going to have to be at the station."

"As long as it's not in an interrogation room," I said. "I don't want Flannery to feel like she's a criminal."

"You can bring cookies if you want, Miss Allison."

I wanted to tell him I missed him. Why was I turning into a complete marshmallow?

"Who else should be there?" I said.

"Since you have a signature now, get Liz Doyle to show up. Flannery doesn't need an attorney, but it never hurts to have somebody on board."

"That'll be Kade Capelli," I said.

"That should do it. They may send somebody over from the DA's office to observe, but they won't be in the room. I'll take her statement, and you can go on and adopt her."

I sat up straight on the bistro chair. "I'm sorry, what?"

"I'm just giving you a bad time, Miss Allison," he said. I envisioned his freckled face. "I always have this picture in my head of you picking up every person you see that can't make it and taking them home with you."

"Thanks, Nick. I think."

"See you tomorrow at three."

Twenty-four hours, I thought as I set my cell phone on the table. I just needed to keep Flannery from doing an about-face for twenty-four hours.

And then what? What if Brenda Donohue didn't get herself

straight in thirty days? We could all do our part to get Flannery on the road to healing, but I couldn't *adopt* her. I didn't even *have* a pile for *that* thought.

I thought about getting up, pacing the kitchen, dragging my hand through my hair, that whole thing, but I forced myself to sit there and breathe and get out of my own way.

Okay. Liz. She would have answers, now that I could officially consult her.

As soon as she answered the phone I knew I had caught her running somewhere. No surprise: she was always running somewhere, which meant I had to fill her in fast.

When I did she said, "This is great. Perfect, in fact. One thing, though."

"Yeah?"

"Don't say anything about the stuff on the website during the interview."

"What web … oh. Yikes, I forgot all about that."

"You really need to look at it, Allison. Without Flannery even in the house, or Desmond either."

Her tone made me stop dangling my leg.

"What the Sam Hill is it, Liz?"

"You'll see. Just brace yourself. I've got to dash, but maybe we could talk more tomorrow? You mind if I join you and Hank at Sacred Grounds?"

"Please do," I said.

After I set the phone down, I went back to swinging my leg until my knee ached. The laptop was on my desk in the corner, but I couldn't bring myself to open it, much less click on the link

Liz had sent me. Every pounding thought in my head told me I was going to be sickened by what I saw. Maybe I'd told Flannery wrong; maybe I did know what was going to happen. Because when I finally retrieved the computer and found Liz's email and clicked myself to the link, I had to wrap my arms around my torso and rock. It was beyond sickening.

The images were stationary, but my eyes rendered them a blur as I jerked from one to the other, unable to stay on any for longer than a repulsive second.

Barely pubescent girls who should have been begging for iPads from their fathers beckoned instead for sex from the slavering creatures who logged on.

Sordid descriptions of the pleasures in store by simply leaving an email message for Topaz.

Names that no woman had given her child.

Tiger Cub. Succulent. Tricksy.

Tango.

Foxy.

My fingers cramped, which was the only thing keeping me from taking the cursor right to INTERESTED? and scalding Elgin "Topaz" Wedgewood with an email. That and the gripping fear that he would find me, find Flannery and bury her in the living grave he'd dug for her, for all of them.

I couldn't stand to look at it anymore. But even after I clicked it away and erased the history and turned off the computer, I could still feel it creeping under my skin and twisting my gut until I leaned over the trash can and lost everything but the memory of those tender body parts, displayed for any sick, demented predator with a laptop.

I went to the sink and splashed water into my mouth, although I knew the taste might never go away. That really was the worst thing about it, the fact that anyone could see it. Including the police.

"God," I said into the sink. "How do you expect us to live in this world?"

I folded, my forehead against the porcelain, and sobbed, so loud and so hard I knew Miz Vernell would soon be dialing 911. But even in the wails I couldn't control, I heard the whisper.

With love, Allison. You live in it with love.

I reached for it. But right then, all I could feel was hate.

I managed to hold it together with the kids that night, which might have been easier if I could have at least talked to Chief, but I still hadn't heard from him. I couldn't decide whether it was pride or straight-up fear that kept me from calling him. By the time I got Desmond to school the next morning, in the van because the rain was coming down sideways, and sent Flannery up to Second Chances swallowed in my motorcycle rain gear, I was frayed to my last thread. Hank would be waiting for me at a table inside Sacred Grounds, and I knew she would keep me from snapping completely.

When I saw Gigi was with her, I almost did. Really? One *more* thing?

"Hey, Miss Angel!" Gigi said as I took myself, dripping, to the table back in the corner. "Miss Hank says all you'll drink is a latte, but Imma try to talk you into something better than that."

She pulled a pad from her pocket and poised a pen over it.

"Somebody want to tell me what's going on?" I said.

"Patrice said she could use some help, with business picking up," Hank said, "and I thought of Gi. Didn't think you'd object. I told you she's a natural in the kitchen."

"No, I think it's … great. Go Gigi, huh?"

Gigi gave me her bug-eyed smile and waggled the pad at me.

"But I still only want a latte," I said. And if I could keep that down, it would be the first thing since before yesterday's sweet tea.

"You're looking rough, Al," Hank said when Gigi had gone behind the counter and I'd dropped into the chair across from her.

"I'm *feeling* rough." I leaned in and touched the hand she was about to use to butter a bran muffin. "I think I might be in over my head, Hank."

"Hold that thought," she said. "Here comes Liz."

I was actually grateful. When Liz leaned over to "hug my neck," as she always put it, I hung on for a second longer than I usually did. When she sat down next to me, her eyes were still scoping me out.

"You saw the website," she said.

I nodded.

"I told you to brace yourself. But you needed to see it."

"Why? I can't get it out of my head. Or my stomach."

"I assume we're talking about a porn site," Hank said.

"Worse than that," I said.

Hank closed her eyes and nodded. "Got it."

Liz put a rain-damp hand on my arm. "I wanted you to have a clear picture of what Flannery's been through. Just in case she tries to soft-pedal it in the interview today."

"And then are you going to erase my memory?" I shook my head at both of them. "Why is this worse than almost everything I've seen with the Sisters put together?"

"Because this is about children," Hank said.

"Speaking of which …" Liz shuffled through the inevitable nest of papers in her gaping bag and pulled out several that were clipped together. "I found out about Tango."

"How bad is it?" I said.

"She was picked up by the police September sixteenth, but I didn't get notice until early this morning." Her eyes rolled. "Took them five days to figure out that she was underage."

"We were a lot faster than that," Hank said.

I squeezed my eyes shut. "Okay, that was a Sunday, right?"

Liz turned to the second sheet in the collection. "Right. Around six p.m. This is weird."

"What?"

"They picked her up on Valencia Street. Not exactly the part of town where you'd expect somebody to be soliciting."

"Can I see that?" I said, and then virtually tore it out of her hand.

"Sure," Liz said. I could feel her giving Hank a look.

Gigi came with the coffee and proudly pulled out her pad again to take Liz's drink order. That gave me a chance to find the arrest report. The suspect, I read, had been apprehended for assaulting a teenage boy in the Flagler College parking lot on Valencia Street, one block from Sevilla. Suspect, who had no identification and refused to give her name, resisted police and had to be restrained.

I didn't doubt that.

There was more as I skimmed down. Her victim told police he only knew her as Tango and that he had been out for a walk when she "came out of nowhere" and "kicked him in the nuts."

Didn't doubt that either. What I did wonder about was why the police happened to be cruising by just then. Like Liz said, that wasn't exactly a part of town known for suspicious activity. The only people I knew who were aware of the Hot Spot were the Chattinghams, but Christine told me they went out there to feed the kids pizza. Did *they* call the cops?

"I'm going to need that back, Allison," Liz said.

"Uh-huh."

"I think she means in one piece, Al," Hank said.

I looked down and realized my fingers were digging into the pages. I handed them back to Liz.

"So what happens to her now?" I said.

"She'll go before Judge Atwell, and he'll make a determination." Liz put her hand on my arm again. I wondered which one of us she was trying to calm. "I don't think it would be a good idea to pass this information along to Flannery before the interview."

"Good call." I set aside the latte, which was probably cool by now anyway. "One woman at a time, right?"

"That's right." She gave my arm a squeeze. "So I'll see you at three at the police station."

"Police station. I have a lot of catching up to do," Hank said to me as Liz turned toward the door, and then turned back.

"Oh, I almost forgot. Bonner wanted me to tell you that he hasn't been able to locate Maharry Nelson in any of the nursing homes or assisted living facilities in the St. Augustine area. Strange, huh?"

When she was gone, I turned to Hank. "What isn't?" I said.

When we gathered in a well-lit conference room at the station that afternoon, Flannery, Nick, Liz, Kade, and I, with a woman from the district attorney's office watching from the other side of a two-way mirror, Flannery told her story with her chin high and her vocabulary in fourth gear. Using words like *exploited* and *coerced*, she related everything she'd told us at Sacrament House eight days before and all of what Brenda Donohue had shared with me. I hadn't heard the part where Elgin had sex with her in her home for six months, but I had, sadly, already filled that in. There was only one surprise.

"I don't want anybody blaming my mom for this," Flannery said, straight at the mirror that wasn't fooling her. "She didn't know what he was doing to me because she was always at work. And I couldn't tell her or he would have made it so she went to prison."

I opened my mouth, but Liz was quick with the hand on my arm.

"How's that?" Nick said.

"I visited Elgin's grandfather in the nursing home with him almost every time he went," Flannery said. "Mr. Wedgewood— senior—liked me so we talked a lot, even when Elgin was off flirting with my mother. She was working there. That's how they met."

Pieces fell into place so fast I gave up keeping track.

"He wasn't even close to dying. He just couldn't take care of himself any more, but there was no way he died—*boom*—just like that. Elgin did it to him."

Nick frowned. "That's a serious accusation."

"I know he did it because Elgin told my mother he would accuse *her* of doing it. He set it up so that if anybody ever questioned it, there was evidence that would prove she killed him."

So that was the power he had over Brenda. I felt myself going cold. Even as much as I'd seen already, I had still underestimated this man's capacity for evil.

"She was afraid the police would believe him and she didn't want to go to prison and leave me." Flannery looked at the mirror again. "She didn't know I knew. I just heard him threatening her, and then he used it to threaten *me* later."

Nick glanced at his notepad. "So that's why you let him take you: because you didn't want your mother to go to prison."

"For something she didn't do." Flannery poked her finger at the pad. "Put that in there."

We were all silent as Nick wrote. Flannery watched him, and then she looked at me, eyes large.

"I just figured something out," she said.

"What's that, Flan?" I said.

"The only reason he was ever nice to his grandfather was because he thought he was going to get all his money. I already knew that, but he really did get the money he came looking for." She tightened her lips. "He got me."

I could see that it was taking all that was left of her old tough shell to hold back the tears. My arms ached to reach out for her, but I could hear Ms. Willa saying, *You can't do all the work for her.* This was strength I was seeing, not toughness.

"I have one question," Kade said.

Flannery, of course, brightened.

"The day Allison and I tried to take you home, Elgin said we'd better be off his property before he got back. But that house doesn't belong to him, right?"

"No. It actually belongs to my great-uncle. He lives in Fort Myers and when he dies, it's in his will that my mom gets the house. All the stuff like the electric bill and all that are in his name because my mom had a lot of credit issues when she was married to my bio-dad." The chin tilted. "But she's working really hard on all that. Which is why I just want to make sure she doesn't get blamed for any of this."

"Were you headed for your uncle when you tried to run away?" I said. "Before Elgin found you in Palatka?"

"Yeah. That's where I wanted to go when Tango and I ... well, you know that part."

Now that the story was out, she wasn't interested in repeating any of it. I didn't blame her.

"We through?" Flannery said.

"Are you tired?" Liz said.

"No, I'm starving. Can we go get pizza or something?"

It was my turn to hold back tears. I was saved by a tap on the mirror-window.

"I'll stay with Flannery," Liz said. "We haven't had a chance to get to know each other."

Kade touched my elbow, and he and Nick and I met the woman from the DA's office in the hall. She was slim and black-suited and professional, but she didn't hide the hunger in her voice. She had *let's get this miserable excuse for a human being* written all over her face. I liked her.

"What do you think, Tara?" Kade said to her.

Tara. Well then.

"She's amazing. I'd put her on the stand in a heartbeat. But here's the thing."

"What thing?" I said.

"We're going to have to turn the charges of solicitation of minors over to Duval County since his business was run out of Jacksonville. But we can indict him on sex with a minor, all of that, here in St. Johns. You heard her: he was having sex with her for months before he started renting her out." She looked at me. "I don't know how you deal with this all the time. I want to throw up."

"I do that a lot," I said. Yeah, I was going to make a lunch date with this woman.

"It can be really hard to make sexual abuse charges stick," she went on, "so we're going to need the mother's testimony as well. We'll send somebody down to Hastings to take her statement."

"I guarantee you Brenda Donohue is going to freak out," I said. "She's not like Flannery."

"Then how about if I go personally?"

Forget the lunch date. I was having her over for dinner.

We all agreed that would work, and Tara said she'd head straight to Hastings. The storm wasn't hitting that far inland as hard as it was hitting there in St. Augustine. I could see the rain slashing into the window at the end of the hall.

"I'm glad we rode with you, Kade," I said. "Can we stop and get Desmond at school?"

"Yeah," he said, and then he grinned at me. "And I think we'd better get some pizza."

CHAPTER SEVENTEEN

Flannery had to settle for one of Hank's pizzas from my freezer because by the time we picked Desmond up the streets were flowing like small versions of the St. John's River. Kade consulted the weather app on his phone while we savored Hank's inimitable crust and sauce around the trunk in my living room.

"They've downgraded it to a tropical storm," he said. "And we're just looking at the front side of it right now."

"Them kindergartners gonna drown if they don't close school this time," Desmond said.

"Tomorrow's Saturday, genius," Flannery said.

She reached across the trunk and wiped a straggling piece of cheese from his chin. Desmond took a swat at her hand. Yeah, they were in brother-sister mode. At least that was one thing I didn't have to worry about. My main concern at the moment was whether Tara was going to get Flannery's mother to talk to her. Maybe I should give Brenda a call and assure her that I wasn't siccing the law on her.

"I could sure use another Coke, Des," Kade said.

Desmond inspected Kade's glass. "You ain't finished the one you got, Cappuccino."

"They want us to leave the room," Flannery said. "Like I said, you're a genius."

When Desmond had chased her into the kitchen, Kade turned to me. "That attorney from CE called me this morning. I'm having a hard time putting her off."

"Pix? She called me and left a voice message."

"What did she say?"

"I don't know. I didn't listen to it."

"You're not even a little bit curious? I am."

"Why?"

Kade shrugged. "Maybe they want you to testify against Troy. Impeach his character."

"I am not—"

"I know," Kade said, hand up. "I just like to see you get all feisty."

"Like you don't have plenty of opportunities to witness that. If you want to find out what they want, I'm okay with that, but I don't want to do lunch." I selected another piece of pizza. "Now your friend Tara is a different story. I'd really like to get to know her."

"Big Al! Look who's here."

The unbridled excitement in Desmond's voice could only mean one thing. Chief came through the kitchen door, covered head to toe in Gore-tex.

"Kade," he said. "Classic."

"Hey, boss," Kade said. "Glad you could …" He pressed his lips together and pushed himself out of the green chair. "Let me take that gear and hang it up in the laundry room before Allison gets on your butt for dripping on the hardwood."

Chief backed into the kitchen and Kade disappeared with him. I let the pizza slice drop back to the tray and tried not to let in every *one* of the scenarios that crowded for admittance to my mind. He was here. Yes. But there could be several reasons why, and I only liked one of them.

"I hear it went well today."

Chief passed through the dining room and sat on the edge of the chair Kade had just left. I could smell the rain on him. Beyond that, I couldn't tell anything.

"It did. They're going to get that piece of slime. Actually, he's not just a piece, he's the entire bottom of the septic tank. We're waiting for the DA's office to … well, you know all that, I guess."

"Yeah, but go on. Your rendition of anything is always more vivid than anyone else's."

I didn't look to see if his eyes were crinkling. I was afraid of what else I might see.

"Have some?" I said, pushing the tray his way.

"I'm good."

"Well, yes." I did look at him then. "You're good at a lot of things. But letting people know where the heck you are when you disappear for days isn't one of them." I put up both hands. "Not that it's any of my business."

"You done?"

"Yes. No. I do want to say one more thing."

"I don't think there's any stopping you."

The only thing that *could* stop me was the clog in my throat. I swallowed it down. "I'm going to worry about you no matter what. But I just need to know if I have the right to ask where you are when you take off without telling anybody."

"I want you to know. That's why I came over here."

I sank into the red chair. "Now I'm not sure I want to know. You're scaring me."

"Classic—"

My phone rang. I ignored it, but Chief picked it up and looked at the screen.

"Tara McClanahan," he said.

"I have to take this." I pointed at him as I took the cell from him. "Don't go anywhere."

"Staying."

"Tara," I said into the phone, my eyes still on Chief. "Did she talk to you?"

"No, she didn't."

The hunger was gone from her voice, replaced by something I didn't know her well enough to name. It sounded like sympathy to me.

I pressed a hand to my temple and focused on the wall across from me. "What happened?"

"Allison, Brenda Donohue is dead."

The air left the room. Chief took the phone from me and put it on speaker.

"Her car was in the carport," Tara said, "but she didn't answer when we knocked. I had a sheriff's deputy meet me there, and he looked in the front window. She was lying on the floor." Her voice softened. "The paramedics didn't even try CPR. She'd obviously been gone for hours."

"Was she ... do they know what caused it?"

"The deputy told me it looked like an overdose, but there's no way to know for sure until they perform an autopsy."

"I don't think she did drugs."

"There were two empty prescription bottles on the coffee table. Both narcotic pain meds. Both with someone else's name on them." I heard her sigh. "I know you don't want to get into this now, but she did work in a nursing home."

"Yeah. She did."

Tara let a small silence fall.

"I'll call Liz Doyle," she said. "I just thought you'd want to know right away so you can tell Flannery. I don't envy you that. She suffered a lot to protect her mother."

"Just get that monster, Tara," I said.

"Oh, don't you worry. I am on it."

Chief ended the call and moved to the arm of my chair. I sank my face in my hands.

"When does it end, Chief?" I said. "It's like the evil just goes on and on and on and we can't get away from it."

"We do stay right in the middle of it, don't we?"

"Do we have a choice? I don't think *I* do."

I felt his arm go around me and I let him pull my face into his chest. The misery pulsed through me.

"I will say this, Classic. It sounds like that poor woman's life was a walking death. When you get to that place, the step into literal death doesn't seem that hard to take."

I sat up to look at him. "I don't think she took that step. I think she was pushed. In fact I know she was. Even if he didn't shove those pills down her throat, he started pushing her there the minute he walked into her life."

"What's going on?"

It was Flannery, with Desmond.

Chief got up and met Desmond in the middle of the dining room. "In the kitchen, buddy," he said. He took the glasses Flannery was carrying and pushed open the swinging door. As Desmond moved past him Chief looked over his head at me.

Nobody can do this like you can, Classic, he said with his eyes. *PleaseGodpleaseGodpleaseGod let him be right.*

Flannery took the news as if she had been expecting it for a long time. Tears slid soundlessly down her face as she tucked herself into the corner of the chair-and-a-half and stared, unfocused, at her knees. But she didn't sob or tremble. She didn't even ask for details. It was as if I had told her the plot of a film she had already seen and it was only the memory of it that made her cry.

She didn't say much of anything beyond "thank you" when Desmond promised that, as her brother, "Imma be here for you." She simply stared as quiet activity went on around her. Kade left to meet Liz and find out what legalities we were now facing. Chief removed the pizza and Hank came with Gigi and Rochelle and a bag full of groceries I knew would be turned into comfort food. Only when Bonner showed up with Zelda, and India arrived with Jasmine, Ophelia, and Mercedes, only then did Flannery stir from her stoic staring.

I couldn't see how she could do otherwise. All the Sisters but Sherry gathered around her in the Palm Row living room just as they always did at the Sacrament Houses when one of their own faced the dark tunnel of crisis. None of them tried to pull her out of it. They were simply there to see her through it.

"You want to talk, you can talk, baby girl," Mercedes said. "Or we can just sit."

"We been there," Jasmine said. She was doing the crying Flannery had yet to do.

Flannery slid her gaze over all of them. "What happened to your mothers?"

Jasmine looked anxiously back at me, but I nodded.

"Mine died from AIDS," she said. "Prob'ly got it from one of my pretend stepfathers."

Ophelia, who sat on the arm of the chair, wiped a tear from Flannery's cheek to make room for the others. "My mama left me with my aunt when she went back to Mexico."

Zelda started to speak, but Mercedes shook her head at her and slid closer to Flannery from her place further down on the red chair.

"Why you wanna know all this?" she said.

"Because I was hoping it isn't just automatic that the same thing happens to you that happens to your mother."

I put both hands to my mouth. Flannery's pain throbbed in my throat, but Mercedes seemed to have no such problem.

"I can't believe I just heard that come out your mouth. My mama raised me on her own and she did it right, just like your mama raised you, and then I got in with the wrong things, just like you did—only I made bad choices. You didn't have no choice, so you don't got to dig your way through a whole lotta guilt like we havin' to do."

"That's right," Jasmine said.

Zelda added an amen. Rochelle's grunt was kind. I let my hands fall to my sides. The rhythm was starting, the one that could sing Flannery right into God's arms.

"But that isn't even the point," said Mercedes, who was by now no more than five inches from Flannery. "This thing we doin' here, this isn't about the past, about some legacy you got handed to you."

"Mmm-hmm."

"You listen now."

"This about what *you* gon' pass on," Mercedes said. "That's why we all gettin' ourselves straight with God and tryin' to give somethin' good back to Sacrament House by workin' in the bow-tique and the garden and the car place and the coffee place." She pointed to each of the Sisters like a maestro conducting a symphony of croons and murmurs. "You way ahead of any of us, Miss Thing, and you got a responsibility to do somethin' with your healin' so other girls don't have to stay in that trap you got out of." Mercedes gave her a slow nod. "That'll honor your mama. That'll make her life worth somethin'."

Flannery put her hands to Mercedes's wrists and let her face give in to the true sobs she'd been holding back for hours. Maybe even since the first time Elgin Wedgewood touched her.

As I cried with her from my place near the stairway, I watched Mercedes cradle "that child" in her arms and rock her as she whispered into her hair. There was no need to look for someone to oversee the Sacrament Houses. We had just found her.

I was awakened from a restless sleep on the couch by my phone ringing in my hand. I checked the time before I answered. Nine a.m. The room was probably still dark because of the storm. Flannery was asleep in the chair, so I took the phone toward the kitchen as I answered Chief's call.

"How you holding up, Classic?"

"I'm not sure yet. How's it going out there?"

He and Kade had left before the Sisters to go out to Kade's house at the beach to shore it up. I opened the curtain on the kitchen door and looked out at a murky mass of gray.

"We've got the house pretty well buttoned up, but he's going to lose a lot of real estate if we don't do some sandbagging. You think Desmond'll want to help? Stan could pick him up on his way out. It would give Des something to do."

"We all need something to do," I said. "Besides, I don't really want us to stay here with Elgin on the prowl and you that far away."

I had already given that a lot of anxious thought and had come to the conclusion that we would all be safer in a storm with Chief than at my house with Elgin Wedgewood on the loose. If indeed he had killed Brenda, he wasn't going to leave Flannery alone for long. Tara had assured me in her last call to me the night before that there was a BOLO alert out on him. I hadn't asked her if Detective Kylie was in charge of that.

"Come on, then," Chief said, "before the storm picks up again, which it's going to." I thought I heard a smile. "I don't want to sound sexist, but you and Flannery could keep us fed while we work outside."

"That doesn't sound sexist; it sounds absurd. Nobody eats my cooking."

"Hank and Joe are coming."

"I'll get the kids up. Do you have an evacuation plan if it really gets ugly?"

"On it, Classic."

I hung up feeling like I'd just been hugged. Maybe we could actually get that in sometime during this day. That and the conversation we never got to finish.

The scene at Kade's was grimmer than Chief had described it. The water had surged past the dunes and into the edges of the sea grass, and the way the ocean rose and crashed, the guys would be lucky to have the sandbags in before whatever was heating up in its dark waters boiled it over onto the path. The scrubby foliage trembled; it was the first time I had ever felt sorry for a palmetto.

Desmond went outside with the crew, after Chief ordered him into his rain gear and told him he'd be staying on the high side. Flannery and I joined Hank and her husband, Joe, in the kitchen. We were immediately shooed to the counter to chop vegetables.

"I want to get this cooked before we lose power," Hank said.

The lights had already flickered several times, and we all paused again as the refrigerator groaned off and then back on.

Hank gave it a dubious look. "If that thing makes it through the storm—"

"We're buying him a new one anyway," Joe said. "And a stove. I can't work under these conditions."

I grinned. We didn't get to see enough of Joe at our fun get-togethers. Come to think of it, we hadn't had a fun anything since the last time we were at Kade's, two weeks ago. We were going to have to fix that.

I stirred restlessly. Or could we? Wasn't there always a death or an injustice or a sociopath coming around the next corner, heading off our attempts at joy? Just as Chief said, we stayed in the middle of it.

But I never just stayed there. I went another mile into it. And another one. And another one.

When were we going to get there?

"You chop one tomato and you're done?" Hank said.

Flannery hopped off the stool beside me. "I would way rather be out there." She peered between the strips of tape on the glass door that faced the ocean, apparently heedless of the rain that tried to slap her from the other side. "It's kind of cool."

"You didn't grow up with storms?" Joe said. Evidently Hank hadn't told him about Flannery's history because the question came out as if he were chatting her up on a plane. "You're not a Floridian?"

"We never lived on the water. Every time we get a hurricane, we go to the storm shelter at the nursing home. My mom sure isn't going to take me to the beach to watch …"

Her voice trailed off. I was poised to go to her if the tears came, but she just pressed her forehead to the glass until the mistake passed.

"I want to go out and help," she said.

"You'll get blown away," I said. "Come on, this knife is calling your name."

"We'll sing while we work," Joe said. "How about—"

"No, really, I'll do it," Flannery said. "Just, please. Don't sing."

The attitude was back for now. I could do for now.

Chief, Stan, Kade, and Desmond came in just as the horizon disappeared completely. Between the fall of night and the final blast of the storm, everything was black and fierce. The power went out just as Hank set the fifth of six steaming casserole dishes on the table.

"Where are your candles, Kade?" I said.

Dead silence.

"Don't tell me you didn't get any—"

"They're here someplace. I just don't remember—"

"Flashlight? Anybody?"

I was bordering on strange, hysterical laughter by the time the Maglites came out and Joe discovered a box of candles in the back of the refrigerator.

"Oh, yeah," Kade said. "I heard they kept better in this heat if you stored them in the fridge."

"Not in that one," Hank said. "You're lucky your butter doesn't melt. Speaking of which, Joe, would you get it out for the bread—"

"Kade."

We all turned to Chief, who stood in the entrance to the narrow hall leading back to the two bedrooms, flashlight in hand.

"Did you leave the door open in the master bathroom, the one that goes out on the deck? Did anybody?"

There was a chorus of nos.

"It was open?" Kade said.

"Where is Desmond?"

"In the other john?" Stan said.

"No."

We made an automatic path as Chief charged across the living room. Before he got to the glass doors, I made another discovery.

"Flannery," I said. "She's not here either." I pushed Stan aside and flew to Chief. "Are they on the deck? I'm going to throttle them both."

Chief shook his head. The lines in his face were deepening. "Stan, check the street side. Kade, out back."

The wind swept the life out of both candles as doors opened and Kade and Stan ran out into the storm, still shoving their arms into already soaked jackets. When Chief pulled open the sliding door to the side deck I pushed past him.

"Classic!"

I didn't answer him. Several inches of water raced across the decking as I slid across it and flung myself at the railing, already screaming my children's names.

Chief's hands gripped my arms.

"Get back inside, Classic!"

"No—Chief—dearGoddearGoddearGod—"

"Listen to me!"

Chief whipped me around to face him. Even with his face directly in mine he had to shout to be heard over the roar of the storm.

"They couldn't have gone that far yet."

"Desmond can't swim! You know that!"

"Kade and I will find them. Stay here—"

Call it adrenaline, or mother-love, call it God himself. Whatever it was, it exploded, and I wrenched myself away from Chief and headed, half-running, half-careening to the back deck and down the steps until I reached the path. Immediately I was knee deep in roiling sea, but I pushed through it until a low wall of it knocked me to the bottom.

I fought for the surface, only to be smacked down again by

another wave, more determined than its predecessor to slam me into what just a day before had been the beach.

The second time I came up I knew Chief was right. I was going to drown if I didn't get out of this, and I was a strong swimmer.

Desmond wasn't.

PleaseGodpleaseGodpleaseGod.

Somehow I got off the sandbar and past the dune, into the thicket of palmettos beside Kade's house. It clawed back at me as frantically as I clawed at it, but I thrashed through its panic-stricken midst screaming, "Desmond! Flannery!"

The wind snatched my voice away. I thought I could hear it being carried off toward the road beyond. When it came again, I froze and strained to hear. Again. It was someone else's voice.

I crashed toward it through the brush, slogging in the water that rose even as I pushed my way forward. The voice wavered on the wind, off to my left, toward the house next door. I turned, shouting "Who is it?" and "PleaseGodpleaseGodpleaseGod!" until words came back at me.

"Allison! Help me!"

I was within a few yards of the house. Water rushed like a mountain fall from the upper deck, curtaining the empty storage area below, and on the other side of it a tiny figure clung to the piling as the water surged around her waist.

"Flannery!"

I plunged through the waterfall and reached out for her, but the storage area was below the level of the ground and I lost my footing and fell headfirst. When I came up sputtering, Flannery was groping for my back.

"Let me carry you, Flannery!" I shouted at her. "Stop fighting me!"

"Where's Desmond! Did you find him?"

I didn't answer as I flung her onto my back, fireman style, and pushed through the water to the low wall that I now knew separated the storage area from the ground above. If I didn't keep moving, panic would take control—because she didn't know where Desmond was.

I managed to get us both back up to the palmetto thicket, but an angry gust threw us sideways and Flannery slid off my back. When I grabbed for her, another pair of hands got to her first, and Stan hoisted her onto his shoulders and reached down to take hold of my arm.

"I'm okay!" I shouted to him. "Is Desmond back?"

"I don't know—"

"Take her in. I have to keep looking."

Once again the storm ripped through me and I was blown sideways toward Kade's. Just as my back rammed into the side of the steps, I was pulled to my feet and held against a chest I knew well. With the breath knocked out of me and lost in the wind, all I could do was let Chief lift me into his arms and carry me up the steps.

As soon as the glass door was forced closed behind us, the roar ceased. But the candlelit quiet inside was more unbearable. Joe sat on the sagging couch, eyes closed, hands clasped, lips moving without sound. Hank and Stan were engulfing Flannery in a blanket, and Kade stood at the other glass door, shaking his cell phone and swearing under his breath.

I looked at Chief and even in the weak light I saw the lines drawing deeper in his face.

"You haven't found him."

"We're still looking."

I pushed away the blanket Hank offered me. "I'm going with you. I can't just leave him out there."

"Nobody's leaving him out there. Let's find out what happened so we're not just running around blind."

Chief nodded at Flannery, who, despite the blanket that wrapped everything but her face, was shivering on the floor between the chair and the coffee table. Still shedding water, I half-flung myself at her and yanked her out to face me.

"Why did you go out there? I *told* you not to—"

"It wasn't like that!"

"Then what was it like?" My fingers tightened on the blanket. "The lights went out and you sneaked out the back door. You knew Desmond would come after you. You knew that so *why* did you do it?"

"Al." Hank's hand was on my shoulder. "I think she's trying to tell you something."

"I am!" Flannery's voice was shrill with fear. "I was in the guest bedroom looking for candles, and Desmond was in Kade's room. I heard him say he found one and I started to go in there and I saw this light like he'd lit it. And then there was this pounding, like on the back door from the bathroom out onto the deck and a big *whoosh* like he opened it. I was, like, 'Desi, don't be a moron,' but by the time I got in there it was dark again and the door blew back open. I thought I saw him going down the steps so I went after him." Flannery clawed her way out of the blanket and pulled at the soaked front of my T-shirt. "I went after *him*, Allison, only I got knocked down and ended up over there."

She pointed to the side between Kade's and the neighbor's, where I'd found her in the storage area. I knew it was the truth. I'd had the same experience.

"I found this on the floor in the bathroom." Kade stood in the opening to the hallway, shining his flashlight on a soot-stained votive candle. I'd seen it there before on the back of the toilet.

"I'm sorry, Flannery," I said.

I tried to get my arms around her, but she stiffened and looked around the room. "Who went for help?"

"Nobody, Flan," Kade said.

"But I saw a car leave. When I was trying to get under the house next door, I saw it pull out of the driveway and go that way."

She pointed south, back toward St. Augustine. Chief crouched beside us.

"Could you see what it looked like?"

Flannery closed her eyes. I watched her struggle to hold tight to her mind while everything else in her threatened to rattle apart.

"It was a car, not a truck or a van or anything. And it was big, but I couldn't see a color. I just thought somebody went to get help."

Chief nodded at me. "All right, Plan B," he said.

He stood up and motioned to Stan, Kade and me.

"I believe you, Flannery," I said. "I shouldn't have—"

"Find him," she said.

I kissed her forehead and followed Chief and the others back to Kade's bedroom. I heard Hank taking over with a sobbing Flannery. I felt like I was being ripped in half.

As soon as Kade closed the door behind us, I said, "He was taken, wasn't he?"

Chief put his hand on the back of my neck. "I think we have to consider it as one possibility."

"Does that make sense, though?" Kade said. "How would anybody know he was even here?"

"We're talking about Sultan." I heard my voice go as far up into fear as Flannery's. "He uses Marcus Rydell's eyes to watch us, just like he did Sunday night. And if he has him ..."

I plunged my hands into my hair and jerked toward the door. Chief caught me by the shoulders and held on.

"Don't go there yet, Classic. Let's just stay with this and see where it takes us."

"Can I say something?"

We all looked at Stan who was at the sliding glass door shining an LED Maglite into the midst of us.

"I don't know what any of this is about but it sounds like we oughta bring the cops in on it."

"I would have done that an hour ago if I had reception." Kade threw his cell phone onto the bed where it bounced aimlessly. "I'da had the Coast Guard, the SWAT team—"

"My truck's the only vehicle that'll make it into town," Stan said. "I'll drive in and notify the police. We're still in St. John's County, right?"

"I should go with you," I said. "I know who to talk to—"

"I think you should stay here in case Desmond shows up, which he still might."

I knew Chief didn't believe that was going to happen. The lines cut so far into his face I could have crawled into them. His eyes gave away what he did believe: that I would go after Detective Kylie with my fingernails and teeth and wind up in a cell.

"I'll go with Stan," Kade said.

"That works," Chief said.

He pulled me out of the way so the two of them could get out the door. He didn't let go when they were gone.

"I'm going to keep looking for him, Classic," he said. "And one way or the other, we're going to find him."

"I can't just stay here and do nothing."

"You're going to do nothing?" His eyes dug into mine, as if he were clearly taken aback. "You're not praying? Because that's what I'm doing."

I swallowed hard. "What are you praying?"

"The only thing I can think of," he said. "DearGoddearGoddear God."

No one slept. Flannery only dozed fitfully in her blanket, pressed as close to me as physics would allow. She woke up every time Chief and Joe returned to shake the storm off of them and see if by some miracle Desmond had come back on his own. Each time they went back out through the glass doors, more of my hope went with them. If it weren't for Hank, praying and listening and folding her hands, I would have lost it all.

Two hours after Kade and Stan left, Kade returned with Nick Kent. A search-and-rescue team arrived behind them, and after questioning Flannery and me, they, too, went out into the now-waning storm to look for Desmond. By then, I knew he wasn't out there.

I took Nick Kent down the hall where we talked in whispers.

"I appreciate you coming," I said. "But why didn't Kylie come himself? Or send a crime-scene unit? He still doesn't believe me, does he?"

Nick chewed at the corner of his freckled lip. "I don't know what he believes. He said he's working it on his end and for me to find out anything you hadn't told Kade."

"What is his problem? Why wouldn't I give Kade all the information ..."

Nick looked away.

"He said that's why he sent you, but that's not it, is it?" I said.

"Nope."

"He wants you to placate me so I'll stay out of the way."

"I'm not going to do that. It wouldn't do any good, right?"

"You're in enough trouble as it is because of me. You can go back and tell him I'm just sitting tight."

Nick chewed his lip for another few seconds.

"As long as I'm here, I might as well have a look around. Have y'all touched anything back here?"

"Just the candle, but Kade can tell you where he found it."

"You think Flannery would walk through it, show me where she was and where Desmond was, all that?"

"Yeah. It would be good for her to have something to do besides beat herself up."

Flannery was actually in the midst of another round of that when Nick and I returned to the living room. Kade was on the couch with her, smoothing the hair that was drying into a tangled clump.

"It's not your fault, Flan," Kade said. "How could you even think that?"

"Because if somebody took him—"

"Who said anything about that?"

"I'm not deaf. I heard you guys talking." Flannery sat up. "If somebody took him, I bet it was Elgin, coming after me."

"Flan, no." Kade got her face between his hands. "Listen to me. You need to stop putting this on yourself and start focusing on believing." His voice left him, and he pressed his forehead against hers until he got it back. "He's my brother too," he said. "And I'm not going to stop until we find him."

When sunlight finally smeared across the water, the ocean was still raising her voice even though the storm and its rain had largely passed. The search team said they would keep looking, that hopefully they would have better luck in daylight. None of them said anything to Chief when he wordlessly followed them back out. Nick had already left by then, after going through everything with Flannery, and Hank and Joe were ready to head back to town. Hank offered to take Flan with her.

"I want to go to Ms. Willa's," Flannery said. "She's going home today, and she's going to need me to check out the nurse."

I suspected Flannery was the one who needed Ms. Willa, and I was happy to let them hold each other up. What *I* needed was to go home and find out which way I was supposed to go. Nick Kent had been right not to believe I was going to sit tight.

After Hank and Joe left with Flannery, Kade assured me he'd tell Chief where I was off to, and that he would keep me informed if he got any news from the team, if he ever got cell phone reception again.

"We're going to find Desmond," he said.

I was delayed a few minutes longer while he cried hoarsely in my arms.

That wasn't the only thing that slowed me down. Although A1A was largely passable, I had to bring the van to a crawl through standing water in several places. I was testing the brakes on the St. Augustine side of the bridge when my phone rang. *Now* I got reception.

I pulled over into the parking lot in front of the fish market and answered, my heart pounding in my throat.

"Yes?" I said.

"Good morning, Ms. Chamberlain," a muffled voice said. "Are you ready to find your son?"

CHAPTER EIGHTEEN

I squeezed the phone. "Who is this?"

"Your only hope. Follow my instructions exactly, and you will see him."

My thoughts spun, but I grabbed onto one. "I want to talk to Desmond."

"After you follow your first set of instructions."

"Put him on the phone!"

"We'll do this my way or no way, Ms. Chamberlain. What's it going to be?"

I twisted the phone away from my ear and pressed my mouth into my wrist. I couldn't mess this up. *PleaseGodpleaseGodpleaseGod, the words.*

I put the phone back to my ear. "What do you want me to do?"

"You've made a good choice. In one hour, go alone to Forty South Palmetto Avenue, Palatka. Ask for Mr. Ozzy."

"Wait." I opened the console and dug frantically for something to write with. "Tell me that address again."

"You heard me, Ms. Chamberlain. One hour. No more. No less."

The call ended. I stared at the phone until it blurred in front of me. He had him. He had my son.

DearGoddearGoddearGod—

Go. Go the mile.

"That's *thirty* miles, God!"

I let my head drop to the steering wheel. What was I saying? I would go as far as I had to for Desmond. And the whisper, no matter what it meant, was still the whisper. God was still there. I sat up and restarted the engine. *Forty South Palmetto Avenue—*

The van shuddered and died.

"No! Nonononono!"

The dashboard lit up, and I trounced on the gas pedal and pushed on the key until it cut into my finger.

"Don't do this to me! Please!"

I stomped on the pedal again, and the engine gasped its way back to life. But it ran rough and the chassis shimmied. It wasn't going to stay alive for long.

Coaxing with my foot, I pulled back onto the road and forced myself to breathe while I thought what to do. There was only one option, and that was to go home and get the bike. The jackal on the phone said one hour, no less. I could change out of Kade's sweatshirt and into riding clothes and still get to Palatka in time. I just didn't let myself think what I was going to be in time *for.*

The van stalled twice more before I reached Palm Row, sealing my decision, until I turned into the lane and saw Hank's car parked in front of my house. I might have backed out and taken my chances with the van if she hadn't pulled aside the kitchen curtain.

Think think think think …

I prayed all the way to the side door for a face that gave nothing away. Hank opened it and said, "You've heard something."

I nodded her back and looked around the kitchen.

"She's upstairs taking a shower. What gives, Al?"

"If I tell you something in confidence as my spiritual adviser, you can't tell anyone, right?"

"What did you do?" she said.

"Nothing yet. But I'm about to, and you have to swear that you'll keep it to yourself unless I'm not back here with Desmond in two hours."

"Al—"

"Please. Promise me. I have to do what he said."

"Who?"

I told her about the phone call while I put on jeans and a shirt from the laundry basket and crammed my feet into my boots. She did nothing except shake her head, but when I stood at the door with the Harley key in my hand, she closed her eyes and said, "The Lord be with you, Al."

"And also with you," I said. "With all of us."

At first the roads were ponded from the storm, but the further inland I rode, the less often I had to drive straight down the middle of the highway to keep my wheels from disappearing into the receding wash. Once I no longer had to concentrate so hard on navigating, I let myself think about the phone call.

The voice had obviously been disguised. I would never be able to identify its owner, but he was definitely male and not uneducated. That ruled out Marcus Rydell.

Which didn't reassure me. Nor did the fact that his tone wasn't aggressive or immediately threatening. The arrogance, the cold certainty that I would do exactly what I was told—that rendered Marcus Rydell a schoolyard bully in comparison. I had no illusion that whoever it was would hand Desmond over to me when I got there. He wanted something from me, and he was going to get it. As long as he let Desmond go, I would do anything.

That was why I hadn't called Chief or Kade or Nicholas Kent. They wouldn't let me risk my life doing this. And I had no doubt that was what I was doing.

The road was potholed where the water had stood and I had to focus on it and on the fact that now that I was in Palatka, I had no idea where Palmetto Avenue was. I saw a Citgo station ahead and signaled a right turn. And then suddenly I was jolted above the pavement by a rock I didn't see until I was airborne.

I forced the front wheel to stay straight, but all I could do was pray that the back one wasn't thrown one way or the other, or the Classic and I were going down. We hit the pavement on both wheels so hard my teeth slammed together and I could almost feel my brain sloshing in my skull. But we were upright.

My jaw wasn't the only thing that had been jarred. If I was going to get through this and get Desmond back, I couldn't let my mind go chasing after what-ifs.

"There is only what is," I whispered.

Then go.

I followed the directions the woman at the gas station gave me, and the address on the cinder block building read: 40 Pal etto Aven e. But I still stared from the bike for several minutes after her grumble faded. The sign above it said Wildwood Convalescent Center.

If this was that jackal's idea of a joke, it was a sick one, and I was far beyond laughter.

I had to be buzzed in through the front door to get to the reception counter. An uninterested black woman cleaned out her ear with her little finger as she asked me what patient I was looking for.

"Mr. Ozzy?" I said.

She examined the wax she'd retrieved. "Is that an answer or a question?"

"I was told Mr. Ozzy was here."

"You were told right." She pushed her chair back and stood up to lean across the counter. "Go down that hall," she said, pointing. "He's in Room 110. And thank the Lord somebody came to see him. Maybe he'll hush up that cryin' he's been doin' ever since he got here."

I headed toward the hall.

"You're welcome," she called after me.

Room 110 was five doors down, and I reached it before her voice faded in the Pine-Sol–scented air. I didn't set myself up for what I was going to see. It didn't matter what shape Desmond was in as long as he was alive.

But when I pushed open the door, it wasn't Desmond's chocolate-eyed gaze that met mine from the bed. Even in the dismal half-light I knew the almost nonexistent eyes that blinked behind the thick, smeared lenses belonged to Maharry Nelson.

It took him a moment longer to recognize me, and when he did, he fought to sit up, but restraints on his wrists kept him latched to the bed rails.

"Maharry, what on earth?" I said.

"You came." His voice crackled with the effort to breathe. "They said you would but I didn't believe them."

My mind spun again, but I forced it to stop right where I was. Think now. Think.

I put my hand up to quiet Maharry and opened the door to the bathroom. It was empty. I crossed back to the hall door and locked it. By the time I got to his bed, the thoughts were coming one at a time.

"I'm taking these things off," I said. "But you have to promise to stay quiet, okay?"

He nodded, but I was sure he couldn't have spoken anyway. His voice contorted into dry weeping.

"Shh, Maharry. I'm going to send somebody back to get you out of here, but you need to help me help you."

"Don't help me," he said. "Help Sherry Lynn."

I got one wrist loose and Maharry grabbed my hand. I was shocked by the icy feel of his bones.

"Where is your oxygen?" I said.

"They brought me here to die."

"Who?"

"Sultan's people. They brought me here to die."

"I don't understand. Why would they do that?"

"Because I shot Sultan. A year ago I shot him."

My fingers froze on the strap.

Maharry let his hand fall to the sheet that only half-covered his diminished body. "I shot him to protect Sherry, and I'll lie here and die for that. But you have to make sure they don't go after her."

I loosened the other restraint and pressed the frigid hands between mine. His pain pulsed against my palms, but it wasn't guilt I felt there. It was the fear of a parent who would sacrifice anything for his child.

"You didn't shoot Sultan," I said. "Your eyesight is so bad you would have had to have been right on top of him and you weren't."

"He had a big back. I got lucky."

"He was shot in the head, Maharry, and you didn't do it. You're protecting Sherry *now*, aren't you?"

Panic seized his face, and he lurched up, gasping. I somehow found the release for the bed rail and got one knee up on the mattress so I could take hold of him. He was no more than a skeleton in my arms as he breathed again, shallow, tearing breaths.

"Okay, we won't talk about that right now," I said. "I'll take care of Sherry, I promise." My inhale was only a little less ragged than his. "I just need to know one thing, Maharry, because my kid is lost too."

He nodded. The drawstring skin around his mouth was blue.

"I think the same people who brought you here sent me to see you, but I don't know why. Do you?"

"The letter," he said.

"What—"

"In the drawer."

The only drawer I saw was in the bedside table. I helped him back onto the pillow before I yanked it open and found a folded piece of paper.

"Is this it?" I said.

Maharry licked at his lips as if he could barely find them. "He said to give it to you and then I could have my nurse."

"When did he say that?"

"Just before you got here. Can you get her for me? The redheaded one. She's the only one who takes care of me."

"I'll find her right now." I leaned close to him. "Maharry, I have to go, but I *will* get you out of here."

"Just find Sherry Lynn," he said. "Tell her to keep running."

I made myself leave the letter unopened as I marched down the hall. The woman I'd talked to before was standing in front of the counter with a flier and a roll of tape.

"I'm calling the authorities about that man's care," I said. "I suggest you provide him with oxygen before they get here."

She waggled her head. "He has oxygen."

"No ma'am, he does not."

She looked at me with the first trace of concern I'd seen on her face.

"And he wants his nurse," I said. "Redhead?"

The woman brushed past me and squealed her tennis shoes down the hall.

"Where is she?" I called after her.

She didn't answer until she reached the door to Room 110. With her hand on the knob she said, "Look on the counter."

I saw nothing on the counter except the flyer, lying face down with four rolled pieces of tape fixed on it for hanging. Dread bit at me before I even turned it over.

IN MEMORIAM, it said—above a fuzzy photo of a smiling Brenda Donohue.

DearGoddearGoddearGod.

My return to the Harley was like a run in a bad dream, thick and horrifying. My mind was the only part of me that raced as Sultan and Maharry and Brenda and Marcus Rydell chased themselves in a surreal circle. It stopped when I finally reached the bike and opened the letter.

Good choice, Ms. Chamberlain, it said. *You will get your son back when you have brought me the rest of my betrayers. Go home and wait for my call.*

There was no whisper from God to go. Perhaps because there was no other choice.

When I got to the house I went straight to the living room to plug my phone into the charger on the end table. Hank was on the couch, holding a sobbing Flannery. My heart stopped.

"What is it?" I said. "Did you hear—"

"No," Hank said. "Hon, come on, tell Miss Allison what happened."

I sat on the other side of Flannery, who handed me her phone. "I don't ever want to see this again."

"Tell me some more," I said.

"I turned it on when I got back because I thought Desmond might call me. It rang just now and it wasn't Desi—it was *Elgin*. He said he's going to get me back because now he has help."

She thrust her face into her hands and rocked. I'd seen that more times than I wanted to, in every woman who came to us in danger of losing her sanity.

"Okay, listen to me, Flannery," I said. "I'm going to call Officer Kent. See?" I put my phone in front of her covered face. "I'm calling his number. He won't let Elgin get near you."

Hank pulled Flannery back into her chest and raised her eyebrows as I waited for Nick to pick up.

"This is about Elgin," I said to her. "Whole separate thing."

I wasn't sure now that it actually was, but if I didn't keep it that way in my head I was going to be rocking right beside Flannery.

The call went to voice mail. I turned Flannery's phone over and brought up her call history.

"Nick, it's Allison," I said. "Flannery heard from Elgin. Here's the number."

I rattled it off and asked him to call me. When I hung up I heard a car door slam. Flannery convulsed in Hank's arms.

"It's okay," I said, running to the foyer.

I had no idea whether it was okay or not. It wasn't. When I peered through the curtain Detective Kylie was getting out of his car.

"Hank," I said, tearing back into the living room, "take Flannery upstairs."

"Is it Elgin?" Flannery said.

"No, baby." I bulged my eyes at Hank. "It's a detective friend of mine. I need to talk to him alone."

Hank practically picked Flannery up and stuffed her under her arm to get her up the steps. Even though the doorbell was on its second insistent ring I waited until I heard Flannery's door close before I let Kylie in as far as the foyer. The thought that he might be coming to tell me Desmond's lifeless body had been found washed up on the beach was only just joining the surreal circle in my head when he greeted me with, "Nothing on your boy yet. Search and rescue has covered everything, but the Coast Guard is still on it."

"He's not out there," I said.

Kylie rubbed the back of his head. "Kent says there's evidence he was taken, but we know it wasn't by Marcus Rydell."

"Oh, come *on*—"

"We picked Rydell up for questioning just before dark last night, before your son disappeared, and we had him in an interrogation room until four this morning."

I could feel beads of perspiration gathering on my upper lip. I had to think, and I couldn't let Kylie see that I was anything but reassured by that news.

"What did you pick him up for?" I said, but as soon as I said it, the sweat broke out on my palms too. Bad idea. Any minute my phone was going to ring and I was going to be told how to bring Sultan his betrayers. I needed to get Kylie out of there.

"You know, I don't even care about that right now," I said. "I just want my son back. Thanks for coming by."

Of all the frustrating conversations I'd had with Detective Kylie, he chose that one to look at me as if he saw me. The defensive mask fell slowly from his face.

"We've been tailing him," he said, "just in case you were right about seeing him here." He kept his eyes on me. "Nothing suspicious until yesterday afternoon when we got him on surveillance opening a package he got in his PO box. Cell phone. Probably a burn phone."

It would be too obvious if I didn't ask the question. I wiped my now drenched hands on the seat of my jeans and said, "It's a crime to get a cell phone in the mail?"

"No. But it's suspicious. Plus he was driving a red Mustang we *know* he doesn't own. Listen, I know you've been up all night." He pointed his chin at the church pew behind me. "You want to sit down?"

"No," I said too fast. "But I do want to *lie* down, so—"

"We followed Rydell out to Ponte Vedra. When he parked at a public beach and walked up A1A in fifty-mile-an-hour gusts and hid under the steps of a vacant rental, we thought it was time to bring him in."

"Then he didn't take Desmond," I said.

Kylie's voice was even. "Why aren't you relieved?"

"Because somebody did!" I said.

"Who?"

A phone rang, and I recoiled like I'd been snakebit. Kylie pulled his cell out of his shirt pocket and barely took his eyes from me long enough to look at the number.

"Fifth time this morning," he said, more to himself than to me.

"Go ahead and take it," I said.

He shook his head and dropped the phone back in his pocket. By then I'd managed to grab a few of my wits.

"You're right," I said. "I'm so exhausted I can't even think."

He waited, eyes alert. It was the first time I ever thought that in there someplace, Detective Kylie might be a good cop.

"If your son ... Desmond, yeah?"

I nodded.

"If Desmond was abducted, Allison, and you get a ransom call—"

"Which would be pointless since I'm practically broke—"

"—you need to let us know. Call Officer Kent if that's who you want to talk to, but don't think you can handle this by yourself because that never works out."

"I know I can't handle it by myself," I said.

It was the only truth I could tell him right now. But it wasn't the only truth he was seeing.

"I'm going to send Kent over here to stay with you," he said. "If you do get a call, he'll know how to handle it."

"Great," I said. "That would be, yeah, do that."

"He's not back on duty until four, but I'll get him in."

"Mmm. Thanks."

He gave me a look that had probably torn confessions out of tougher suspects than me, but I held on until he was out the door. I let myself fall against it and listened as his car left Palm Row.

"Coming down," Hank said from the top of the stairs.

Flannery was already at the bottom, holding her arms out to me. "Is he going to help find Desmond?"

"Absolutely." I hugged her close and looked at Hank.

"I'm thinking that just to be on the safe side with this Elgin thing, you and Flannery ought to go to Second Chances. Close the shop and hunker down with the Sisters and when Nick Kent gets here, I'll send him over there."

"Sounds like a plan," Hank said. "And you?"

"I'll wait here for Nick. Kylie's sending him over."

My cell rang in the living room. I went cold.

"I need to get that," I said. "Y'all go ahead."

The call was on its third ring when I picked it up and pulled out the charger cord. My hands were so slick with sweat it shot out of my hand like a bar of soap and shot into Flannery's path. She picked it up.

"Miss Allison's phone," she said into it. "She's right here—"

I snatched it from her and retreated to the bookcase, pressing it hard into my ear.

"Bad choice, Ms. Chamberlain." The voice was more menacing than before.

I looked over my shoulder. The kitchen door was swinging.

"I've done everything you told me," I whispered.

The back door closed.

"You let that cop in."

"Cop."

I groped at my memory. Kylie wasn't wearing a uniform, and his car was unmarked.

"My mistake," the voice said. "Detective. That's worse, Ms. Chamberlain."

Hank's car started out front. I waited until its voice dissolved into the traffic on Cordova before I said, "I got rid of him. I didn't tell him anything."

"How do I know that?"

"Because he left. If I'd told him about this, he'd still be here, tapping my phone ... You said I could talk to Desmond after I went to the nursing home."

"He's in transit right now."

"To where? Here?"

Silence.

"Please," I said. "Just tell me what you want me to do."

"Bring the betrayers."

"What betrayers?"

"Do we have to draw you a picture, Ms. Chamberlain? Oh, wait. You've already seen it."

His muted laugh crawled under my skin.

"What picture? What are you talking about?"

Silence again. This time I stared into it, and saw the bloody portraits on the auto shop wall.

"You know," he said.

"The women in exchange for Desmond, that's what you want."

PleaseGodpleaseGodno—

"You're getting ahead of yourself," he said. "Get them all together in one place. I will find you."

I stared in horror at the phone when he ended the call. I was already getting them into one place.

Fingers shaking almost beyond my ability to tap in the number, I called Hank. She didn't answer. I hung up and headed for the door, but I stopped before I opened it. If Sultan or whoever was calling me knew I'd let Detective Kylie in, the house was being watched, so either he or his informant would try to follow me.

But that didn't mean he'd succeed. A motorcycle could go places a car couldn't.

I broke every traffic law in St. Augustine, short of driving right down St. George Street. I cut across it at Orange Street and then shot inside the square that housed Faux Paws and White's Jewelry and pushed the Classic between White's and the Silver Feather just as a woman in the Crystal Clear Gallery poked her head out the door.

"Sorry," I said. "Wrong turn."

I parked the bike illegally next to a Dumpster and ran until I hit the next mall, beside the schoolhouse. The usual crowd of souvenir hunters let me disappear among them until I came out two doors from Sacred Grounds. For once I was grateful for their hunger for junk. I took a breath and pretended nonchalance as I made my way down the sidewalk. The only thought in my head was *PleaseGodpleaseGodpleaseGod.*

I was about to make the final leg up the stairs to Second Chances when Patrice hissed to me from the front porch.

"Hank needs you inside," she said.

I ducked under the railing and followed her in. Hank was at the same far table where she and Liz and I had talked a two-day lifetime ago. Flannery was crying again.

"It was Elgin, Miss Allison," Flannery said when I reached them.

"What was?"

"On your phone when I answered it."

I closed my eyes. "Flan, no. How could you even tell? It was disguised."

"It's a software voice changer. He used it all the time on his smart phone when ... it was *him*! You have to believe me."

"I do." I closed my eyes and breathed. "Hank."

"Yeah."

"Who's upstairs?"

"Mercedes and Jasmine and Ophelia. I was about to call Liz to bring Zelda over here and then head to Sacrament House to get Rochelle. Gigi's here, in the kitchen."

"Don't," I said. "Leave Flannery with Mercedes and you go find Chief or Kade and tell them what's going on so one of them can take care of Flannery."

"Al," Hank said, "I don't *know* what's going on."

"I'm not sure I do either, but just do it okay? Trust me?"

She gave me a grim nod.

"Take Flan up the inside stairs."

"Right. Where are you going?"

"I'm going to Liz's place to get Zelda."

She didn't ask me why. I wasn't sure I knew, except that I had to make it look like I was rounding up all the "betrayers."

Hank and Flannery cut to the inside hallway that led to the stairs and I went to Gigi in the kitchen.

"Don't ask me any questions, Geege. Just tell me if there's a back entrance."

She simply bulged her eyes and pointed. I emerged into the alley just as my cell rang. It was the same number.

"I'm trying," I said into the phone. "You have to give me time."

"Mama?" a thick, young, frightened voice said.

"Desmond?"

"I'm at Sacrament House, Mama," he said.

And then the phone went dead.

The only thing that kept me from tearing up the steps of either of the houses when I got there was that Desmond hadn't said which one he was in. When the curtain parted in the front window of Sacrament One and the too-big cream-colored palms came through and waved, I ran for it, shouting his name.

His hands disappeared from the window, but it wasn't Desmond who opened the door and shut it behind me. It was Elgin Wedgewood.

"Surprise," he said.

Without the voice disguise he was far less convincing. I felt like

I could take him out at the knees again, just as I had before. Hope rose as I turned to the window to see my son, and found Sultan between us. In his hand was a gun, just like the one Nick Kent carried. Maybe it was smaller, but it could have been an AK-47, as large and murderous as it looked to me.

I didn't know whether it was fear or revulsion that wrapped itself around me and squeezed. I had only seen this man twice. Once when he was still physically whole and powerful enough to rule his hellish world. And once after that world had been replaced by the one he was imprisoned in now, with a crippled body and a misshapen face and a patch over the eye that was no longer of any use to him. He was no uglier now than he had been the first time.

I edged toward Desmond, who was on his knees on the chair where Flannery had pulled out the stuffing. Sultan jammed the wheelchair between us and shook his head at Elgin, whose breath I could feel on the back of my neck. He stepped back.

"I've met all your demands," I said to Sultan. "Your women are on their way here, all but Sherry, who I'm sure you've already taken care of."

I heard Desmond gasp, but I couldn't look at him.

"And they say I can't get women to perform for me any more," Sultan said.

"So I can take Desmond home, then."

"He can go wherever he wants. But he'll be going without you, and I think we both know what that means: right back where he started." He turned his misshapen head toward Desmond. "Unless he wants to come with me. I am the boy's father after all—"

"I ain't leavin' without her."

Desmond's voice was stronger than it was on the phone, and it frightened me. One word over the line could provoke this man.

"It's okay, Des. I just want to ask Mr. Lowery some questions, and then I think we'll both be out of here."

Elgin spit out a laugh. Sultan dismissed him with a one-eyed look.

"Ask me anything you want, Ms. Chamberlain," Sultan said. He let the gun rest on his thigh.

"What do you want with me? I never did anything to you."

"You tried to destroy my life. I understand that's what you're about with men."

"I'm not the one who shot you. You may not recall, now that your brain has been scrambled, but I was facing you when you went down. You got it in the back of the head, so there's no way—"

The gun was once more in his hand, black square barrel pointed at me.

"One of my whores shot me," he said. "I'm about to find her and take care of it. But it wouldn't have happened if it weren't for you."

The unscarred places on his face darkened, creating an even more macabre picture. It made me fear far more than what that gun could do.

"You took Geneveve. Her and everything else I worked for."

"That *you* worked for?" I said. "They did the work you forced them to do—"

"You destroyed it!" His voice was suddenly as wild as it had been controlled five seconds before. "You made it impossible for me to get any of it back."

"Not exactly impossible," Elgin said. "You and I—"

"Shut up."

The expletive Sultan shot at him sent Elgin into silence.

"It will never be the way it was," Sultan said to me. "*You* are responsible, and *you* are going to pay."

"So why don't you just shoot me and get it over with?" I said.

"No!"

Desmond was out of the chair and wedged between Sultan and me before I could stop him.

"You shoot me first!" Desmond screamed at him. "'Cause I rather be dead than be any kin to you!"

Sultan narrowed his only eye. "Get him out of here."

"Desmond, sit down," I said.

But Elgin shoved me into the chair and grabbed Desmond by the Harley insignia on the front of his T-shirt. With an almost effortless heave he threw him against the plank-and-cinder-block bookcase and left Desmond, slumped and limp, on the floor.

I screamed his name and tried to go to him, but Elgin stood over me. His eyes, however, were on Sultan. Somewhere amid the profanity, I deciphered—

"Enough of this! Where is my girl? You promised me if I helped you get your kid, you'd get her back for me."

"She's on her way." Sultan had recovered command over his voice and turned it on me. "You can't control this situation."

"Then what do you *want?*"

"What we all want, Ms. Chamberlain. Revenge."

"That won't give you your life back."

"No. But someone else can." He nodded at Elgin. "See who just pulled up. No, let's all see. Open the curtain."

He was pointing at me. I went to the window and yanked back the curtain Geneveve had hung there.

A BMW stopped at the curb. I stared as the driver's door opened, and Troy Irwin stepped out.

CHAPTER NINETEEN

My mind ceased to track as the passenger door flung open and Flannery belted from the car and took off across the street toward Sacrament Two. Elgin tore outside, leaving the screen door flailing in the wind, and grabbed her just short of the koi pond.

I started for the door, but something clicked into place, and I knew it was Sultan's Glock. I could only watch as Elgin passed Troy at the curb on his way back to Sacrament One with a kicking, screaming Flannery thrown over his shoulder like a bag of Owen's fertilizer. Troy said something to him with no visible response from Elgin. When all three of them came through the front door, Flannery was the only one talking.

"You said you were going to *help* me!" she screamed.

Her eyes were right on Troy.

"You see, Ms. Chamberlain." Sultan's voice oozed sickening charm. "My life is not over after all."

Flannery pounded Elgin with both tiny fists, and I could see his face taking on the same monstrous expression it had worn when he slapped me aside to get to Brenda.

"Flannery!" I said. "Stop, baby."

"Everybody stop," Troy said. He swung his gaze across the room as if he were running a board meeting. "Go across the street, all of you, and wait in the other house. I need some time alone with Ms. Chamberlain. That was the agreement."

Elgin glared at Sultan, who nodded and said, "Give me the girl."

Elgin deposited Flannery into Sultan's arms and Sultan locked her against him before she could even think about pummeling him. But he couldn't lock down her voice.

"Don't let them take me, Miss Allison!"

"Hey." Troy's voice was like a velvet fist. "I said I'd help you. Just be patient."

Flannery gave him a hard stare and spit on the floor in front of the wheelchair.

"You can't let them take her, Troy," I said, even as Elgin pushed them both out onto the porch and slammed the door behind him.

Troy ignored me and went to Desmond, who was still motionless against the bookcase. "What happened?"

I pushed him out of the way and knelt beside my son. I could feel his breath on my hand as I pulled his face toward me.

"He's out cold but he's still with us," Troy said.

He lifted Desmond up from his armpits and hoisted him over his shoulder.

"What are you doing?" I said.

"I'm getting you two out of here before they come back. Back door this way?"

"I'm not going to let you—"

But Troy was already halfway through the kitchen. When I got to him, he had the door open.

"Where can we go that's cut off to cars?" he said.

I stared at him.

"Ally, come on—"

"There's nothing but alleys between here and West King," I said. Not because I trusted him, but because the Whisper was louder than it had ever been.

Go the extra mile with him. Go!

It pushed me through the door and after Troy, who jogged across the backyard and into the vacant lot beyond where the Johnson grass parted at his waist as he mucked through. I kept my eyes on Desmond's head, bobbing over Troy's shoulder.

PleaseGodpleaseGodpleaseGod let this be You I'm hearing.

When the narrow field gave way to the alley behind C.A.R.S., Troy turned and looked at me, eyes confused.

"I have no idea where we are."

"Almost to West King," I said.

"Is there a place we can stop so we can call an ambulance?"

I followed his gaze skyward. Rain was starting to fall again, and his face was scarlet. Desmond was dead weight on his shoulder.

I pointed toward C.A.R.S. As we drew closer I could see the remains of tattered crime-scene tape hanging from the gaping side window. The shards of glass had been removed, but no one had boarded it up. The HOGs must have been too occupied with securing their own houses.

I held back the tape for Troy and let him pass me with Desmond just as the shop lit up with lightning as sharp as the jagged glass that was swept against the wall.

"What can I lay him down on?" Troy said.

"There are some cushions on the couch in the office," I said. "But he had better be right here when I get back."

Troy closed his eyes. His face was beginning to go gray. If he did try to make off with my son he wouldn't get far.

When I returned with the cushions, Troy was on the floor with Desmond in his lap, lifting his eyelid.

"He's starting to come around," he said. "There's a bump on the back of his head, which they say is a good sign. He'll be okay."

"What do *you* know, Troy? Nothing about this is okay."

I dropped the cushions in a line on the floor and rolled Desmond off of Troy's lap and onto them. Then I dug in my jacket pocket for my cell.

"I already called 911," Troy said. "They're sending the paramedics."

"You don't mind if I double check that, do you?"

Even as I said it I realized my phone was with the Harley. The push to follow Troy had been so strong, so divine, but here I was in a vandalized building on West King Street with the man who had obviously orchestrated this entire nightmare.

Love another mile, I was told. Sternly. There was no room for an answer.

"All right," I said. "I'll wait here for the ambulance. You get a head start on the police, because this time when I tell them what you've done, I'm going to camp out in Detective Kylie's office until he—"

"I've been trying to get him all day."

"Proactive as usual," I said. "Troy, please don't try to snow me. Just go. You've already turned Flannery back over to her pimp. My son is unconscious, thanks to you, I'm sure—"

"No. That's not how it went down."

Troy got to his feet and pulled me up by one arm. I struggled, but he pushed me into the counter and pinned me against the edge until I gasped.

"Just listen to me for five minutes," he said. "And then you can tell them anything you want. Please."

Please. I hadn't heard that word come out of Troy Irwin's mouth in thirty years. Not in that tone that said *I need you* and expected nothing in return. The desperation in his eyes was only that of a man begging to be understood. The Troy Irwin I had come to despise did not beg.

"Until the paramedics get here," I said.

Within me something sighed. Troy loosened his hold just enough to stop the counter from digging into my back.

"I *was* in on it,'" he said. "I thought you took everything away from me, and I was going to take everything away from you."

"You already told me this," I said.

"Just listen. I went through the school, told them I wanted to give them money for their athletic program, and they put me with the coach—"

Skeeter Iseley flashed through my head. Desmond saying "Roy" was hitting on her in the office. "Is there nothing you won't stoop to?" I said. "You dated his teacher so you could get *information* from her about my *son?*"

"She said—"

"You don't even have to tell me what she said. She told you right where he came from, didn't she?" I shook my head. "But you knew that ..."

"She had already looked into his history. She had his biological father's name."

"Why are you telling me this?"

I pulled at my elbows to push his arms away, but Troy caught me and spun me around. I was trapped against him. Ten feet away, I saw Desmond stir.

"I found Lowery, and I made him an offer," Troy said. "I would set him up with anything he needed for his business, and he could get his son back, and we'd both have our revenge on a mutual enemy."

"Stop!"

He didn't. His breath was hot in my ear. "He turned me down at first, but then he called me and we made a deal. I would set him up in Vilano Beach, and he could take over the town, have a bigger thing going than he ever had here. All he had to do was get Desmond and let me be there when he took him away from you. He had it all set up with his business partner."

"Marcus Rydell is not his business partner."

"Not Rydell," Troy said. "Elvin."

"Elgin."

"And then you showed up at the courthouse."

"And the rest is history—"

"Ally—listen." His arms tightened. "I couldn't go through with it."

"Yet here you are."

Desmond whimpered.

"By then I knew I was in deep with a psychopath. I had to let him get Desmond so *I* could get him. I knew he'd keep our agreement to let me be there, and I tried to get Kylie on the scene."

"But Flannery—"

I heard a vehicle pull up, but Troy didn't flinch.

"I didn't know anything about that until I got to the Vilano Beach house last night. Elgin had Desmond there, but he was raging about *his* kid. Apparently Rydell was supposed to snatch her, but he had disappeared and Sultan couldn't control Desmond by himself so that Elgin could go after her, not unless they tied Desmond up or drugged him." Troy jerked me closer. "I couldn't let them do that to him. I told Sultan I would get the girl and call them to meet us at the place on San Luis. I thought I could get Kylie to be there. I need you to believe me."

"Why?" I said. "Because you had a miraculous change of heart on the courthouse steps? You could have fooled me."

"Do you remember what you said?"

"I said a lot of things." I wasn't sure how much longer I could stall him and keep him from seeing that Desmond was struggling to open his eyes. By then I was beginning to think I had only imagined that someone else had arrived.

Troy turned me around, and my breath caught in my throat. I was looking into a guileless face with longing in its clear blue eyes. "You said you loved me, Ally. And I couldn't get past that."

"Let her go."

Troy's eyes darted to the gaping window. Before I could twist to look there, too, he shoved me behind him and once more I was pinned to the counter, this time by his back pressing against me. Over his shoulder I saw Kade step into the shop, shoes crunching on crushed glass. The Glock he held high with two hands was pointed at Troy.

"I said let her go."

"Take it easy," Troy said. "You put the gun down, I get out of the way."

For the second time that day I heard the metallic *click-clack* of a slide bar being pulled back.

"Kade, no," I said. "I'm okay. This isn't what it looks like."

Troy's head turned to me. In the same instant I saw the surprise in his eyes, the air cracked. Something white crashed to the floor, accompanied by a man-child scream.

Through a choking cloud of dust, I saw Desmond up on his elbows, heard him crying, "Cappuccino!" Troy threw himself into me as another chunk of the ceiling smashed to pieces.

"It's okay, Desmond," Kade said. "Just a warning shot."

"Kade, don't," I said. "Troy, step away."

Troy nodded and pulled himself off me, but his finger pointed at Kade. "Put that thing down before somebody gets hurt."

Kade followed him with the barrel of the gun. "That was the plan."

"Not a good one."

"Mr. Chief!"

Chief was behind Kade, who didn't turn to look. The gun shook in his hands.

"Come on, son. He's unarmed."

"He's never unarmed!"

Troy took another step away from me and put his hands up. I saw the resignation in his shoulders.

Kade swore softly and lowered the gun. "I was just hoping he'd give me a reason."

"Darn the luck, right?" Chief said.

"Mama!"

Desmond was sitting up, neck craned toward the street edge of the gaping window. Elgin Wedgewood's image registered in a flash before three sharp retorts blasted in my ears and Troy was thrown back. I hit the floor with his weight on top of me.

The world was once again surreal. Troy being rolled off of me blurred with Desmond crawling to my side. Chief shouting to Kade morphed into a siren screaming through the blood that soaked my palm as I pressed it to Troy's chest.

The only thing that came clear was the hand reaching up to me. Troy tugged me down to his lips.

"Why do you love me, Ally?" he said. "Tell me."

"It's all God, Troy," I said.

He closed his eyes. The pinch of arrogance and the twist of entitlement smoothed from his face.

"Big Al."

I turned to Desmond. He was still sitting with me in a splash of Troy's blood.

"We got to find Flannery," he said.

Her face flooded back to me, mouth open, screaming at me from Sultan's hideous lap.

DearGoddearGoddearGod where is the end?

"Kade!" I said.

He came out of nowhere, lip blossoming, shirt slit at the shoulder.

"We got him," he said.

"Call an ambulance."

"Done."

"And stay with Desmond. Where's Chief?"

"Outside talking to Kent."

"I love you, son," I said to Desmond and got to my feet.

I had to stagger a few steps to get my balance. As it was, I nearly fell into Chief at the side window everyone seemed to be using like an entrance.

"What are you doing, Classic?" he said.

"We have to find out about Flannery."

"What—"

"Last time I saw her Elgin was taking her and Sultan to Sacrament Two. Then he ends up here. Will you take me back there?"

Chief's gaze bored into me, hard. With his eyes still on me, he said, "Nick."

I tried to pull away from Chief, but he held fast.

"You finished with me?" he said. "I need to get Allison out of here."

"Sure," Nick said. "Kylie can question her later."

Someone else called to Nick and he hurried off.

"Thank you," I said to Chief.

I didn't see that he was limping more than usual until we were almost to the Road King. We were all going to have scars from this, including Troy if he made it. I just hoped I'd have a chance to help Flannery heal from hers.

The rain had slowed to a misty drizzle. When I could finally see Sacrament Two, someone stood on the porch, screaming into the front window. The someone was Sherry, and the twenty-two revolver she pointed at the window looked as old as Maharry himself.

I half fell from the Road King and once again staggered to get upright as I hurled myself across the street. Chief shouted something, but I kept going until I tripped onto the bottom step. It was Sherry's voice that stopped me there.

"I shot you once, Sultan," she said, tone now calm as death.

"And I'll do it again. Only this time, I'll make sure you don't come back."

"Sherry, don't do it," I said. "He isn't worth it."

She didn't turn to look at me. It was as if she'd known it was only a matter of time before I would appear so we could come full circle.

"That's right, Miss Angel," she said. "There's nothing left there but evil. I just want to take it out of this world."

I waited for the warning click I'd already heard twice that day, but it didn't come. I still had a sliver of time.

"It's not about him, Sher," I said. "It's about you. If you do this, he still wins."

"How do you know that?" she said.

"Because I feel it. You can too. You told me you know things just like I do." I moved up another step. "You know this, Sherry."

At last she turned to look at me and nodded. And then her eyes startled and her hands flew up. I saw the gun hit the porch and slide as Chief's arms came around me and pulled me with him off the steps. Bodies rushed past us and I heard a door open.

"Hands up, Lowery—it's over."

It was the first time I had ever been glad to hear Detective Kylie's voice.

By the time the sirens and the questions and the exits with people in handcuffs had faded, Hank was there with Jasmine and Mercedes and Gigi. Ophelia had arrived with India, Bonner and Liz with

Zelda. Flannery had fallen into Kade's arms when he brought Desmond, and I sank against Chief as he held my son and me to his sides. There was silence among us all as we stood by the koi pond and watched both our homes being wrapped in crime-scene tape.

It was as if the houses were being held back from the urge to fight evil with anger and hate, just as I was. And it was in Sherry and Kade and Flannery and perhaps Detective Kylie. I knew that in some lingering, grasping way, it had been in Troy Irwin's insane plan as well.

As I crossed my arm over Chief and watched Officer Man-Child clank a padlock on the door to Sacrament Two, I knew something else. We would all stay locked up, unable to get to the world we so wanted to change, if we didn't give in to loving another mile. No matter what that meant in the lives of the six women who clung to each other now—or to the six of us who worked every day to give them hope.

"I wanted to live there, but now I don't think I can."

I looked at Flannery. She stood apart from Kade now, small and ashen and drained of the fight that had held her together.

The Nudge pushed me toward her.

All right God, I answered as I reached my arms out to Flannery. *But this is as far as I go.*

I could have predicted God's reply. *You've come too far to say far enough.*

CHAPTER TWENTY

The Things To Be Sorted Out Over The Next Several Weeks pile resembled a sizeable landfill. Or, as Owen put it, we had more issues than the United Nations, more mysteries to solve than Sherlock Holmes. Et cetera.

Owen himself was one of them. We didn't discover—until he asked the paramedic who was attending to Rochelle to check out a nick in his side—that he was suffering from a flesh wound caused by a bullet.

"Is there anybody who *didn't* have a gun pointed at him today?" Nick Kent said.

We finally pieced together from Owen, who gave us far too many details, and Rochelle, who offered almost none, that they had been working in the garden in the back part of Sacrament Two's backyard when they heard someone, who they eventually discovered was Flannery, screaming inside the house. Rochelle saw, to use her few words, "a big bad-looking white guy" cross the street to Sacrament One, while Owen got a look in the window at Two and witnessed Sultan holding a gun on Flannery, forcing her to go to the front window and keep watch.

"I told Rochelle to stay there and I'd go in and help the little girl," Owen said.

When we pointed out that Sultan had a *gun,* he said he thought he could handle a paraplegic with one eye. He obviously couldn't. He wasn't in the door half a minute before he took one in the side.

"You're lucky he missed," Nick Kent said.

Owen looked at Flannery. "Luck had nothing to do with it. This little girl saved my life jumping him from behind."

I pushed aside all thought of how that could have turned out. What *did* happen provided enough angst. When Rochelle heard the shot she ran to Sacrament One to call the police. According to Flannery, Sultan sent Elgin across the street to Two to find out what Troy was doing. Elgin must have seen the back door open and gone after him just before Rochelle got there.

I spent that first night in the hospital with Desmond, where they insisted he be observed because he had been unconscious for over twenty minutes. It had certainly seemed like longer to me. After that a number of things demanded our attention. Brenda Donohue's funeral was one of them. The legalities of putting Flannery in my care as a foster child was another.

By far the most nerve-racking was Chief petitioning the DA not to charge Sherry with the attempted murder of Sultan a year before, since she had done it to save my life, or with intent to kill, which, Chief argued, was an attempt to save Flannery's life. While the DA looked into it, Bonner used the money he'd offered me to bail her out so she could take care of Maharry. There was no bail set for Sultan or for Elgin, but I still had to call the jail daily to reassure Flannery that her former pimp was still in the cage he belonged in.

Six days after what we began to call D-Day, Chief and I went with Sherry to get Maharry from the Wildwood Convalescent Center in Palatka where, just as he'd told me, Sultan's people had taken him. Chief was there at the request of Tara McClanahan, since Sherry was leaving the city proper, and to notify the manager that he had filed a lawsuit on behalf of Mr. Nelson. Maharry looked little better than he had the day I was there, and I wasn't sure he was going to survive weeping and wheezing in his daughter's arms.

The day before our trip to Palatka, I had wondered out loud to Chief why Sultan had involved Maharry in the whole ransom thing.

"He was probably just messing with your head while he was waiting for the call from Troy Irwin telling him to bring Desmond to Sacrament House."

"He succeeded," I said.

Chief reached across the bistro table and pulled me toward him by my elbow. "There's no messing up your head, Classic."

If there was more he wanted to say, it was cut short by Flannery, presenting us with Desmond's latest caricature. It showed her with Desmond and me, her wild tendrils falling over the two of us like the leaves on a weeping willow.

"Nicely done," I said to Desmond who was standing beside her, face headed toward a pout. "So what's with the face?"

"She sayin' this missin' somethin'." His voice pitched upward. "I didn't miss *nothin'*."

"Yes you did, bro." Flannery turned the drawing to him and poked at it. "Hello, where's Mr. Chief?"

Desmond's eyes went straight to us. "I don't know," he said. "Where you at, Mr. Chief?"

I didn't know even now, as I stood in the hallway with Sherry waiting for a doctor to finish examining Maharry for his release, how Chief had answered that. I'd escaped from the kitchen, claiming a pressing urinary issue. I had no idea where Chief was at anymore, and as more time went by, I was more afraid to find out.

"Miss Angel?" Sherry said.

"I'm sorry," I said guiltily. "What did you say?"

"I said there's something else I need to tell you."

I had already accepted the fact that the stream never ended, so I nodded her on.

"It's about Sultan."

"Okay."

"I didn't think he knew I was the one who shot him. That wasn't the reason I wouldn't tell you. I was just afraid he thought it was Daddy, you know, because of where the shot came from."

"He had to know Maharry couldn't have done it from that distance."

Sherry shook her head. "He never really knew Daddy. But I figured something out."

"Okay."

"You know that big Lincoln we had in the shop for a while, the one the guy said nobody else in town could fix?"

"I remember that, yeah."

"When they were booking me last Sunday, I saw the guy who brought it in. He was being booked too."

"Elgin," I said.

"Then it *was* Flannery's pimp. I guess Sultan sent him in there to get a closer look at Daddy."

"And to gank the keys," I said.

She gave me a puzzled frown.

"Too much time with Desmond," I said. "So ... how do you know Sultan decided it was you who shot him?"

"Because." Her gaze swept the floor. "The day we found those horrible pictures on the wall … the one of me had a bullet hole in the forehead."

I felt as if one had gone through mine. I reached for Sherry, but she leaned away.

"You need to let me finish before I chicken out," she said. "I wasn't the only one Sultan was after, but I *was* the one who shot him. I thought if I left town it would draw him away from all of you and Daddy."

"Where did you—"

"I took the money from Daddy's drawer, and the gun, and I took a bus to Jacksonville because after what Flannery told us, I thought that was where he might be. It took me a while, I don't know—"

"Nine days," I said. "Jasmine was keeping track. You were gone nine days."

Sherry closed her pale eyes and took a few breaths. "I had to do it, Miss Angel. I knew where to find the street women, and I paid them some of the money to get information about the local pimps." She nodded as if she wanted me to nod with her. "I also told them about us and where they could come when they're ready to give up the life that wasn't a life. Anyway, I finally found out where Sultan was working with some other pimp named Topaz, and when those girls told me they were into child prostitution I almost found Sultan and shot him then. But then one of them told me he and Topaz left town, and I knew he was coming back here. I had to take the bus, though, so it took me too long to get here."

"I'm thinking you got here just in time," I said.

"But I left Daddy at the hospital. I thought he was going to be there until the money came from the sale of C.A.R.S. But I still left, and they almost killed him. It's just too much, Miss Angel."

I put my hand to her face. This time she didn't pull away.

"You think I don't have that feeling just about all the time, Sherry? It's just one thing after another after another in this thing. Every Monday I say I'm going to quit, but then I don't."

"Why? Nobody would blame you if you did."

"It's not a matter of blame … or shame or guilt. It's a matter of making the choice between loving and hating. And you do it over and over and over again. And just when you think you'll never hate again, somebody like Jude Lowery comes back from the dead and you have to face it one more time."

"So it *doesn't* end."

"I know it will someday."

"When?"

"When we love our way to the root of it."

She was quiet for a moment. I was sure she was musing just as I was about where those words were coming from.

"I never could get into working with Mr. Schatz in the garden," she said.

"You and me both," I said. "I'd kill every tomato on every vine, just walking past them."

"But I heard him telling Rochelle something one day that … well, I'm not good at saying stuff like this the way you and Mercedes are, but he said every plant was meant to grow, but if you let the weeds get to the roots, they don't have a chance." She pulled her shoulders to her earlobes. "Do you think there was ever any good in Sultan? Because if there was, maybe somebody could have loved it out."

"If anybody could have, it was Geneveve," I said, "and that didn't happen. I think the weeds got to him and choked out his soul long before any of you met him."

The door opened and a nurse with a smile that said, *I have been threatened with unemployment if I'm not nice to you* told us Mr. Maharry was free to go. I prayed that very soon, Sherry would be too.

On Monday the first of October, a week and a day after D-Day, Hank and I decided it was time to pull all of us together at Sacrament One, which was now back open. We used chicken marsala and the Telling of Their Tale as the context, but all of us who loved them were more concerned about their being spread out all over St. Augustine in the interim. There was no room for them all to move into Sacrament One, which was their first choice. Jasmine was staying temporarily with India, and Sherry was with Maharry in an apartment Rex, Ulysses, and Stan got her into. An advance on the C.A.R.S. deal, Rex said, although I was sure they would never accept repayment from Sherry. As for Rochelle, Zelda volunteered to stay on with Liz to make more room, but Owen wouldn't hear of it. He practically remodeled his entire upstairs so Rochelle could stay up there and be close to me.

But I didn't like her being separated from the Sisters just when she was beginning to talk. I didn't like any of them not being with the others. They weren't ready for that, and the near-frenetic way they hugged and kissed and pulled at each other when they came together that night was proof of it.

The feasting on yet another D'Angelo Special did scrape them off the walls and each other so that we could at least hear what had happened to them on D-Day while the rest of us were, as India described it, "Being held hostage and shot at and rescued like y'all were in a Clint Eastwood movie."

"Who?" Flannery said.

"Lord, I'm getting old," Bonner said. "Let's hear it. Somebody start."

Ophelia raised her hand. "Right after Hank left Flannery with us up at Second Chances—"

"Before I could even get the door *locked*," Hank said.

"That man came in."

She covered her mouth with her hands, and India slid an arm around her shoulders, bracelets dangling in the sudden silence.

I shrugged at India.

"Troy Irwin," she said quietly.

"I just lost it," Ophelia said. "It was like it was all happening to me again."

Suddenly it was happening to me, too. "Ophelia, I am so sorry—"

"Me and Mercedes, we were trying to get between him and Ophelia," Jasmine said, "'cause we was thinkin' he come up there after her."

Mercedes let out her signature, "Mmm-hmm. We so focusin' on her, we didn't even see he was takin' Flannery till they was out the door."

"My turn," Gigi said. "I was out on the porch waiting on a table, and I saw them, only I didn't know what was going on. The guy was all talking to Flannery, telling her he was just taking her back to you so I thought it was okay."

"I don't see how you could be thinkin' that," Zelda said.

I touched Gigi's shoulder. "I do. Go on, Geege."

She shook her head and pointed at Kade. He turned his head and nodded at nothing in particular.

I had been worried about Kade all week. No one had been there to witness him holding a gun on Troy except Chief, Desmond, and me, and we assured him that first night that we saw no reason for that information to go any further than us, especially since Troy was still in intensive care and would likely go to prison if he did recover. I suspected Nick Kent had an idea, but when I was questioned later, nobody said anything about the damage to the ceiling. Maybe it was assumed to be part of the general abused condition of the whole building.

But even at that, Kade had kept his distance since D-Day. When I called he was pleasant but reserved and apologized for being tied up right now. Chief said he stayed in his office during the workday. Even Flannery mentioned to me that he must be mad at her because he wasn't answering any of her texts with his usual funny retorts.

This was the first time I had seen him in person since that day, and I was disturbed by the sallow look of his skin and the difficulty he was having meeting anyone's gaze. Now with everyone's eyes on him, I watched him shrink into himself and I knew why. Shame could take many shapes, but it was always impossible to hide completely.

"Okay so Mr. Kade got there right after that," Gigi said, obviously impatient with the delay, "and he was going upstairs and I told him Flannery already gone with a guy that—and I said this, now—that looked like him only older."

I was frankly amazed that Kade didn't get up and leave. He didn't actually have to. He pulled so far into himself, nothing remained of my son but the shell he now hated, because it looked like Troy Irwin's.

"So what happened, Kade?" Flannery said.

"No big deal," Kade said. "I called Nick Kent and gave him Irwin's phone number. I figured it had GPS."

"How come you knew his phone number?"

"Flan," I said, "let him tell the story."

"By the time he called me back Irwin was at C.A.R.S." He shrugged. "You know the rest."

Flannery lifted her chin. "I know you held Elgin down until the cops got there, which totally makes you my hero."

"Chief had that handled," Kade said.

And then he did stand up and weave through the bodies to get to the kitchen. I followed him, catching the door before he could close it. I found him on the back stoop. He sat dismally, nails digging into the concrete on either side of him.

"Stop it, Kade," I said.

He lifted his hands.

"I'm not talking about that. I'm talking about what you're doing to yourself."

I sat beside him. The first niggle of autumn had teased a leaf from the pecan and blown it to the step. Kade flicked it off with his finger.

"I'm not who I thought I was," he said, eyes straight out over Owen and Rochelle's garden.

I kept mine straight too. "Who did you think you were?"

"Not a person who could shoot somebody."

"You were protecting me, Kade. I would have done the same for you."

I felt him stiffen. "Would you be disappointed that he stepped away so you didn't have a reason to bring him down?"

"Maybe not him," I said. "But Sultan probably. Or Elgin."

Kade looked at me. His face was pinched with pain.

"Why *not* him? After everything he did, why don't you hate him?"

"Seems like we had this same conversation about a month ago," I said.

"Then I guess there's no reason to have it again."

"I think there is."

"Why?"

"Because now I have a different answer. Maybe even the right answer."

Kade stared down at his hands.

"We all have a choice," I said. "We can live our lives the way somebody else tried to shape them. Or we can live them the way God wants to shape them if we give God a chance. Guys like Sultan and Elgin and Marcus Rydell probably didn't even know they had a choice. Troy knew, and he chose to let his father and then my father and then his own power do it for him."

"So what's the difference?"

Kade's voice was flat, but he didn't leave, and I went with that.

"The difference is that the down-to-the-core evil people never had any other kind of shaping. Troy did."

"From who?"

"I didn't realize it until recently, but Sylvia did. I knew she raised me, but I never thought about the influence she had on him. In some small way, she brought him up too."

Kade looked at me again. His face struggled with itself. "Is that what he was telling you when I got there? Is that why you defended him?"

"I defended him because in the end, he was trying to save Desmond and Flannery. But you already know that."

"That's not all of it. The way you were looking at him when he lost consciousness. There was something else." He pounded the heels of his hands on the step. "I didn't get that from you. I got his drive and his hate and his—"

"Look at me."

He turned away. I grabbed his face and forced it close to mine.

"You were born with Troy Irwin's passion and intelligence and wit. But the Capellis raised you, Kade. They gave you the tools to become who you are, and so far you're doing a pretty good job with that. I don't know what you got from me, but I know what I can give you now."

I watched his hands come up. I knew he was going to pull mine away, and I had to let him do it. I had just given him a choice. I couldn't take it away from him.

Slowly his fingers curled around my wrists, as damp and slimy as mine ever got, and he left them there.

"So ... God," he said. "That's the only way out of this, right?"

"No," I said. "It's the only way through it."

His face gave in and he pulled me roughly into his arms, with none of the finesse of his biological father, and all of the awkward, clumsy, bottomless love of his mother.

Kade left not long after that, asking me to give his apologies to the group. He did stop on the front porch and look back at me. "I forgot to tell you that I scheduled a meeting for us and Chief with Pix Penwell. Wednesday at eleven o'clock."

"I'll try to make it," I said.

When I turned to go back inside, Hank was waiting.

"You ready?" she said.

I let Kade take his place in the back of my mind and joined her and the rest of the group in the living room. The Sisters looked mystified as India spread a snowy cloth on the coffee table and Hank set a cruet of oil in the center. Bonner placed a pillow on the floor in front of it, and I took Mercedes's hand.

"What, Miss Angel?" she said.

"This is a special night for you, Merc," I said. "You're graduating."

Immediately she shook her head. "I ain't—I'm not ready to leave here, Miss Angel."

"We wouldn't hear of it," India said.

"Then what—"

I put my hands on Mercedes's broad shoulders. "The board came together and we prayed and we feel Nudged to make you the Sister in Charge of Sacrament House."

"Amen, now," someone said.

"That's right—"

The rhythm rocked in, and Mercedes looked at me with eyes like liquid gold.

"You've healed into this, and just like you told Flannery, now people trust you. Not just the Sisters, but all of us. Especially me."

I turned to Hank, who had the cruet open.

"If you'll accept, Merc," she said, "I'll commission you."

I had never seen our Mercedes without words. But the stunning grace with which she nodded her fine head made words unnecessary.

And so in the name of our Lord Christ, Hank anointed Mercedes. With the hands of her Sisters and her mentors, she was prayed into her new way of being. The Nudge was at peace.

But as the Sisters left that evening, half to go in sundry directions, their longing spirits made it clear that something had to be done to keep them together.

The next day, Tuesday, was Flannery's first day at Muldoon Middle. Although she walked into the place with her chin ready to take it over, and although Desmond vowed he would turn his attention from maidens in distress to "any fool thinks he gonna mess with my sister," I spent the whole day wondering what things were going to look like when I picked them up that afternoon.

When I drove up in the van, Skeeter Iseley had already stationed herself on the sidewalk for duty. The Nudge was immediate.

Go—

I know, I get it.

I got two things, but I knew only one was from God. The other was just a little housekeeping detail.

"No motorcycle today," she said when I joined her. "No Harley."

"No room for two passengers," I said. "Did you by any chance get a new student today?"

She adjusted the sunglasses. "No. Why?"

"Just wondered."

Check. Now on to the God-thing.

"Would you like to have coffee sometime, Skeeter?" I said.

If I had asked her to the prom she probably wouldn't have looked more dumbfounded.

"We have more in common than you realize," I said. "Starting with being used by the same man. But it goes deeper."

"Deeper," she said. She was obviously too flabbergasted to come up with a synonym.

"We both care about the at-risk kids," I said. "You obviously do or you wouldn't have gone to the trouble to look into Desmond's history and share it with a virtual stranger." Her jaw dropped, but I went on. "You understand the obstacles they face. I have a way of helping them knock those down. Maybe we can help each other."

She looked as if she were waiting for me to drop another shoe. When I said nothing, she nodded.

"All right," she said. "Coffee. Sometime. Anytime."

"I know where to find you," I said, and stepped away to locate my kids.

It was too bad mosquitoes didn't transform into butterflies the way caterpillars did. But there was hope for Skeeter Iseley. I could feel it.

"We need to celebrate Flannery's first day," I told her and Desmond when we'd all climbed into the van.

Flannery sniffed. "What's to celebrate? All those kids are so immature."

"That's what I'm sayin'," Desmond said.

That launched them into the inevitable banter, during which I observed Flannery in the van's rearview mirror. She was always going to be more mature than kids her age, and some adults for that matter. Some of that came from her fight to be who she was made to be, and it was good. But some emerged from experiencing things no child her age should ever have to live through. No child. No woman. No anyone. I didn't need a Nudge to tell me I had to stay on that until no one suffered such things, or until I died. Whichever came first.

Flannery requested Georgie's, I suspected because she hoped Kade would be there. Desmond had never been, so they set off to inspect the jukebox while I looked for a table, and discovered who *was* there.

Yates Chattingham slipped from his stool beside Christine at the soda fountain and came to me, both hands extended. The better half of my mixed feelings pushed me to take at least one of them.

"Will you join us for a minute?" he said. "We haven't wanted to bother you with all that y'all have had to deal with, but we'd really like to talk to you."

I looked around for Desmond and Flannery, who were curling their lips over the musical selections, and nodded at Yates. I might have a few things to talk about as well.

"This has to be a divine appointment," Christine said when Yates ushered me to the stool between them. "What can we get you?"

"Nothing," I said. "I'm with my kids. So ... how did you know we've had a lot going on?"

Christine turned a pretty shade of pink. "They didn't give me any details. They just said it's been a little rough."

"Who are 'they'?"

"I can tell you, right, because you already know they're in NA?"

"They?"

"Rochelle and Gigi."

"Oh," I said.

"You didn't know I'm their sponsor."

"No." I pulled my hand through my hair because what else was there to do when you felt like an idiot?

Yates came to the rescue. "Christine and I were just wondering, and you may not know this with everything else happening, but do you have any idea what happened to Tango? We haven't seen her since, when, Chris?"

"The night she was arrested for pounding a teenage boy a block from the Hot Spot?" I said.

I watched them both, but they just looked at each other, faces blank.

"So where is she now?" Christine said.

"My source says she's been sent to the juvenile correctional facility." I craned my neck for sight of Flannery, who was now examining the menu with Desmond at a table where two milkshakes had already appeared. "I would appreciate it if you wouldn't say anything about that in front of Flannery. She doesn't know yet."

Christine's eyes drooped. "So she and Tango ... worked together."

"And now Flannery has a chance and Tango doesn't," Yates said.

"Ms. Chamberlain obviously can't take all of them in, Yates."

"I didn't mean that—"

"What ticks me off is that Tango is in jail. I only got to talk to her twice, but I thought we were getting somewhere."

"Which is probably why she was kicking that kid's butt instead of offering him her services," I said.

Christine pushed her Coke aside so she could grab my wrist as she went on. I was getting the impression that she couldn't speak unless she was touching the person she was talking to. I found myself not minding it.

"What we need is someplace where they can go while we work with them," Christine said. "I've checked it out, and there is nothing like what we had in Atlanta."

"I keep telling you, start something," Yates said.

"Big Al! Whatchoo want to eat?"

I held up a finger to Desmond and slid off the stool.

"I need to get over there before they order an entire buffet," I said. "But I would like to talk more sometime."

"How about Friday night?" he said. "After you talk to the kids at the Hot Spot. You'll do that, right? I mean, isn't that what you do? Give people hope?"

"That's what I hear," Christine said.

I gave her a smile. "Gigi and Rochelle talk too much."

Christine shook her head. "I didn't get that from them. I mean, not in those words. I heard that from Pix Penwell."

I was once again reduced to "oh."

"Big *Al*."

"Go," Yates said. "We'll see you Friday."

All right, already, I said. Not to the Reverend Chattingham. To God.

"I am not cooking dinner for you two tonight," I said when we were back in the van.

"Thank goodness," Flannery said. "Kidding. Just kidding."

"We don't gotta go home and do homework, do we?" Desmond said, as if that were tantamount to swallowing thumbtacks.

"No," I said. "We're going to Ms. Willa's."

"Good. I still haven't gotten to check out those nurses."

I nodded at Flannery, but that wasn't why we were headed there. Ms. Willa had called me that morning and said that, one, "these people" were *not* working out for her and, two, she had a proposition for me. That could mean anything from hiring Flannery to take care of her (not happening) to her taking over the running of Second Chances (not happening either).

It was neither.

With Flannery and Desmond sitting right there to hear it all from the couch, she hit me with her plan.

"There's only one of these nurses who knows what he's doing."

"He?" I said.

"You know I'm not racist—or sexist. He's blacker than the ace of spades, but he takes good care of me. The rest of them."

She blew off *the rest of them* with a loud sniff. I was still recovering from the blatant political incorrectness.

"But he can't be here all the time," she said to Flannery, who answered with, "Well, no doubt."

"Here is my proposition."

I straightened my back, thinking I was ready.

"The Sisters are still scattered hither and yon," she said.

NANCY RUE

Desmond's brow puckered. "I don't know nothin' 'bout no hither and yon."

"All over the place, genius," Flannery said.

"So I will donate this house so they can all live here. New ones can start out at the ones you have, or whatever you want to do with that. But there's room for at least eight here."

"They aren't qualified to take care of you, Ms. Willa," I said. I was already having nightmarish flashes of Zelda telling her she better get straight, and Rochelle grunting at her across the tea table.

"If you would let me finish."

"She hates it when you interrupt," Flannery said.

"They are not going to take care of me," Ms. Willa said. "My nurse is, when he's on duty during the day. And then you and these two children can do whatever else needs to be done for me, which is a whole lot less than those doctors think, I can tell you that."

"That's true," Flannery said. "I'm in."

"You're in school now." I did the habitual fingers to the temples. "I love you, Ms. Willa, but I can't be running over here—how's that going to work in the middle of the night?"

Ms. Willa looked at Flannery. "Is she going to let me finish?"

"You just have to keep talking," Flannery said. "She'll listen eventually."

"*What?*"

Ms. Willa all but said, "*Tsk-tsk.*"

"Sorry," I said. "Explain. Please."

"You won't have to come running over here because I won't be living here. The Sisters will be living here. I will be living at your house. You have four bedrooms."

Even Flannery's mouth fell open. I was fairly certain Desmond's lower lip would be hitting his lap any second.

"My house," I said.

"Not for free, obviously. You would be handsomely paid, both before my death and after. Don't tell me you don't need the money, because I know you do. And with two children to raise now ... do you have any idea how much that's going to cost you?"

I closed my eyes. "Um, okay, this could get complicated, legally speaking."

"Not according to Jack Ellington. I talked to him this morning. He's drawing up the papers."

"He hasn't said a word to me about it."

"Of course not. Attorney-client privilege."

"Since when is Chief your attorney?"

"Since I decided I can't trust anyone else in this town but you people." Ms. Willa gave her blue mane a nod. "Well?"

"Ms. Willa, I don't know what to say."

This time she barked at Desmond. "How hard is it to say yes?"

Nobody had an answer to that one. The best I could come up with in my dazed state was a promise to think about it.

That promise was easy to keep. I couldn't think about anything else until Wednesday when I got to Chief's office to walk over to Chamberlain Enterprises with him and Kade.

"I know about confidentiality blah blah blah," I said before my seat even hit the chair, "but you could have given me some kind of warning about Ms. Willa."

"Like what?" he said, eyes crinkling.

"Like 'Hey, Classic, you're about to be hit by a Mack truck.'"

"This is more fun."

"It isn't fun. I don't know what to do. It would be perfect for the Sisters. You should have seen them this morning. It was like a funeral at communion."

"That's not the part you don't know what to do with."

"Ya think? Aside from the fact that God is doing nothing to help me make this decision—"

"Maybe God figures you should already know. That's how it works for me when I already have all the information I need and I'm still saying, 'help, help.'"

I stared at him, my next words sitting wasted on my lips.

"What?" he said.

I shook my head. "Aside from that, would *you* want to live in a house with two teenagers and an eighty-something year old woman who can't keep her—"

"Are you going to be living there?"

"Of course I'm going to be living there!"

"Then that's exactly where I want to live."

I could only stare as the crinkles softened. That was how Kade found us when he opened Chief's office door and said, "She's here. You want to join us in the conference room?"

"Here?" I said, stupidly.

"I thought we should do this on our own turf," Kade said. He looked from one of us to the other, said, "Five minutes?" and backed out.

"Chief," I said.

"Tonight, Classic," he said. "I'll pick you up at dusk."

"The kids—"

"Kade's lined up."

"Dress code?"

"Leathers. You'll need them."

As he took me by the elbow and ushered me down the hall to the conference room, I didn't care what the powers-that-were at Chamberlain Enterprises had to say. Nothing else could surprise me.

And then it did.

I had never seen Pix Penwell before. She fit the corporate-power-suit mold, until she opened her mouth. Her soft drawl had not been replaced by the staccato executives all seemed to acquire with their stock options. But, then, Troy had been a great actor too.

"You're obviously all busy people," she said, "so I'll just get right to the point."

"Which is?"

She surprised me with a smile that didn't appear to come from the Mr. Potato Head kit. "Your reputation precedes you, Ms. Chamberlain. All right then, as you know, your father left a considerable number of his Chamberlain Enterprises shares to Troy Irwin."

"Yeah, I figured that out the day my father disowned me." I bit my lip. "You know what, I'm sorry. Forgive my sarcasm. It's the only way I can keep from spitting when anyone mentions my father."

Pix Penwell turned the smile on Chief. "Do you have a spittoon in here? Because I'm about to mention him again."

"She'll control herself," Chief said drily.

"Wait," I said. "Did you say my father left a number of his shares to Troy? I thought he left all of them."

She turned back to me. "I'm getting to that. What you probably *don't* know is that your father willed those shares to Mr. Irwin with the caveat that should it ever be discovered that he mismanaged corporate funds in any intentionally illegal way, the rest of the shares would go to you."

"I'm sorry, what shares?"

"The ones your father put in trust, which have been there for over ten years. Even with the downturn in the economy, they're still worth a great deal."

"Define 'a great deal,'" Kade said, but I put up my hand.

"I won't take the money."

I heard Kade choke. Chief pinched the bridge of his nose with his fingers. Pix Penwell's face was a puzzle.

"I don't think you understand what we're talking about here, Ms. Chamberlain. Two million dollars worth of help for your program can make up for a lot of resentment. You could use it to—"

"I didn't say I wouldn't use it," I said. "I just said I wouldn't take it. For myself."

I looked at Chief, and at Kade, who was a virtual puddle on the other side of the table. "Can we make it so that the money goes directly to Sacrament House?"

"We can do anything you want," Chief said.

Ms. Penwell tapped the folder in front of her with a chiseled nail. "There's one more thing. That two million dollars is in the trust fund. There is another million in CE shares."

"Sell them," I said directly to Kade.

"They aren't worth as much right now as they will be when we get the company back on its feet," she said. "You might want to hold onto them for a while."

Only because she seemed truly concerned did I reach over and squeeze her hand. "I'm sure you're going to turn that ship around,

Ms. Penwell," I said. "And I hope you get going again in the direction my grandfather had in mind when he built it. But I personally don't want anything to do with it."

She looked at me like a girlfriend across a lunch table. "I hope the fact that your father provided this for you softens the past a little bit for you."

"Actually it doesn't," I said. "That was my father's final slap in my face. I'm sure he thought I would be at the reading of the will, which I obviously wasn't, and that I would know that money would never come to me, because he never thought this would happen."

"He didn't think Mr. Irwin would do what he's done."

"No. He just didn't think he would get caught."

I left the table a millionaire with a very sad heart.

I gave Kade a half page of instructions regarding Desmond and Flannery before Chief and I left that night. Kade promptly crumpled it into a ball and said, "I know how to handle my siblings."

When Chief and I stepped out onto the side porch, I stopped and listened to the repartee on the other side of the door.

"Should I offer the shares to Kade instead of selling them?" I asked. "He could have an influence on CE if he wanted to."

"It's a thought," Chief said. "But it's not the one I want you to have tonight."

He took my arm and pulled me with him down the steps and across the lane. When we reached the Road King, he folded his arms across a leather chest.

"Any other thoughts you want to leave here? You can pick them up when we get back."

"I don't want to think about the money," I said. "I know we can do a lot with it, and I can't wait to see the Sisters' faces when I tell them, but it doesn't really change the root."

"Go on."

"Money can't take the place of working their way through. It can't erase what's happened to Ophelia or Flannery or any of them."

I reached for my helmet, hanging on his handlebar, but Chief stopped my hand.

"We're not taking this with us. Keep talking."

"It gives us a chance to help more women and provide more for the ones who are already in the family. Maybe build a recovery center for the young girls where that school never got built on San Luis."

"Lots of good maybes."

"But I'm afraid of it, Chief. I've seen it take people and twist them into something they were never meant to be."

Chief lifted my chin. "You're not Troy Irwin, Classic."

"I don't hate him anymore."

"I know."

I watched his eyes. "And what about you?"

"Ah." Chief handed me the helmet. "That's a question we can take with us."

The Bridge of Lions lifted us over Matanzas Bay and carried us out to Anastasia Island with the watercolor sky fading to our right and the moon already making a light-path across the Atlantic on our left. By the time we left the condos and golfing clubs of St. Augustine Beach behind, I knew where we were going. Chief was right. It was a place with no room for anything but the freedom to be.

Chief pulled the Road King to the Intracoastal Waterway side of the low, flat bridge that separated the sunset from the moonlight. He took my hand and helped me off the seat behind him and together we crossed to the side that faced the ocean and her rising silver moon. We stood shoulder to shoulder, not touching.

"Don't look behind you, Classic," he said.

"Why?"

"Because you're going to go where your head points."

"Okay," I said. "I don't need to look behind me anymore."

"I do. Just for a minute."

"You're going to tell me about Joy."

"I am." I looked up to see him slitting his eyes sideways at me. "And I want to do it without any interruptions from you."

"Did you bring duct tape?" I said.

But I pressed my lips together, and I listened. Listened to a story about a man named Jack Ellington who at thirty-five thought he had found the love of his life. She seemed to have found hers, too. They had everything in common. Both lawyers, both loved motorcycles and hiking and places like Red Deer, Alberta. They were married in Colorado after they passed the bar, but soon after, the man named Jack Ellington felt that the wife named Joy was holding something back. He pressed her, and she confessed that she had been married once before, very young, but she hadn't told him because she wanted

Jack to be her first. It was all right again. And then within six months of their marriage Joy received a job offer out of the blue from a firm in central Florida.

I did stop Chief there. "You told me nothing comes out of the blue."

"No," he said. "It doesn't."

He turned again to the moon and the story.

So the man named Jack Ellington took his wife named Joy to Orlando and found a job with a firm doing not-very-satisfying work. The marriage, it seemed, was not very satisfying either, not to Joy. The details were not important. The root of them was. The job had not come out of the blue. She had sought it out, because her first husband lived in central Florida. She didn't want to be with him again. She simply wanted him to see her with her tall, handsome, accomplished husband so that he would know that he had let go of the best thing that had ever happened to him.

I snagged on that phrase too, but I let it go, let Chief go on.

It all came to an ugly head one day at a Harley rally. Husband number one was there, and Jack Ellington recognized him from pictures he'd found that Joy still kept. He had never begrudged her the past. But he couldn't be the Band-Aid for it.

"I filed for divorce the next day," he said. "And I came up here with Stan because I didn't know where else to go."

"Why didn't you go back to Colorado?"

"Because I couldn't go back to a place where I thought love was real. It was better to be here and be reminded that it wasn't."

I looked away from him, to the moonstruck ocean. "And then?"

"Then I found you."

"But then you thought you were reliving that whole story over again."

"Classic, I'm sorry—"

"I'm not Joy."

"I know that. I always knew that. But I had to go see her."

I turned slowly. "Telling no one where you were going, of course."

"Yeah."

"Well?"

"I told her I didn't hate her anymore."

"And?"

"She thinks I'm crazy. Never felt more sane."

"Anything else?"

"What do you want me to say?"

"That she's a shriveled-up chain-smoking attorney two facelifts into her sixties."

"That's about it."

"Then why are we having this conversation?"

Chief turned to me until I could see nothing but a leather chest and the eagle eyes that had the power to take me to the mountaintop with them.

"Forgive me.

"Done.'"

"Marry me."

"Yes."

"You sure? What does God say?"

"What's God saying to you?"

Chief looked down at me, the prekiss look all over his raptor face. "God's saying we'll never go far enough."

"Interesting," I said. "God's saying the same thing to me."

The kiss was almost enough to carry me away from that place. But I was still aware, in the Nudge and the Whisper and the Knowing that made me who I was, that the wretched past lives of the Geneveves and the Tangos would always be behind us, pushing us forward. And that the new Zeldas and Ophelias and Sherrys would always be ahead, waiting for us to offer them a scrap of hope. Some would turn into Mercedes and Jasmines and Flannerys. Others would never know the new lives that beckoned from San Luis Street.

Even as Chief lifted me off my feet and shouted, "Yeah, baby!" in his best Desmond voice, I felt God's pain for all of them.

But stronger, always stronger, was the Nudge, whispering, *Go another mile, my prophet.*

Go another mile.

... a little more ...

When a delightful concert comes to an end,

the orchestra might offer an encore.

When a fine meal comes to an end,

it's always nice to savor a bit of dessert.

When a great story comes to an end,

we think you may want to linger.

And so, we offer ...

AfterWords—just a little something more after you

have finished a David C Cook novel.

We invite you to stay awhile in the story.

Thanks for reading!

Turn the page for ...

- **Why St. Augustine**
- **More about the Nudge**

Why St. Augustine?

I always do a lot of thinking about where I'm going to set a story, especially a series, because I have to live there in my mind for such an extended period of time. I also consider the setting to be a character in itself, so it has to be right for the role. We got to be good friends, St. A. and I (and my husband and my daughter, and my grand-daughter ...)

◻ I grew up in Jacksonville, Florida, which is just north of St. Augustine, and visited at least once a year for field trips during elementary school, and probably three times that often for out-of-town guests who wanted to see the sights. I never got tired of its history and mystery and artistic appeal. I'm still not.

◻ It is definitely a town with a facade, though. Between the tourist industry and the wealth, both old and new, the place has a strong image to uphold. I didn't know about the West King Street culture until I took a carriage ride and interviewed the driver about parts of town she never took the tourists to. That made St. A. a perfect metaphorical character.

◻ I spent four different weeks there at different times of the year. Jim and I explored every lane and alley on our Harley and frequented many of the places Allison does. The Spanish Galleon (now closed), the Monk's Vineyard (still for sale), Georgie's Diner, The Bunnery, Columbia, the Santa Maria, the F.A. Café, the A1A Crab Shack (now closed), J.T.'s Seafood Shack, the St. Augustine Harley Davidson dealership, the Hot Shot Bakery, 95 Cordova, and O.C. White's are all real. So much investigative work was tough, but somebody had to do it.

¤ The goal of my first research visit to St. A. was to locate a home for Allison. Found Palm Row the first afternoon and knew she lived there. The house I redecorated in my mind was for sale (and still is as far as I know), and I actually considered setting up a showing with the realtor so I could see the inside, but I couldn't bring myself to pretend I was in the market. Hank would not have approved. The house took on a life of its own anyway.

¤ Kade's beach house at Ponte Vedra is also real. My little family and I spent a week there last summer and lived through a major tropical storm. While hubby and daughter were battening down the hatches, I was imagining Desmond and Flannery caught in the wind and driving rain. It was all I could do not to go out there after them. This is why I take people with me when I do research.

One of the saddest things (among many) about finishing this trilogy is that I won't be going back to St. Augustine as often. When I do, I know that Allison and Chief and Desmond and Hank and the Sacrament Sisters will always be there. I hope the place is as alive to you as it has become for me.

What If You Feel a "Nudge"?

In *Unexpected Dismounts,* India says to Allison, *"Not everybody can bring home a hooker."* She's right (in spite of the fact that later she actually does). I myself am not as involved in social justice ministry as Allison is. But I do know about God-Nudges. I think all of us who are paying attention have felt them. The question is what to do about it. Most of us aren't going to go buy a Harley and start a ministry that has the potential to consume our lives. But all of us can do something, and I'm convinced all of us are called to. So—a few thoughts on what to do when you know you're being Nudged by God. These are things that have worked in my own experience.

- *Get some confirmation.* Does it come up in other places, both likely, as in your Bible reading, or unexpected, as in from your teenager? It's not so much about asking people what they think. It's about being aware of validation that comes without provocation. Some people call it synchronicity, others name it "out of the blue." You get the idea.
- *Then do some internal research.* Intentionally take time to search yourself and ask, "What's my motivation? Guilt? Maybe a chance to get some recognition? Or something deeper, more real?" I like journaling for that, but if you'd rather be shot than write in a diary, long walks, horseback

rides, and drives in the country work just as well. I spent a lot of time on the back of our Harley before I accepted the call to write a trilogy on things I knew absolutely nothing about.

◻ *Count the cost.* That isn't hedging. Jesus himself told us to do that before we make a commitment. Just about any significant Nudge is going to require some sacrifice. Maybe not giving up your spare room to a prostitute (or two), but probably some time, a little cash, an old way of thinking. Consider, too, the effect obeying a Nudge is going to have on your relationships. It's okay to discuss all that with God.

◻ *Find out what's already being done in that area.* If you're Nudged to tutor homeless kids, you don't necessarily have to set up your own shop downtown; it's just as obedient to volunteer with a program that's already up and running.

◻ *Start small.* Even Allison just took on one woman (and her kid), with the intention of getting them quickly back on their feet. That would have been huge in itself. One small step could be all you need to do, or it could be the beginning of many. Too many people, however, have burned out quickly because they tried to do too much too soon. God's good at only giving us so much to do at a time.

◻ *Keep balance in your life.* Allison wasn't as good at that as I wanted her to be. Bonner, India, Chief, and Hank were constantly reminding her to take some time to rest and enjoy. Guilt can make you feel like you can't do that because the people you're serving don't have that "luxury." I try to keep this old adage in mind: "If the Devil can't make you bad, he'll make you busy."

- *Continually check in with God.* My own quiet time is a sacred ritual of asking questions. How am I doing? Am I on the track you want me on? Am I making it about me instead of you? Am I really helping or am I just doing? God gives the Nudge in the first place so it only makes sense to let God guide us as we edge forward.

If you'd like to be in community with other people who are Nudgees, you're welcome to join us on "The Nudge" a (mostly) weekly blog, which you can find at http://tweenyouandme.typepad.com/the_nudge.

Acknowledgments

People have told me they actually read the acknowledgments in a novel, just to see what breathed real life into it. I thought I was the only one who did that. Since I'm not alone, here's a peek at the folks who shared their breath with me.

Rich Petrina, the unfortunate man who tried in vain to teach me to ride a Harley. He introduced me to the riders' philosophy that we have always come too far to say far enough. I believe him (but I still can't ride a motorcycle …)

The warm, hospitable **people of St. Augustine and Ponte Vedra Beach, Florida,** whose eyes never glazed over when I started a conversation with, "I'm writing a book …"

My daughter, **Marijean Rue,** whose research assistance led me to **Rory Evans** of the St. Johns County Family Court. Thanks to them, Desmond's adoption and Flannery's plight did not come purely from my imagination.

Drew Etter, whose considerable expertise in law kept me from breaking into a cold sweat when writing about corporate things. Besides that, he rides a motorcycle.

The **Reverend J. Mark Forrester,** Vanderbilt University Methodist chaplain and director of the Wesley Foundation, as well as my friend and spiritual director, who always helps me make theology real. Really real.

Jackie Colburn, who has allowed me to see a prophet in today's world and not run the other way.

The works of **Abraham Heschel** and **Rami Shapiro**, whose understanding of prophets both biblical and contemporary opened the strange new world for Allison and for me.

The entire editorial and marketing staff at **David C Cook. Don Pape,** who took a leap of faith for this trilogy. **Ingrid Beck,** whose patience with me is angelic. **Karen Stoller,** who believes enough to keep on marketing Allison et al. **Renada Arens,** who has the thankless task of keeping me on track with details, and **Amy Konyndyk,** my liaison with the cover design team, who knows how to capture a vision.

My virtual assistant (yes, there really is such a thing), **Leah Apineru** of Impact Author Services, who may be personally responsible for your knowing about this book. She is the reason you can actually find me on Facebook. In case you want to …

My editor, **Jamie Chavez (www.jamiechavez.com),** who truly is one of the best in the business, and who has cared for Allison and her crew like friends. We cry in all the same places.

My husband, **Jim Rue,** who taught me all I needed to know about packing heat for this book and who, more importantly, takes me anywhere I want to go on his Harley. We have never said, "Far enough."

The Academy for Spiritual Formation, Academy 31 class. I am a different kind of Christian because of them. And so is Allison.

My agent, **Lee Hough,** to whom this book is dedicated. We have come far together, and for that I am so grateful.